RECLUSES

Terry L. Vinson

RECLUSES

DOUBLE DRAGON

introvert—*(psychology)* a *person* who tends to *shrink* from *social* contacts and to become preoccupied with their own thoughts

loner, lone wolf, lone hand—a *person* who avoids the *company* or *assistance* of others

hermit—a *person* who retires from *society* and lives in solitude; a recluse; an anchorite

THE ISLE OF TRANQUILITY, PART I

Well, here it is ten minutes 'til noon and she's still among the missing. Didn't even bother to cook me up some brunch before traipsing off on one of her infamous island jaunts. Damned if I'll ever comprehend that woman's mindset. It's like she's always late for an appointment she never had. You'd think three blessed months on this island would've altered such behavior. No matter ... I'll do enough relaxing for the both of us. First off I'll heat up some of those frozen waffles and wash 'em down with a pot of the stoutest Joe I can take. Second, I'll toss on a pair of swim trunks and kick back by the pool with an icy beverage and the last of Pop's many bestsellers. Funny, in a tragic sorta way, that it took a global catastrophe for me to get rightly acquainted with the crazy bastard's life's work. Whatever, I'm sure Pop is peering straight up from the fiery pits of hell with an expression of fatherly pride at the mere concept. Sadistic jackass ... long may you simmer in Satan's crockpot.

I was thinking of giving the Internet another shot, but why waste precious time and effort on such a hopelessly lost cause? No way it's been miraculously revived overnight ... same with the satellite TV and radio transmitter. Frozen solid as my waffles, no doubt—dead as the swollen ranks of wandering corpses that make up the world population these days. Ah, no big deal anyhow. I never cared much for the Web except for the occasional porn surf. TV sucked sewer fluid and the radio was a wasteland of crappy music and still crappier political babblings.

The fact is, I ain't at all ashamed to confess to feeling damn relieved at the whole turn of events. I'd been spouting off for years about making a permanent move to Pop's little island getaway and living the rest of my life on cold beer and processed foods.

Other people's opinions be damned—what exactly is so wrong about living one's life in peaceful solitude? I could care less about said opinions—everyone possesses an asshole as well—but why shouldn't I, as an only child, enjoy the fruits of my father's labor? The only thing that kept me from making tracks years ago was Jenny and her passion for high-society living. She always felt the need to wear that mask of wealth ... to show off whatever new bauble or toy came into her greedy possession. Me, I never gave a rat's hairy hind leg about putting on airs. Never was my style to flaunt. Don't get me wrong ... I loved the unlimited supply of cash and all the artificial happiness it brought me ... but the status thing never meant squat.

6

Besides, one who spends a large majority of his youth doing time in assorted rehabs finds it a bit difficult to feign a high level of class.

Jenny was always the actress while I played the part of bumbling stage hand. No doubt her friends always pondered, and more likely asked her outright, why she stayed with such a societal misfit as yours truly. To that I respond with two simple but extremely forceful words ... prenuptial agreement. Though admittedly I have to say there is a bond there, however threadbare. Twelve and a half years is a chunk of time, after all, especially amongst the blue-blood crowd. As far as Jen and me, there is a massive gray area between hate and love, mostly consisting of a thick, crusty layer of reluctant tolerance. The socialite and the boozy, drug-addled recluse—Howard freakin' Hughes and Madonna ... together forever. Who would have ever thunk it? Well, off to nuke some waffles, then to peruse the old man's vast library of meaningless but obviously lucrative words.

Thirty-eight minutes later:

Ah, another sun-drenched, carefree day on Slacker Island. What else could a guy ask for? Lounging poolside with a frosty cold beverage and a good book? Guess I should withhold judgment on the "good" part for a later date. Dad's works were never that well received by critics, but that sure didn't sway the buying public a single iota. I lost count years ago how many movies were adapted from 'em. Dozens, I'd say, though I never

7

personally watched more than four or five. Never went in for guts 'n' gore, end-of-the-world scenarios, or futuristic soap operas, so that pretty well eliminated anything made from one of the old man's writings. Snooty critics aside, I remember reading in his obit where he'd sold something like one hundred and sixty million copies of his books worldwide—enough to afford houses on every freakin' coast and this modest little sixteen-room abode here, parked smack-dab in the center of the Pacific with no sister island in sight.

Damn, isn't life ironic, though? Pop would be having a knee-slapping field day with the world's present-day fix, though he never was big on zombie-plague tales, if I recall. Called 'em all redundant and lifeless, that last part said while flashing a sour smirk he often flashed in lieu of a genuine smile. What a cheery, fun-filled dude my old man was. Money and riches never made 'im happy. Booze only added to the misery. Five or six ex-wives didn't exactly add joy to the mix. Still, I think if he could picture the weird, wild happenings going on about now, even his ultra-cynical butt might be capable of cracking a grin.

Let's see now ... twelve-forty-four and still no Jenny. Probably packed a freakin' lunch ... anything to put additional time and space between us. Not exactly sure what I did to irk her off this time. Rarely am. Sometimes my very existence seems to be enough. Probably something to do with falling off the wagon for the umpteenth time, though I'd have to lay some of that particular blame on the old man. For one thing, I definitely inherited my love for the hard stuff from his boozy old soul. For another, it ain't my fault he left behind enough gin, vodka, and tonic on Slacker Isle to inebriate half the free world, or at least those still remaining upright with a working pulse.

Ah, well, they say time heals all wounds, and damned if time isn't the one commodity least likely to expire in these more-than-trying times.

On to the reading before all the melted ice transforms my gin and tonic into a slushy.

Chapter one, then, of Raymond J. Striker's best-selling collection titled LONERS *... wow ... now isn't that conveniently fitting?*

BOOK 1 - THE BUNKER

Prologue

Prologue: *Killian's Lair*

Killian fears the girl isn't going to make it. Worse yet, he feels her imminent passing a certainty. It seems merely a matter of time. He is no doctor, far from it, but in terms of potentially fatal symptoms, she possesses so very many. Shallow breathing, a rapid pulse, and a skin tone that grows paler by the moment. Gently patting her chilled forehead with a damp rag, he experiences a sudden rush of shame in the helplessness of the situation. Though he'd pawed through the contents of the first aid kit numerous times, there seems to be nothing available to offset the gradual shutdown taking place within the girl's motionless frame.

Despite the cruelty of such thinking, he can't help but ponder if she'd been better off expiring out there with all the rest. At least then the end might've been somewhat merciful and without the undue suffering of the slow, agonizing demise that surely waited.

Moments earlier he'd finally managed (spilling a half bottle of peroxide in the process) to slow the bleeding from the deep gash at the underside of her throat by first applying the necessary pressure and then securing the area with a heavy gauze wrap. Ditto the open wound behind her left knee and the bloodied knot at the back of her skull. Having laid her on the living room couch, the whole of which swallowed her like a shallow pit of quicksand, Killian then steps back to survey the unholy mess he's made of the tiny living room area. No matter, he realizes with a lengthy, resounding sigh that holds just a tint of desperation.

It isn't as if there isn't ample time to tidy up. Collapsing onto a nearby bean bag, he watches the girl's narrow midsection rise and fall inconsistently and wonders how long she has and if she will ever again regain consciousness. Killian closes his eyes in search of a moment's peace just as the bunker's filtration system hums to life.

Contradictory as it is, he can't help but both praise and curse his late uncle within the same fevered thought.

It has been just short of an hour since he'd carried the young girl inside and secured the shelter's outer doors, and he has yet to take proper inventory of their strange new surroundings. Outside the thick stone walls, the grounds continue to grumble and groan like a caged beast and Killian believes the earth could soon open up and swallow them whole, though at the present he is far too fatigued to dwell upon such probable catastrophe.

As it is, the memory of the girl's rescue is of the hazily blurred variety. He is finding it extremely difficult to believe many of his own actions in the past three hours, much less the reckless heroics that had seen him horse-carry the girl inside what he'd previously deemed to be his very own exclusive safe haven.

Running blood-smeared fingers through his already sweat-coated coif, Killian leans forward with both elbows propped atop his knees and reviews the replay as fragmented segments began to take shape in clearer, sharper clarity.

Chapter 1

Day One Flashback: *Upheaval*

Toppling over into the gravel drive just as the ground to her left swells and expands like an overinflated balloon, the lithe figure rolls gracefully beneath a nearby SUV, though such actions are more by accident than purposely seeking cover. Just as the Jeep is tilted to a tipping point by the cracking, heaving surface, the girl dives forward and gains clearance, miraculously suffering only a mild bump on her forehead in the process. The back of her head is already matted in crimson, as is her upper chest as a fresh neck wound gushes forth its freely flowing contents.

Weaving toward the house on her hands and knees, she watches the two-story brick structure implode a section at a time. The tiled roof peels itself free as if assaulted by monsoon winds. The front porch supports bend and snap like toothpicks beneath a sledgehammer's merciless blow. A foot-long crack forms in the red brick near the entrance, as if pulled apart from the inside by some monstrously oversized rib-spreader. A picture window explodes just as the front door entrance sails off its hinges, showering the gravel drive in a whirling mix of glass shards and oak splinters that slap the girl's exposed flesh like a dozen separate wasp stings. She falls back onto the vibrating earth with her hands blocking her eyes, her shoulder-length brown locks coated in debris. Curling into a fetal position as the ground rocks and trembles beneath her, the girl repeatedly screams out the names of those she fears have already fallen victim to similar scenes of horrific destruction. As the surface beneath her continues to buck and rumble, she peers between splayed fingers and can feel tiny specs of submerged glass that blur her vision to a watery haze.

"Dear ... God, what ... is ... this?" she mumbles between sobs, managing to rise to one knee as the structure before her crumbles into itself like a Styrofoam cup crushed within a solid steel vise. Attempting to stand while wiping both eyes with bare forearms that seep crimson from dozens of open wounds, the girl is oblivious to the thousand-plus-pound SUV that is being rolled toward her like a jagged bowling ball, shoved forward by dirt, clay, and rock swells that better resemble murderous ocean waves at the center of a building squall. Shoved forward onto bloodied knees as the ground rises beneath her, she is equally unaware of the man sprinting wildly toward her from the opposite direction. The girl manages only a choked whimper as the man first grabs and then tosses her over his left shoulder, the tiny patch of ground she'd previously occupied battered into oblivion less than a full second later by a serrated man-made boulder constructed of twisted metal and fiberglass.

"Wha— ... w-who? W-who y-you?" the girl babbles, though more from shocked bewilderment than true protest as the breath is slowly beaten from her lungs by the man's upper shoulder. The man, nearly twice the size of the squirming parcel atop his back, does not respond as he lumbers forward

14

with his eyes to the ground, lest either of his booted feet sink into the constantly shifting earth. A small duffel bag bounces atop the opposite shoulder, its connecting strap cutting a deep crease into the loose flesh of his ample midsection. Behind them, what remains of the SUV vanishes into the ever-widening sinkhole where the center of the homestead previously stood.

Overhead, the skies are a psychedelic mix of coal black, dark blue and luminous orange, swirling in both clockwise and counterclockwise fury from various directions, as if pregnant with funnel clouds on the verge of impending birth.

Huffing and groaning like a strained locomotive, the man lumbers up a steep upgrade leading into a thicket of overgrown shrubbery that pulsates with each subsequent earth tremor like some giant oceanic life form. With surprising grace that belies his considerable bulk, the man dodges and darts between the scattered weed clumps and saplings within to emerge into a vast clearing. With the girl having gone limp in his grip, he briefly glances upward into the swirling mass of maroon-shaded clouds overhead just as the first tennis-ball-sized clumps of hail plop into the ankle-high grass at his feet. It is just as he begins to descend a gravel-coated downgrade that the pelting subsides a bit, and he is able to keep from toppling forward by using the girl's bulk as a counterweight. The icy spears transform into a torrential rain as he slows at the base of a pear-shaped hillside practically engulfed in kudzu growth. The wind at his back is monsoon-strong, deafening. He feels he has but a precious few moments before he and the girl are scooped up like so much bagged trash and slung skyward.

Laying the girl face down as gently as circumstances allow, he sidesteps the shattered trunk of an ancient oak and reaches forward into the undergrowth with fingers outstretched like a blind man groping for hidden wares.

The man becomes acutely aware of a shrieking cry, a siren's wail that somehow pierces the howling winds. Glancing at the girl, it is obvious she is beyond such dramatics.

It isn't until he is able to rip away several layers of loosely tied vine and secure the squared outer edges of the trapdoor that Killian realizes the screams are his own. It has been nearly a calendar year since his uncle revealed the location of the bunker's well-camouflaged entrance, and he can't help but fear just what he'll find behind the stout wooden planks, or better yet ... what he *won't* find, such as suitable shelter from the hell-storm presently assaulting them from above and below. He'd loved the man no end, and there was no doubting either the man's intelligence or work ethic, nor that he'd possessed the wealth to complete such a project, but he also knew oh-so-well of Uncle Raymond's ultra-eccentric reputation. With that final thought at the forefront, Killian half-expects to pull the door ajar and find nothing more extravagant than a shovel-dug hole in the side of the hill with perhaps a jug or water, a carton of Winston Lights (his uncle's favorite smoke), and a few rolls of toilet paper serving as "survival" gear. Even worse, a flimsy lean-to constructed of cardboard or bamboo walls. What he finds instead is yet another blockade, this particular one of the solid steel variety and void of any type of knob or handle.

Twisting about, he leaps through the first entrance and lifts the girl to his chest, her blood-drenched hair entombing the whole of her face with the aid of the hard rain that only seems to have intensified until he can no longer visualize anything beyond a four-to-five-foot range. Hauling her inside the minuscule opening, he leans her against the inside of the wooden door and turns his attention back to the barricade at hand.

Jutting from the ground to his right is a silver metal pole, where a numerical keypad sits atop a flat marble surface about the size of a tea saucer. Crazily, Killian first assumes this to be a calculator, but then recalls the bizarre e-mail he'd received from Uncle Raymond several weeks earlier. The message had revealed a numerical code that Killian had instantly recognized as his father's birthday: three, twenty-seven, fifty-six.

Instinct motivates him to step over and quickly punch in the same five-digit number onto the pad's large hard plastic keys.

The thick metal door swings open with a mild sucking sound as if pressurized from within, and Killian laughs aloud. Wholly without his aid, the door reseals with the same whooshing sound and brings to mind the inner hatches on a submarine. The interior air smells metallic somehow, like wet coins.

Carrying the girl into a stony, narrow, dimly lit tunnel that favors a concrete sewer pipe, he takes barely a half dozen steps before facing the identical twin of the steely entrance at their backs. A sharp, resounding cracking noise causes Killian to fall roughly to one knee, though he does manage to maintain a firm grip on the girl. He believes the plank entrance to be little more than scattered kindling at this point, and tries not to contemplate his own fate (and the girl's) if the keypad combination had been wrong or even punched in incorrectly.

As was the first, the second door is provided with an identical keypad, to which Killian provides the exact same code, albeit punched out with a wet, badly shaking forefinger. The door slides smoothly ajar, though a bit slower than the first and with an even more resounding hiss of decompression. He lugs the girl inside with what little energy reserve remains intact, the scent of her blood loss piercing the otherwise antiseptic odor within. Killian's eyes dart about spastically as he takes rapid inventory of their new world. The lighting within isn't overly bright but is sufficient without being murky. The squared stone walls are painted light green, the rock ceiling smooth but unpainted. The floors are slickly tiled. Killian can only imagine the time and expense Uncle Raymond sacrificed on such a project, only to miss its inaugural unveiling.

It won't be until he discovers a fairly well-stocked first aid kit and completes treatment on the girl's wounds that a suitable tour is taken of all that encompasses his late uncle's bunker. An odd feeling of soul detachment will soon follow; a state of surreal bewilderment Killian will learn to not only accept, but actually *savor* as the once- essential element of time gradually becomes a non-factor.

Chapter 2
Day One: *Settling In*

With the girl (who appears to be no older than fifteen at the outset) sufficiently bandaged and her comatose condition unchanged, Killian eventually snaps from his self-imposed daze to better explore the shelter. Every few moments, as if set on some unseen timer, a low rumbling sound builds and soon crests before fading, as if an army of giant excavating machines were digging a tunnel just outside the stony walls.

Moving forward to the front room, which he'd so hurriedly bypassed in order to find the girl a soft place to lie down, he discovers an area perhaps twelve by twelve feet in circumference. Its contents include a large metal desk, top bare save for an open but powered-down Apple laptop and a legal pad with several assorted pens and pencils. A single high-backed chair faces a trio of mounted thirteen-inch TV monitors spaced approximately a foot apart.

Pondering the meaning of such a peculiar setup, Killian steps forward and leans both elbows atop the chair's cushioned top. Checking his watch, which somehow survived the random mayhem unscathed, he sees it reads 4:26 PM. Why this matters is a mystery, but he finds the power of such knowledge soothing in itself. A sense of order, perhaps, in a universe now sadly devoid of such.

Scanning the desktop, which appears miraculously dust-free, he is able to make out what is written across the legal pad's light blue cover. Scribbled in black magic marker, perhaps a Sharpie, are four simple words that invoke an instantaneous response.

INSTRUCTIONS TO LIVE BY

After rereading the phrase aloud several times, Killian begins to giggle uncontrollably until fresh tears roll down his dirt- and grit-smeared cheeks. After a time, his ribs begin to ache and his limbs grow numb. The thought that he might accidentally wake the girl from her deepened slumber only adds to the absurdity and thus the fit resurges forth unabated. Laughter transforms to a hacked, wailing cry. He collapses onto the cool tile and assumes a fetal position with balled fists pounding his chest in frustration. Mucus spews from his nostrils in gooey streams.

It is a full five minutes before he regains a semblance of composure.

Retrieving the legal pad while clearing his eyes and nose with a series of forearm wipes, he calmly begins to read in merciful silence as the tour recommences. His uncle's narratives are brief, to the point, just as the man himself had been. There doesn't appear to be a single wasted syllable. A man of few words was Uncle Raymond. A well-respected architect who had designed upscale office buildings and entire medical wings from Philly to Phoenix, Raymond Briggs had been a lifetime bachelor with a legendary temper and very few friends within the industry. Once retired, he'd gone into seclusion, having been labeled a wealthy crackpot by family members whose only interest in the man had been the supposed fortune he'd accumulated through the years. The crackpot talk had become prevalent in the wake of his constant speeches of the doomsayer variety, not to mention the rumor mill tidbit that he'd been planning on constructing a state-of-the-art fallout shelter.

True, Raymond (nicknamed the Mad Hatter by Killian's older sister) had been a man of precious few words. Few words but vital actions, especially regarding the darkest era mankind would ever suffer; the era of the end.

The hum of the purifiers kick in just as Killian settles into the chair and flips to the first page of the legal pad, wherein he discovers a hand-drawn blueprint titled "Lair of the Still Living." Despite the continued rumblings outside the stone chamber, he is soon pulled into a blissful state of oblivion.

A quick note before class begins:

***

To my dear nephew Kill-Joy [Uncle Raymond had pinned this nickname on Killian from a very early age] ... *I truly hope you have survived to peruse this rather grim operating instruction, and if so, that you were able to save a few others as well.*

Knowing that your penchant for privacy and solitude match my very own, I believe this not to be the case, but you can't blame a (deceased) old man for hoping you won't be trekking alone through the

22

psychological minefield ahead. You have a long, hard road ahead of you, Kill-Joy. Use this manual (six years in the making, as is the bunker itself) as a stepping stone for what is only the beginning of your new existence. The next chapter is totally up to you and those others who have found the will to go on in these, the darkest of times. I wish you nothing but luck in the strange new World all mankind will now inhabit.

You loving uncle, Raymond

Uncle Raymond's *"Instructions to Live by"* Part I:

(In case I'm not around to explain in person; a distinct possibility considering my advanced age and questionable health)

The entrance (welcome to your new home):

As you no doubt have already noticed, there are not simply one, but two entrances to the lair. This may seem a bit in the way of overkill, but in terms of logical thinking, it is simply a matter of security. The second door is there just in case the first is somehow breached, thus providing an added sense of safety. Each contains three inches of stainless steel girth with an internal triple-bolted lock. They are, of course, sealed airtight, as is the entire lair. Concerning the structure as a whole, and to perhaps ease minds, I'd be remiss in not mentioning that the outer shell is constructed of high- strength steel (HSS) and an additional four inches of solid

23

concrete intertwined with rebar (reinforced steel bars) for added flexibility, which I have a feeling may prove to be invaluable.

Communications Room (The "room with a view"):

Allow me a posthumous apology for the lack of style regarding the desk and (un) matching chair. No excuses, I went for the cheap, though I can honestly state that few other items contained within this lair can boast the same. Once powered up, the monitors allow a view from three distinct angles outside the bunker (an admission here: setup of these units was of the true nightmare variety, even more so than the construction of the shell and interior rooms ... hard to fathom but nevertheless true).

This is to provide at least a glimpse of the outside world, whatever remains, thus eliminating the natural curiosity one might feel to depart the safe haven for a brief "look- see" that might prove deadly to all involved. The cameras themselves are completely user friendly, require no adjusting, and are housed in a titanium casing that is completely waterproof, and, unlike the aforementioned furniture, they hardly came cheap.

The Apple laptop is Internet ready, for whatever good that might prove over time.

If nothing else, the built-in word processor might provide useful. There are extra legal pads and writing utensils within the desk's trio of drawers.

As you will no doubt notice more sooner than later, there are no clocks and calendars present. I am (was) a firm believer that man doomed himself with time restraints. It's time (pardon the horrific pun) for the big rewind, so to speak, and to leave the past exactly where it now lies ... in ruins. I'd suggest creating a new calendar, á la the Mayans or Aztecs, and pace your days, months, and years as you wish. Just a suggestion, of course, but it isn't as if such a chance comes along very often.

Pathways to Safety/Sealed to Perfection (purely precautionary measures)

Between each pair of connecting rooms lies a relatively short passageway (seven feet in length) that is centered by what I like to call a "crash seal," this being a sliding barricade that essentially segments each room into an individual space. These doors will only activate in case of a traumatic breach. They are an inch and a half thick and once again, the seal they provide is airtight.

Living Quarters (The "rest and recreation" room):

This is the largest (fifteen by eighteen) of the lair's rooms, since logically the living space is where the majority of one's time might be spent on a daily basis. Again, I must apologize in advance for whatever misguided purchases were made in the name of "entertainment," as I am less than an expert in such matters. The young clerk at Best Buy might well have taken advantage of such ignorance. Regardless, the space provided houses a large-screen TV (52' plasma) with floor mount; a combination DVD/Blu-ray player, and a

CD/cassette AM/FM stereo system with twin speakers.

You will find that the spiral-designed combination DVD/CD holder contains a rather varied collection of programs and musical choices. Again, I must apologize for the "all over the map" approach, as it is rather difficult to assume individual tastes. I went for old, new, popular and iconic. Hopefully my choices will allow for a welcome diversion, though the term "time-killer" might well serve as more appropriate.

The sectional couch is genuine leather and might be a bit stiff until broken in, while the twin bean bag chairs were admittedly a "spur of the moment" purchase in a split second of weakness while attempting a bit of decorative style. In retrospect, it is obvious I am woefully inept at such matters, though you will notice at least the colors do match.

The John (the "mother nature calls" room):

A personal note: this was, without a doubt, the most difficult space (ten by twelve) to map out, design and construct within the lair. The toilet is built atop an eight- hundred-gallon self-sustained septic tank forged from titanium. It goes without saying that the crew I hired to dig out and insert said tank were not without their puzzled looks, despite the pretty penny I doled out for the job's successful completion. The sturdy construction does not ... I repeat, does NOT guarantee damages will not occur as the earth shifts (i.e., earthquakes, tremors and the like). If such a calamity occurs and the tank is

26

ripped or torn from the flooring foundation, the backup will obviously be considerable and you will have to find an alternative to prevent the spread of germs. I can only say good luck, as I have no easy solution to the problem of human waste buildup.

The shower does contain both hot and cold running water (to use the modern vernacular, this was a true "bitch" to pull off), though the user(s) would be wise to limit overindulgence in fear of an inevitable water supply shortage as days pass. I would suggest no more than three (brief) showers a week per person. There is a reason the supply room inventory contains a healthy supply of deodorants and colognes.

Remember, water to *drink* is much more valuable than water to bathe.

The basin was added mostly for washing/scrubbing small clothing items. Sorry, but a washer/dryer combo just wasn't in the cards. Water usage would be a serious issue, as would the power drainage from a dryer unit.

Sleeping Quarters (the "sack-out" room):
Simplicity in itself, as I never was one for bedrooms overloaded with items more fit for the living room such as televisions, stereos, or computers. This room is about restful slumber and nothing else.

It measures twelve by twelve and houses two sleeper-peutic beds designed for the most comfortable sleep possible. A tinsel-steel clothesline (from which a privacy sheet can hang) halves the room at the center in case solitude is required. Additional sheets, blankets, and pillows are available in the supply room.

Kitchen (The "come 'n' get it" room):

At a mere six by eight feet, the smallest of the lair's spaces, but I believe significantly roomy for its intended purpose. The two-burner stove will boil the water and heat the canned goods sufficiently. Adding the mini fridge was questionable, since dairy products will only keep for so long before ruination and fresh meat isn't worth the bother as long as suitable packaged food is available (being a strict vegetarian, I simply couldn't stomach the thought of even the tiniest of meat lockers). I guess in the end I decided it one of the few extravagances provided within these impersonal stone walls. So ... if one does desire a chilled drink of water or fruit juice, so be it.

There are ample cups/mugs (3), glasses (4), dishes (5) and utensils (to include not one but two can openers) within the lone mounted cabinet.

Gym (The "keep the old ticker stout" room):

As a lifelong jogger and self-proclaimed health freak, I couldn't resist adding what is possibly the most unnecessary space within the lair. Still, if the future resident(s) are anything like me, it might well turn out to be the most appreciated. I'm afraid it is quite cramped at a mere ten by thirteen, and I originally had planned on adding another Nautilus machine, but I certainly hope it suffices for whoever finds it useful. The manual treadmill is nothing elaborate, but offers four degrees of difficulty from beginner to athlete. The Bowflex equipment is from my personal gym, and was used sparingly once my health began to deteriorate a few years back. It provides quite the workout, and I have included a user's manual. The last item is the heavy bag, which is sand-filled and weighs upwards of eighty pounds if unchained. I have provided the heaviest padded gloves (with wrist guards) available to avoid injury to the knuckles and wrists.

If nothing else, you can utilize the treadmill handles as clothes hangers.

Supply (The "everything you'll need to scrape by and more" room):

Here we have housed the essentials. Food will, of course, need to be rationed depending on the length of stay. I based quantities on what I liked to call the "radiation" factor, thus utilizing the old Cold War theory on how long one must avoid exposure to radiation following a nuclear holocaust. Though you may be facing an altogether different scenario, it remains one of the better (not to mention realistic) doomsday survival plans. I was actually amazed at how much I could pack into a relatively small (ten by twelve) space, although there is admittedly little room to maneuver. The water takes up the majority, though I did manage to relocate a few of the larger jugs to the generator room.

As for said inventory, I have included:

Food items:
Purified water:

Twenty 5-gallon jugs and fifteen additional of the single-gallon variety. This of course is to be utilized for both consumption and to refill the hot water heater and toilet reservoir. Of course, space limitations prevented a larger supply. I calculated this to be an eight- to ten-month (up to a calendar year) supply if properly rationed. Of course, this depends on the number of residents housed. A single survivor could stretch this out to as long as sixteen months.

Canned goods:
beef stew (twelve cans)

assorted soups (no water required—twenty-five cans) assorted packaged noodles/pasta (requiring water—two dozen packs)

assorted canned fruit in their own juice (twenty cans) assorted canned vegetables (twenty-four cans)

assorted canned meats (tuna, chicken, etc—twenty-four cans) canned coffee (2 cans instant)

Packaged foods:
crackers (low sodium)—two boxes w/four packs each rice cakes (sugar free)—six packages

animal crackers (low fat)—three packages

cereal breakfast bars (low sugar)—three packages of six

Bottled liquids:
fruit juice (enriched vitamin C—eight half-gallon jugs)

Vitamins/medications/toiletries:

multivitamin for men (three bottles of 100 pills each) multivitamin for women (same quantity as above) vitamin C supplement (three bottles of 60 each) rubbing alcohol (two bottles)

aspirin (three bottles—fifty tablets each)

cough/throat drops (two boxes—twenty-five drops each) hydrogen peroxide (two bottles)

Pepto-Bismol (three bottles)

Band-Aids (two boxes of assorted sizes) gauze (two boxes)

surgical needles (2)

cold/flu medication (two boxes—twenty pills each)

cold/flu medication (liquid—two bottles) toothpaste (Colgate—four large tubes) floss (four rolls)

toothbrushes (4) mouthwash (one bottle)

soap (Ivory—six bars; Olay—six bars) shampoo (three bottles—anti-dandruff) hairbrushes (two)

combs (two)

razors (three packs of twelve—disposable) shaving cream (three bottles)

liquid soap (three bottles) hand sanitizer (three bottles) grooming scissors (one)

toilet bowl cleaner (one bottle) Windex cleaner (one bottle) sewing kit

assorted candles (twenty-two count) matches (six boxes of 100 count)

oil lamp

lamp fuel (one canister)

air filters (six—one filter change for each purifier)

31

And ... last but certainly not least ... toilet paper (twenty-eight 1000- sheet two-ply rolls (talk about essentials!)

Clothing:
wool sweaters—size large (two) wool sweaters—size small (two)

winter jackets (hoodies)—size large (two) winter jackets (hoodies)—size small (two) undershirts—size large (two) undershirts—size small (two)

briefs—size large (three) panties—size small (three) sweat pants—size large (one) sweat pants—size small (one)

parachute shorts—size large (one) parachute shorts—size small (one)

athletic socks—men's one size fits all (three) athletic socks—women's sizes 5-10 (three) tennis shoes—sizes 10 and 11 (one each) tennis shoes—sizes 6 and 7 (one each) hiking boots—sizes 10 and 11 (one each) hiking boots—sizes 6 and 7 (one each)

Note: Obviously picking sizes was a colossal crap shoot. After mulling it over for a time, I went with large for men's sizes and small for women's. If small children are a part of the equation, I'm afraid improvising will be necessary. As for the aforementioned sizes, I'd personally rather appear a little baggy than be constricted, and it isn't as if looking "stylish" is the least bit prevalent anymore.

Note #2, the sequel: As you might have already noticed, each room is equipped with a first aid kit, each of which has been mounted onto the wall for easy access. Call me paranoid, but it just seemed logical not to have to sprint the length of the lair if an emergency arose.

Generator Room (The "only thing that now separates us from the Caveman" room):

Briggs & Stratton Vanguard Series, model #040234 (12-20 kW, 16,000 watts, fully automatic, air cooled), fueled by liquid propane. Operating instructions taped onto unit.

I'd rated at least a dozen brands and assorted models and found this one impressed above all others for reliability and dependability. Since most standby generators are built for outdoor setup, I was forced to add several extra air modifying units to prevent carbon monoxide buildup within the lair. After lengthy consideration, I had decided that a portable unit simply wouldn't provide the necessary power. The connecting propane tanks hook directly into the unit, and will provide approximately a month's worth of fuel (if used no more than ten to twelve hours daily). There are twelve additional cylinders (as my goal was a calendar year's worth of power). My suggestion: limit fuel usage to six-eight hours daily if possible. I have provided an ample supply of candles and an oil lamp as alternate light sources.

Air modifier/purifier and filters: Units are located in the living room, bedroom, and generator room. Filters good for up to 120 days; one backup filter for each located in supply room. I'd advise operating at least one purifier (living room during day; bedroom at night) for up to 10 hours per day.

A final note: *Pardon me for the "Will and Testament" tone here, but I find it a necessity if legalities ever surface that question my actions. The original plan for this state-of-the-art survival shelter was solely for my family's use. With the not-so-recent falling out between myself and said kin, the word "family" is now defined by a single individual, my nephew Killian. Upon the event of my untimely demise, I pass sole ownership to him and whatever other survivor(s) he deems worthy to share both the structure and provisions found inside.*

Sincerely, Raymond Briggs II

***

Tucking the legal pad beneath one arm, Killian rises with great effort, as if he'd been sitting in place for several hours instead of just under fifteen minutes. The constant throbbing at his left shoulder is an even match for the soreness of his right ankle, injuries no doubt suffered in the mad dash for safety with the girl in tow. He thinks it a perfect time to search out a glass of water and a handful of aspirin, departing the comm room with a slight limp for his initial exploration of the structure.

"Show me what you've done, Uncle Ray," he mutters weakly as the grounds outside the bunker grow mercifully silent.

Chapter 3
Day One: *The Grand Tour, However Brief*

He gives the girl a quick once-over, her curled position on the couch unchanged, before trekking through the short tunnel that separates the living room from the sleeping quarters. Just as advertised, therein lay twin beds (meticulously clean and neat) and a wire clothesline that runs the length of the relatively short space. Still another tunnel and he enters and then quickly departs the bathroom, the weak smell of disinfectant tapping his nostrils. The kitchen looms next, the sight of the two-burner stove causing his stomach to mumble and groan almost instantly with a deep-seated hunger he'd hardly been capable of registering. Next the gymnasium swims murkily into focus.

Killian soldiers quickly on, as the mere thought of physical exertion seems to increase his level of fatigue and minor injury tenfold.

The generator room follows, and Killian inspects the machine briefly, just long enough to ensure the aforementioned operating instructions are indeed taped to its side.

The supply room is, as his uncle had mentioned, packed tightly with only the narrowest of space in between stacks of clearly marked items. Some (mostly canned food and medicines) are stocked inside clear plastic containers with the individual drawers labeled.

It takes little time to search out and find the aspirin, and after a brief struggle to remove the top from the childproof bottle, Killian palms a trio of pills and a gallon jug of water that is simply labeled *From the Tap* in Sharpie in his uncle's uniquely defined writing style.

Lumbering back into the kitchen on wobbly legs, he pulls the plastic twist top from the jug, tosses the pills to the back of his parched throat and drinks greedily, rationing be damned. Ignoring the slight twinge of urgency at his bladder, he bypasses the bathroom and stumbles into the bedroom, piling clumsily atop the neatly made bed to his right.

Before unconsciousness sweeps over his senses like a billowy black cape, Killian thinks momentarily of the girl and wonders if and how long she will retain a pulse. In his dreams, he sees the face of his late uncle, whose overly pasty visage appears frozen in a perpetual grimace. The scene alters; his uncle is now completely naked and calmly, robotically waiving goodbye while being gradually swallowed by a dense maroon-shaded fog at his back. Killian attempts to run toward his uncle in order to obtain a firm hold and pull him back from the blood-colored mist, but finds his limbs in a particularly frustrating state of paralysis that seemingly can only exist in such nightmares.

"Not your fault, my boy," his uncle moans though the horrible grimace remains unchanged.

"Remember ... not your fault...."

Mercifully, Killian sleeps without further interruption.

Chapter 4

Day Two: *Getting Organized*

Waking in blurred increments as if heavily sedated, he practically falls from the firm comfort of the mattress to the cool tiled floor, his injured shoulder screaming its disapproval. Hanging his head while sucking in several deep breaths, he remains on all fours for several moments before rising with a pronounced groan. His button-up cotton shirt hangs crookedly from his torso, and his blue jeans are stiff with dampness.

Peering downward before taking an initial step forward, he notices his left foot is sockless. Turning about to scan the floor near the bedside, he resembles a drunken stew bum pondering the whereabouts of the previous night's hooch. With the missing footwear nowhere in sight, Killian rambles forward in an uneasy gait. He locates the jug of water from the previous day's expedition and gulps down several swallows before a bout of intense nausea threatens its successful descent.

"F-f-fuel..." he stammers as the air purifiers kick in for the initial concerto of the morning, "gotta ... find some ... grub. T-that's what ... I need. Haven't ... haven't eaten anything since ... since..."

By practically sticking the face of his watch flush with the tip of his nose, he reads the time as 9:17 AM.

"Almost a ... d-day ... a full day without so much as a n-nipple ... n-nibble. No wonder I'm ... so damn ... wrec ... weak."

37

Breakfast consists of a can of beef stew (unheated, as desperation simply does not allow for the time or bother) and a full package of saltines, all washed down by the remains of that initial jug of water. Afterwards, Killian's lower gut aches from the wolfing of the meal, the execution of which is a gluttonous blur.

Cautiously entering the living room on bare feet (having discarded the remaining sock), he has an overwhelming sense of foreboding as his lungs are forced into instantaneous lockdown. The pulse pounding in his ears and at the base of his neck grows ever louder as he nears the girl's prone form, whose curled position appears frighteningly identical from the night before.

"Um ... he ... hello? Are ... are you ... awake ... uh ... okay?" he babbles timidly, instantly regretting the attempt at vocalizing a greeting that inadvertently sounds as if it had been spoken by a spooked six-year-old on the verge of tears.

Though unresponsive, the girl's narrow chest does visibly expand and deflate, and Killian exhales in relief. Kneeling onto the edge of the leather couch, he gently checks her bandages. A bit later, having turned her onto her back, he subsequently cleans and replaces the gauze on both the neck and knee wounds. Utterly exhausted from the process, he soon plunders the supply room for more food (canned chicken), water, aspirin, and a handful of vitamin supplements. While gorging, he vows to start organizing the bunker and form a plan of action for what will be his (and perhaps the girl's) inevitable departure back to the world beyond.

Instead, within a half hour of finishing his second meal since awakening, he slumps back toward the bedroom and passes out cold. This time, the experience is utterly dreamless.

His watch reading 2:37 PM, Killian arises with just a bit more pep than following the previous slumber.

"Damn ... just call me Rip Van Wrinkles," he croaks hoarsely while running stiff fingers through an ever-stiffer coif that feels as if it had been dipped in honey. He can smell his own odor: a thick, rancid BO mingled with just a tinge of stale urine.

"My kingdom for a suds-filled Jacuzzi."

He laughs at this, the process burning the back of his throat. Sitting on the corner of the bed, he notices the top blanket still mostly intact and figures he'd hardly moved while slumbering.

After procuring a towel, bar of soap, and bottle of shampoo from supply, he enters the miniscule shower (wondering exactly what race of *Pygmies* Uncle Raymond had designed it for) and allows the fairly warm but far from steamy streams to cascade his battered form for a full ten minutes before the water goes ice cold. It is during the toweling-off period that he notices the grotesque bloating of his midsection, which appears twice its normal size. Not an attractive sight, he muses, considering it wasn't exactly lean to begin with.

"Probably just stopped up from all the stress," he decides without alarm, hoping the dull ache located there soon translates into a healthy bowel movement. He forces a grim smile while massaging the massive swell with both hands.

"Maybe I'll start using Uncle Ray's little gymnasium after all."

First things first, he concedes, prioritization is goal one. Find out exactly what's going on outside the bunker walls before getting situated on the inside. Dressing in a fresh tee-shirt (a bit on the snug side), sweat pants (slightly baggy), and socks (one size fits all), he strolls purposefully through the narrow hall, giving the girl only a passing glance to ensure her condition has remained stable. Once confirmed, he moves on to the comm room.

Instantly mesmerized, he sits for nearly three hours scanning the trio of monitors, trying to ascertain exactly where such meticulously placed cameras could have been mounted on the mountainside to provide such clear, breathtaking scenes. The laptop remains untouched throughout the marathon, though the blatant disinterest isn't at all purposeful. It is more the hypnotic effect of peering through the camera's eyes that makes all else around him pale by comparison.

Camera one (viewed from his left) appears to focus on the wooded hillside Killian himself had descended to reach the bunker's hidden entrance. Camera two (centered) zooms in on the entrance spot itself, where a dark, jagged hole has replaced the wooden door that Killian had heard shattered in the storm. Thick waves of greenish vines hang over the black chasm like flowing tendrils. The overall view covers a six- to eight-foot area on either side of the formerly hidden doorway, as if Uncle Raymond had expected visitors, whether they be of the welcomed variety or just the opposite.

Knowing his favorite uncle, the latter would've been the safer bet by far. The exact focus of the final camera (far right) is a mystery. On display is a flat clearing with a thick patch of what appears to be evergreen shrubbery on one side and a line of ancient pines on the other. The clearing is perhaps three to four feet wide, though a precise estimation is impossible, and resembles the type dug out by a once-active water source having recently gone dry. At the moment, a slim stream, no doubt created by the recent storms, is clearly visible down the trail's center. Leaning back with his bare feet atop the desk and looking every bit the haggard sentinel, Killian finds himself drawn to the enigmatic clearing again and again.

"What exactly were you looking for here, Uncle Ray?" he ponders while running a flat palm across the fine growth of stubble at his chin.

"What are ... were you expecting?"

More than once he ponders why he wastes time on such a fool's folly, but remains mysteriously drawn nonetheless. He figures his uncle might well have set up the cameras for no other reason than to provide an enigmatic time-waster.

It isn't until the loud grumbling of his overextended gut snaps him to that he departs his post for the bathroom. Grimacing from the building pressure of an enraged bowel, he practically sprints through the living room, shooting the girl the briefest of glances before nearly tripping over the nearest beanbag in startled reaction.

For a moment, he is able to ignore the pain and desperate need for relief, the soles of his feet squeaking loudly as an impromptu break dance leads him back toward her.

Though her eyes remain closed and her body motionless, it's the obvious alteration in her positioning that has him once again looming over her like a ravenous vulture prepping to feed.

The girl now lies squarely on her back, her arms stiff at her sides as if called to attention. One ankle is crossed over the other in a pose of casual bliss.

Unconsciously holding his breath, for an instant he considers waking her with a gentle shake or forceful vocalization, but hesitates and instead checks her bandages without actually touching them. With bleeding no longer an issue as evidenced by the lack of stains on the gauze, Killian quietly sidesteps away and resumes the original mission.

While crouched on the toilet seat like a perched gargoyle, he cannot help but feel both equal parts elated and fearful of the girl's possible recovery. The former emotion is natural, he concedes with a silent nod. After all, he had saved her life and should be viewed as a hero of sorts. As for the latter, he hasn't a blessed clue of its origin.

The flushing sound that soon follows isn't nearly loud enough to drown the girl's moaning cries, a piercing banshee-like scream that sends Killian crashing to one knee outside the bathroom entrance.

He realizes in that horrible moment that the fear is indeed real, no matter its mysterious source. A large part of him wants to hide, to squirm away on all fours and duck behind the nearest available barricade (generator room perhaps?). It is several tense moments and only when the girl's wails have transformed into weakened sobs that he finds the courage to rise.

He eventually reaches her. Her positioned is unchanged. Her eyes are closed. Her ankles remained crossed. Her breathing is shallow and her complexion as pale as ever. With badly shaking hands and with feet of clay, Killian studies her for several minutes through unblinking eyes, expecting (and clearly dreading if so) her eyes to widen and her lips to part with still another siren-like screech. Instead, the lone movement remains the gentle rising and falling of her upper torso.

Tiptoeing back in the direction he came, Killian heads to the supply room and retrieves a bottle of Pepto-Bismol, tearing away the childproof top with a single twist and sucking down the equivalent of three full adult doses.

"Shit ... I needed that," he spews through pink-coated lips. It is another half hour before he finds the intestinal fortitude to reenter the living room side of the bunker.

Two additional hours of playing glazy-eyed sentinel to a trio of unchanged images (the last hour of which is viewed in murky shadows lit only by sparse moonlight) and his eyes grow red and itchy with grogginess. Hugging his knees to his bloated belly, Killian resigns to collapse in the chair in lieu of the bedroom (thus saving himself an additional nerve-splintering trip through the living room). His dreams are few but fitful; the faces within blurred and unrecognizable, as are the static-filled voices that accompany them. Actions have no middle ground and are either maddeningly slow or executed at warp speed. All told, they mean little but are strangely troublesome just the same. Nightmares in *mini-blurb* form. Killian wakes only once and ignores his aching bladder in fear that any semblance of noise (save the ever-present purifiers kicking on and off throughout the night) might serve to refuel the girl's phantom cries and send him spiraling off into a permanent state of madness.

Chapter 5

Day Three: *Frozen Images*

Finding his gut maladies more acute than ever, breakfast is kept to a bare minimum (a glass of juice and a cup of steamed ramen noodles). Having arisen at nearly half past ten in the AM, Killian is shocked to discover his energy sapped despite the extra slumber.

Sleeping upright in the less-than-roomy chair has left a slight crick in his neck and added a new dose of misery to a still-sore shoulder. Dry of mouth and with great trepidation (his hands go ice cold; his scalp tingles like mad), he checks on the girl and finds only a slight variation in her position; her ankles have uncrossed and her right arm now rests folded across her midsection. Her bandages appear sound and unstained.

Though fearful of the possible reaction, he reaches down and places the back of his left hand ever so delicately against her bare forehead. The flesh is warm, but without obvious fever. Backing away, he wonders how long she can last in such a state without water ... without nourishment. Stepping sluggishly toward the comm room, it strikes him as bizarre that the helplessness of the girl's situation isn't the psychological burden to him that it should be. As it is, he views her plight as no more than a worrisome irritant; a discomfort that, much like his distended, constantly groaning stomach, he wishes would simply go away.

45

He assumes what he has begun to think of as the "day-watch" shift, leaning back with bared feet propped and frequently shifting eyes scanning the trio of monitors in true department store security guard fashion. An hour or so in and having witnessed nary a movement (all three views are beginning to resemble still paintings), Killian shifts his focus to the laptop. Balancing it atop his knobby knees, he powers it up and watches the black screen transform to a dark blue. A few select keystrokes find the Internet Explorer icon (only two others grace the screen saver Uncle Raymond has created, those being Microsoft Word and Excel).

"Ohhh, always the joker you are," he blurts between giggles, "what exactly am I supposed to do with *Excel*, Uncle Ray, balance my checkbook? Then again, I can't see dictating very many letters or writing the old memoirs in *Word* either. What a freaking card you are ... um ... w-were." This final omission having placed a serious damper on the previous bout of levity, he quickly double-clicks the Explorer icon while wearing a deep frown.

The default search engine is Yahoo!. The home page loads in less than thirty seconds, and Killian sits dumbfounded at a frozen image he is unable to escape as the page remains in suspended animation no matter how many times he attempts to navigate to a more serene landscape. He reads the headline aloud numerous times though unaware he is doing so.

"The End of it All," it simply reads. Not exactly Pulitzer material, but brutally honest and without even a hint of the mass media's usual (former?)

46

hyperbole. Then again, why exaggerate something that needs no such doctoring? What's true is true. Cold hard fact is cold hard fact. Besides, the accompanying photo, spread out over the length of the page, says more than any mere words can express. Not that the White House smoldering and in ruins isn't shock enough, but it's more the background images that give justice to such a bold, horrific headline. The entire capital city resembles an enormous bonfire, with not a single high-rise upright and a dozen separate funnel clouds of smoke rising into an orange-tinted sky that looms much too low and appears pregnant with mayhem.

"Oh ... god ... it is ... it's ... real...." is all Killian can manage while right and left clicking like mad on a dead mouse. Since he is unable to navigate down the page, the article is limited to the top two and half paragraphs. In it he reads such spirit- demolishing terms as "*billions feared dead*" (he is forced to reread this several times in order to wrap his mind around the word 'billions') and "the planet as a whole seems to literally be imploding upon itself." A half hour passes, the image now sewn indelibly into his subconscious, until he is finally able to escape its magnetic pull. He'd always heard people talk about not being able to look away from such disasters, auto crashes being the usual culprit, but had never before experienced the phenomenon firsthand. Nodding solemnly while powering down the laptop, he realizes with great irony that he'd most likely been entranced by the biggest crash of them all ... the crashing and burning of Mother Earth.

The girl now sleeps on her stomach with her arms tucked beneath and her narrow hips tilted slightly to the right. As is now his habit, Killian tiptoes by without benefit of either inhaling or exhaling. He has begun to think of the living room area as that single room inside a haunted house that all must avoid in order to ensure survival. As badly as he wants to check the television for a working signal or the stereo for an operating radio station, he talks himself out of such attempts with an ease that barely masks a building shame. He is deathly afraid of a barely teenaged girl who is apt to die unless he forces the issue of proper healing. Blowing out a long breath as he reaches the bathroom, he aggressively massages his inflamed midsection with gnarled fingers.

"Once I check the generator and prep some lunch, I'll see if I can wake her.

Yeah, well ... maybe after lunch, but it has to be done. It ... I ... can't keep avoiding it. What the *hell* am I so spooked of anyway? She's just a kid, for Christ's sake," he grumbles, taking a seat on the cool porcelain to await the latest mucus-filled explosion from his nether regions.

"Just a kid who's gonna kick off unless I at least ... try to help."

Washing up afterwards, Killian becomes acutely aware of a detail he'd somehow overlooked in the two and a half days since being incarcerated in his late uncle's survival bunker.

There wasn't a single mirror or reflective device in the place.

***

Foolishly, he'd thought a light lunch of tuna on saltines and a cup of black coffee wasn't going to irritate his stomach. Instead, he finds himself perched atop the porcelain goddess for the third time in less than an hour. Dreading the mission ahead (he has begun to think of the girl as some hopelessly infected and possibly contagious lost cause), he attempts a mild diversion by continually rehashing the curious subject of mirrors, or in this case the lack thereof. With the generator and air purifier filters (save the one mounted in the living room) checked and double-checked, he'd executed an extensive walkthrough just to verify the mirror theory as fact. Sure enough, not a single glass reflector present (including the living room, which he'd inspected in double-time mode). Mulling it over with great effort, he can't come up with a single hypothesis of how or why his uncle would omit an item so commonplace in people's everyday lives.

An item found in homes (usually in several rooms if not all), in virtually all forms of transport, public bathrooms, pocketbooks, and purses. An item used casually and professionally, by the vain and not so vain. An item the majority took for granted as easily accessible no matter the locale, be it a lonely street corner or a brush-infested jungle. How could anyone forget to add even a single mirror to the inventory list for a shelter built exclusively for long-range survival?

Then again, if he remembers correctly, Uncle Raymond hadn't exactly been the well-groomed type. The man had always held that "mad scientist" look, what with the stringy locks that resembled coiled wire and the thick, gray-streaked beard that looked as if it hadn't seen a comb since its stubbly inception (*the kind of beard you could hide things in,* he'd heard his mother quip more than once).

Perhaps his uncle simply didn't deem the need for reflection necessary, or better yet, just plain old forgot. Though he'd been a certified genius, it was a known fact that an overabundance of intelligence had its side effects, such as lack of common sense when dealing with the more mundane facts of life. Regardless, that first attempt at shaving was liable to be quite the adventure. Perhaps he could use the big-screen TV's reflection as a substitute. With that in mind, he meanders toward the living room with all the enthusiasm of a death row inmate making his way to the gas chamber.

***

The girl is sitting up as he enters, her coltish legs pulled tightly to her chest, her chin submerged in between. The gauze bandage hangs loose like a broken shutter from her left knee. It is several moments before Killian can manage to exhale the breath he'd so hastily sucked in, much less form a string of intelligible words.

"H-hey ... are ... are you awake?"

Obviously caught off guard, she openly cringes, hugging herself ever tighter into a ball of quivering flesh.

"S-sorry to surprise you … I didn't mean to … to sneak up," he offers, sidestepping the same beanbag that had earlier threatened to trip him up. "You've been out for … for a while. I was beginning to worry. I mean," he continues through a strained smile that better resembles a pained grimace, "you've gotta be about ready to eat the wallpaper by now … that is, if there were any."

"W-who are y-you? Where is … this place?" the girl croaks timidly, having elevated her head just enough from the crevice of her knees for the words to be audible. He sees her raise an unsteady hand to the bandage secured to the underneath of her chin and feel about gingerly.

"I'm … my name's Killian. As for the bun— well, I'm afraid this is home for now." "Is it…your house?"

He kneels slowly and sinks into the alternate beanbag on the far side of the tiny space, careful not to overcrowd the girl.

"Well, no … it's … well, technically it's not a house at all. It's more like a shelter.

My uncle had it built in case … in case it was needed. Who might you be, miss?" "K-Kayla."

"Proud to make your acquaintance, Kayla, though I wish it were under more pleasant circumstances."

Gradually lowering her legs, the girl sits upright until she faces him, though their eyes have yet to meet. She folds her arms at her groin and keeps her chin lowered so as to not yet reveal her face in its entirety.

"Was ... was that your uncle's house that ... that crumbled out there?" "Yeah, it was. I barely saw you in time to sa ... to get you out of there." "The house ... it ... it melted."

Fighting a mad urge to laugh aloud at both the girl's choice of words and her mechanical, emotionless delivery, Killian feigns a cough instead.

"It was a mess, all right. There was an earthquake and a ... a really bad storm.

We're ... safe in here though. You don't have to worry."

"I'm not an infant, mister," she replies scornfully; "you don't have to be so patronizing. I ... know what was going on ... what caused it all. My ... dad always used to say the end was coming, that the world was just asking for it. Guess he ... didn't know, like, how prophetic those words would be."

Small in stature as she was, a "walking twig," his uncle might have said, there was a maturity in her tone that went well beyond her years. Perhaps it was just the shock of what she'd witnessed over the past several days leading to their present incarceration, but Killian cannot help but acknowledge the vibe that this isn't just your average, ordinary preteen. Curiously, there is a twinge of familiarity with the girl that holds no logical merit.

"Um, sorry about the tone. I was just trying to set your mind at ease." "Have…things improved at all? I mean, is it, like, over?"

52

Feeling as though his left foot is falling asleep, Killian shifts his bulk atop the beanbag and barely avoids toppling off altogether.

"So far, so good. We've been ... inside for ... well, this is the third day, and it's been fairly quiet. I was actually considering venturing out to find you a doctor if your condition didn't ch—"

"Third day?" the girl interrupts, her high-pitched tone suddenly void of the previous hoarseness.

"Yeah, you've been conked but good. Sorry about my bandage work. Don't claim to be an MD. Fact is, it's probably about time we changed those out. I was afraid the neck wound might need stitches. Luckily for you, it seems to be healing on its own, 'cause I'm certainly no whiz with needle and thread, even if we had any."

"What h-happened?" she inquired, gesturing weakly with an index finger toward the wound beneath her jaw.

"Not really sure, but you were bleeding like a stuck pi—um, losing some blood.

Probably some shrapnel from the house or my uncle's SUV. That thing was rolling toward you like a spiked bowling ball by the time I—"

"What was ... I doing out there?"

Verbally dumbstruck, Killian struggles with a response but eventually can only go palms up with both hands. This is his first experience in dealing with an obvious case of amnesia, and it seems psychology is no more his specialty than healing physical wounds.

"I'd wrecked the ... my van a few hundred yards north of Uncle Ray—my uncle's place and by the time I reached the house, you were standing in the driveway with all hell breaking loose around you."

Finally, the girl's head rises completely and she brushes several lengthy strands of strawberry blonde locks from her forehead. With her slim face and large eyes, Killian is instantly reminded of the actress Dakota Fanning in her preteen years.

"Mister ... can I have a drink of water?" she asks, the greenish hue of her eyes containing an almost supernatural glow. Though her face is predictably gaunt and still quite pale, there is a chiseled quality in her features that previews the beautiful young lady she is sure to grow into.

"Of course ... are you hungry?" he replies, rolling clumsily off the beanbag. His knees pop wildly as he stands. "Think you could eat a bite?"

The girl nods, reaching back to massage what had once been a golf ball-sized knot on the back of her head.

"I can try, I guess. Got any cold pizza?"

Killian laughs at this, a hearty, deep cackle from the pit of his still bloated, constantly growling gut. The girl does not join in the jocularity, but instead lies back down on the couch and turns her head in the opposite direction.

Double-timing it to the kitchen, he feels a faint cramp at his midsection as an icy chill races up his spine and to the back of his neck, the hairs there standing out like quills. It takes every bit of self-control he has not to race back to the living room to see if he'd imagined the entire conversation. What keeps him moving forward is the possibility that such an insane notion could prove true, and that if he were to go back and find the girl again comatose and unresponsive, that he might well join her.

**

As the girl sips tea from a steaming mug, Killian busies himself with the flat- screen TV and stereo in an attempt to gain any outside news. It isn't a difficult confession to admit he's purposely avoided such endeavors since sealing off the bunker, and not solely because of the girl's languishing presence. Simply put, he was terrified of what he would see or hear, a worst-case scenario being *nothing at all* on both counts.

Predictably, the television proves a woeful failure; channel after channel of either pitch-black nothingness or jagged lines of static. As for the radio, a half hour of station scanning across both FM and AM lines proves equally fruitless until a faint voice pierces the crackling drone like a glorious beacon.

Nearly maxing out the Sony system's volume control, Killian positions himself between the twin speakers and shoots the girl an excited glance. In return, she seems hardly to have noticed while staring straight ahead with the oversized mug clasped tightly in both hands.

For the next hour plus, neither hardly budges as the weary-toned host of what is announced as KBGY Talk Radio spews forth the latest in projected death tolls and countries under siege by what is now being labeled *Days of Reckoning* by whatever media still exist.

"Enough already ... my kingdom for a dose of heavy metal," Killian eventually concedes with an accompanying groan that screams mental fatigue. Poking the power button with an extended finger, he relishes the relative silence even as his bowels seem to reignite with sudden movement. He had spent the previous few hours feeding and rebandaging the girl, who had gone practically mute during the process.

"You want another aspirin?" he asks her offhandedly, having grown a bit peevish from an overall lack of response.

"No. I think I want to sleep now," she replies stoically, placing the empty mug on the tiled floor while resuming a prone position on the couch.

"Sounds like a plan. See you in the morning ... or whenever we both wake, whichever comes first, I guess. Goodnight then, Kayla."

The girl has already rolled over and seemingly dismissed his very presence. He thinks of bringing her a blanket and reconsiders as the temperature feels a tad muggy. Instead he reaches down and retrieves the mug and departs, having given up on further conversing in lieu of a much-needed siesta. He checks the monitors one last time and finds the tranquil, moonlit landscapes as unchanged as ever. Despite the stern warning issued in Uncle Raymond's survivor manual, Killian will venture out to check the landscape (and hopefully breathe some welcome fresh air) the following day. If nothing else, he decides while paying the bathroom a final visit (hopefully) for the night, it will free him up from the girl's strangely uncomfortable company.

Chapter 6
Day Four: *Weather Events of Note*

Killian wakes layered in a cold sweat, the cotton tee he'd worn to bed stuck to his torso like moistened paste. A low rumbling sound echoes throughout the structure, much like the aftershocks from that last series of earthquakes that had led them here.

Reaching out, he places a flat palm against the cool stone wall as if to halt the tremors with his touch.

The vibrations are weak but unmistakable. A short prayer escapes his dry, chapped lips.

Miraculously, the rumblings halt almost immediately. Before drifting off, Killian experiences a particularly grisly dream wherein the bunker is flooded by a virtual ocean's worth of blackish, foul-smelling water filled with floating entrails and indistinguishable body parts. While splashing about and searching for an exit from the rising waters, he dog-paddles into the living room and sees the girl crouched atop the flat-screen TV like a perched gargoyle.

"Oh, but I *do* know you, mister—" she screeches with maniacal glee, frothy spittle flying from her curled lips as her dark green eyes roll back to reveal blackened pits. Her fingers are freakishly long, and begin to stretch and flex with reptilian grace.

"You know me too, don't you? Ohhhh yessssss, you know me sooooo weelllllll…" she wails, diving

58

toward him and vanishing beneath the gooey, tar-colored waters.

Killian hasn't a clue if he actually screamed aloud once the clawlike vises gripped his ankles and began to tug. In retrospect, he believes he probably did. Shrieked and then whimpered like a terrorized five-year-old who'd just heard his first bona fide ghost story. If possible, he would have openly dared even the bravest souls not to have done the same.

***

As if strictly obeying Murphy's Law, Killian rises to find his wristwatch has stopped at exactly 2:14 AM. Using a forefinger to tap the glass and then the back of the watch, he sees it has no effect.

"Aw yeah, that's the old college spirit..." he spits sourly, tossing the now- worthless piece of jewelry aside; "... just CPR it back to life. What a moron..."

Dressing in the same white tee-shirt and sweat pants from the night before, he starts toward the kitchen to boil water for coffee and instead makes a quick beeline for supply.

The large-size wool sweater is a bit tight, though his feet slip into the size eleven hiking boots as if specially designed with his feet in mind. He eyes the thick winter jacket with its bulky design and leaves it behind for now, hoping it won't be a necessary item anytime soon. As is par for the course since their arrival at the bunker, his stomach churns and aches with the sudden flurry of activity. Despite this, he craves nourishment and figures it wouldn't at all be wise to be running on empty with such an event-filled day ahead. In truth, there is a palpable relief in escaping the dreamscape world for reality, however unsettling and unpredictable the latter.

***

Once in the kitchen, he leans on the hard oak kitchen counter while sipping steaming black java and tries to recall the last semi normal weather conditions before the many and varied storms had turned the atmosphere inside out.

"It was fairly cool for mid-September ... highs only around sixty or so. Ten or fifteen degrees colder than the norm, I remember 'em saying. Things were already getting mighty strange before the big hammer fell," he mumbles between cautious sips. Lord, how he missed fresh milk or half and half to cool his morning caffeine. "Could be winter in Greenland or summer in the Mojave out there ... sure can't tell a blessed thing by those monitors."

He feels the girl's presence behind him before her words verify it.

"Don't want to interrupt whatever conversation you're having with yourself," she says without a hint of humor, leaning hard against the outside wall and peeking inside. "But can you, like, spare another cup of whatever that is you're drinking?"

"Um, sure. You ... like black coffee?"

"Never tried any, but it smells worth checking out."

Taking a few steps forward, the girl momentarily grips the side of the counter for support. Her face has regained a bit more color, but maintains a slight ashen quality.

"You sure you ought to be up? I mean, I could bring you a cup," Killian suggests, turning to refill a lidless metal pot with water from a gallon-sized jug.

Once more, her choice of words suggests levity even as the delivery implies anything but.

"No, thanks. I'm going to end up with bedsores unless I get my lazy ass in gear."

Several uncomfortable (at least from Killian's point of view) minutes pass as he prepares the coffee.

"Sugar?" he asks after filling the ten-ounce mug approximately halfway.

The girl shakes her head, reaching to take the cup from his visibly shaking hand. "Going somewhere?" she asks after an initial sip, followed by a slight grimace.

Bending down to retie his left boot for no other reason than to avoid the girl's intrusive glare, his response is delayed and for a second he even considers lying, though he cannot validate the impulse to so. It isn't as if he has anything to hide.

"Well, I was considering a ... little excursion outside these stone walls just to see if things are as bad as advertised."

The girl snickers into the half-empty cup, motioning with her free hand toward the comm room.

"Really? You might want to check out the monitors first."

With a deeply creased brow, Killian discards his own mug and passes the girl without response. He'd scanned and scoped the same trio of bland, tranquil images for three days running without even a hint of dramatic (or otherwise) change, and both his heart and mind raced with even the slightest possibility of alteration.

"Brace yourself, Mister ... from what I saw, it ain't pretty," he hears the girl blurt out in a semi-mocking tone, and Killian can't help but ponder (and not for the first time since her awakening) her level of mental stability.

Mockery or not, what he witnesses upon arrival within the comm room vindicates the girl's warning tenfold. Standing upon entering, he takes a seat soon enough while falling into a virtual trace—his bloodshot, spastically darting eyes pass from one screen to another and back again with mechanical, computerized precision.

"Aw, now, how can that ... how can any of this *be*?"

He points at each screen individually, starting with the far left and moving gradually to the right, though pausing a bit at the center monitor for what a film director might label "dramatic effect."

"How can it ... *that* be real?"

The girl has slipped in behind him, still gripping the mug in both tiny hands. "I dunno, but I'm pretty sure we're, like, both seeing the same thing. Glad to know my cheese hasn't completely slipped off the old saltine."

Even in his present state of awestruck wonder, the girl's latest stab at humor (delivered with a slight nasal whine in her usual ultra somber tone) strikes Killian as strangely familiar. Regardless, he is unable to further contemplate the origin of sameness while so fully entranced.

Monitor one (formerly of the wooded hillside to the left of the bunker's entrance) is awash in a swirling brown murkiness that Killian can only relate to a giant-sized aquarium in desperate need of cleaning. Without the occasional floating branch or weed formation, one would be hard pressed to immediately identify that the entire landscape is indeed completely submerged by raging floodwaters. Suddenly recalling the previous night's tremors, Killian's scalp begins to tingle and itch, the hair on his forearms growing instantly erect.

Monitor two (focused directly on the bunker's previously intact faux wooden entrance) depicts a similar scene, though there is the added bonus of what appears to be a car or truck bumper entangled in a thick thatch of weeds (the latter of which seems to tighten like squid tentacles with even the slightest shift of the mangled metal).

Monitor three (the mysterious "clearing" scene) is easily the most effective at defining the overall scope of the devastation, with its wide-lens setting allowing an expanded view of fast-churning waters of at least ten- to twelve-foot depths.

"Looks like the dam busted all right," he hears the girl mumble, followed by a series of loud sips. "You won't be going out there without scuba gear."

"I ... I need to check the perimeters..." Killian babbles, rising so quickly and clumsily as to almost overturn the chair. "Check for leaks ... find something to ... to plug 'em with."

"Mister?" the girl asks coyly as Killian sails about the comm room checking every nook and cranny. "Um, mister?"

Groping the floor in blind panic, he balances precariously on the very edge of hysterics.

"I'm a little busy right now, kid. G-give me a second, all right?" "But ... mister, don't you think—"

Galloping toward the entrance, Killian runs the index finger of his right hand the length and width of the steel door's tightly sealed frame. He then pulls the digit back to eye level to check for even the smallest sign of moisture.

"Good ... good ... she's dry as a hollow bone. Gotta ... gotta check the rest ... make damn sure…"

"Slow down, mister ... can I tell you somethi—"

With a cocked brow, he turns on her wearing a hideous grin that appears borderline predatory.

"*What* then?"

"I woke up two, three hours ago and saw the same thing," she replies morosely, waiving toward the monitors, "checked the whole place and didn't see drop one of uninvited wetness."

His grin gradually fades to a spastic frown, his upper lip quivering uncontrollably. "Sooooooo, what I'm trying to say is ... no need to darken your drawers over it. Looks like Uncle Roy did a bang-up job waterproofing the joint."

"Ray," he croaks, turning away even as the flesh of his jowls turn beet red. "His name is ... was Ray ... Raymond Briggs."

"Oops, my bad. Anyway, I was just trying to, like, save you a coronary."

Strolling away with as much civility as he can muster, Killian fears a tooth might soon crack beneath the severe gnashing.

"Appreciate it, Kayla, but I think I'll give it a go myself ... just to ease my own mind, you understand."

The reply that follows is laced with a level of sly, overt sarcasm usually associated with adults, and one that might well call for immediate verbal retaliation if not for the source.

"Go for it, Ace ... like, plunder away. Just remember, this girl don't know CPR, and probably wouldn't use it if I did."

"I'll take my chances, thanks," he manages, picking up his pace toward the rear of the bunker just to lengthen the space between them. He thinks he might've heard her whisper something as he trudges away, though the thumping of the hiking boots make it impossible to be sure. Regardless, he feels instant relief once out of her sights. Insane as it seems, a part of him wants to prove her wrong concerning possible chinks in the shelter's armor, as long as such a breech doesn't birth a life-threatening scenario. Just a small, harmless leak would be fine, he deduces, just enough to prove the little snot wrong.

***

The girl was dead on, as it turns out. Not a single drop of H_2O is detected, even in the bathroom, which he'd figured to be the prime suspect for a nasty backup of some type. After spending an additional five minutes staring at the monitors in dumbstruck wonder, Killian returns to the kitchen to find the girl calmly munching on a cracker. Her left brow arches quizzically as if to inquire about his findings. Curbing his anger in the face of such obvious smugness, he once again reminds himself that he is dealing with a twenty-first-century teenager.

"Well, inspection is complete and, happily, my findings match your own. We appear to be as snug as a bug in a rug despite the murky depths beyond."

"Yep ... told ya so, worrywart. The kid may be young but she ain't, like, stupid." Despite himself, Killian grins as the outer layer of his anger peels harmlessly away.

"So it seems. Sorry to doubt you, but I've always been, well ... the paranoid type."

"Snack?" she offers, reaching over to cradle a pack of Saltines. "Um, yeah sure, whatever you're having."

"Tuna on Premium she is, then."

Leaning against a far wall with folded arms, Killian rotates his focus from the girl to his booted feet. Having already discarded the overly warm sweater, he feels a slight chill that is weirdly comforting. More thirsty than hungry, he has a sudden craving for an ice-cold beer and wonders if he is coming down with a fever. As if on cue, his troubled midsection groans and murmurs. He has settled on a most logical explanation for the continuing belly misery; that being a particularly nasty stomach virus whose origin shall forever remain unknown. Staring down at the inflated end result, he can only hope the symptoms soon begin to fade.

"So what grade are ... were you in?" he finally asks with no genuine interest but merely to break the stilted silence.

"Eighth. We were supposed to dissect a frog in biology next week. Hard way to get out of being grossed out, but I can't say I'm sorry I missed that. I was even thinking about faking a virus. Dad would've never bought it, though. He knew me too well."

"When did you see your folks last?" he asks, hoping to jar her bleary memory about how she'd ended up in front of his uncle's imploding homestead.

"I ... can't remember. I've been trying, *really* trying to, like, figure out how I got here and where that placed them. It's all blank ... just nothing there. I must've really took a shot on the melon, huh?"

"Yeah, I'd say you probably did. I can't for the life of me figure out why you were standing in my uncle's yard."

"Sorry...can't help you there, Ace," she shrugs, sipping water from a plastic cup. "Maybe it'll come back to me in time. Anyway, I appreciate the rescue ... I guess."

This time, it's Killian whose brow arches dramatically while regarding the girl through squinted eyes.

"You ... guess? What's that mean?"

Tilting her head upward to meet his gaze, there is a twinkle in her eyes that is the definition of youthful mischief.

"It means what it sounds like, Ace..." "Please, call me Killian."

"It means what it sounds like, Mr. Killian. I shouldn't have to spell it out to my new adult guardian, right? You see anything in those monitors that predict a happy, carefree future for anyone lucky or downright stupid enough to have survived?"

Peering back down at his boots, Killian's next spoken words sound hollow, even to himself.

"Well, I'd say it's preferable to *dead*, yes." "Really? Please expound..."

"Expound on why it's better to survive to live another day?"

"Let's just say, I need reassurance from a more mature standpoint."

"Kid, I'm no expert on anything, but I would always prefer to stand above ground than be buried six feet beneath it."

The girl's expression and tone turn dark, her upper body visibly stiffening. "Easier for you to say, Mr. Killian ... easier to say and easier to accept if things don't go your way."

"How so, Miss Kayla?" "How old are you?"

"Turned thirty-eight last month, but what's that—" "You married, Mr. Killian?"

68

"Divorced several years back, but I still don't see—" "Children?"

"No, fortunately, as it turned out." "What was your job?"

"Bug assassin."

Her face contorts in comical confusion.

"Pest control," he says, stomping down his right heel several times as if crushing a swarm of invading insects.

"How long?"

"Oh, six ... seven years now, but I've had several so-called *careers* since getting out of the Army."

"Your favorite job *ever* would be?"

Lifting his gaze to the stone ceiling, Killian's answer is almost immediate.

"I'd have to say ... security guard duty at Hahn ... um, that's an Air Force base in Germany. Did flight line duty for two years. Easiest gig I ever had. Worked mids mostly ... that's midnight shift. Didn't have to put up with anybody's shi—, uh, was pretty much on my own with no supervisor breathing down my neck."

"You graduate high school?"

"Oh yeah, seems like a lifetime ago."

The girl claps her hands and sighs heavily, causing Killian to flinch as if she'd taken a poke at him.

"So, let's recap then…" "Recap ... recap wh—"

Pacing the tiny space behind the counter, the girl seems to no longer acknowledge his presence, as if rehearsing a speech meant for a later time and place.

"You experienced high school.

"You immediately leapt into the real world of work and responsibility.

"You joined the armed services and obviously did some adventurous traveling along the way.

"You enjoyed the rare experience of loving the job you were paid to do. "You experienced the love of a soul mate, or at least a person whom you presumed to be your soul mate at the time.

"You experienced sex with someone you truly love, or at least loved at the time. "You got married.

"You made money.

"You spent money.

"You took trips ... vacations ... did things ... *saw* things.

"Can you confirm all these things as being affirmative, Mr. Killian?"

"Killian ... just *Killian*, okay kid?" he blurts, feeling a gradual rebirth of agitation. "Kayla, Killian, just Kayla, okay?" she responds sweetly, though her blistering gaze reveals a different persona might soon make an appearance. "So did you experience all the things I've mentioned or not?" "Yeah, sure....sure I did. What's the point already?"

Leaning her elbows onto the counter and placing her squared chin into waiting palms, the girl suddenly appears a decade older. The bandage at her neck hangs askew, and Killian can see the scabbed-over gash there.

"Well, I haven't. Can't honestly check off a single one, and now it looks like I never will. So who's got it worse, you think, a middle-aged bald guy with a pot gut or the fourteen-year-old whose tits resemble California raisins and who's yet to sprout her first pubic hair? I haven't done SHIT yet ... haven't accomplished anything ... and probably never will!"

Though thoroughly enraged by the brat's unexpected descent into self-pity, Killian finds an immediate response impossible to verbalize.

"I saw the images on the laptop. There is no future. We probably won't ever leave this cave. We'll survive only as long as the supplies last before slowly wasting away."

"Listen, maybe it isn't as bad as it seems…" he pleads, surprising himself with the conscious attempt at consolation.

"Admit it, Ace," she snarls, backing toward the sleeping quarters, "you saved me to spare yourself the isolation. You just didn't want to be alone, did you?"

"Excuse me?"

"Or maybe you're just a lonely old perv looking to cop a feel on the sweet innocent girl who owes you her very life? Maybe steal her virginity and make her your apocalyptic sex-slave?"

With that, Killian instinctively raises an open palm as to ward off further accusations.

"Whoooaaa now ... just a minute here, kiddo…"

"You just try it, Ace, and I'll rip your sagging sack off! You keep those w-wiener- grabbers away from me or I'll ... I'll k-kill you!"

Tears flow from her eyes in thick streams as she turns away, and Killian is unable to fend off the

71

wave of pity pounding his chest cavity at the very sight. A scared young child stands before him, challenges him, acting out in order to survive mentally what she'd already accomplished from a physical standpoint. As she vanishes beyond his line of sight, Killian shouts a final verbal folly that, for the first time in recent memory, is fueled solely by complete and utter honesty.

"Kayla, listen ... I saved you because it was the right thing to do. That's all ... it was the right thing ... to do."

He listens to the girl's distant sobs for several minutes before retreating to the gym for the first workout session since their incarceration.

Less than ten minutes on the treadmill (beginner's setting) and five punching the heavy bag leave him totally spent, though he can assume such a pathetic performance can be tied directly to a state of already-present mental fatigue.

He finds the girl fast asleep in her bed and totally submerged beneath the covers.

The relief he feels at this discovery is immeasurable, as he is woefully unprepared for further conflict.

Following a brief shower and still more time spent atop the toilet, he splits the remaining afternoon hours between the comm and living rooms.

While the comm room monitors reflect no obvious change, the living room radio provides more than its share of drama, the majority of which is not of the positive news variety.

72

With the earlier station having faded to a low static hum, Killian scans the dial in both FM and AM mode, and is only seconds from powering down in defeat when a barely audible human voice seeps from the twin Kenwood speakers in a whispery moan. Shoving his left ear almost flush with the left speaker in lieu of cranking the volume and possibly waking the girl, Killian crouches like a jungle cat and is instantly enthralled. He will later doubt the validity of what he actually heard, believing in part that he had dreamed the incident or at least a sizable portion of its content.

"This is Sid the Kid on KYJV radio, Rock One-Oh-Three! I am now in hour seventy-six of this live broadcast from what remains of our studio, and hoping and praying that someone ... anyone ... is left out there to listen. I'm on my sixth pot of coffee since this marathon started, so please forgive the occasional lapses of reason or moments of dead air. As I've repeated at least a few thousand times in the past three days plus, I have ... still have four lines open at six-three-six, four-five-eight, ROCK. Needless to say, I'd like ... love ... hell ... adore to hear from anyone receiving this continuing drone.

"The story of my own survival is beyond miraculous, though I'd bet there are similar tales to be told out there in the vast wasteland of the former planet Earth. Once the quakes, fires, and funnels hit and turned the station into a gin mixer, I found myself planted beneath the console in a state of disbelief and making some mighty tall promises to a higher power I'd previously disavowed a decade or two ago. I can't truly say how long it was before I crawled out from the wreckage ... since I was clocked squarely on the noggin by falling debris, but what I found amidst all the ruins was the miracle that is somehow, some way, allowing this broadcast. My producer, Bud the Chud Wilcott, lies buried beneath what had been the second floor of our mountaintop hideaway. The thin glass around his booth was hardly a safe haven. I've been calling out to him since the ... walls caved in ... the walls, the floors ... the heavens. I guess there can only be so many miracles doled out to a single structure.

"The only other staff member on duty had been Walt Cooper, our combination IT techie and maintenance man. I can only assume he was tucked away all snug and comfy inside his office when the hammer ... hammers ... fell. A great guy, Coop. None better in the find 'em, figure 'em out and fix 'em business. Rest in peace, my young friend.

"How we remain powered up is beyond all reasonable logic. I have to believe there is a plan behind it ... and so I rattle on if for no other reason than for others to hear that they are not alone. It isn't like the craziness is over ... far from it, I'd wager. For one thing, the outside temps have dropped like a stone, pardon the pathetic pun, since the last series of tremors. It seems the seasons are now changing every half hour instead of the usual once-every-four-or-five-month timetable. Things have gone horribly askew, to state the painfully obvious, good listeners. I've picked up a few scattered broadcasts besides my own, but most fade within a few seconds or crap out altogether before an understandable message is relayed. Be that as it may ... as dark as it may seem out there to one and all ... and right about now that's surely as dark as a coal miner's bunghole, Sid the Kid has made a vow to both himself and the man above.

"Trapped and cornered like a wounded rat and hurting like hell from what I'm pretty sure are a broken left forearm and one nasty-ass concussion, as long as the power grid holds out, along with yours truly, the Kid flat-out refuses to leave the air ... sleep and or pain killer-induced stupors be damned! Being that our website appears permanently down for the count for obvious reasons, if you can get to a phone ... cellular, landline, pay or otherwise, give me a buzz, people! Let me know you're out there! And ... if you can possibly remember to do so, bring the Kid a bottle of Tylenol of the extra-strength variety along with a pint ... no ... no ... make that a quart of Jim Beam's finest corn mash! In the meantime, I'll juggle my everlasting rants with a tune or three from the classic rock vault, and this broadcast will continue unabated 'til either the station crumbles down the side of Mount Juliet or Sid the Kid's gas tank runs completely dry! Rock on, Planet Earth! Survive, thrive, and rock on!"

Having shoved the couch flush with the stereo, Killian spends a full hour with Sid the Kid (who'd sounded anything but youthful) at KYVJ radio, eventually passing out to the thundering guitars of the Foo Fighters' sadly ironic (considering the circumstances) "Long Road to Ruin." During that span, Killian notes with marked sadness that Sid has yet to receive a single call from the outside.

Chapter 7

Day Five: *Deep Freeze*

Having awakened to the hauntingly familiar sound of static where KYVJ had previously belonged on the dial, Killian tries to shrug off the whole experience as a mind-fog induced hallucination, though under more careful scrutiny he knows such a theory simply doesn't fly. Thus, he decides the best path to follow, at least where his mental stability is concerned, is not to scrutinize at all. The gloomy alternative, that he has actually borne witness to what had sounded like a textbook "doomsday" broadcast of sci-fi fame, is far too deflating and depressing to consider.

Tucked loosely into the wool sweater he'd so rudely discarded the day before, Killian sips the final remnants of his third cup of coffee since waking and feels his bones begin to warm despite the formidable chill. In spite of the latest cosmic shock supplied by the trio of monitors, he finds his emotional state surprisingly calm. Perhaps, he decides, it is simply a matter of "enough already" syndrome, wherein the beaten and battered senses toss out the proverbial white flag in surrender. No matter the reason, he cannot help but relish that the inner panic button seems temporarily out of order.

A glass of juice and a handful of crackers have done little to quiet the internal war bombarding his midsection, but he has wisely abstained from a heavier breakfast in fear of spending the remainder of the morning balanced atop the bathroom toilet.

"Is that what I think it is?" the girl's voice chimes softy at his back.

As further evidence of his unruffled demeanor, Killian isn't shaken in the least by the sudden intrusion. He starts to respond but stops in midbreath, his lips parted only slightly.

"Have ... did I go into, like, another coma? No way ... that happened overnight," she continues, and he can sense her slow, deliberate pacing as bare feet slap against slick tile. He hears her teeth chatter lightly together.

"Feels like a hockey game is gonna break out in here any minute."

Slurping the last of the lukewarm beverage, Killian fights temptation and remains mute.

"Listen, um, I ... I'm sorry about ... freaking out the way I did. I ... was just ... like,

I lost it, is all. I guess it all hit me at once, you know? My family ... my friends ... everybody just ... probably just ... gone. It's ... it's scary. I've never been ... you know ... alone. It may make me sound like a squalling little kid, but I really, *really* miss my mom and old man ... old-fashioned a-holes that they could be at times."

The high-backed chair squeaks loudly as Killian whirls about. The girl is wrapped in the bed blanket from ankles to neck, her bangs standing straight out like porcupine quills.

"You're not alone now. I'm here. We have each other to see this through," he begins, keeping his voice purposely stilted and as void of emotion as possible in fears anything more might trigger yet another unwelcome scene. "Once the weather settles and it appears safe to do so, we'll venture out and ... maybe find things aren't as bad as they look."

"Maybe. I guess there's always hope, huh?" she replies, looking past him back toward the monitors. "But seeing something like that sure doesn't do much for the odds, does it?"

Craning his neck to redirect focus back to the visions at hand, Killian is unable to mount even the slightest argument.

"Well, maybe it's just a passing front ... similar to the one that caused the flooding two days ago. Probably won't last any longer either. Sooner or later, the skies are gonna clear and stay that way."

Before walking away, the girl's tone grows noticeably chipper, and Killian cannot help but dread the inevitable transformation surely to come.

"Wow. Bet the Weather Channel people would have given up a decade's pay to be able to cover this wacky scene."

He can only nod his head in total agreement and continue to soak in the ghastly imagery on display while secretly pondering the consequences if such conditions remained unchanged or possibly even grew more extreme.

The metamorphosis was dramatic, to state the obvious. From what little was visible from the virtual whiteout on display, the surrounding landscape was now a massive iceberg, as the river of flood waters from days previous had transformed overnight into a liquid-free, rock-solid tundra that held everything in its path in suspended animation. Killian could only guess such a phenomenon possible with a temperature drop of at least sixty to eighty degrees, possibly more. He thought back to the days before the quake, when the daytime highs had hovered near the seasonally normal sixty- to sixty-five degree mark.

"That means ... it has to be thirty ... forty below out there," he whispers, feeling a fresh wave of chills tickle his spine.

"You say something?" the girl yells from what he presumes to be the kitchen area.

"Uh, yeah, I was ... just thinking out loud."

"Okey-dokey. I'm heating up some water for ramen noodles. You game?" "Sounds good. Be there in a minute."

Finding it more and more difficult to put on his game face, Killian has long since decided not to speak of the previous night's radio broadcast. For the time being, he thinks it wisest to tread atop eggshells while in the young girl's fragile presence.

***

They each sip nosily from prepackaged cups as waves of steam massage their respective faces. While Killian leans against a far wall, Kayla props against the counter with a single elbow for support.

"If I could fit inside this cup, I'd surely take a dive into the warmth," she says with a wide, toothy smile that at least appears sincere. "I am truly appreciative to the man upstairs for the ability to boil water in times like these. Well, the man upstairs and your uncle, of course."

Forking a mouthful of noodles, Killian quickly swallows with only a token amount of chewing.

"It is a might chilly in here at that. I guess Uncle Raymond didn't give a heating system much thought. We'll just have to bundle up 'til it passes."

The girl pauses while lowering the cup to her neck as to allow the rising heat access to her now bandageless wound.

"Sorry I called you a perv."

"Actually," he says with a playful wink, "that's balding, pot-bellied perv."

Kayla giggles like the young teen she is, her usually pale cheeks instantly glowing beet red.

"No harm, no foul. I ... understand ... *understood* your reasons. I don't think there is a right or wrong way to handle a ... situation like this, but going a little crazy is to be expected."

"Do me a favor, then ... okay?" she asks, pushing the noodle cup aside before repositioning the blanket around her shoulders and neck.

"What's that?"

"Please refrain from the going nuts part, at least where I can see you." Killian holds up a three-finger salute and nods.

"You got it, kiddo. Not where you can see it, and that's a promise." Kayla returns his nod and gestures in the direction of the comm room. "Well, now what, Chief?"

Rubbing his arms briskly through the wool sweater, Killian shivers involuntarily.

He gauges the temperature inside the bunker at around the fifty to fifty-five degree range and falling.

"I'm gonna give the air filtration system a quick look-see, then I'd say we'd better rummage the supply room for all the clothing and extra blankets we can find."

With mission in hand, the two move forward as a team for the first time.

Lingering doubts aside, Killian can't help but look upon the girl with a renewed trust. There is a flicker of hope that maybe, just *maybe*, she'll turn out to be an asset and not a hindrance to their prospective survival.

***

"Anything?"

"Listen for yourself ... a virtual crackling static concerto."

"Well, shit! Without TV, the Internet, or a radio, how are we supposed to know what's going on out there?"

"Easy, kiddo, remember where we are. Concrete and steel bunkers buried inside mountainsides aren't exactly conducive to radio waves and the like."

Kayla sighs and tucks herself ever farther into the tunnel of blankets she'd created.

Having been careful to bypass the spot on the dial once occupied by Sid the Kid of KYVJ radio fame in fear of an updated broadcast of similar grisliness, Killian otherwise discovers the radio landscape a literal gravesite for dead air.

"How's the memory reboot coming? Anything yet?"

"Still pretty foggy, though I get the occasional flashback," she says, her teeth chattering with each pause, "but so far I can't, like, piece much together."

"Don't worry, it will ... just takes time. I caught a shot on the back of the head once playing football and couldn't remember anything that happened in the game even though the other guys told me I was on the sideline watching and cheering 'em on. The human brain is one temperamental instrument."

Turning away from the radio to the flat screen, Killian suppresses a yawn. "Enough of that...let me try the boob tube."

Kicking inside the blankets, the girl shrieks in comical frustration.

"Gawwddd, I never thought I'd miss blogging this much. Like, what did people do before power, before lights ... before *Facebook*?"

Killian laughs while flipping through a seemingly endless array of blackened television screens, and for the first time notices his own breath escaping in a faint but visible vapor trail.

"Oh, they probably sat around the campfire and watched their toenails grow."

Showing no evidence she'd either heard or if so comprehended the joke, the girl's eyes grew wide with fright.

"You know, my dad used to tell my brother and me about those *dark days*." "Yeah ... and what bleakest of days might that be specifically?"

"Oh, you know ... before cable TV and the Web. He could even remember the *pre-MTV* era!"

Pausing in his fruitless clicking of the remote, Killian manages to remain straight- faced in his purposely morose reply.

"Hey, I felt his pain ... just a child you understand, but I recall having only three or four working channels to watch."

With only her nose, eyes, and forehead showing from the wool and cotton barricade, the girl nods sympathetically.

"My dad said the same thing. No cell phones, either, so texting was out. I guess folks just didn't communicate much in your day."

Turning his head to hide the twitching at the corners of his mouth, Killian readjusts his own array of blankets and leans back on the second of the two beanbags he'd piled together to create a single bed. Having fought off an earlier bout of nausea following the dinner meal of tuna sandwiches and chicken noodle soup, he occasionally belches up a mouthful of bile that torches his ravaged throat.

"Yeah, that talking face-to-face thing does take some getting used to, for sure."

Effectively cocooned, they each remain in the living room and fall asleep amid the repeated hum of the air purifiers.

Chapter 8

Day Six: *Gut Check*

"I've got an idea if you're game."

"If I'm ... game? What kinda game?"

"Oh, um, pardon my *old man* speak. It means if you want to." "What?"

"Well, working out is a great way to elevate body temperature. We can take turns on the treadmill."

"Beats sitting here stiffening up, I guess."

"If nothing else, it'll help us work up an appetite for lunch." "I vote for hot soup!"

"Ditto."

"Did oh?"

"There I go again ... sorry. It means ... me too."

The morning had brought no relief from the cold as the bunker's interior temperatures seemed to have dropped an additional five to eight degrees. Camera images saw little change as well, the girl comparing them to "peering out from inside an ice cube." Several cups of steaming hot coffee follow, the girl allowing a bit of extra time to warm her hands over the burner. Killian excuses himself both before and after their shared breakfast of java and cereal bars, shuffling toward the bathroom with cramps so intense he's broken a warm sweat despite the overly chilled air. The bouts of nausea are also growing worse, and he can't help but worry that perhaps the initial diagnosis of a simple stomach bug was not only a bit premature also a woeful underestimation.

"Hey, I feel better already. Well, better in some ways and worse in others ... like, I'm warming up but my feet and knees are killing me!"

Killian flashes a pained smile before refocusing on the Bowflex, which he'd managed to work into a fairly graceful curl position despite the overabundance of clothing.

"No pain ... no gain."

"Yeah, well, I'm about fed up with the pain part. Your turn," she says, jumping off the track with a youthful grace Killian can never recall possessing. She flips the black hoodie back to reveal a slight coating of perspiration atop her forehead.

"Anyway, I was starting to feel like my pet hamster. Think I'll do some stretching."

Adjusting the speed to an even lower setting, Killian climbs aboard with a grimace. He glances over at the girl and sees her brow crease in puzzlement.

"You ... feeling okay? You look kinda sick."

"It's just my stomach acting up again. Hasn't been right since I ... since we got here. Must be the radical change in diet setting it off, or maybe it's just craving a Big Mac and fries."

"Could be, all right, and if so, all I can say..." she says, grinning, "... is *ditto*."

***

While the girl fixes a lunch of hot tea, chicken noodle soup, and ham spread on crackers, Killian performs what he had come to think of as "drive-by" monitor checks. With the freeze-dried look still firmly in place on all three, he takes a moment to sit and consider the bleak future ahead if such arctic conditions become a permanent state.

Though it is much too early to dwell upon, it is only a matter of time before supplies become an issue. They have done well thus far, limiting meals to the bare minimum with no in-between snacks, but it is the water supply that holds the most concern.

Before rejoining the girl, he's made the decision to begin strict rationing unless weather conditions change drastically within the next three days. This means using the supply for drinking and cooking only, eliminating the daily birdbaths both have enjoyed. A little BO is easily tolerated, he deduces, in comparison to a slow, agonizing death via the dehydration route.

"Soothing, ain't it?" she asks, slurping a spoonful of steaming soup, her gloved hands practically engulfing the small cup.

Killian shoots her a wink and tips his cup forward as to offer a toast. Vapor trails abound, whether originating from the boiled liquid refreshment or their own trembling, parted lips.

"Mama's milk ... sure hits the spot."

For a change, Kayla inhabits the bean bag while Killian's prone form covers the length of the couch. Both are well-cloaked save for their hands and face, with the girl having discarded her hoodie for a purple-shaded sweater with a Minnesota Vikings logo.

"So tell me more about your last job ... the bug-terminator thing." "Exterminator. I always preferred pest technician ... made me sound brainy."

"Pest techie? Yeah, that does sound better but maybe a little on the snotty side. I always, like, wondered why anyone would want to kill things for a living. Not that I'm a bug lover or anything like that. I've stomped my share into pudding over the years, but..." she shudders as if she'd just tasted something particularly sour, "... I'd hate to spend, like, my whole day doing it."

Setting his cup aside, Killian reaches up to adjust his own headgear, an aviator- styled hat with fur-lined earflaps that was easily a size too small.

"Well, as we older folks are apt to say ... it's a ... it was a living. Probably not gonna be much of a call for it now."

The girl merely shrugs and waits for him to continue.

"Money wasn't great but it paid the bills. Company provided a truck and fuel.

Hours weren't bad unless a job took me too far out of town. We covered a wide range ... twenty, thirty miles from the city limits. Too much competition to turn folks down that had a pest problem."

"So you debugged mostly office buildings or what?"

"We did some commercial spraying, but it was mostly residential." "You mean people's houses?"

"Yeah, most people signed up for the once-a-month service, but a few were quarterly. Spring was the busiest ... it could get pretty dead in the winter months when the little beasties went into hibernation."

Leaning up, the girl's face was suddenly full of color; her wide-eyed expression filled with interest. Every so often she'd reach up and give the healing wound beneath her chin a light scratch.

"So what did you like offing the best?"

Scratching the substantial beard growth at his own chin, Killian hesitates momentarily as his eyes grow faintly distant.

"Rats, by far ... they're carriers of a lot of nasty shi—um, stuff. Roaches were the toughest, no contest. We were constantly forced to change pesticides just to keep pace with their built-in immunities to the stuff. Termites were a big moneymaker, but you had to be specially trained to treat for 'em. I never got licensed for those. We put out traps and poisons for moles and mice. Spiders were always high on the hit list. Nobody but *nobody* likes a spider, and of course there were tons of ant issues during the spring months."

"Probably got to know your customers pretty well, huh?"

"Yeah, my route didn't change too drastically, so there were a few regulars. You had to treat them a bit different ... give 'em added attention so they'd maintain the contract even in the colder months."

"Ever see any snakes?"

"A few, but all were of the harmless variety ... usually rat or king snakes."

The girl pauses to yawn, the bags beneath her eyes growing increasingly pronounced.

"You look tired," Killian says before suppressing a mouth-stretcher of his own with a gloved hand.

"Been waking up a lot the last few nights," she replies a tad morosely, "keep dreaming I've passed out in an ice-cream truck."

"Take a nap if you'd like. Supper's on me tonight. I'll even do the dishes." "There are no dishes, old man," she sneers playfully, "we use paper plates." Killian shrugs and loses his top layer of blanket in the process.

"Oh, yeah, there is that. Anyhow, you just rest up, kiddo. It's not like either of us has an appointment to keep. I'm gonna have a cup of tea and stare at the monitors a while."

"Killian?" she asks softly just as he's broken free from his cocoon and started toward the kitchen.

"You want me to bring you a cup?" "No, no thanks."

"What's up?"

"You miss your family ... I mean, your folks?"

"My family's long dead, kiddo. Kinda glad they missed out on all this otherworldly misery."

"How about your wife ... kids?"

"No wife ... long since divorced. Luckily, that devil-spawn of a woman never bore me any ankle-chewers."

"So what happened to your marriage ... that is, in case I'm prying where my nose doesn't belong."

"No, no, it's all right. It's an old story," he begins, peering toward the stone ceiling with a purposefully distant glance. "Let's just say we had a personality conflict..." he glances back toward the girl and arches a brow dramatically, "as in ... she didn't possess one."

After a short pause, the girl laughs long and hard at this, though the giggle-storm is eventually overtaken by a coughing fit that is every bit as raucous. Killian provides a soft pat on the back as he strolls by.

"Oh, you're a card, old man. Thanks for the deep insight." "Not a problem. You live ... you learn."

"And with that ... I think a nap is definitely in order," she says, suppressing still another yawn.

"Let's just pretend I've adopted *you* as my only offspring, what say?"

Wiping the building moisture from her eyes with a woolen sleeve, Kayla still struggles to regain complete control.

"S-sure thing, Daddy-O. Oh, my aching gut."

As if on cue, Killian soon bypasses the kitchen for still another toilet seat pit-stop.

Rising from the throne, he peers down at this latest deposit with a mixture of confusion and stark fear. It is a shapeless blob; a dark crimson mass that brings to mind a two-word description that Killian finds more frightening, more disturbing than any earthquake, funnel cloud, or ice storm. Two words that a mere natural disaster-fueled apocalypse cannot begin to touch. Those words are *death sentence*. Death sentence via the cancer highway, to be exact. As his hands begin to shake and tremor in true detox fashion, he involuntarily jerks forward and vomits onto the glutinous mass.

As he rinses his mouth and begins the mental preparation necessary to act as if all is well in the girl's presence, Killian cannot shake the irony-laced thought that winds and rewinds without mercy:

Life's a bitch and then you...

... and then you die.

Eventually another familiar refrain breaks the monotony, though it is far less than comforting in its own right:

What goes around, comes around.

Killian wishes, *prays*, he could fend them off in equal measure or at least find a worthy distraction for temporary relief. Sipping his tea in silence as his midsection aches with renewed vigor, he finds self-pity his only true ally.

***

They eat in relative silence, and for this Killian is eternity grateful. The girl appears haggard, even more so than before her three-hour nap. He begins to wonder if perhaps both of them haven't come down with a similar malady, though she shows no signs of physical illness save for her rundown look and lack of energy. Of course, he understands that in her case it might simply be the result of the walk-in freezer-type conditions. Not so easily explained as his own health issues. As it stands, he finds the scent of food sickening to the point of dry heaving, much less the actual flavor.

"Glad you chose soup of the mixed vegetable variety," Kayla finally says between spoonfuls; "a chicken noodle overdose was a definite possibility."

"Understood, kiddo. Personally, I'd gladly hand over the keys to the kingdom for a steaming plate of three-cheese lasagna and a loaf of garlic bread."

She watches him continue to stir his bowl without ever taking a bite. "You don't hurry up and down that you're gonna be chewing ice cubes."

Pushing the bowl aside, he collapses atop the bean bag and begins the nightly insulation process. Believing the interior temperature to be hovering around the thirty- five to forty mark, they had broken out the last of the blankets from supply and split them between the living and sleeping quarters.

"Guess I'm still full from the tea party. You can have it if you'd like."

"Stomach issues again?" she asks solemnly, obviously not the least bit fooled. "A little ... no big deal. I'll just hold out for a sizeable breakfast. So ... any luck rebooting those long-lost memories?"

"Nil. Heck, maybe it's better I don't know every detail. Maybe ... it's one of those, like, mental blocks that sprang up for a very good reason."

"Maybe it is at that, kiddo," he nods after finding no viable argument to render, though finding an inexplicable relief in her continued lack of memory.

"When ... do you think this will ever break? The cold ... I mean."

"I ... just don't know, Kayla. We can hope it ... gets better. Wish I had a better answer."

"Wish you did too," she smiles despondently before rolling over onto the couch with a yawn and vanishing into the multiple layers of bedding.

The dreams return after several nights' respite, no doubt fueled by memories of the bloody stool and preemptive fears for a possible repeat performance.

***

Killian sits quietly before the monitors, sipping an iced-down beverage of some sort (a specific taste sensation is, predictably, lacking) from a comically oversized glass mug. He is wearing his pest control uniform; a white, button-up shirt with company logo embroidered about the left front pocket, tan Dockers pants, brand-less white tennis shoes and to complete the look, a bright orange shaded ball cap with Pest-Away *embroidered in dark red lettering. He'd sincerely hated that cap, as had his many coworkers. One had remarked it was the perfect desert island headgear, as a plane couldn't help but spot its bare-ass ugliness from a hundred miles away. Removing the cap and tossing it into parts unknown, he peers down toward his left foot and spots old reliable; his three-gallon B&G sprayer, the metal cylinder rusted and dented in all the familiar spots, the nozzle bent just slightly near the handle. Beside the sprayer lies a blue steel, snub-nosed revolver, the occasional plume of smoke escaping its stubby barrel.*

A low pecking sound redirects his focus back to the monitors, from which he no longer visualizes the freezer-burned landscape but instead smooth, sandy dunes sparkling beneath what appears to be a blazing noonday sun. No longer do the monitors reflect three separate images, but a trio of sameness that is eerily unchanged from one to another, as if all are focused on the same exact strip of beachhead. Feeling an urgent need as the dryness of the images seem to parch his throat simply by existing, Killian gulps greedily from the frosty mug that never seems to empty no matter the level of consumption.

The incessant pecking noise returns, and this time he is able to identify its origin.

He doesn't feel the mug slip from his grasp but hears shattered glass at his feet nonetheless. Practically falling back and out of the chair, he instinctively reaches for the sprayer he'd once so lovingly nicknamed Bon-zooka after his ex-wife. His lips quiver in futility in an attempt to react to what he sees with either a coherent, formed sentence or, most likely, a piercing scream.

The image of the man fills all three monitors, though from strikingly altered poses.

Monitor one is a full frontal shot. Two is an aerial view, looking down from perhaps ten to fifteen feet. Three is photographed from the rear at approximately the same three-to-five-yard distance.

Shouting (though impossible to hear within the bunker's granite walls) and gesturing like a man possessed, the man has an overstuffed duffel bag slung across his shoulders. Killian knows the face oh so well; every deep crease and pockmark, the scar that starts out floss-thin just below the left eye but gains thickness as it trails toward the jawline. The caterpillar-thick mustache and red, curly, overlong hair that is nestlike in all its ruffled glory.

After countless refrains, Killian is able to effectively read the words the man so frantically screeches.

Let me in, you goddamned traitor...

Let me in or I'll have my friends force their way in...

... and you really don't want that, no, sir...

... nooooo, you really don't want them as houseguests...

The man then spreads his arms messiah-like, and Killian finds himself leaning in to the first monitor (frontal view), squinting to better visualize the surrounding sand— sand that begins to shift and sway in billowy waves. Sand that is fast becoming the color of a tar pit—the blackest of black, like an oil spill come to life.

It is when he views the second monitor, the rear image, that Killian is able to readily ID the swirling seas as an army of German cockroaches, the majority as large as a man's hand. They quickly bury his unwanted visitor up to the knees, though the man appears not only without fear but weirdly amused. Somehow, as if peering through a two-way mirror, the man locks eyes with Killian and grins while playfully waiving a raised forefinger from side to side. As his lips part to speak, Killian clearly sees a half-dozen or more of the bloated army spew forth onto his bared chest like birthing arachnids.

... better let me in, Kill-Joy ... fair is fair, don't you agree? ... I want what's mine, you rotten son of a bitch...

Killian feels a scuttling sensation trail the whole of his left leg between his Dockers jeans and instinctively swings away with the heavy metal

95

cylinder. Surprisingly, the fierce snapping of his femur is totally painless, but as he attempts to drag himself from the comm room for an as-yet-unknown safe haven within the bunker, the searing pain at his groin is like lit coals against the most tender of flesh. Tossing the cylinder aside, his senses are filled with the overwhelming stench of copper.

His uniform shirt is bloodsoaked; his Dockers spattered from groin to ankles; his formerly white shoes now a blackish crimson.

He panics at first but then realizes the blood is not his own. The relief of this is palpable, but painfully brief in duration.

Limping on whatever leg is still completely intact (the memory fades as to which), Killian reaches the bathroom to see a crawling army spew forth from the toilet in slimy droves.

Stomping and swiping (and surely shrieking), he manages to dodge the flow and shuffles into the generator room. He attempts to close off the sections as he goes but the emergency seal doors are apparently as shattered as his leg.

Crouching behind the generator like the insects he once vowed to eliminate but now attempts to evade, he can think of no worthy defense to employ.

A looming shadow soon fills the entranceway, and Killian can hear the clicking of literally millions of tiny legs on the slick tile flooring.

What he fears to be his last waking thought is of the "ain't it ironic" nature as he bows his head in defeat and prays the end won't be quite as horrible as feared.

A hand slaps down on his left shoulder with great force. A tiny, blemish-free hand that might possibly belong to a young girl—the shockingly strong hand pulls him airborne just as a river of roaches fill the spot he'd previously filled.

"Not to worry, Ace..." he hears Kayla spout cheerily, "it ain't the bugs you need to be worrying about, no, sir."

Hanging airborne, Killian is swung about like a marionette on a string.

They are face to face, grown man and teenaged girl, their noses positioned mere inches apart.

Kayla shoots him a wink, revealing a hollowed-out eye socket from which an impossibly bloated roach struggles to free itself. Her breath reeks of ancient decay. He watches in dumbstruck horror as yet another mutated insect, this one with a roach's body but the elongated appendages of a daddy longlegs spews forth from the scar beneath her chin.

"Nope ... you got bigger worries than bugs these days, don'cha, Kill-Joy?"

***

This time, he is certain the scream that awakens him is in full Dolby stereo mode, though its release inside a thicket of covers is at least sufficiently muffled. He lays awake for the remainder of the night and early morning, unable to successfully decipher a coherent meaning to *all* elements of the dream. Eventually resigned to defeat, he rises for that day's initial trip to the john. Needless to say,

97

despite a desperate need to evacuate his bowels, Killian spends several tense moments checking the toilet's inner workings before cautiously taking a seat.

Upon inspecting the results of his latest bout upon the throne, all thoughts of nightmarish realms are instantly replaced by similar horrors based in a more realistic setting. The mucus-laden specimen of the previous day has been replaced by a spool of what appears to be pure blood, so clear and without solid formation it looks as if he's drained a particularly nasty wound directly over the toilet bowl.

"Oh, that can't be good," he murmurs through chapped lips, his remaining breath forming a frigid vapor trail that serves as tangible evidence that the overnight temperature has dropped even lower.

"Not good at all."

Chapter 9

Day Seven: *Being of Sound Mind and Freeze-Dried Body...*

"So what triggered it, you think?"

"Some of the eggheads on CNN pointed toward the meteor shifting the planet's axis. Guess it'll always be speculated on, but we'll probably never really know for sure."

"My dad was always preaching on it, saying it was getting close ... the way the world was going, I mean."

"Yeah, well, I'd been hearing doomsayers yap about it since I was your age or younger. I always figured for a nuclear meltdown, what with all the third-world nut jobs owning the hardware to pull it off these days."

"Guess it really doesn't matter now, huh?"

"Probably not ... water under the bridge." "Want another cereal bar?"

Killian waves her off with a gloved hand, flecking away tiny crumbs from the snack he'd just polished off, though it had been a laborious task to do so.

"Better gulp the rest of that beverage there, Ace, or you'll be sucking on a green tea popsicle veerrrry soon."

"Nope, I'm done."

"Old man, you're not eating enough to keep a hamster alive. So, like, what's the story?"

"Same old same old. Talk about your rotten timing, this is one extremely stubborn, nasty stomach bug. For your sake, I hope it isn't catching." He stops short of spilling his guts, so to speak, about the bloody stools and extreme aching that seems to intensify by the hour. His mind naturally races to a worst-case scenario ... that being the Big C of the pancreatic variety, a condition he'd always heard was in the top two or three in the *Worst Ways to Expire Top Ten*. Again, this is hardly a theory he desires to share with his fellow inmate, as he can only imagine her reaction.

"I still think all you need for an overnight cure involves a steak sandwich or two and a plate of salty fries," she says, pausing to shiver beneath multiple layers of clothes that serve to triple her body mass. "Think about it ... we're surviving on preservatives alone. God help me, I swear I'd kill for a Caesar salad 'bout now, and I don't even eat the damn things!"

"You been taking your vitamins?" he scolds through squinted eyes, the aviator headgear hanging slightly askew as a few curly stray hairs stick out from beneath like probing antennae.

"Yes, *dad*, I most certainly have, and you?"

"Well," he hesitates long enough to exhale, temporarily cloaking his face in a cloud of whitish fog, "haven't really been able to stomach pills since ... well, whatever the day before yesterday was. I'll get back to it, though, soon as I can learn to hold 'em down again."

He can feel the young girl's eyes probing him long before she speaks. "Straight up ... like, you ... okay?"

"Oh, yeah, I'll shake this off in a day or two."

Shrugging playfully, he forces a grin and can practically hear the beard growth crackle as if tiny ice shards had broken free with the effort. "Like you said, more than likely it's the survival diet menu that's at the core of it."

Reaching out from beneath the covers, she smacks him lightly on a comically padded shoulder.

"Yeah, and besides, we'll both freeze to death long before something else can off us, right?"

"Easy money, Miss Kayla, easy money." "Say *huh*?" she asks with a frown. "That's a safe bet."

"Oh ... like in a wager ... gotcha."

They fall into a comfortable silence, something that hadn't been possible a few short days previously.

Earlier, following the morning monitor check (unchanged with not a single sand dune in sight), Killian had performed the daily duties of refueling the generator and checking the air filters. Bad enough was the fact that the supply of generator fuel was vanishing at an alarming rate, despite limited power usage and a nightly blackout, but infinitely worse was the condition of the air filtration system. Located in each room within the bunker save the supply and generator rooms, the system had been his uncle's ultimate creation against the radioactive particles present in the wake of a nuclear incident. Though Killian had no earthly idea where the fresh air supply was being pumped from, especially considering the present elements outside the bunker walls, what was obvious was the battering each unit was taking from said fact. Each unit (roughly the size of a small microwave) appeared freezer burned, its inner filters coated in slick layers of icy spears that in at least one case (the living room unit) was beginning to penetrate the outer shell. As horrific an image as dying from the cold was, such terrors paled woefully in the face of passing from a lack of breathable oxygen.

He's already used half of the available replacement filters, and future swaps appeared impossible with the interiors frozen solid.

After waking from an unexpected nap of unknown length, Killian sees Kayla has departed the living room; he can hear her banging around inside the kitchen.

Resembling a lurching hunchback with the mountain of covers atop his back, he scoots toward the stereo with the intention of scanning the dial for signs of life. When the radio remains lifeless, he is less surprised than simply frustrated, poking and punching the power-on button until his thumb goes numb. He checks to ensure the plug has properly penetrated the outlet, and isn't at all shocked to see it has. Cursing under his breath, he starts to turn toward the flat screen when Kayla reenters carrying a serving tray.

"Don't tell me ... radio's fried."

"More like frosted ... cheap piece of crap. The cold plays hell with electronics," he spits, unable to mask his anger and instantly regretful. Perhaps sensing his frustration, the girl flops down onto the nearest bean bag with a resounding sigh, her own blanket wrap spreading out like some massive alien pod sewn from cotton and wool.

"No great loss. The top forty was, like, really lame lately. I never was into country pop, and rap gave me a instant migraine. As for talk radio, all I ever heard was blah ... babble ... blah ... babble, *politics* this and *sports* that ... like I said, no great loss. Tea, monsieur?"

"No thanks."

"It'll warm the cockles, whatever the heck a cockle actually is." "Go for it ... I'm waterlogged as it is."

"It's all about the heat, baby ... not the flavor. I really wish your uncle would've added a box or two of cocoa into the mix."

Despite its static-filled greeting, the TV being in working order is an instant tension-reducer, and Killian sits back with a lengthy exhale of his own and slowly begins flipping from one blank screen to the next.

"Maybe we can pick up something from one of the local networks."

Seemingly staring through the screen with unblinking eyes, the girl's tone is suddenly void its normal sarcastic edge, replaced by a casual acceptance that Killian finds a bit unnerving. He watches her sit the tea cup atop the serving tray and then push it aside, steam rising from the twin cups in synchronized plumes.

"I ain't exactly expecting the Weather Channel, Ace."

"Probably a good thing," he wisecracks, the role of cheerleader having unexpectedly switched in a matter of seconds, "Don't need some hot-air-spewing meteorologist telling me something I

103

already know from staring into those monitors. But, hey, if the long-range forecast includes heat and humidity in any way, shape, or form, I'm all ears."

Obviously not impressed by his attempt at levity, the girl buries her head into the bedding quagmire and mumbles a final declaration.

"Just wake me if you find the Disney Channel, okay?"

"In that case, sleeping beauty, you may be in for a looooonnnnng nap."

With apparently no response forthcoming, Killian returns his bleary focus onto the task at hand, though the constant barrage of futility is making it increasingly difficult to stay positive. His midsection, though not currently grumbling or moaning due to his lack of substantial intake, is nonetheless as hard as a stone slab and in constant ache mode. He dreads his next bowel movement more than death itself, which of course is highly ironic considering the former might well be a forerunner to the latter's inevitability.

His appetite is practically nil for obvious reasons, though there is little logic in starving to death with such a varied plethora of other options currently on deck. Lack of breathable air would surely lead to anoxia, and then there was the definite probability of death by pneumonia if the temperatures continued their downward spiral. Last but surely not least, there was the ever-popular expiration via drowning and/or blunt trauma if the bunker were to implode from either a buildup of floodwaters or a powerful enough quake. Already their supply of drinking water was beginning to freeze within the plastic containers, a problem solved easily enough with use a cooking pot and working stove, but what happened if or when the generator fuel ran out? A complete lack of power coupled with below-freezing temps would surely mean a slow, agonizing demise.

As he continues to surf the digital graveyard known as HDTV, Killian occasionally shifts focus to the pile of blankets covering his bunker mate.

Not surprisingly, forty-five minutes of additional channel-surfing nets zero results.

Rising from the floor as quietly as possible so as to not awaken the girl, Killian resembles some sort of mythical swamp creature ascending from a muddy bog as at least a half-dozen blankets drag along behind.

His latest excursion to what he now thinks of as the "bloody throne" yields similar results to the last two, and he can only bow his head in despair. The color appears darker now, like freshly poured tar with swirls of maroon tossed in for good measure.

Without memory of the steps that brought him there, he finds himself seated in the comm room with roughly half the previous blanket cover now missing. Still, the warmth is sufficient to trigger yet another nap. It's the cold, he construes in his last waking thought before passing out, the bone-chilling temps that trigger this constant need to slumber. He gives the trio of monitors a final wearisome glance, his eyelids slapping shut without relaying the message to his brain what they'd viewed in those final few blinks. Perhaps because the change, the oh-so-faint alteration, had been so minor in what his subconscious deemed the grand scheme of things.

***

Tipping the jug, he pours the remainder of the water onto his scalp and feels the majority stream down his spine before spattering onto his bare feet. Although barely cooler than room temperature, it nonetheless births shivers of chilled ecstasy that in turn evokes a faint cry of joy that is almost sexual.

"You're hogging the juice, boy," the old man grumbles, scooping up a fresh gallon jug, twisting, then tossing away the top in one fluid movement. "How's about saving some for the rest of us?"

The old man, dressed only in boxer shorts and a pair of sagging black socks, chugs a mouthful before handing the container over to the elderly woman to his left. She slurps greedily, licking the excess from her chin through a toothless maw before pouring an ample supply onto her bony shoulders and similarly narrow chest, which is covered only by a thin white tee-shirt. Killian feels his gorge rise at the sight of the old woman's sagging breasts through the soaked tee. Reaching up, he slides a sweaty palm over his forehead and whisks away a handful of sweat onto the nearby wall. His entire body radiates waves of fever, as if he were lounging inside a cramped, hot-rock-heated sauna.

"Ain't planning on anything sinister, are ya, boy?" the old man asks with a grin, his dentures as white as the freshly driven snow.

106

"You can be trusted, can't you, dear?" the old woman adds while waiving a gnarled finger back and forth like a fleshy pendulum. *"With an old family secret, I mean?"*

Looking past her, Killian sees the gray walls of the bunker coated with wide sheets of perspiration, as if they inhabited a sweat gland built of stone and steel.

"Why, sure he can, dear," the old man replies with a sly wink. *"This one's a keeper. Invited him inside the homestead every month for almost a year, and haven't laid eyes on a single bug since."*

Suddenly overcome with dizziness, he falls to one knee and inhales. The heat that pelts his senses is akin to a mouthful of boiling water, as if he'd stuck his head inside a raging furnace.

"Heat gettin' to ya, young fella?" he hears the old man ask as the woman giggles maniacally in the background.

"Well, you know what they say..."

A different voice, all too familiar, finishes the old man's sentence.

"If you can't stand the heat, Kill-Joy, old salt, best to stay the hell outta the kitchen." The air goes instantly frigid.

***

Killian wakes with fright, tossing the blanket cover from his face as a low gurgling noise escapes his parched throat. With a series of hacking coughs, he gradually regains a sense of reality, rubbing each eye with the back of a gloved hand. Placing both

107

elbows on the desk, he rests his chin atop clenched fists and peers slowly upward toward the monitors.

"Hey…" he croaks, blinking rapidly as if to shake away any remaining cobwebs. "Hey, hey, hey now … what do we have *here*?"

The smile is crooked, warped, and from an outsider's perspective might even be considered a tad on the demented side. Even as his horrible chapped lips crack and separate like dozens of miniature slash wounds, Killian is beyond caring. It is the first smile of total sincerity he has experienced in recent memory.

***

"Oh my god … like, when did this happen? Were we out *that* long?" the girl gushes wide-eyed, her mouth hanging agape.

Killian stands to her right, temporarily able to ignore the building urgency at his lower abdomen.

"Apparently the winds of change blow in like a freight train."

"I mean, like, they used to bore us to tears with all that global warming jazz, but this is straight up ridiculous!"

"The way those icebergs are breaking loose and swirling around out there, I'd say the outside temps must've soared seventy, eighty degrees."

Wearing a deep frown, Kayla readjusts the multiple layers of cover around her neck and shoulders. "But won't that mean…"

Killian shrugs, still unable to refrain from breaking out in a grin despite the considerable cons of the situation.

"Yep, flood waters yet again, at least till a dry spell of considerable length plays out."

"Aw, rats. I thought as much," she replies with a pout.

"Hey, cheer up, kiddo," Killian counters, reaching out from his own self-made tent of blankets to pat her on the back. "Whatever happens is a step up from iceworld, agreed? At least we can toss the *'moving away from the sun'* theory out the window."

"True. I just hope the heat-up out there translates to a warming trend in here very, very soon."

"No doubt about it, kiddo. It shouldn't take long with a temp swing that extreme. We'll be shedding these bed accessories in no time flat."

"Speaking of which, is it lunch or dinnertime, do you suppose?" "Take your pick."

Swinging about on a single heel, the girl squeals playfully as if pinched and shambles off toward the kitchen. As has been the case countless times since their forced imprisonment, Killian is again amazed at the young girl's emotional flexibility.

"Dinner it is, then. What say you, King Killian? Would you prefer tuna on white or potted meat spread and saltines?"

Though the response is real, Killian plays his comical grimace for humor.

"Either sounds perfectly disgusting. Oh, and no more tea, okay? I'm holding out for some ice-cold lemonade for a later time."

"Gotcha, Ace. You just keep watching those bergs float away and yell if you see a Coast Guard rescue boat sail by."

Gingerly retaking his seat behind the desk, Killian is instantly re-entranced by the amazing visuals. The dull gray images of the previous three-plus days have long faded, replaced by a rapidly shifting kaleidoscope of colors, easily the most exhilarating of which is the occasional flash of blue tinged with bursts of bright sunlight. Equally mesmerizing, if not more so, are the jagged sections of solid ice that crack and collapse with frenzied regularity, as if literally being hacked apart by some enormous, invisible axe blade.

Hours later, even though the entire landscape had been a solid mass of frozen floodwaters for as far as the camera's lens could stretch, layer upon layer is torn asunder until the sun's joyous rays acquire complete domination.

While washing down remnants from a serving tray filled with potted meat spread on crispy saltines, Killian is forced to turn his head away from the spectacle (as well as his young cohort) to wipe away a building tear. Before darkness shades the final stage of the massive meltdown, both he and Kayla are able to shed several of the blankets that have been their savior as interior temperatures begin a gradual rise.

Killian's fifth (and final) bowel movement of the day is a cramp-filled excursion into uncharted depths of physical and mental anguish. Despite this, and the predictably bloody, grisly outcome, his sleep is deep and fueled by an inner calm. An inner calm reached when a single word has reclaimed its rightful place in his frazzled state of mind. That word, however tenuous and fleeting, is *hope*.

Chapter 10

Day Eight: *Reruns and Relapses*

"No offense, Ace, but your uncle must've been one ... weird dude."

"I believe eccentric is the PC word you're fishing for, kiddo." "Nope ... I'd say weird covers it juuuussst fine."

Having stripped down dramatically in the twenty-six hours since waking to find a new, vastly improved climate, Killian and Kayla share a bag of cheddar-cheese-flavored rice cakes while viewing a DVD pulled from Uncle Raymond's selected stash. Earlier, Killian had managed (before stomach/bowel issues intervened yet again) to check the air filtration systems, all of which seemed to be no worse for wear since the sudden temperature surge. The ice build-up had melted away, leaving minimal damage.

"Hey, in his defense, I don't think he had your age group in mind when he picked these out."

"Nooooo! Ya think?" she barks sarcastically, feigning shock. "Exactly what age demographic was he aiming at then, Sherlock?"

Perched atop a bean bag with his back tilted forward and his shoulders slumped, Killian is adorned in a purple sweatshirt and matching pants, a far cry from the headgear and pile of blankets that had previously served as required bunker attire.

As for Kayla, a ludicrously oversized hoodie and blue jeans is the wardrobe of choice, and

Killian is again left to marvel just how tiny the girl is once all the winter layers have been shed.

"I'd say more the over-twenty to twenty-five crowd ... those he foresaw as future leaders of a new world order."

"Guess he figured all you *old dogs* as worm dirt, huh?"

His head slumps forward even as he is unable to refrain a muffled giggle. "Yeah, I'd presume. You want to put in something else?"

Pawing through a cardboard box packed with DVDs, the girl's face is a frozen mask of indifference that amuses Killian no end.

"Ohhhh, so many classics to chose from. We have *The Civil War* by Ken Barnes..."

"That's Ken Burns ... great documentary filmmaker. That's a long one but worth the time. I saw most of it in ... um ... saw it on PBS five or ten years back."

"Pass. Like, I can't stand a movie where I know the ending," she says, flipping it aside.

"Next we have a series of *National Geographic* specials...most of 'em covering historic places and landmarks."

She begins to flip them faster, pausing only to read an occasional blurb on the back of the DVD boxes.

"My god ... it's all history and geography! I might as well be in school..." "I think ... that's what he had in mind, kiddo, at least partly."

"What do you mean, partly?"

Focusing on the currently inserted disc, where a montage of viscerally entrancing war-torn images

(World Wars I and II) flash across the screen in vivid HD, Killian slides off the bean bag until he sits posed on his knees with crossed arms.

"From his selections, I'd say Uncle Ray was hoping that whoever ended up in this bunker would watch and learn, and once they were able to brave the outdoors…"

"Learn what? What good is this…" she struggles to finish, waiving an accusing finger at the screen, where a stack of horribly emaciated nude bodies are being shoved into a manmade ditch, lit afire, and burned in a Nazi death camp.

Killian interrupts just as the picture shifts to a still shot of Hitler standing before the German masses with a clenched, shaking fist raised high into the air.

"He wanted me, you, *whoever* made it out to start over to … learn from previous mistakes. Dreamer he was, Uncle Ray wanted a better world to emerge from whatever disaster purged the old one."

"Geee-sus, Ace…" Kayla says, leaving her mouth agape as she falls back onto the couch with a hand stuck tightly to her chest, "…you are truly freaking me out! I mean, like, you sounded exactly like Mr. Childers, my seventh grade American history teacher."

Waving her off, Killian remains silent while reaching over to up the television's volume.

"I mean it, dude … you channeled the man perfectly. Scaaaaaa-ry!"

The girl soon collapses into a deep slumber, leaving Killian to ponder his uncle's true motives. It seemed the entire bunker setup had been designed for outsiders to discover and use, certainly not for the man himself. Perhaps his uncle had suffered from a fatal disease and completed the shelter knowing he wouldn't be a part of either its active use or the aftermath to follow. Reaching to massage his ever-tender, ever- bloated midsection, Killian wonders, mostly without fear, if he might have contracted a similar fate.

***

"So how's the sandwich?" she asks offhandedly before taking a large bite of her own, the left side of her mouth coated in mayo.

Pausing after a small bite, Killian tilts the sandwich toward his nostrils and carefully parts the bread before taking a brief sniff.

"I dunno ... you ... do you smell something funny?"

"Canned chicken seemed okay when I opened. I figure the chilly spell we had might've added shelf life to 'em if anything."

"Yeah, but maybe it's the condiments. Something smells rotten and we ain't anywhere near Denmark," he continues with a weak smile, pushing the barely touched food aside before leaning ever harder onto the kitchen counter. His complexion is chalky; his eyes bloodshot; his skin texture like semidried paste.

Reaching into the icebox, Kayla pulls out a glass container marked Miracle Whip, screws off the top and sticks her nose to the lid.

"Nope ... smells fine to me, and I get the feeling you'd surely know it if it was starting to turn even a little bit."

"Yeah, guess it's just me and this stomach bug. Wish I had a pesticide I could swallow to kill off the little SOB."

"Ya think maybe..." the girl begins before halting abruptly to take in another mouthful. It's been twenty-nine hours since the meltdown, and she has finally shed the hoodie for a long-sleeved (but still woefully oversized) cotton button-up.

"What?" Killian finally asks after a lengthy pause wherein the girl seems to have purposely avoided finishing her thought. "Do I think what? You have a theory regarding my misery?"

"Well, you mentioned the bug spray ... the poison. You ... think maybe it's the cause? I mean, like, maybe from your job."

Grimacing, Killian starts to take a sip of water but barely manages to wet his lips. "Nah, can't see it. I always took the necessary precautions on the job. Besides, if the stuff was gonna bother me this much, I figure I'd have known right away ... like an allergy or something."

Tossing a final bite into her mouth, Kayla gives the morsel a token chew before quickly swallowing.

"Thought so ... sounded stupid even to me. Pardon a pesky kid for talking out her butt-hole?"

Slumping away, Killian raises a hand and waves her off.

"Not a problem, kiddo. At this point, I'm open to any and all speculation." "Where ya headed, cowboy?" she asks, shoving their used papers plates

116

into an oversized black trash bag, the second to be filled to overflowing since their incarceration. "Gonna monitor the monitors for a while ... that is, unless you want to toss a fresh DVD into the player instead."

"No, thanks, Ace ... no more of that history homework for this girl. Meet you there in a few."

"You got it," he mumbles, already having vanished from her line of sight.

Stepping away from the trash bag after resealing the top with a wire tie, Kayla's nostrils flare at the sour stench floating about the room. It isn't until she circles the counter and invades the exact space Killian had previously occupied that it becomes painfully clear that the building trash has nothing to do with the sickly smell permeating the air.

Fighting her gag reflex, she is forced to quickstep from the room with tear-filled eyes.

***

Feeling as though heavy chains had latched onto his eyelids, Killian stares at the center monitor with his chin tucked lightly against his chest. He has nodded off several times in the past few minutes, the girl's constant dialogue doing little to fend off the building drowsiness.

"Yep, sure looks like it's drying up out there. Water in that ditch is two, three feet high at the most...

"Ace, I gotta give credit where credit is due. Your Uncle Roy might've been a little short-sighted on, like, heating issues and DVD choices, but when it comes to water sealing, he is ... was ... a cer-teee-fied genius. A swarm of beavers couldn't have kept us more high 'n' dry..."

If not for an absolute zero reading in both the energy and motivation departments, Killian could have worked up quite the guffaw from the "swarm of beavers" comment.

As it was, he could only manage an occasional nod as the young girl's dialogue continued unabated and seemingly without the need to pause for air.

"... and I still don't have a Sherlock Holmes clue how or, like, *where* the fresh air is pumped in from. I mean for four days solid we were trapped in the center of an ice cube. From where in the name of the Mad Hatter did the flow of oxygen originate...?

"... and not to inject a note of sourness, but I do, like, wish he'd thought of the building garbage dilemma. Another week and we'll be praying for nose plugs...

"... seems to me if the water level keeps dropping and the sun keeps popping out and saying hi that an expedition might be order, right, Ace...?

"... Ace, are ya with me? Hey, grandpa ... wake up!"

Stretching his arms high and wide, Killian turns to the girl and weakly nods. "Y-yeah, kiddo ... I'm listening. Y-you were talking about ... the, um, lack of a garbage disposal and sunbathing, right?"

"Yeah, something like that," she smiles between tiny bites from a box of saltines.

The monitors reveal flood waters that appear to be rapidly dissipating, the most likely culprit being consistently stout winds and two full days of blazing sun since the meltdown commenced. Meanwhile, the bunker's interior temperatures seem to have leveled at a still slightly chilly but reasonably comfortable level, allowing for long-sleeved shirts but completely eliminating the need for an accompanying jacket.

"So tell me, Ace, other than your ex, whom would you most *dislike* spending bunker time with?"

Killian pauses to frown before executing a textbook double-take. "Say ... what?"

"Sorry, didn't know I tossed any, like, teen-speak in there. I said, whom would you least enjoy being stuck with in this oversized sewer pipe? I'm talking anybody ... past or present."

"Lord, girl ... where do you come up with this stuff?"

Her stoic expression unchanged, Kayla shrugs without response. "Restless minds and all that ... use it or lose it."

Scratching casually through his grayish brown hair (the gray having become the dominant shade over a frighteningly short duration), he squints fiercely as if attempting to recall a long-faded memory.

"You did say the ex doesn't count?"

"Affirmative ... that would've been much tooooo easy." "Anyone, past or present, right?"

"Aha ... so you were listening."

"Afraid this one's pretty easy too..." he says with a toothy grin, and Kayla barely refrains from wincing from the foul smell of his breath.

"... fact is, I think I'd have even *preferred* the old ball and chain."

"And the loser is?" she asks cheerily, though careful to pause a few moments before inhaling.

"Tell ya what, kiddo ... I need a few minutes to properly stew, so you go first."

Rubbing the healed scar beneath her chin, Kayla leans back onto the couch and pulls her slender legs to her chest.

"No competition in my case either," she grins, her eyes sparkling with mischief. "The person I speak of is a walking, talking turd of a human being named Donald J. Bond, or 'JB,' as he was referred to by the few retarded souls stupid enough to hang with 'im."

Struggling not to giggle aloud despite the many and varied pains wracking his entire being, Killian nevertheless arches an eyebrow in sincere curiosity. He could almost see the fire spewing from the young girl's nostrils.

"So what exactly was Mr. Bond's major malfunction?"

"Too many to list ... believe it or not, despite our present predicament, there ain't enough time to cover all that nasty boy's warped ways. Allow me instead to, like, hit the lowest points only."

The girl then inhales deeply as if preparing to submerge under water. Smelling the foul odor of his own passed gas, Killian quickly covers his groin with a blanket in an attempt to block the scent.

"The floor is all yours, kiddo ... I am truly intrigued."

"Well, it started in the third grade ... Miss Garner's class. She had a girl-boy-girl- boy seating policy, and I was unfortunate enough to, like, draw JB Bond as my rear seat copilot. The kid's breath smelled like a wet dog's butt even then. I ignored him as best I could, but the constant reek spewing from between the boy's lips was impossible to *brush* off, so to speak. I tried handing him a TicTac once and the retard stuck it up his nose. Speaking of that, his fingers were constantly digging for gold in those oversized nostrils of his ... and he'd wipe those nasty, gooey nose-burgers on the back of my desk! I kid you not, he smeared 'em on like jam on toast. Oh, and the farts! I won't even go there! He'd wait till Miss Garner was talking and let 'er rip ... full steam ahead!

I always pitied that boy's poor mother for having the unfortunate task of having to wash out the racing tracks from his undies!"

"K-Kayla..." Killian manages to stutter between howls while raising a shaking hand airborne. Seemingly entranced by her own rant, the girl never seems to notice her slowly collapsing cohort crumble to the floor.

"He never left me alone that entire year ... and kept up the harassment steady for the next four. Somehow, we always ended up seated near each other for at least two classes a year. It's like the smelly little runt planned it that way ... blueprinted it and then bribed the faculty so he could, like, continue to curl my hair with his sewage breath and

121

butt biscuits! He was, like, a puss-coated scab given human shape!"

"Kayla ... c-can I ask you ... s-something…" he blurts with what little air remains in his battered lungs. Bent over like a pretzel stick, the severe throbbing pain at his ribs has at least served to temporarily overtake his stomach in the *worst misery of the moment* sweepstakes.

"It wasn't just in class, either. He followed me around on breaks, licking his grubby little fingers till they were dripping ooze and then wiping them on my face and chin. I swear, like, his spit reminded me of my cat when it had diarrhea. No matter how I screamed and cursed at him, he never let up. My big brother would beat 'im to a pulp and tell 'im to stay away from me, but it never took. I think, like, in some ways the sick little worm even enjoyed it!"

Attempting a last-ditch intervention, Killian finds neither the required oxygen nor energy to complete even a single sentence.

"Did y-you ... did h-he…" is all he can manage as his laughter is soon transformed into a grotesque dry-heave of hysterics.

"And last year ... this last school year, he shows up at my house on his motorized scooter and wants to know if I'd go to the movies with him! Can you believe the colossal bag on this boy to *ask me out* after four years of such inhuman torture? I swear to the man above, like, if I'd been holding a blunt instrument at that moment, JB Bond could have added 'toothless' to his many disjointed physical attributes!

"Soooo ... short story longer, just knowing I have to share the same planetary space as Donald Bond is bad enough, but ten minutes inside this bunker with that walking poop-stain would, like, be enough to have me searching for the nearest piece of cutlery, 'cause one of us was gonna have to go…"

Arising to a sitting position, Killian is forced to suck in several strained breaths before attempting to verbalize a response.

"I was going to ask," he finally manages, wincing with each word while hugging his ribs with both arms, "did you two ever date?"

Rolling her eyes, the girl feigns a gag while pointing a forefinger into her open mouth.

"Dating…? Did you just hear anything I said? The boy was an anal wart with feet.

Why in the good Lord's name would I want to be seen with him in public?"

"Well, kiddo, I hate to break this to you, but that particular anal wart with feet was, more than likely, on a single-minded mission all those years."

"That being?" she frowns, looking every bit the preteen Madonna.

"The kid had a big-time crush on a certain curly-haired cutie named Kayla."

"Strange way to show it, wouldn't you say? I mean, like, I can't see many of my gender being impressed with a boy's nose- and/or butt-picking prowess."

Finally able to breath normally, Killian climbs back atop the bean bag he'd so clumsily exited and becomes aware of the cramps slowly twisting his lower colon.

"Hey, he was a kid. He wanted your attention at any cost. Dumb as it sounds, to a nine-or ten-year-old boy, *any* attention from the girl of your dreams is good attention."

"Well, regardless of his warped romantic intentions, I hope to never run across anyone even half as repulsive. To spend time with someone like that in such close knit quarters as these is, like, justification to find the nearest jagged cliff and take a swan dive."

"Good enough then, kiddo. If JB Bond comes a-knockin', I'll be sure to send him and his nose-burgers on their merry way to the next bunker down the line."

Adjusting her position on the couch until she sits posed in lotus position, the girl claps her hands with such youthful exuberance Killian can't help but regain a bit of pep despite the impending ills to come.

"Okay, your turn then. I've spilled my guts ... so I hope for something similarly smarmy from yours truly. I already know it ain't the ex ... so the suspense is killing me. Like, spill already…"

The smile having rapidly faded, Killian now wears a pained grimace that only magnifies his haggard appearance tenfold. The harsh squint returns, but with a noticeably darker edge. The girl can't help but think that her savior has aged a full decade in just over a week.

"Afraid the loser of my choice doesn't come with near the level of humor, so bear with me, kiddo ... that is, if you really want to hear it."

"I'm all ears," she answers, though a reluctant wariness has replaced the previous sparkle in her eyes, "nothing you can't tell me."

"Yeah, I think you've matured to way beyond your years this past week. "Anyhow, with all that's happened in the past nine, ten days to this planet, from the quakes to the tornadoes to the hurricanes and fires, a person can't help but feel pity for the majority that bought it ... that didn't make it through whatever disaster they were witness to. Fact is, kiddo, I can only think of one solitary individual whose dying is ... was probably a good thing, at least for those of you ... of *us* who might survive to see a rebuilding."

"Let me guess ... your mother-in-law," she injects with a bit of nervous humor, though it is quickly obvious that such a lame attempt is not only fruitless but mostly ignored.

"Decent enough guess, and I'll give you a point for being on the right track, but no."

If anything, his demeanor shifts further and further into a dark, distant mode Kayla finds equally fascinating and frightening.

"It is ... was a family member, though. The name was ... *is* Oliver ... referred to by most as 'Ollie,' and..." he pauses to sigh heavily, as if somewhat reluctant to continue, "the evil rat bastard is ... *was* my father."

"Your ... dad?" she whispers cautiously.

125

"Yep, ain't it sad?" he answers through a spite-filled squint that causes the fine hairs on Kayla's arms to stand at attention.

"Did he, like, beat you and stuff?"

"Nah, it wasn't your stereotypical child abuse scene. Papa Ollie didn't drink, didn't smoke, didn't cheat with the ladies, and never raised a hand to me."

Thinking he would continue, Kayla paused several moments before speaking up. "Then, why ... what did he do that was so, like, *evil?*"

"Sorry, kid. I ... um..." Killian stammered, standing suddenly and pacing about the tiny room like an expectant father. "I'm not up to dishing out the dirty details just yet. Take my word for it ... Papa Ollie was a real prize, and about the last person you'd want to spend any face time with in any situation, much less one as ... dire as this."

"Is he ... do you think he's still alive ... out there, I mean?" she inquires timidly while watching his frantic pace increase to spinning top proportions.

"Not likely, unless they found a safe haven for three hundred more of his kind when all this crazy shit nailed the fan."

Shocked more by the amplified volume of his tone than the cursing, Kayla scoots as far to one end of the couch as possible.

"I mean, how much time could they have had to move 'em all ... and when push came to shove, who would put forth the effort to save such scum when there are ... *were* so many decent folks in trouble?

"You'd figure they'd leave 'em to rot ... to fend for themselves. Talk about your ironic justice.

126

That's what I'd have done, just toss the master keys into the nearest trash bin and head for the hills…"

His voice growing shriller by the word, Killian's gestures grow comically animated as arms wave about in circular fashion while the attached hands clench and unclench with an almost timed regularity.

"… I wouldn't have given it a second thought … not a twinge of guilt in leaving garbage like him behind to drown like a rat or be scooped up and hauled away by a friendly funnel cloud or two … it ain't like the world would shed a tear, is it?"

How she is able to summon the courage to interrupt such a vile rant isn't nearly as astonishing as the response to follow.

"Was your dad … in a hospital?"

The pacing stops abruptly in midstep, as if he has body-blocked a brick wall. He turns to the girl and stoops until they are eye level, though he is using both hands to vigorously massage his perpetually engorged midsection. Though the volume of his words has toned down considerably, almost to the level of a raspy whisper, the glare of madness is still present in both rapidly blinking eyes. Kayla does not cringe at the sudden intrusion, but instead, miraculously, holds her ground with a level of maturity well beyond her years.

"A hosp—no, kiddo, he isn't … wasn't in a hospital when the big, bad bell tolled. As far as I know, Papa Ollie never suffered a sick day in his miserable life. No, it prides his only son to announce that his father was in state prison when those damn meteors splashed down in the Pacific

127

and things starting turning to shit. Papa Oliver was in state prison and on *death row*, no less. Now, ain't that just a barn-dance hoot? The murdering bastard was slated to die in less than six months before Mother Nature intervened to shorten his sentence."

"Who ... did he ... I mean, why was he there?" she asks, matching him glare for glare, though careful to speak softly and avoid sounding the least bit interrogative. She has heard, after all, what such unabashed curiosity did to a certain feline.

"Papa Ollie was on death row on a charge of homicide in the first degree," he replies stoically, tilting his head a bit to the left as the stomach massage slows a degree.

"He ... killed someone?"

"Sweetie," he grins, "one doesn't land on death row via a five-finger discount or jaywalking."

"Who ... but who did he—"

"Well," he interrupts, rising, spinning about on his right heel and performing a technically sound about-face maneuver. His whole deportment is instantly transformed to cheery, upbeat mode, a change that scares the young girl far more than the exasperated ranting that came before. "I guess we've gone this far, and I do owe you a full explanation after that booger-smearing boyfriend tale."

He stands before her in an at-ease pose with his hands now tucked neatly at his lower back. The girl can smell the odor of rot about his person, and the stench is no longer limited to merely his breath. Years earlier, around the age of eight, she'd found a dead cat in the woods behind the family home. The

128

foul smell of that stiff, dead feline is eerily similar. She'd often heard and read the term "stench of impending death," but never truly experienced its stomach-churning aroma until now.

"He murdered a sweet, caring young woman named Cassandra, or 'Cassie' to her many friends.

"Cassie was my mother."

For a brief flash, Kayla is no longer sickened by the odor emanating from her savior, as the air has locked in her lungs and throat like powdery dry ice.

"Lucky me came home from school one afternoon to find my ... to find her body laying face down in the kitchen floor with not one, not two, but three eating utensils sticking from her back like metallic quills," Killian continues, his tone growing increasingly robotic even as the room pacing begins anew, albeit at a much slower rate of speed.

"I'd never dreamed a human body could hold so much blood. She was ... she was practically floating in her own juices. It just ... didn't seem ... real ... possible.

"I mean, hey, I was a kid of the seventies after all. We weren't hardened by all the brutality and violence that future generations watched so routinely on TV, movies, videogames ... not to mention your local newscasts.

"Anyhow, for a second, I mean just a blink or two before cold, hard reality kicked me upside the head like a rented mule, I thought mom was playing some sort of elaborate practical joke. My mom was that way ... always good for a laugh no matter the

129

level of mental cruelty pop was doling out to her at the time."

Sensing Kayla's building curiosity at the contradictions in his story, Killian halts the marching to lock eyes with his young, wide-eyed audience.

"Don't misunderstand ... Papa Ollie never laid a hand on her before the murder, least none that I knew ... and for good reason. Reason number one; mother never would've put up with it without scooping up the nearest frying pan ... she was one tough bird. This leads directly into reason number two: Papa Ollie was a bit of a chickenshit, pardon the crudeness. Even as a kid I understood and accepted the old man as the type who had run from every fight he'd ever faced. You could practically see his yellow- streaked spine glowing through those damn polo shirts he always wore as casual, away from the office attire. I never met Grandpapa Ollie; he'd died when I was a baby, but I can only deduce that my pop came from a long line of mealy-mouthed cowards whose natural instincts were to always choose flight over fight.

"Tell you one thing ... the *pussy* gene is one this boy never inherited. I may end up being bald as a billiard ball and as wide as I am tall, but running from conflict is something I will ... *not* ... do, and with the big-time changes all around us, I get the feeling there'll be tests aplenty in the bravery department."

As he resumes pacing, Kayla seizes the opportunity to cut to the chase in fear of his story possibly veering off the main plotline.

"So if he were such a chick—such a coward, how did he ... work up the courage to k-kill your mom?"

"I wasn't there, kiddo, so that little mystery will forever remain so," he answers sharply, his arms flailing about as if he were attempting to take flight. "The cops found him in a park a few miles from our house, feeding the pigeons leftovers from the lunch my mom had fixed him that very morning. He freely confessed to her murder and didn't even bother playing innocent or the self-defense card. Then again, he never gave the media or law enforcement a clear statement on what led up the event, just kept mumbling something about how 'he'd just ... had enough' and wished he hadn't waited so long to do 'what he had to do.' He was sentenced to die and dragged off to state prison.

"I only visited him once, when his older brother and my court-appointed guardian practically dragged me along. It had been over a year since the killing. I had just turned fifteen. I cannot put into words how much I despised that son of a bitch. Sad thing is, I'd hated him *before* he took away my mother. By the time I sat across from him with only a clear glass shield between us, the level of loathing was immeasurable."

Shifting uncomfortably within the couch's mushy confines, Kayla annunciates her next works carefully, realizing she's verbally tiptoeing atop an active minefield.

"Did you ... speak? I mean, like, didn't you ask him *why*?"

131

His booming, sarcastic howl shatters her veneer of cool, and her entire body tenses and coils in anticipation of a potential outburst.

"Did I ... did I ask him why?" he repeats mockingly, flashing a ghoulish smile. "Jesus wept, girl, what a notion ... you must have ESP, 'cause in point of fact, that single word was the *only* thing I could manage to spit out over that prison phone. Somehow I managed to mouth it, though it may have been a silent scream for all I know. I was only a year older than you, kiddo. Imagine that ... a year older than you are right ... now."

Once again, he kneels over and down until the space between them is sparse. "I indeed did inquire of the murdering bastard who helped create me why he'd ended my mother's life and left his teenage son's in a shambles.

"Wanna know his answer? Wanna know what Mr. Sensitive offered up to his only son? The son, by the way, that he barely acknowledged on a year-to-year basis or bothered to speak to for weeks at a time. Wanna know what golden nugget of insight ol' Papa Ollie barked out in that crucial moment?"

The girl swallows hard but otherwise remains still.

"Through the same cold, emotionless stare I'd grown so very accustomed to he said, and I quote ... *'It was time for a change.'*"

She hears a low clicking sound escape the base of his throat, followed by a full- body shiver that concludes with him standing upright with both hands gripping either side of his head. The flurry of movement creates a slight breeze that slaps Kayla's nose and fills her nostrils with a putrid stench that almost triggers an involuntary gag.

"Time ... for ... a ... change. Can you beat that for some vague psychobabble horseshit? From there, he gently hung up the phone and arose from the chair, then nodded for the guard to take him away. I never contacted nor heard from crazy old Papa Oliver again. I did, however," he continues, releasing the grip on his skull and raising a single forefinger airborne, "periodically check with the institutional powers that be on just what date they planned on ending his miserable life. As is the way of the modern justice system, due to appeals by various bleeding heart types, that joyous day had yet to surface before the recent doomsday scenario made it a moot point."

Turning his back, Killian shambles forward a few steps as if shackled at the ankles. With his scraggly beard, disheveled coif and semihunched back, he resembles a homeless derelict on the verge of total collapse.

"So that's the story, kiddo. Now it's official, I guess; you are imprisoned with the son of a lunatic. Not sure why I decided to share such a heartwarming tale, but it certainly wasn't meant to shake you up like I'm pretty sure it did. Sorry about that..."

"No, you were just being honest. I asked for it, remember?"

"Yeah, well, I could've made something up that wasn't quite as mind-numbing. You ... I forget sometimes how ... young you really are."

"Not to worry," she smiles, the majority of built-up tension having left her neck and shoulders. "I'd say I've aged considerably in the last week."

"Touché, young woman, touché. If you don't mind, I'm gonna lay down a while." "Sure, Ace. My ears are bleeding from all this gabbing anyhow. Go get some rest. Breakfast will be on me."

Killian stumbles away in a shambling gait, cradling his midsection and leaving a vapor trail of sickly aroma in his wake.

Left to navigate the rest of the night alone, the girl gives the monitors a final look- see (darkness has fallen) before settling in for a few select hours of the DVD documentary *VIETNAM: Winning was never an option*.

She sleeps on the living room couch, mostly to avoid her bunker mate's rancidity.

Sometime during the night, she awakens to the shrieks that his nightmares have birthed.

After a time, the verbal outbursts wane, and a fitful slumber ensues. Tomorrow, she feels, is an important day. Perhaps even a vital day.

A day that just might ... that *should* dramatically alter everything about the future to come. Maybe, she muses, it is indeed time for such a change.

***

The nightmare is unique in that it is segmented into two distinct chapters, the fragments created by a troubled, fitful sleep that sees him awaken with each toss, turn, and twist within the crumpled,

134

soured sheets. Unlike the majority of dreams, which begin anew with fresh plotlines as a new round of slumber ensues, this particular screenplay remains intact despite the wakeful interruption, as if his subconscious flat refuses to move on until the story unfolds in its entirety.

__Chapter One__: He and the girl share the living room couch in front of the television, their respective images outlined in the dark, grayish haze of the blank screen.

"I found a DVD at the bottom of the box," the girl announces flatly while flipping the disc from hand to hand, "it's unmarked ... figured we might as well, like, give it a whirl."

"Plug it in then, kiddo," he responds calmly enough, though an unexpected wave of inexplicable apprehension floods his senses. Grinding his teeth as his scalp grows feverish and his heart races like mad, he realizes he is on the verge of a panic attack the likes of which he has never before experienced.

With the DVD player powered up, a sea-blue screen erases their images. Blue soon gives way to clear, crisp imagery, and he is forced to shove clenched fists into the sides of each thigh just to avoid screaming aloud.

"Ah, pooh," the girl grumbles, "looks like another documentary."

He doesn't attempt a response, for fear his voice will crack like that of a prepubescent teen.

An elderly couple stand with their backs to the camera in what appears to be a dimly lit basement or attic. A single light bulb hangs from the ceiling several feet to their right, the only other object visual being a trio of cardboard boxes stacked nearby.

The woman is slightly humpbacked and thus a full foot shorter than the man. Her entire upper body appears to be wracked with spasms. The man, completely bald except for the bushy gray patches around each ear, reaches over and pats the woman gently on the back in an obvious attempt to console. Several voices can be heard in the background, though no one else appears before the cameras as the couple stand before the red brick wall like hostages before a firing squad.

"I don't get it ... like, what's the plot?" he hears the girl inquire, the thundering at his temples threatening to drown her out.

"Don't do it ... please ... just ... don't..." he hears the elderly man beg as he continues to pat the woman's back with a visibly shaking hand.

The off-camera voices respond in kind, one much louder and emotionally charged than the other.

"Listen to h-him ... we won't tell anyone ... we promise we won't tell."

"Just shut the hell up, grandpa," a quaking voice instructs; a voice instantly recognizable from a previous dream. "I ain't decided what to do with you yet. Just cut out the whimpering for a minute and let me think, goddamn it!"

"Let's just cut out, man ... we got what we came for..." still another mystery guest bellows from what sounds like a far distance. This voice, too, is vaguely familiar. The images begin to *scramble and retract like fallen pieces of a jigsaw puzzle before fading to a white, milky haze...*

Chapter Two: *"This is, like, lame ... talk about amateur hour," he hears the girl's voice echo just before the television screen reappears in ivory, static-laden flashes that eventually piece together for a full image.*

"I'm giving it another minute or two and pulling the plug on this lousy home movie."

His limbs are numb with an utter paralysis only found within such dreamscapes; otherwise he would gladly trump her suggestion long before the aforementioned sixty seconds were up.

"Looks like they skipped right to the ending."

With his back still turned, the elderly man has sidestepped over and is blocking the woman as to protect her.

"Not her!" he pleads, his voice crackling with emotion. "She's ... she won't tell, god help me, she won't tell!"

"Yeah? How can you be so sure, gramps?" the off-camera voice spits sarcastically. "What's gonna keep her from singin' like a bird? I hear old ladies can bear one helluva grudge."

"S-she won't ... she j-just won't..."

"I'm supposed to take your word for that, am I?"

"She h-has Alzheimer's, you son of a bitch!" the old man whimpers, practically engulfing the woman as they both crumple slowly to the planked floor.

"I'll bet," the man laughs cruelly. "Show me a doctor's slip, old man."

"The house is clear, man, now let's make tracks!" the second mystery voice chimes in, again from what sounds like a mountaintop away.

"You sure? I know I heard somebody or something movin' about upstairs." "I checked every room ... every closet ... it's clear, now let's move!"

"We can't have no witnesses, man ... no loose ends, you get it?"

"Whatever, asshole ... just ... just do what you have to, then, and let's get out."

A sharp clicking sound ensues—the unmistakable sound of the hammer being pulled back on a revolver.

"Sorry, old-timer ... my heart bleeds if what you're sayin' is true, but I just can't take the chance..."

Much like the full-body paralysis, he finds his vocal cords equally useless, and the desperate plea he so desires to verbalize sticks in his throat without release.

"Uh-uh ... looks like the geezers are going down!" he hears the girl announce with a frightening mix of youthful glee and unbridled bloodlust.

The sound of the first shot is badly muffled, as if the television's built-in speakers were unable to process the full amperage of the blast. The old man's head jerks back as a wide crimson stain spreads from between his shoulder blades. A second shot, this one completely muted, opens a dime-sized hole at the base of his neck. As his life source spews

138

forth in a volcanic eruption, the old man shudders before toppling over in a spastic lurch.

"Boy-howdy! One down, one to go!" the girl chirps, and he feels a sickening wave of nausea as hot bile fills his throat.

The old woman, her face shielded by lingering shadows, rolls over onto the man's still frame and embraces him with her pale, spindly arms.

"Just stay still, grandma," the man instructs sternly; "don't make this any harder than it has to be."

The old lady raises a hand palm up, as if to ward off the evil standing off-camera. "The Lord is my shepherd ... I shall not want ... he—"

The bullet removes three of her fingers and she prays no more... The screen goes black just as a second shot rings out...

Killian wakes with a garbled scream; garbled due to the outpouring of vomit from his mouth and nostrils. Rolling over from his stomach onto his left side, he becomes aware of a sticky wetness coating the sheets. Utterly disgusted but unable to muster the strength to rise and escape the foulness, he manages to clear his throat and wipe the excess from his nostrils with a dry section of sheet before passing out yet again.

His last conscious thought is a prayer that if indeed death intercedes during the night, may eternity be void of dreams in any way, shape or form.

Chapter 11
Day Nine: *Foxhole Confessions*

Kayla had heard the term *projectile vomit* many times, usually amongst her small circle of friends as they rated the looks and/or charms of the boys at her school; i.e., a particularly unattractive specimen was disgusting enough to be projectile vomit-*worthy*. They had deemed said term catchy, cute and original, and it held a special place within their building vocabulary of teen-speak. Openly gagging, she backs from the kitchen with her jeans and v-necked tee soaked in warm, sticky bile.

Lying face down on the tiled floor, Killian attempts to push himself upright and manages only to throw up yet again before collapsing onto the puddle with his bared chest.

"I ... g-get m-me ... to the couch. I ... I'll ... j-just need to ... t-to lie on my ... my back," he mumbles as pinkish fluid drips from his nostrils to congregate within his already saturated mustache.

Straining and struggling like a cripple attempting to locate his lost wheelchair, he eventually makes it up to all fours before being pummeled by a fresh fit of dry heaves.

Peering up through bleary eyes, he cannot locate the girl. "Ka-Kay ... Kayla?"

His throat is afire; his chest aches and throbs, and his midsection feels strangely displaced, as if it has been literally turned inside out. The ultrabitter taste of upchucked Pepto-Bismol coats his tongue. Splashing about in his own fluids, he is aware of a kaleidoscope of colors to include pink (of obvious origin), yellow (stomach acid perhaps?) and (most frightening by far) a red so dark it is borderline ebony.

"N-need some ... some he-help here, ki-kiddo."

The attempt to push himself to his feet goes horribly awry as he ends up toppling onto his back with a jarring thud and slamming the back of his skull on the countertop.

Before everything fades to black, Killian sees a blurry image of someone kneeling over him. The girl, he deduces, coming to his aid after all. He figures her level of fear at the mere sight of him is probably to a degree she's never before experienced. As he drifts in and out of consciousness, he becomes aware of a slight but palpable pain at the underside of his left elbow. There is a sudden pressure felt there, followed by instant relief. Darkness falls yet again.

Chapter 12
The Final Day: *Paradox*

His eyelids seem welded shut, but with several minutes' worth of rapid blinking, they eventually do separate and allow for a gradual return to sight.

She has indeed managed to get him to the couch, as he can feel the give of the cushions beneath. More importantly, the blanket atop his chest and arms seems void of wetness, as do his mouth, chin and nostrils.

"You finally coming to, sleepyhead? I was beginning to think your family ancestry included a Van Winkle of Rip infamy."

The girl's voice is such a welcome, somehow homey sound that he would surely crack a smile if physically able.

"You got some serious tummy issues, Ace. Here, I brought you some tea…"

Though her voice was clearly heard to his left, when he looks over with vision still terribly marred by a glazed gumminess, he sees no one is there. Peering over the blanket tucked tightly beneath his chin, he gradually scans the room with the same result.

"Ki-kiddo? You ... where are you?"

Silence—the kind where one could literally hear a pin drop-the eeriest quiet of all. "Y-you ... got ... my ... my tea, kiddo?"

He hears only the faint throbbing of the pulse at his temples and the ruffling of his own hands beneath the blanket as they try to free themselves to the outside air.

142

"Kay—Kayla?"

Raising his head just slightly from the pillow ignites a sudden wave of dizziness.

He blacks out momentarily and awakens to see the girl leaning directly overhead.

"I hear you call out?" she asks, reaching down to pull a loose hair from his cheek. "Oh ... well, I ... I th-thought I heard you before. Y-you were ... said s-something about t-tea…"

"Tea? Nope ... think you were dreaming again. Don't think you're up to ingesting anything at this stage, am I right?"

"I-I guess n-not. Th-thanks for ... well, cleaning ... me up. I know it's ... it's a mess."

Turning away, the girl's tone is noticeably grim.

"Don't ... thank me yet, Ace. In the long haul, you might not be so ... appreciative."

His right hand emerges from the blanket in a feeble attempt to rub the bleariness from his sight.

"I ... I'm so ... weak. I ... think I was throwing up ... blood back there." "Yeah, it was blood ... and lots of it."

"I ... must look ... like hell." Her back remains to him.

"Pale as the freshly fallen snow, but I have to admit ... tough as nails ... a true glutton for punishment."

Killian tries to smile but can only manage a sneer.

"I s-sure don't ... feel t-too tough. Day old ki-kitten could ... take me out a-about now."

"Well," she replies after a drawn-out sigh, "it's a problem all right. What to do now..."

Even through the haze, he can see her shoulders are badly slumped and her head bowed.

"H-hey now, k-kiddo. This isn't y-your fault. My ti-timing never was very good. I mean, it's ... it's not like you can call the nearest doctor for a ... house ... house-call."

She finally turns to face him, a single tear having dug a prominent groove into what appears to be a hastily applied makeup job.

"No, no ... that is out of the question, for sure."

"It's ... okay, kiddo. Don't fr-fret. I must've had this ... condition long before all this ... other stuff happened. Just ... wasn't meant to be for me, that's ... all."

The girl nods solemnly, her eyes darting wildly about as if to prevent locking on his. Despite his many and varied physical ailments, the heartache felt in light of the young girl's sincere misery over his plight might well be the more excruciating by far.

He had meant to safeguard her through a future littered with dangers and uncertainty; to play a part he'd never before desired—that of guardian. Now she would be alone—so very young and alone—to face those fears and unknown hurdles without him. Surely if a single drop of bodily fluid remained within his hollow husk of a body, he would have cried it out at the very premise.

"No, it wasn't ... wasn't meant to be at all," she agrees, bowing gingerly at his side.

"I know you probably don't feel much like talking, but can I ... ask you something?"

He swallows several times, his throat ragged and sore from the constant gagging and heaving.

"S-sure, kiddo. Shoot…"

"Have you ever felt so guilty about something that ... it made you, like, question something you did that, at the time, you knew for sure was the right thing to do?"

"I ... I'm not s-sure I understand."

The girl takes his exposed hand and holds it, squeezes it.

"Killian, did you ever do something so bad it made you feel ... I dunno ... evil?"

"E-evil?" he repeats as his left brow arches dramatically. "Th-that's a pretty strong word. I ... think everyone has done ... things ... they've regretted later ... but evil is a bit ... harsh."

She massages his hand gently but firmly, her eyes suddenly wide and gleaming. "Come on, we can be honest with each other, can't we? Just like that trade-off on the person we'd least like to spend time with in this bunker, remember? That was fun, wasn't it?"

When his only reply is a bemused frown, she continues in as serious a tone as he can remember her utilizing.

"I ... need some advice ... some counseling on this, Killian. I'm really, like ... confused."

Coughing weakly, he swallows yet again and breaks her stare to briefly study their surroundings. The bunker seems overly dark, as if utilizing only emergency lighting.

"Did ... is the generator running? Kinda dim in here..."

"I shut it off to save power," she replies flatly, now using the thumb of her right hand to massage his left palm. "Please, Killian. I need to know..."

Inhaling deeply, he focuses on his blanketed feet at the edge of the couch and discovers merely wiggling them a Herculean task. His head and neck are strained due to awkward positioning, but he is unable to muster enough strength to remedy the problem.

"Oh ... okay. I'll try. Give me a minute to ... think about it."

The girl squeals with delight, a sound that warms Killian's heart despite the decidedly off-kilter request.

"Give me something good, okay? I ... need to know for my own ... peace of mind, you might say."

She helps him to lean up and straightens the pillow beneath his neck. He sighs with relief and pauses an additional few seconds. He feels faint and is forced to take deep, pained breaths between sentences.

"All right, then. This ... this happened several years ago. I c-caught my wife cheating with a co-worker. They were ... had been meeting at a hotel fairly regularly. I ... got messed up on ... on pain pills and decided to confront them both. Things got ... real ugly real fast and I hurt the guy pretty bad. Long story sh-short, the little weasel ended up in the hospital with a fractured skull and I ... spent year and a half in state prison for aggravated assault and ... d-drug charges."

146

"You were in ... jail?"

"Yeah, and I ... deserved it. I got what was ... coming to me ... no denials."

As the room goes momentarily silent, Killian scans the room between dizzy spells and becomes aware of subtle changes he cannot quite put his finger on. The air is thick with rot; the type usually associated with feverish infections gone long untreated.

"So you did ... do feel guilt over the act ... I mean, the act itself?" the girl asks while letting go of his hand and standing, her knees popping loudly.

"Yeah, s-sure I did. I made a mistake ... a dumb one. Those two deserved ... each other. I almost ruined my life over my w-wife's transgressions."

"That doesn't sound like guilt, Killian. It sounds more like ... you're sorry you got caught."

"N-no, I felt bad about hurting the guy. He wasn't worth ... soiling my mitts over ...

I was ... am better than t-that."

Once again facing away from him, the girl's tone grows suddenly cold and vindictive.

"Damn it, Ace, that's not guilt ... that's more like self-pity." "I d-did my time and never once felt sorry for myself." "So you feel no guilt now?"

"No. What's done is done. Its past hi-history," he croaks between ragged, wet coughs.

"I'm not talking about that."

He pauses to cough into his palm, half expecting the palm to be coated in blood, and replies only when he sees it isn't.

"Not ... not talking about ... what?"

147

"I'm not talking about the thing with your wife and her boyfriend."

"Then ... what are we talking about, k-kiddo? Now ... I'm the confused one."

Without speaking, she departs the room in a sprint, leaving him to struggle with the blanket that has literally bound him to the couch from the waist down.

He is unable to loosen the portions that are tucked beneath his body weight, and gives up the fight with a strained huff just as he hears the girl reenter the room with a resounding thump.

"Look familiar?" she asks angrily, her lips pursed tight and shockingly pale in the aftermath.

She flings the small duffel bag to the floor between them and carefully studies his reaction.

"Ye-yeah. I ... I think so," he answers flatly, though his doe-eyed expression reveals a plethora of repressed emotions. Perhaps as a diversionary tactic, he tries to cough into his hand but is unable. His flesh, clammy as it is, begins to tingle as from a mild electrical shock.

"You *think* so? Let's, like, clarify this then: that is your duffel bag, isn't it?" "Yes, it's ... mine. Listen, kiddo, I can explain..."

He closes his eyes and sucks in a lengthy breath, fighting off yet another dizzy spell. Beneath him, the previously padded couch feels as hard as stone.

"Explain what, Killian? Why should you have to explain anything to me? Why is it even my business?"

"I take it ... y-you did ... you looked ... inside."

148

Her defiant stance unwavering, he finds the challenge of matching her intense glare impossible.

"Goes without saying. Why the grave concern?"

Wriggling about on the suddenly unforgiving couch, he catches a quick glance of the wall to his left, executes a comical double-take and then pauses to rub his eyes.

"Wood ... planks? What's ... wh-what's going on? Where—"

"Stick to the program, Ace," the girl commands, clapping her hands fiercely as if to refocus his attention.

"Wh-what do you mean, Kayla? What ... p-program?" "Just want to hear you say it, that's all."

"I-I'm not feeling too g-good, kiddo," he mumbles, giving the alien wall a final, worrisome once-over before pulling the blanket snugly to just below his chin. "Can we ... get back to this g-game a little later?"

"Sorry, Killian, but there is no later."

Taking a step forward, she bends down and retrieves the duffel.

"I think you need to tell me about this, I mean, since I do have a vested interest." She unzips the bag and pours out the contents in a single fluid movement. "Maybe I'm just paranoid ... jumping to conclusions the way teens so easily do. You tell me."

Killian watches in apparent despair as she scoots and scatters the items across the floor with a booted foot, almost toppling from the couch in a brief, pathetic attempt at retrieval.

"What does ... it matter," he says between coughs, focusing more on the tiled floor than the items themselves, "that stuff ... has no value now. W-what does it matter ... where it came from or ... where I got it?"

"Just call me curious ... guess it's that damn teenage thing again." "Kayla, I…"

Among the assorted bundles of cash bills, most of which appeared to be of the fifty- to one-hundred domination, are several diamond bracelets, rings, and a coiled bundle of perhaps a dozen pearl necklaces. Despite the theatrical revelation and its potential ramifications, Killian finds himself entranced yet again by the flooring beneath, as he clearly recalls the bunker's being of the smaller, Jerusalem stone type instead of the larger, glazed style on display.

"Just looking at that stash brings to mind many varied scenarios, none of which involve anything legal."

"I ... it's not ... what you thi—"

Rearing back a leg, she kicks several bundles of cash and the wound pile of pearls into a nearby corner.

"Quit babbling like a brain-dead idiot and tell me where you got this *SHIT!*"

"I ... stole it, okay? Is that what you wanted to hear? I ... burglarized a house," he replies weakly, coughing harshly into his palm once again. This time, a small smear of crimson does indeed coat his fingers in the aftermath, though Killian finds he is neither shocked nor as concerned as he ought to be.

The girl reaches down and picks up a trio of rings, all of which sport gold bands and diamond settings. She tries each of them on, and Killian is amazed to see at least one fit perfectly onto her left ring finger.

"Feel better now?" she asks, holding the finger away from her as if to rate its look. "Tell me, Killian, is confession *really* good for the soul?"

With great strain, Killian manages to pull himself upright, rubbing both eyes yet again as if to clear away a final buildup of cobwebs. Squinting, he attempts to stare through the darkness of the outer rooms at his front and back. The surrounding walls are, as he'd previously discovered, planked instead of solid stone. The tile floor is undeniably of both a different color and style. A boom box of unknown brand name sits atop a badly scarred lamp table minus the matching lamp.

"Kayla ... where ... where are we?"

"I see it's wearing off ... must be an extremely gradual process," she answers as if speaking to someone else.

A fresh coughing fit bends him over, splashing the blanket with maroon spatters. "Did you ... d-did you move us ... s-somewhere?" he mumbles, wiping the dripping fluid from his lips and nostrils with an extended shirtsleeve.

Tossing the rings aside like cheap baubles, she leans down onto her haunches and studies him with a creased brow. The expression she displays is equal parts pity and bemusement.

"No, Killian ... no I didn't move us. Fact is, you haven't moved for quite a while." "But the room ...

the bunker," he whimpers, "nothing looks ... th-the same."

"I'm sure it doesn't. Tell me, do *I* ... look the same?"

Wiping his nose yet again and leaving a dark smear across his stubble-covered jawline, he turns to her wearing a warped, bloody smile that is the definition of grisly.

"Do you ... wh-what did you mea—"

"It may be too soon, but look closely ... look long and hard," she instructs, speaking slowly as one might to a small child.

"What are you ... w-what the he-hell's wrong with you?" he barks angrily and is instantly drained by the effort.

"That's a shame. I really need for you to see the big picture," she replies with a heavy sigh. Standing erect, she begins to roll up her shirt sleeves and slowly pace the room.

"While we wait for ... the inevitable, allow me to share my guilt-trip story."

"K-Kiddo," Killian whispers weakly as fresh trails of blood leak from both nostrils, "I suggest ... you make it the Reader's Digest v-version. Afraid I'm ... drifting here."

In scanning him from head to feet, the girl amazingly maintains a stoic, unemotional deportment.

"No problem, since you might find certain aspects strangely familiar." "'Zat right? F-fire away then ... " he says, glassy-eyed, having tucked his bloodied hands back beneath the equally stained blanket.

"My guilt stems from cowardice, Ace. A blatant, yellow-bellied, chickenshit cowardice that I will never ... *can't ever* forgive myself for. I could've at least tried, you see, but instead I hid myself away for self-preservation and listened while those I love ... those that loved me without condition were systematically slain in cold blood. By the time I snapped out of it and decided to act, it was far too late ... for them. But, you see, it wasn't about them, it was about saving my own hide at any cost. I knew that then and know it now. I refuse to ... even try to justify my non-actions."

Pacing with a single hand tucked behind her back, the girl shoots Killian the occasional glance to ensure he remains conscious and at least somewhat coherent.

"Don't get me wrong ... I'm not delusional enough to think I could've saved the day and come out unscathed. Most likely I would've joined the others as just another victim. But ... I will never know, will I? Still, here I stand to testify to my own woeful lack of backbone."

"Who was sla—who are these ... v-victims you m-mentioned?" he blurts, resting an upper arm across his forehead.

"My foster parents," she replies, having temporarily halted all movement. "My foster parents and ... my half-sister."

There is a pause that Killian measures as eternal in length as his body as a whole free-falls into a state of complete meltdown. Nerve endings shriek for relief; his pulse seems to fluctuate from rapid to nonexistent and back again within the same

153

labored breath. His vision grows bleary to the point of complete blindness. Still, through all this, he finds he needs an answer ... wants an answer.

"Wha-what h-happened to 'em?"

Though he can no longer visualize the girl, he can feel her warm breath slap his cheek.

"Two-part answer there, Ace.

"First, you watched two of them die.

"Second, you murdered the third yourself before adding a fourth body to the mix." He begins to cough; a dry, hacking, powerful cough that threatens to toss him from the couch. When it does subside, Killian opens his eyes to a hazy landscape of swirling colors and shapes. His throat ravaged and bleeding, he is unable to respond. Curling onto himself, he uses the blanket as a makeshift cloaking device, even pulling his head beneath the coppery-smelling covers.

"I was upstairs the whole time. I'd just arrived home that morning and was worn out from the bus ride so I was deep asleep in my sister's room when you showed up for your monthly bug spraying, or so you told my folks anyway.

"Obviously it was a setup from the get-go, 'cause I heard my father ask you why you were a week early for the service, and also why you hadn't driven the company truck but your personal vehicle. I actually started to come downstairs until I heard you dole out the first threat. By then your buddy had burst in and it was ... it was too late. My sister had been ... doing her homework in the kitchen, and I heard you tell her to stay with you while your

154

partner forced my parents down into the cellar at gunpoint."

The portion of the blanket covering Killian's head begins to shift slowly from the left to the right and back again in a continuous "no" motion. A low grunting noise ensues, like the soft moaning of a sick infant.

"You both had run across my half-brother in prison, I take it. Jake had always been my foster parent's biggest regret, though I know for a fact they tried for years to straighten him out before an armed robbery sent him packing upstate. It doesn't take a master detective to piece together the rest; somewhere along the line, Jake must've spilled his guts to you or your buddy about the safe. Maybe you promised him a cut. I'd like to think he wasn't involved in such a vile plan, but deep down, I have to figure he most certainly was. The last I'd heard, Jake wasn't even up for parole for another year, so he either didn't think you two had the guts to carry it out, or trusted you for his third once he got out. Either way, if he had any part of it, Jake deserves a special place in hell."

A hand emerges from the blanket, tugging downward until a sweat-coated scalp and forehead protrude. Killian's words are badly garbled between hacking coughs.

"I ... it wasn't supposed to ... I d-didn't th-think…"

"Obviously you were on point for casing the house, though it does amaze me just how you managed to work the exterminator bit to such ironic perfection. I mean, it can't simply be a matter of *coincidence* or dumb luck that your spray route included my parent's home, can it? What would be the odds? I can only speculate you bribed your boss somehow, possibly even promised him a cut of the action."

"It ... all j-just went b-bad ... Tommy was cr-crazy ... I ... I couldn't c-control…"

"I heard the shots and ... tiptoed down the stairs into the kitchen in my bare feet.

I ... s-saw you standing there holding my sister while you yelled down into the cellar." "I don't ... sister? I can't ... recall ... but ... no one w-was supposed ... to get hu-hurt ... he ... agreed that we'd ... take the s-stash and le-leave them all ... loc-locked up in the b-basement ... "

"I had a choice. Make a stand or ... run away. I could have ... should have at least tried to save my little sister. Instead, I crouched behind the kitchen counter and saw you drain the life from her with a single slashing motion. I ... saw the spray of ... burst from her wound and onto the kitchen wall."

The exposed hand inches the blanket down a tad more, revealing a set of bushy, disheveled eyebrows. The voice remains severely muffled, though there is marked improvement in the pronunciation as the constant coughing has temporarily subsided.

"Listen ... who ... whoever you are ... I ... it was Tommy, all right? Tommy was ... he went crazy ... maybe he was all ... along, but ... I begged him ... n-not to off the ... old folks ... he j-just kept cu-cussing me and ... ignoring ... threat-threatening…"

156

"From that point on, everything went ... well, hazy, dreamlike. I ... did consider, very briefly, pulling a carving knife from a nearby drawer, but then you see, fright usually overpowers rage once the heat of the moment passes. Instead, I took off through the living room and headed for the front door. From there, I ran outside and ... took shelter inside my father's minivan, though the first vehicle I'd run across in our driveway had been your pickup. I say yours, but it was probably stolen, right? All part of the grand scheme, I'm sure.

"Anyway, at the time, I wasn't sure why I'd taken the time to rummage through the unlocked toolbox hitched to the cab. I dunno ... maybe it was a subliminal thing ... advice from a higher power perhaps. I didn't have the keys to Dad's van, but figured I could sneak back in after you'd gone, so I curled up in the back floorboard and covered myself with the extra-large sun visor that Dad always kept stashed for instant access.

"Lying there smelling my own fear and nauseated with guilt, I heard your partner's threats, your desperate rebuttal and the single gunshot that followed. I barely refrained from rising up and taking a peek at the outcome. Ten minutes seemed to pass, though in hindsight it was probably no more than three or four. Guess it took you that long to find the keys. I heard the driver's door swing open and damn near peed myself. I heard your heavy breathing; could almost smell the panic spewing from your pores. Of course, at the time I would've thought it a safe wager that it was your partner climbing behind that wheel, even though I'd never laid eyes on him. You see, all that I'd *heard* indicated a clear-cut Alpha Dog, and it surely wasn't you."

The hand tugs downward an inch further to divulge a set of rapidly-blinking, deep-set eyes that are horribly bloodshot.

"He ... he wanted ... he g-got greed ... greedy ... was g-gonna shoot me on the p- porch, then ... drag-drag me back into ... the house and f-frame ... make it lo-look like ... a one-man rob-robbery ... I was j-just defend ... defending myself..."

"I don't know how long you drove before I ... I snapped. Maybe an hour, perhaps even three. You'd been blasting some god-awful rap music that in retrospect was your biggest mistake, since you couldn't have heard a grenade detonate from that backseat, much less the unintentional racket I was making. In between the bone-jarring bass and curse-filled lyrics, the occasional newsflash talked about the rash of earthquakes and freak storms popping up in the wake of that meteor landing in the Pacific. Guess you were listening to see if anyone had discovered your crime, though logically such worries were sadly misplaced. My mother used to joke that they lived so far out in the boonies that even the most sophisticated GPS units needed handwritten directions to find 'em."

Once the blanket sags to just below his chin, the definitive madman is put on display; a madman donning a blood-drenched mask and lunatic's grin. The madman's lips squirm and wriggle, but no longer form anything resembling human language.

"I figure Jake told you and your partner that my foster father was a semiretired physician. He made a good living for a small-town doctor, though the jewelry you'd raided was mostly made up of family heirlooms. As for the cash bundles, he and mother never trusted banks. Many of their generation didn't, I understand."

Still blinking at warp speed, he attempts to focus on the individual kneeling mere feet away. Though the voice is vaguely familiar, something vital has changed.

"Being a country doctor, my father had a bad habit of leaving his black bag in the minivan. It wasn't as if he had to worry about thieves, you understand, but it is possible some of the medications could have been ruined by fluctuating temperatures.

"It seemed to take hours of pawing through the contents to find the right potion, then another marathon of unknown length to find, unwrap, and fill an empty syringe. By the time I had the right weapon locked and loaded, I was so drained that finding the courage to use it was going to be another miracle entirely."

Laboring to roll onto his side as the blanket coils around his torso like a flexing anaconda, Killian can only visualize the figure as a swirling, shapeless blur.

"Well, as fate would have it, about the time I'd lost all hope of working up said courage, the first tremors hit as a ... booster shot of sorts. At first I thought we'd already crashed. The rumblings were so loud it even drowned out that god-awful hip-hop garbage. Then I heard you begin to yell and curse as the tremors grew worse. We swerved so hard a few times I thought we had already started to roll. I guess it all came down to what fear was worse; dying in a car crash or allowing myself to die in a car crash without at least attempting a little payback. After all, there was the distinct possibility you'd survive said crash. On the other hand, chances were slim for this girl making it out alive from either the impending wreck or being discovered stowing away in the back seat. So, somewhere amid all the busy, noisy havoc, I threw caution to the wind, reached up and over and planted that syringe deep into the back of your neck."

The blanket gives way with a sudden snap and Killian barely avoids toppling to the floor. Balanced completely on his left side, his arm is pinned beneath and is instantly paralyzed. As if to compensate for this sudden loss of circulation, his vision begins to gradually clear.

"I heard you gasp ... hard to believe through all the hellacious racket ... but I heard it. I heard it and it made me smile. Even as I glanced out the passenger's window and saw what looked like three ... a *trio*, mind you, of funnel clouds ascending a nearby clearing. Even as I glanced through the windshield and saw the asphalt peel away like overripe banana skin. Even as the earth beneath us appeared to be opening up to swallow that damned van whole, you couldn't have wiped the smile from my face with a Louisville Slugger."

"K-Kay ... Kayla?" he stutters, wide-eyed, his lips bubbling maroon. "L-lady ... have you seen a ... young girl ... we need to f-find h-her..."

"The actual crash is a mystery, as I believe I'd already been slung to the back of the vehicle and smacked my head on the rear door handle. Hard to say ... I woke with so many cuts, scratches, and bruises that it's a sure bet I was tossed around like a rag doll until we finally rolled to a stop in that ditch."

"W-where is ... Kay-Kayla? Wha-what h-have you ... d-done to ... with ... her?" he stammers, staring at the figure through his right eye as the left has temporarily stuck shut from drying blood.

"Found you crumpled in the front seat with only the tiniest of bruises on your forehead where you had obviously kissed the steering wheel upon impact. After reloading the syringe, I administered a booster and then decided to take a walk just to see where exactly you'd taken us. By that time, however long we'd been out, the sky had cleared and the storms had moved on, but the damage was on a massive scale just from the looks of the highway and surrounding landscape. We were in the middle of nowhere ... not a home in sight, just acres and acres of pastureland. Oh, you had a hideout in mind. It was just a matter of finding it. The van started like a true champ, but steering her out of that ditch was easier attempted than accomplished, let me tell you."

His left eye unsticks with a loud pop and he reaches up to rub away the blurriness with an extended forefinger.

"Lis-listen ... I ... need help ... the ... there is a ... girl that ... that's missing ... and I ... I think I'm ... dy-dying…"

"Found your uncle's house up the road a few miles. Good thing, since the van wasn't going to go much farther with all the leaks she'd sprung. Plus, the roads were all ripped up with large sections missing and the occasional sinkhole to dodge.

"Long story a bit shorter, I found the house unlocked, deserted, but with a note left on the kitchen table. The handwritten message your uncle left was kind of a ... well, an invitation, I guess you'd say. He had headed south to visit an old war buddy once that meteor had landed, figuring the end was near for one and all. Guess he had some loose ends to tie up. He'd left a handwritten map to what he referred to as his 'shitstorm bunker' and wished luck to whoever utilized it in the aftermath to what he called *god's final spring cleaning* of the planet. A strange but apparently wise man, your uncle."

Though she stands at the center of a wavering aura coated in squirming, zigzagging lines that he cannot seem to shake from either eye, the woman's overall appearance begins to take shape.

"The ... girl ... if I'm not ... ar-around she ... she's gonna ne-need a g-guar- guardian…"

"Though in the process I'm fairly certain I pulled or strained every muscle in my possession, I got us here, but mister, I have to say ... you were one heavy slab of dead weight."

The woman pauses, rising to pace the limited space in a graceful, light-footed gait Killian finds weirdly familiar.

162

"Just like when I'd risked being caught pillaging your pesticide supplies back at the house, I can't really tell you what drove me to drag you here. I mean, I could've easily left you in the van or discarded you in the nearest asphalt and gravel sinkhole.

"I'd heard tales of retribution and the ... power it employs, but up until now never experienced it first-hand."

"Listen, M-Miss ... I ... I know what we ... what Tommy and me ... I did b-back there was ... wr-wrong, but ... it's ... it's the past now ... like the ... th-that whole w- warped, un-unfair, ungodly society we ... we lived in ... it's a-all the distant ... past. I ... we need to f-focus on the ... girl ... I'm getting weaker ... you have to help m-me ... find her. She may ... may be ... hurt."

The woman ceases the pacing and turns to him, kneeling down yet again.

Placing her left hand firmly atop the couch arm directly beneath Killian's tilted noggin, she runs her right gently through his sticky coif.

"Killian, Kayla isn't hurt. Kayla ... is dead."

In attempting to reach up and slap her hand away, Killian finds the numbness now affects all available appendages. The flesh of his face begins to tingle and go numb even as he feels his bladder release a warm trickle down his right thigh.

"She ... h-how? I was ... just w-with her."

"No, no, you weren't just with her, Ace. You killed her back at my ... our house three days ago."

163

Her grip on his hair tightens like a vise as Killian's lips part to release the most pathetic of silent gasps.

"Kayla was my fourteen-year-old sister, you bastard."

"N-no…" he spews angrily from beneath gritted, red-stained teeth. "I … I was just with her … in … in the bunker. We … we've been … taking c-care of ea-each other for … over a week … almost t-two."

"Listen up, asshole, and allow *me* to clarify for *you* the rather colossal disparity between fantasy and reality," she barks irately in response, releasing her grip but not before giving his forehead a forceful shove. She stands and takes a single step back with her hands posed atop her hips. Straining to refocus following a brief bout of whiplash, Killian searches the woman's bland features for a semblance of familiarity but finds none. She is slim but not overly so, with wide hips for such a narrow torso; her hair is short and shaded strawberry blonde. Her eyes are a dark brown and sear into him like twin branding irons.

"We've been shacked up inside your uncle's storm shelter for the past seventy- one hours plus, not counting sack time I enjoyed elsewhere. In that time, I've been administering into your veins via syringe the drug *diphenhydramine hydrochloride* at three- to four-hour intervals. This particular medication is normally used to treat allergies, but like many antihistamines, can and will alter a person's thinking through a barrage of psychotic hallucinations, especially if doled out with the careless abandon I've exhibited. Got to say, you've been a walking, talking soap opera on wheels the last three days; fascinating to no end the sci-fi twists and turns a guilty mind can create.

Quite the mindbender, I'd guess, with the limit being only that of the imagination. I bore witness to laughing fits, crying jags, secret door codes, air filtration maintenance techniques and some really intriguing one-way conversations."

"Ly-lying ... you ... you're ... hiding her ... from me. You ... you kid-kidnapped us from ... the bunk-bunker," Killian croaks, staring at the woman through moisture-filled eyes from which spurt bloodstained tears.

"You murdered her, Killian, just like your buddy Tommy took apparent glee in blowing holes into our foster parents. Our mother had Alzheimer's. Alzheimer's, for Christ's sake ... rarely even recognized her own husband or her foster children, but that wasn't about to stand in the way of the *haul of the century*, was it?"

"To-Tommy was ... cr-crazy ... I couldn't ... couldn't stop h-him..."

"Couldn't stop yourself from slashing my kid sister's throat with a serrated blade either, I suppose."

In a final bolt of energy, Killian sits upright and stares her down with a firm jaw and eyes ablaze.

"I ... saved that girl, you lying B-BITCH! The ... quake ... she was ... just ... just standing there waiting ... waiting to die ... I pulled her a-away, damn it! I ... pulled her ... away."

Placing a high-top tennis shoe-clad foot firmly against his heaving chest, the woman pushes him down until he lays flat atop the wobbly couch, which creaks and moans its disapproval.

"You only pulled yourself away, you selfish, soulless bastard. It was always about you ... even within these apocalyptic hallucinations I've witnessed. You alone were gonna survive until the guilt surfaced: the deep-seated kind that chews away at the subconscious of even those of your questionable ilk. It was guilt that brought Kayla back to life, Killian, but you were never going to be able to save her."

"I ... I did sa-save her. The storms ... the quakes ... there was no future without ... without an adult to wa-watch over her. I was ... going to guardian her ... to ... protect her once we left ... the bunker and explored ... the ... what remained."

The woman snickers, twisting about to face the silver, twin-speaker boom box. "What *remained*? Here's a sample of what remains, Ace ... have a listen…" she says smarmily, twisting a single knob and stepping away with a slight bow.

Following a brief blast of static, the familiar guitar riffs of a recent pop song slices the dank air like a carving knife through warm butter.

"T-tape ... CD ... don't mean a th-thing," he frowns, spitting up a fresh glut of blood into his already saturated beard.

"Uh-huh ... I see. How about an old-fashioned station seek, then?" she replies, reaching over to poke an unseen button.

Between static waves are heard multiple ten-second blurbs covering a frenzied mix of musical genres (pop, rock, rap, classical) and voices both male and female, the latter of which seem to all be discussing a similar subject.

"... are simply the best of the best. Someone tell me I'm wrong! The United States of America has been shaken and stirred many times before and we have always, I say always, come out a stronger nation..."

"... terrorism did not break us ... natural disasters have come and gone ... and here we sit braced for another strike with our heads held high and our resilience unwavering..."

"... the cities struck the hardest are logically going to receive a bigger chunk of the immediate federal aid ... the rural townships will be more dependent on neighbors helping neighbors, as it has always been..."

"... It is now estimated that North America was the second hardest hit in terms of overall damage from the quakes and freak storms with South America in the unfortunate lead..."

"... fatality totals are, of course, unofficial, but thus far the U.S. total stands at just under six and a half million people from coast to coast, the majority of that from the hardest-hit East Coast. Meanwhile, India seems to be the least affected with a reported thirty-six thousand killed in last week's mayhem..."

She punches yet another button and all goes quiet.

"Satisfied, Nostradamus? The planet is far from toast. Everyone realizes it was one hell of a speed bump, but from what I've seen on CNN, we'll get over it in due time ... that is, as long as another Colorado-sized meteor doesn't swan dive into the Pacific anytime soon."

"C ... N ... N? How have you ... seen..." he asks so weakly that the final few words are mouthed but woefully inaudible.

"Your uncle has a flat screen in almost every room of that house. Nice generator out back with ample fuel, to boot. I've ... taken the liberty of making it my second home. That is ... when I wasn't out here flipping coins over what exactly to do with you. I've decided to leave your ill-gotten booty here for your uncle or perhaps the property authorities to find. Fact is, they're liable to receive an anonymous tip here in a few days to ... assist in solving the mystery of my family's death and my disappearance."

She glares at him disdainfully, crinkling her nose in disgust.

"Seems the special diet I put you on has ... made the decision for me."

Far too weak to respond verbally, he is only able to cock an eyebrow quizzically.

"Oh, yes, I'm afraid you've had quite the appetite. Not sure what you *thought* you were eating all that time, but I'd wager it tasted *nothing* like the stuff I pulled out of the bed of your pickup."

Reaching into her back pockets, the woman retrieves the mystery objects before whipping her hands around and displaying them in opened palms.

"I ... grabbed these out of a much larger bag, pausing only ... long enough to read the labels on the first pack. Guess I figured they ... they'd do the trick if given the opportunity. I ... never would've thought it'd take so many of the damned things to..."

Tilting his head forward as much as his weakened state will allow, Killian strains mightily to recognize the small black packets filling the girl's hands.

It is painfully obvious once recognition is achieved in his wide, terror-filled eyes. He glares from the packs, labeled *Enforcer Rat Bait Pellets*, to the woman, then back again, his entire body trembling with rage.

By the fourth time their eyes lock, the woman tosses the packs into a darkened corner and looks away.

"Don't ... don't you judge me, you son of a bitch! You ... you kill ... murdered my family in cold blood! I ... I'm ... doing the world a favor," she cries, her lower lip quivering as the faux persona of toughness quickly evaporates.

Wracked with spasms, Killian spits up yet another glutinous mass of vomit and blood.

"I ... didn't know it would ... take this long to ... I wanted it to be quick. I ... didn't want all this suffering. I'm not ... like *you*, damn it!"

Reaching back down for the duffel, she pulls a final object free from its folds. Discarding the bag, she cradles the blue-steel revolver to her narrow bosom.

"I tried ... really tried to end it this way, but never found the courage to ... to pull the trigger."

As his spasms cease, she steps forward, wiping the gun clean with a purple- shaded cloth before laying it ever so gently in his lap.

With consciousness fading, he begins to resemble a human slot machine as his eyes roll back and down several times.

"There. See if you can find the same balls to end your own life as you did to snuff out my sister's," she sobs, wiping her eyes with a bare forearm.

The new burden of weight on his deadened thighs is extreme. The mental command to remove said weight goes unheeded by a set of equally paralyzed hands.

"I'd say good luck ... but that would be in really bad taste."

Through the rapidly darkening haze that is his eyesight, Killian sees the woman stroll away toward a wooden stairway. He is temporarily blinded by an intrusion of extraordinarily bright light. His mouth fills with bloody bile and the majority spews forth from his nostrils in fire-hose fashion.

"Goodbye, Killian. Best you spend the time you have left making amends to the man upstairs. And by the way, my name is ... was Pamela," he hears her say just before a loud creak and subsequent slamming of a door. He thinks he hears a muffled cry and is unable to clarify if it had originated from the woman or perhaps himself.

The vivid light is swallowed by an ebony cloak. As the woman had advised, Killian begins to pray. He prays for forgiveness.

He prays for leniency, knowing in his heart of hearts that an inner guilt had driven his subconscious to create a fantasy world where he might make amends for such horrific acts.

He prays for the young, innocent soul he took and those he assisted in taking. He prays for the woman who has taken his.

Finally, he prays for the strength to reach the revolver at his lap. For this, he prays like he has never prayed before...

***

"By god, that is one beautiful sight," he bellows, glaring up into a blazing sun through the splayed fingers of his left hand. Though the outdoor temperature is a bit cooler than expected, the sunlight instantly warms any exposed flesh at contact.

"Yes, it is ... and just take a big whiff of this air! Sweet as a freshly baked cinnamon bun, she is!" the girl replies happily, dancing about in a circle and waiving her arms like twin windmills. They leave the bunker door open behind them and neither even bothers to give it a second look while making their way up the gravel path and dirt clearing.

As expected, he blazes the trail, keeping a six-to eight-foot lead. The narrow duffel bag swings between his shoulder blades like a pendulum blade, while his baggy khakis hang comically low from the trio of water bottles hanging from his belt.

"Six weeks of staleness, kiddo, will make one appreciate Mother Nature's minty breath for certain."

The girl bounces and hops along behind him, having already pulled the cap from her skull and stashed it within a large black garbage bag hanging from one shoulder.

"Where to now, Ace? Do we head to the nearest metropolis and search for other survivors or what?"

"I'd say priority number one is finding a running vehicle, if such a ride still exists.

We can't be lugging around this stuff forever. Right now I'd settle for a wheelbarrow with a flat tire."

"Agreed, Daddy-O. My feet are gonna be blisterin' up and bleedin' by nightfall." Dashing ahead, he crests a steep hill before kneeling down for a breather. "Whew. Looks like I should've utilized that gym equipment a bit more. Only been walking ten minutes and I'm bushed already."

Sucking in and then inhaling several deep breaths, he scans the trail ahead for any signs of the paved two-lane that had originally led him to Uncle Ray's property. As has been the norm since exiting the bunker, they are surrounded by dense forest on all sides. Strange, he ponders, how the trees and foliage appear undamaged despite the glut of horrific storms in the past six weeks.

"Kiddo?" he finally shouts, "you answering nature's call or what? We need to put down some serious tracks before nightfall."

"Kiddo?" he repeats, standing as various cracking noises ensue from both knees.

The wind, having been a non-factor since their reintroduction to the great outdoors, makes it presence known with a sudden gust that forces him to block his eyes with a raised forearm. Looking skyward, he sees a foreboding buildup of black clouds just to the east.

"Hey, Kayla!" he yells, tossing his duffel aside and scrambling back up the slope.

He feels his skin grow instantly feverish. His lips and the inside of his mouth are suddenly bone dry. His eyes itch and the desire to reach up and pull them from their sockets is immense.

The trail is deserted, though at the bottom of the hill, a hill that wasn't nearly as lengthy when originally scaled, he clearly sees the entrance to the bunker standing wide open.

"No, this ... this can't be," he whimpers sheepishly, his lower body dangerously close to lockdown mode, "we've ... we've been walking the trail for ... maybe a mile or more."

Stumbling downhill, he hits the brakes so abruptly he barely refrains from toppling forward and rolling the rest of the way down.

The girl is standing just inside the bunker door. She is waving at him to join her. Her expression is grim; her complexion ghostly pale. Behind her stand two figures he doesn't instantly recognize until they step out from the shadows and pose to either side of her. The old man has a gaping wound at his chest from which a swarm of fat roaches spew forth, some of which land atop the young girl's neck

173

and shoulder. The elderly woman is missing the majority of her lower jaw, the remaining upper plate chomping down in a continuous biting motion as if she were attempting to speak.

The young girl nods solemnly and leads the old couple inside, not bothering to shut the door behind them. Moments later, he sees a balding, middle-aged man emerge from the entrance in a bright orange prison jumpsuit with the words This Way To Death Row *stenciled on the chest in bold black lettering. The man grins and waves,*

exposing a toothless maw and purple-shaded gums, before vanishing back into the hole.

Whirling about, Killian sprints back up the hill and practically leaps to the other side, his throat blood-raw and a dull ache ravaging his midsection.

Freezing in midstride, he halts mere feet from the tip of the silver revolver's barrel.

The woman stands with her feet wide apart in the classic shooter's pose.

"You just turn around and head on back down that hill, Ace," she says sternly while gently pulling the hammer back. "They left the door open for a reason."

The man tries to scream, but vomits up a thick glut of blood instead.

***

The barrel is inserted between chattering teeth. The hammer is pulled back with a snap.

Somewhere in the blinding darkness, two distinct sounds emerge.

174

The first is a flat clicking sound ... the second a human cry of unbridled anguish.

THE ISLE OF TRANQUILITY, PART II

Damn, pop, I thought short story meant short, as in brief? Another chapter and I'd be on the extra-crispy side. Sucked down the last of my firewater a freakin' hour ago! Bitchin' and moanin' aside ... not a bad chronicle overall. Have to confess I never saw that ending coming. Guess maybe you earned your rep as the King of Twists.

Whew! Better relocate to the mansion before I start the next chapter or I'll be peeling off layers of cooked flesh like a shedding snake.

Eighteen Minutes Later:

Watch reads 1:46 PM and still no sign of Jolly Jen. Maybe she's planning on camping out on the other side of the island. Who knows? She might've packed enough provisions to last a week. Well, as long as she stays outta the booze cabinet ... ha!

Hey, if my bitter, less-intelligent better half would rather spend her day sweatin' to the oldies in the humidity of the tropical forest or blistering her tootsies on the hot sand, more power to her. Me, I got the old AC blowing at full blast and an equally chilly refill in hand. No better way to ride out the impending apocalypse, at least for a man who so relishes his solitude. Jen had another name for my antisocial ways, referring to me as a selfish hermit and saying that it wasn't just that I didn't care for others, but loved myself so dearly that there was no more room in my heart for anyone else. Boatload of soap opera crap, I say. I have cared for many others in my time. Just a few examples— whoever the dude was in Tennessee who came up with the formula for Jim Beam whiskies ... loved that man dearly. Also the genius who first decided to lop off a piece of cow and toss it onto a heated grill ... why I'd hug the stuffing out of 'im! Spent a hefty sum of my youth engaged in unprotected sex with hookers of the female persuasion, so to the man or woman who invented prophylactics, here's mud in your eye! There ya go, Jen my dear ... three prime examples of why you're wrong yet again! So I didn't appear too concerned once the reports popped up about mass cannibalism in Central America... it wasn't exactly happening in my backyard.

Consequently, I wasn't exactly bitin' my nails to the quick when it was confirmed that the deceased were coming back to life and looking to human flesh as their preferred menu item. It was Texas, for crap's sake ... who really cares?

Point of fact, wasn't it I who first suggested we hop in the jet and head to Slacker Isle once it was apparent that human munching upon human wasn't just a fad and had gotten far too close for comfort? I mean, it didn't exactly take a sledgehammer to conk this boy over the noggin to realize something was tragically amiss once he saw bodies squirming free from the grounds of the family cemetery. Had to practically wrestle Jen into the jet kicking and screaming to save our hides as she ranted and raved about saving her kin. Never mind the Phenom had room for four bodies ... there wasn't exactly time to round up the relatives while a passel of *famished corpses were clawing down the front door. Speaking of claws, Jen damn near skinned me alive as I taxied down the private runway. Had to sock her across the jaw just to settle her down, and that was no easy task considering the fight she put up. Hadn't touched that woman in anger during all the turbulent years of our marriage, but there simply hadn't been any choice that day. Sometimes I think she actually blames me for keeping us alive. Gotta say, there are moments I wish she'd hopped in the other family jet and we'd flown off in opposite directions. Since virtually the whole damn family owns a pilot's license, it wouldn't have been much of a stretch.*

Anyhow, enough reminiscing already. Comfy leather Barc-O-Lounger ... check. Icy drink of the alcoholic variety ... check. Air conditioning cool enough to induce chill bumps ... check. Onto chapter two ... okay, pops ... thrill me...

BOOK 2 - THE BIOSPHERE

Diary Entry #3, Day 343 Project Codename: Introvert Recording Time: 5:34 PM
Biosphere Location: Dinning Hall Documented Activity: Dinner Meal Aftermath

I've got company. Call me nuts, I've been called much worse, but I ain't alone in here anymore. Seems as though the salad days are history, for sure, and that simply ain't fair. Maybe it's all in my mind ... a bad-ass mix of daydreams and night screams. Could be that I've gone off the deepest end imaginable, but I truly don't believe that. Its just too damn easy an excuse. Shit! All this and only twelve blessed days away from celebrating anniversary numero uno.

(SHORT PAUSE)

Actually, I figure it's all part of whatever colossal mind-fuck head game the suits are playing. Some kind of endurance test, no doubt, to see how I react or don't react. Gotta give the eggheads credit where credit is due, though. If it ain't dreams, the special effects are about as realistic as they come. I knew science technology had come a long way, but this shit is mindnumbing. Plus which, they sure as shooting knew which button to push. Out of all the warped scenarios I painted for 'em during the interview phase, I have to give 'em props for picking the one most likely to test my sanity. But then, I can't help but fume over the fact that I

179

apparently made it so damn easy for 'em. I mean, did my personnel file open up this particular set of menus? Was it the numerous blood tests? The multiple choice psych exams? I don't see how it's possible, but I guess I woefully underestimated the power of lab coats, clipboards and loaded syringes.

No big shock, when push comes to shove. I should've known it wasn't a kosher deal from the get-go. The dollar signs pulled me in and set me up like the proverbial bowling pin. No better than a stinkin' rat in a trap at the mercy of the bastards pulling the levers and pushing the buttons. Whatever, it's damn obvious there ain't no way out at this juncture. Just have to bite the bullet and learn to cope. Prove 'em wrong in the process. Prove to 'em I ain't no pushover just 'cause of my ... social insecurities. Have to set my jaw tight, pucker up my bunghole till it's leakproof, and hope that they eventually get their jollies and return my peaceful little world to seminormal.

(SHORT PAUSE)

Still, the whole enchilada pisses me off no end. To coin a well-worn phrase, I didn't sign up for this shit. Unfortunately, I'm pretty damned certain no one involved in this little experiment gives a raccoon's furry ass cheeks about any hurt feelings on my part.

Off to the rec room for a game or sixteen of pool just to divert the old noodle, followed by a steamy shower and perhaps a bout of pre-nap masturbation. After that, we'll just have to see if the carnival of souls returns for a record-breaking third straight night. Got to confess, I'm hoping they've packed up the tents and moved the hell on...

Diary Entry #4, Day 343:
Project Codename: Introvert Recording Time: 11:36 PM
Location: Biosphere Sleeping Quarters Documented Activity: Downtime Preparation

Damn, but I'm still wired for sound. Should be dead on my feet about now, considering the gauntlet just completed. Six games of eight-ball, a three-mile trek around the b-ball court that was more sprint than jog, and capped off by twenty-five additional minutes of whipping my own ass at *H O R S E*. Afterwards, I crawled into the shower and couldn't even muster enough energy to choke the drumstick. Figured I'd be nice and comatose before the old honeydew melon struck the pillow, but NO! By the time I'm done polishing the choppers and shaving the stubble, I discover a newfound burst of vitality that serves to widen the eyes and bulge the bloomers! Guess it's just the apprehension stokin' the fire. After all, the last two nights have been no picnic.

Have to find a way to wind down ... blow out the inner pilot light. Wouldn't those uppity jackasses just love to see me go to pieces on my own? Yeah, that's probably it. They plant the seed and then back away, hoping I go bananas—a victim of my own self- induced hallucinations. Good luck

181

with that one, you Nazi bastards! Ain't ... gonna ... happen. You picked the wrong guinea pig, assholes.

(LENGTHY PAUSE)

(sighs heavily) Sheesh. These are the times I do find myself craving a bit of chemical sleep-aid action, be it of the over-the-counter or prescription variety.

Diary Entry #1, Day 344:
Project Codename: Introvert Recording Time: 02:47 AM Location: Biosphere Living Area
Documented Activity: Interrupted Downtime

(whimpering) This a-ain't right, man ... it just ain't ... right. Ho-how can this really be ... really be hap-happening (sobs) ... I don't ... deserve th-this ... h-horseshit. She ... she always told me ... w-we had some kinda psychic connection. B-but I never ... never believed it ... never believed the shit was for real! Fuck! C-can't stop the bleedin', no matter how tight I tie it off. Th-think I'm getting ... dizzy; getting harder to breathe.

If you ... if any of you egg-headed assholes are still upright and listenin', you'd ... best be scoping out the nearest exit ... 'cause I gotta tell you (laughs hysterically) ... the girl ain't likely to leave any witnesses behind. Take my word ... mercy is a word she ain't the le-least bit familiar with! Oh ... god (whimpers) ... I stepped right into th-the fucking

182

trap like a blind rat sniffin' a boulder-si-sized chunk of cheddar. I ... I wonder ... if love, tr-true love ... mi-might still s-save the day?

(LONG PAUSE)

... wishful thinking ... at b-best.

God, but I su-surely didn't ... sign up ... for (sighs) ... this ... (sobs)

(LONG PAUSE)

Diary REWIND:
Entry #1, Day 1
Project Codename: Introvert Recording Time: 8:18 AM Location: Biosphere Living Area
Documented Activity: Initial Inhabitation (HISSING SOUND)

Is this thing on? Echo ... echo ... echo! (laughs) This is (**segment deleted**) ... whoops, damn! Forget I ain't supposed to use my real name. Half hour hasn't passed and I'm breakin' rules already (laughs). Any-who, three months of red tape, interviews, vein-poking and a ton of paperwork but I'm finally, officially sealed in. Heard that entranceway close up behind me ... sounded like the top of a giant pop bottle being peeled off. I take it the time for backin' out has passed me by. Like I'd ever consider such a thing. May sound melodramatic and downright corny as hell, but this is truly a dream come true for this here boy. No shit,

I foresee the easiest calendar year of my life, hands down. Three-sixty-five of complete solitude ... peace ... serenity ... and best of all ... nobody to share it with! Society ... you can choke on it! I'll worry 'bout year two when that bridge presents itself ... and no doubt the cool five hundred grand I'll be pocketing for my troubles will surely make the transition back to society a hell of a lot smoother. Plenty of options available with that kind of stash ... yes, sir ... maybe even slap down a big fat deposit on my own deserted island! Well, I'm off to unpack and check out my new digs! This is Mercury control signing out! (laughs)

Diary REWIND:
Entry #2, Day 46
Project Codename: Introvert Recording Time: 14:26 PM Location: Biosphere Library
Documented Activity: Daily retrospective/questionnaire

Today's query: *Did I truly loathe those around me or simply find it extremely difficult to deal with my peers in normal societal settings?*

Man, these questions are sure heavy on the vagueness. Did I *hate* everyone I met? No ... can't honestly say that. Growing up I had friends like everyone else. Met a kid named Scott Hastings in the second or third grade and we hung pretty steady till his family moved away the summer before ... I believe ... my sixth grade year. Best buds, we were. Middle school was tough, gotta admit. I didn't fit

184

into any specific clique ... jocks, brains, nerds, dopers, etc., etc so I guess it was around that time I started to crawl into my shell, so to speak. As an adult, I just found being around people, in general, a bad experience. Most of 'em are phonies ... never met one without an agenda of some sort. Well (pauses ... laughs) maybe just one, but I digress. Anyhow, the only agenda I ever had was to steer clear of 'em as a whole. Hell, I gave it my best shot for thirty-six some-odd years.

After a while, I stopped trying to fit in and just ... well, existed. Shitty life to most, I'd wager, but I was okay with it.

Thinking back, my folks could've easily qualified as loners. Kept to themselves as a rule. Maybe the condition is inherited. I dunno. Don't really care. As Popeye was apt to say *I yam what I yam*. Tough tits to anyone who takes offense.

Dairy REWIND:
Entry #3, Day 106
Project Codename: Introvert Recording Time: 10:13 PM Location: Biosphere dining hall
Documented Activity: Daily retrospective/questionnaire

Today's query: *Save for anyone outside your immediate family, did you ever feel love for someone?*

Awww, shit, and a-wwwwaaaay we go! I knew it! I knew this was coming!

Took 'em over three months, but I never had a moment's doubt it was floating around on somebody's clipboard! Have you ever loved (laughs)? What's next; was your heart so badly broken that it simply could not be sufficiently repaired and effectively drove you into seclusion (laughs)?

(LONG PAUSE)

You butt-clowns already know about Mindy. Why should I be forced to replay that whole stage play? I watched ol' Doc Thick-Goggles typing away on his laptop as I spewed forth the gory details ... well (laughs nervously), most of 'em anyway. Can't say I'm really up to treading that manure-coated ground again ... not just now. Gimme a (groans) ... just gimme a second to gather my thoughts, damn it.

(LONG PAUSE)

Okay, bozos, you get your way ... but you're only getting the condensed version and I don't really give a warm, steaming mound of crap whether you like it or not.

(SHORT PAUSE)

Mindy and I met on the 'net via the *Friends First* dating site. We e-mailed back and forth for a month or so ... exchanging photos and the like. Typical juvenile horseshit I'd always despised, but hey ... in truth I never had a chance in light of what

186

I call the pull of the Four Horsemen, that being *young, lonely, horny,* and *stupid.* Logical thinking never had a chance. Eventually we hooked up via Ma Bell. Then, against my very best judgment, we agreed to finally meet in person.

Physically, we were the perfect match. Sweet Mindy was no bathing beauty, for sure. Short stringy hair, chubby cheeks riddled with freckles and the frequent acne breakout to go along with an equally pudgy figure. Girl had a rear end the shape of soggy beanbag. On the other hand, I'm ... I sure as hell wasn't any prize in the looks department. My own brother used to call me *ugly as a jagged stump*, and for good reason. But, hey, twenty-something virgins can't exactly be picky, right?

Back to my older sibling Jake for a sec ... you can quote me on this; he's a backstabbing, pinheaded smartass for whom I wish only the shittiest things in life. Right back atcha, bro!

(SHORT PAUSE)

Sorry 'bout that ... settling petty family scores at this late date is kinda fruitless, I guess.

Back, then, to the lone love of my life. Promised I'd make this short, for my own piece of mind. Mindy and I hit it off like gangbusters ... (pauses) ... well, at least as *gangbusters* as two such staunch antisocial misfits can. Cliché time ... apologize in advance ... Mind and I were like two peas in a pod. Equal opportunity detesters, you might say. Well, not quite equal. Fact was, Sweet Mind was off the charts in terms of pent-up rage

187

(laughs) ... waaayyyyyy off the charts! More off the charts than anyone is apt to believe in fact (laughs)! As it turned out, I was Mr. Fucking Congeniality compared to my dimple-kneed sweetheart, and Lord did I adore her for it! Girl could keep a secret like nobody's business, as well. Hell, we'd been seeing each other for over four months before I got the first faint whiff of her dirty little secret, and even then it took her planting several not-so-subtle hints.

Before I divulge said secret (pauses) ... make that *if* I divulge said secret ... allow the following disclaimer; though this boy was accused as a willing accomplice, charges were soon dropped due to a woeful lack of evidence. Having Mind testify in my behalf certainly didn't hurt either. Then again, she was only telling the truth. Sure, I knew of her little hobby in its later stages, but sure as hell didn't participate in any shape, form or fashion. Amazing (laughs) ... the girl truly must've loved me, troll looks and all. How else can you explain her testimony in my favor considering ... well, considering I'd been the one who'd sicced the cops on her in the first place. As for what she did ... I love her no less. I was a bit shocked at first—who wouldn't be, for shit's sake? I got over it. Do I regret turning traitor on my one and only soul mate? Damn straight I do. Every minute of every fucking day. Hell, boys, look where it got me. In the end, I think our love survived due to what I *didn't* divulge to that jury as opposed to what I did.

(SHORT PAUSE)

188

A little confession here, people. Afraid I'm gonna have to pull a George Washington, as in *I cannot tell a lie*. No, I did not participate. Yes, I did rat my girl out in the end to cover my own cowardly ass. Finally ... no, I did not disapprove of her actions ... not the basic principle, anyhow. Can't say much for the methods, but then again it's damn difficult to judge a condition you can't even begin to understand. As for Mindy and I ... said it before and it bears repeating—two peas in a pod.

The last words she ever worded to me were *"greet you soon, my love,"* while being escorted from the courtroom to await sentencing.

That, my friends, is the day I live for, be it in this world or the hereafter. I was a lucky man to meet such a special woman. To ... embrace the unconditional love this special woman offered. A woman of principal. A woman of determination. A woman who understood. A woman who ... forgave. A woman I'll one day be proud to again have by my side. I'm ... a little bushed, fellas. No more secrets spewed forth this night. Like I said, I have to deliberate. Call it a matter of honor. Didn't you ever swear not to tell something? Cross your heart and hope to die and all that happy crap? Anyway, it's time to crash, meditate and rejuvenate. Gonna dream of my sweet Mind, just waiting for me on the other side with open, outstretched arms. Later, gators...

Diary REWIND:
Entry #1, Day 293

Project Codename: Introvert Recording Time: 5:13 AM Location: Biosphere lavatory Documented Activity: Undisclosed

Wow. Fucking *wow*. That was ... man, that was truly some wacky shit.

Waaaaay too wired to get back to sleep, so I figured now was as good a time as any to work off some nervous energy. Besides, figured I'd better make a quick pit-stop to empty the bladder or I'd be soon be wading in a lake of pee. Damn wonder I didn't saturate the bed already!

If what I had was a dream, and shit, it *had* to be, right? I mean, what the hell else explains it (laughs nervously)? I've had some lulus in my time, guess we all have, but brother, this one was one of those nightmares you don't just experience, but survive.

My heart was beating like a friggin' bass drum ... felt like my chest cavity was gonna split open and give birth! Shit if it all didn't seem as real as the little brown package I'm about to mail! She ... Mindy looked exactly the same ... sounded the same, but it wasn't her appearance that made me yellow my briefs ... it was what she said and how she said it. My god, I'd seen her emit that level of rage before, but never, ever directed at me! Details are growing blurrier by the second. Good, who the hell needs 'em? After all, sleep is my best friend here inside the intro-sphere. A real timekiller, ya might say. A few more nightmares like that last one and my heart's gonna shoot out my throat like a mortar shell!

Damn, but it is truly a soothing relief to be staring down my own reflection in the mirror and see all parts and appendages still present and accounted for (sighs heavily). Yeah, I'll say it ... say and by God mean it ... it's good to be alive!

More later...I have a sudden craving for a double-packet of chicken á la king. Only wish I had a quaalude or two and a six-pack of cold beer to wash 'em down with!

Diary Entry #2, Day 344:
Project Codename: Introvert Recording Time: 03:21 AM Location: Biosphere supply room
Documented Activity: Unrecognized Activity

(cries weakly) ... no-nowhere else to ... hi-hide. No ... don't m-matter anyhow. Bleedin' out like a ... stuck-pig as it is. She w-won't even have to ... sniff me at ... out. Can ... proba ... bly j-just f-follow the blu-bloody slug t-trail right t-to me.

(giggles softy) ... so all this time ... they ... weren't dreams, nor w-were th-they s- some egghead-c-created special effect. M-more like visions ... war-warnings. Not that ... I c-could've convinced anybody ... outco— (pauses, breaths heavily) ... outcome still ... the same. Sitting ... fu-fucking d-ducks, just th-the same. Must have followed ... the ... our connection all the w-way from wh-whatever facility sh-she escaped fr-from ... well, it's just (coughs) like they s-say ... a wo-woman scorned and all that ha-happy cr- crappy ... (laughs) Hope whom ... whoever finds this ... can ...

w-will learn something ... never ... e-ever pi-piss off
a wo—

(LENGTHY PAUSE)

(screams) Oh ... g-god ... sh-she's pl-playing
with m-me now ... must h-have pulled the m-main
pow-power switch ... (sobs) ... oh Mindy ... this is n-
no w-way to ... treat ... a ... s-soul-ma-mate ... (sobs)

(SHORT PAUSE)

(the faint clanking of a solid object striking
hard tile and subsequently sliding away)

(a distant voice) ... sh-shit ... dropped th-the
record-er ... w-well, th-they can pro- bably figure ...
out the end-ending (laughs nervously) (low
scratching sounds)... M-Mind? I-is th-that y-you, b-
babe? (sniffing noises)... I'm ... so so-sorry. I'm so
... damned ... sorry (sobs)... can y-you ... forgive ...
me? I never ... stopped l-loving you, b-babe ... I was
j- just scar-scared, that's all ... I-I kept th-the ... your
secret. I ... didn't tell. I was ... tempted ... but didn't
tell ... didn't even ... h-hint ... can you p-please for-
forgive...(faint growling that gradually grows
louder)... oh s-shit ... I ... I guess n-not...

(Screams that quickly grow weak and muffled)

(a series of frenzied ripping/snapping/crunching
sounds mingled with a low, purring growl—
followed by several minutes of low slurping noises)

TAPE CLICKS OFF

Day 345:

Project Codename: Introvert Time: 08:17 AM

Location: Outside Biosphere Main Entrance
Documented Activity: Shift Change

"Don't lose your shirt, doc. We've got another team on the way. ETA is oh-nine- hundred. Meantime, I'll have Jenkins and Weaver escort you and your staff to the chopper landing pad. No need to take undue chances when we have no idea what we're dealing with."

The larger of the two men whirls about and gives the open entryway a quick, apprehensive once-over. Decked out in full chemical gear, his movements are predictably robotic. A few feet to his rear stand three similarly clothed individuals, each of whom busies himself by prepping whatever testing gadget is to accompany them inside.

"I understand as head of security these are your decisions to make, but I would highly advise you wait for backup to arrive," the smaller man counters fretfully, his ankle-length lab coat flowing behind him like a magician's cape from the blustery desert winds. With his pencil-thin build, he is forced to lean into the wind to prevent toppling forward into the larger man.

"No worries, doc. We'll be in and out in a blink. Just have to test the interior air for toxins ... biohazards. I'm not about to camp out in the—"

His hands atop his hips, the smaller man scoffs aloud, peeking over the tip of his wire-rimmed

193

glasses and nodding toward the entrance's thick solid-steel door, which appears to have literally been *folded over* from the top.

"You truly believe a chemical weapon is responsible for *that?*"

"It's required we check, doc. Precautions, you understand. Now, please follow my men to the chopper pad. We'll meet you there in a few minutes with whatever findings become available."

The smaller man smirks, lowering his head and nodding in apparent disbelief. "Well, sir, allow me a sneak preview of the findings *already* available…"

"Not necessary, doctor. We'll be gathering samples as well as taping for a video log. Now, if you'll just fo—"

"Well, I sincerely hope you brought a shovel for your samples, Mr. Watts," the other man rants, whipping off his glasses and waiving them about like a chalkboard pointer, "or … in the case of the comm room, I'd seriously consider sending in my best puzzle-solver to reunite all the scattered pieces."

"Believe me, Dr. Jarvis," the larger man says in a tone that is as bitingly sarcastic as it is consoling, "with twenty-six years in law enforcement at every level … there's nothing in there that's liable to surprise and/or shock this boy."

Turning on his left heel, the diminutive scientist refits his glasses and bolts off to join his coworkers in heading away from the violated facility, but not without a final vocal testament.

"Oh, I wouldn't bet the family farm on *that*, Mr. Watts."

194

The other man seems to contemplate the words for several moments before turning to the men in his charge with final instructions. Moments later, he leads them through the open space with a handheld video blazing the trail.

***

"It's been a half-hour, young man. How long are you going to sit on your hands?" "As I've told you already, Dr. Jarvis, I'm awaiting word from my superiors before moving in. There is the safety of you and the other staff members present to consider." "Still no radio contact?"

"Affirmative. Probably just a glitch caused by the biosphere's unique design." "I've described the massacre we found inside those walls. Isn't it obvious whoever was responsible is still inside?"

"Try to calm yourself, doctor. An answer is mere moments away."

Standing with a meticulously spit-shined boot propped atop the helicopter's landing gear, the uniformed man appears posed at attention as he looks past his would- be interrogator and raises a set of binoculars in order to scan the desert landscape beyond. Groaning, the doctor tucks his hands to the pit of his back and begins to frantically pace the length of the chopper. A few yards to the right stand the remainder of his staff; two women and two men, all of whom fidget nervously and sport similar expressions of pained apprehension. Opposite, the three armed guards stationed to the craft's left resemble their erstwhile leader in terms of both physical stiffness and emotional detachment, unmoving and peering off into the distance through darkened visors.

"We've got a live one," the leader shouts, momentarily lowering the binoculars and blinking rapidly as if to retool his vision before confirmation. As he barks orders, emitting the emotional equivalent of a toaster oven, he maintains an enhanced visual of the subject at hand.

"Just emerged from the biosphere opening. Practically nude ... looks bloody and shaken ... most likely possessing open wounds. Harris ... Weaver ... don masks and assist with extreme caution. Sweep subject with Geiger meters and acquire blood sample. Set up an outer perimeter at least seventy-five feet from the pad."

Following a brief assemblage of equipment, the two guards sprint (perfectly in step) in the direction of the biosphere just as Dr. Jarvis steps over to join his staff in a makeshift huddle.

It takes the guards less than two minutes to reach the stumbling, seemingly incoherent subject. The anguished screams commence in roughly half that time.

***

Despite having lost both shoes somewhere along the rocky terrain, Dr. Jarvis pays no attention to the burning pain at his heels, though he is relatively certain without looking that blood flows freely from countless gashes. He is also blissfully unaware of the shrieking sob that spews unwavering from between his badly chapped lips like the ancient mating call of some mythical desert creature. In a sadly ironic twist, his snow- white lab coat trails behind like a surrendering flag. Trudging forth even as his speed appears to decrease with every lumbering step, he doesn't dare risk even the briefest of glances over either shoulder. A lifelong atheist, he nonetheless discovers a sudden talent for prayer. It isn't until his battered lungs have completely evacuated their contents that he is forced to slide to a clumsy halt, practically diving headfirst behind a wrecking-ball-sized boulder and submerging his shoulder into the slender truck of a budding cacti.

Wincing from the assortment of aches and pains racking his fragile frame, he struggles mightily for air intake while managing to crawl his way toward the boulder and plant his bony shoulder blades against its considerable bulk.

While staring into the lifeless, barren landscape fronting his slumped form, Jerrod Jarvis finds neither the courage nor energy to turn about and seek his pursuer.

Desperate to halt the bellowing groans escaping his parched throat, he attempts to breathe through his nose but fails, instead leaning to one side and vomiting hot, yellowish bile onto a nearby shrub.

Rolling over onto his back, he covers his head with both hands and begins to sob uncontrollably. He first ponders the grisly fate of the initial set of rescuing guards ... the look of disbelief on their usually stoic mugs just seconds before they are shredded and segmented like so much beef cattle.

He then replays the death of their stalwart yet ultimately foolish commander, whose brave stance and fruitless gunplay results in a severed arm, gutted midsection and ultimately decapitation by the single swipe of a descending claw. He replays the demise of the remaining guards via ghastly images of slashed throats, torn appendages, and flung entrails.

He thinks of his colleagues ... Becker, Kennard, Sanders, Eklin ... and how he saw them butchered and dismembered with such gruesome precision while attempting a similar sprint to freedom that has, at least thus far, spared his own life.

Finally, as his breathing becomes less frantic and his pulse begins to stabilize, he thinks of Wayne Grogan Fowler, the specimen hand-picked from literally thousands of potential candidates as the biosphere's lone inhabitant. The chosen one that Dr. Larry Becker, the joker of the staff, had labeled *The Hermit from Hell* in reference to the man's recent, rather infamous dealings with law enforcement and the scandalous murder case he'd previously been tied to. He has only moments to contemplate Fowler's possible involvement in the massacre at hand when a low shuffling noise effectively diverts his attention elsewhere.

Turning around, he raises his head ever so gradually, leaning his skeletal chest against the boulder while propping his chin atop its jagged top.

The young woman is completely nude and literally bathed in partially dried, tar- shaded blood from head to toe, her shoulder-length hair matted to her skull and forehead as if glued into place.

"D-Doctor J-Jarvis?" she whimpers, blinking rapidly and limping forward with her arms crossed over her breasts.

"Yes ... yes, child," he replies with a nod, rising gingerly to his feet while removing the lab coat.

Stepping around the boulder, he moves toward her and gently cloaks her within the coat's flapping folds.

"My god ... where did you come from?" he asks, holding her as she kneels weakly onto her knees, then backing away several steps to scan a seemingly deserted landscape beyond.

"The ... the biosphere, I ... I think. It's just so ... hard to recall de-details."

Jarvis gives their surroundings a final, twisting glance before squatting down to address her at eye level. He tries to think back and cannot accurately recall if any of Watts' initial security team had been women underneath the bulky chemical suits.

"Maybe ... it's better that way," he whispers in reply while strangely hesitant to step forward to console the trembling woman, whose age he can only assume as being between twenty-five and thirty. Her hair, though soaked and caked over to appear darker, is obviously red under normal conditions, her freckle-coated face as round and robust as the rest of her slightly chubby frame. There is, he briefly muses, something eerily familiar about her.

"D-doctor?" she asks between sobs. "Yes?"

"Did you ever ... trust someone completely? I mean ... trust them to never ... *ever* betray you?"

199

Jarvis leans up several inches, enough to effectively scope the valley beyond the woman's crouched form.

"Trust? Um ... yes, I suppose," he answers, obviously distracted.

"What if ... they swore to never ... break that trust? What would your reaction be?"

A sudden breeze slaps his haggard face and tiny specks of sand peck his eyes.

Wiping away the residue with pinching fingers, he then studies the girl a bit closer. She is no longer shaking, her eyes pulled wide and her left brow arched inquisitively. He thinks she is suffering from the initial stages of shock ... perhaps only minutes from a complete mental and physical meltdown. If indeed she's witnessed the same level of carnage within the biosphere's walls as he, such a reaction is far less than unexpected.

"I ... I'm not sure. Take a deep breath now. We ... may need to move on very soon. Do you think you can wal—"

"I trusted a man once. Only time I'd ever done so. Trusted him completely and without reservation," she blurts, tea-colored spittle flying from between tightly pursed lips. Allowing the lab coat to slip from her suddenly taunt shoulders, she gradually begins to rise.

"Told him my secrets. Told him my dreams. Told him ... of my curse." Planting a forefinger to his own parched lips, Jarvis attempts to shush her. "Please ... miss ... just settle down ... don't speak so lou—"

"I warned him, you know. Warned him of what I'd do if he ever dared betray me," she continues, baring teeth stained a dark maroon. Teeth that, Jarvis notes with no small degree of terror, appear freakishly oversized for her mouth. Oversized and thick at the base, but with grotesquely sharpened tips. *Piranha teeth*, he thinks crazily.

"The day I was sentenced ... convicted mainly due to his testimony ... I looked over at him and told him of our next meeting," she says seductively, placing the tip of her left pinky finger between clenched teeth. A finger, Jarvis quickly notes, that seems queerly elongated from just moments earlier.

"He ... apparently misunderstood my message ... big time."

Jarvis stumbles forward a step, waving his arms in windmill fashion in order to halt the girl's increasingly loud rant. He backs away just as abruptly once the transformation becomes all too evident.

The girl's forehead begins to expand and then deflate, as if the skin beneath were lined with air bladders.

"I ... um ... my god ... are y-you ... o-kay?" Jarvis mumbles while unconsciously continuing to flee in the opposite direction. He watches the woman's hunch forward with a resounding crunch as her spine bends and contracts.

"You see, I'm not real sure what he read from my lips that day," she growls as the flesh of her cheekbones and forehead split open as if parted by some invisible scalpel.

"Oh ... sh-shit ... you ... you're the one ... the one w-who…" Jarvis stammers while yearning to turn and dash away, though the scientist within effectively nixes such a notion as the woman's miraculous conversion continues.

"But what I said to that turncoat bastard, Doctor Travis, was this…" she spits in a guttural tone more animal than human…

"… *eat you* soon, my love."

She throws her head back and howls, her breastbone exploding from within before instantaneously reshaping itself. Just before dredging up the intestinal fortitude to turn and flee, Jarvis sees the blackish fur spew forth from seemingly every square inch of her hunched form.

"Mi-Mindy Jor-Jorgenson…" he sobs, lunging forward with a wobbly gait and discovering his legs as woefully drained as the bone-weary psyche giving them direction.

"Oh ... m-my ... g-*god* ... Min-dy ... Jor-gen-son…"

Doctor Jerrod Travis, psychiatrist in charge of the Introvert Project, is barely able to cover an additional fifty feet of soft desert terrain before being lifted airborne by a set of vise-like claws. He feels little pain in the series of vicious, lightning-quick slashes that effectively segment him into three separate portions.

***

The woman covers the three-mile trek back to the waiting SUV in less than fifteen minutes. She

202

uses pre-prepped containers of soapy water to clean away the excess of blood and gore before donning a fresh pair of jeans and a cotton tee. A paved two-lane beckons in the distance, as does a new lease on life. Though careful to remain characteristically pessimistic, she nonetheless holds out faint hopes for a more social existence. Trust, she knows, is as hard to give as it is to get. Still, there is always hope…

***

Some forty-five minutes after Mindy Jorgenson has turned onto the nearest interstate and mingled into traffic, still another helicopter drops onto the landing pad adjacent to the biosphere's lone entryway.

The pilot and crew, predictably armed to the teeth, quickly depart the chopper and descend a steep grade toward said entryway, only to stop dead in their tracks approximately ten yards from the opening.

Several gasp aloud, while others fill the air with exasperated profanities.

The twin M-16 rifles are the same they are issued to carry, each buried deep into the sand butt-end first.

Sitting atop the barrel end of each is a severed head. The first is of an older gentleman wearing thick glasses at the end of his pointed nose. His left eye remains open … the socket of the right a hollowed-out chasm from which several fat flies emerge. A note attached to the jagged ruin of his neck reads *The Doctor is Out*, and has obviously been scribbled in blood, perhaps even that of the victim.

The second displaced noggin is that of a younger man each guard instantly recognizes from past news footage as the individual chosen as the biosphere's lone tenant.

Wayne Fowler's mouth is stretched impossibly wide in a permanent scream of unspeakable agony, the illusion made ever more gruesome by the absence of his upper lip, which appears to have been torn away.

The note beneath the serrated stub of his neck simply reads *Traitor*.

THE ISLE OF TRANQUILITY, PART III

Well, this one certainly proves Pop wasn't at all adverse about upping the gore content at the expense of good taste. Lord, he must've been in some god-awful mood to dredge that one up. On second thought, when was the man not in a god-awful mood? Only times I saw him even mildly amused was when his latest divorce was nearing closure. If only his admiring public had some insight on the real man ... the hard man ... the arrogant man ... the cruel man ... the man who seemed to take great pleasure in first dismissing and then openly despising his only son. The man who always ... freakin' always had to have the last word, be it aloud on in print.

Sure, I dipped into the family cookie jar a few times ... well, a few hundred times, but it wasn't as if the filthy rich old bastard couldn't afford a withdrawal now and then. I mean, what's a sports car or the occasional new set of threads when you owned million- dollar homes in three states, or better yet procuring a freaking island paradise all to yourself! So what that he had to foot the bill for a lawyer or two to pull my fat out of the legal fire? I'm ... I was his son for god's sake! Would he have rather his lone offspring rot in jail on mostly trumped-up drug charges? Actually, I'm pretty damn sure he would've done just that if not for the beating his precious reputation might've taken in the aftermath.

Fact is, the real hate Papa Striker felt for his only begotten son didn't start till that circus of a

*court trial. Cranky old bastard couldn't stand the
negative imagery that surfaced to "stain" his rep,
and naturally turned to me as a convenient target.
Could I help it that some drunken indigent chose
such an unfortunate time to stumble into the damn
street and directly into the path of my Porsche?
Sure, I'd downed a Beam and Coke or three ...
maybe six, but even sober I'd never have braked in
time to prevent spreading that smelly bum all over
the pavement like ham on rye. Besides, the old souse
didn't even have a family ... not a soul gave a
swirling shit, so why shatter a young man's life at
the expense of such a complete waste of space?
Luckily the jury agreed, though I did hear
rumblings of mass payoffs and the like courtesy of
the old man and his well-deep pockets. It was soon
after that he cut off my monthly allowance, removed
me from his will, and officially declared me a "lost
cause," even sending one of his many legal cronies
to my pad in Palm Beach with lump-sum check in
hand, along with a handwritten note stating he
never wanted to see or hear from me again.*

*Well, tough shit, Daddy-O. If you were looking
up from whatever river of fire in which you wade,
you sure as hell must've noticed me at your funeral.
I was the one wearing the frozen smirk in light of
the news that you'd not only left me in your will
after all, but named me sole beneficiary. Must've
been one helluva hard choice between me and all
the exes. In the end, guess the self-serving prick
must've considered me the lesser of many evils.
Blood is thicker than water and all that sappy shit.*

Damned if I don't feel like a Jacuzzi session isn't in order. After, that is, a quick refill at the bar. Whew ... getting harder to walk a straight line, Amigo.

Twenty-two minutes later:

Lemme see now ...: quarter of three and the stubborn bitch is still out there playing Jungle Queen. Ah, the hell with her anyway ... who needs the constant pouting and dirty looks? I always was happier spending time with the smartest, funniest, best- lookin' guy I know ... me! Hey ... that calls for a drink! Damn, too much gin and not enough tonic ... just how I love 'em!

Ah, water temp is just right. Gotta give the old man credit ... he sure knows how to pick a generator. Damn thing's the size of a tractor-trailer, runs 24/7 but rarely needs refueling. Paid a pretty penny for that hulking SOB, for certain. Bravo, Richard ... bravo! Money well sent ... spent. Wow ... better slow the firewater intake. Don't wanna be too soused when the old lady shows up bucking for a brawl.

Oh-kay, then. Back to storytime. Better be a damned good one or I'm liable to drift away for a nap beneath the suds.

Babble on, Daddy-O ... babble on...

BOOK 3 - THE CABIN

He awoke bathed in a cool sweat, no doubt having moaned in muffled anguish before shaking himself to with a bellowing shriek. In the deafening silence of the surrounding forest, his agonizing screams had the effect of a detonated grenade within narrow cave walls.

Rolling from moistened, crumpled sheets that reeked of month-old sweat, he didn't bother to check the illuminated alarm clock sitting atop the headboard. Hours, minutes, days, months, or even years had ceased to matter long ago. Besides, the nightly *banshee howl*, as he had come to label it, was nothing if not consistent in both execution and moment of release, usually sounding off like clockwork between one and two AM. Cold hard fact was, such rigorous attention to detail had always been the calling card of one Joseph Perry Clifford, a habitual, sometimes annoying trait that had been grooved into his psyche at an early age.

Dragging his bare feet down the thickly carpeted hall toward the kitchen, he paused momentarily at the bathroom entrance before bypassing it in a lurch, as if pulled forward by some unseen force. As was the nightly ritual, the inner thirst won over the aching bladder in a first-round TKO.

"Midnight snack awaits…" he muttered, clicking on the kitchen light while shielding his eyes with a raised forearm. A fresh outbreak of chill bumps coated his neck and arms as the chilly night air began to gradually overcome his elevated body temperature.

"Gotta sooth the parch ... feed the craving. Priority number one. Quench the ol' gullet, yes, sir."

Pulling a tall glass from a nearby cabinet, he then turned about and began searching for the bottle he'd so efficiently begun to empty the night before.

"Now, now ... don't be shy. Come ... to ... poppa."

Stumbling into the living room while unconsciously massaging his upper chest with the fingers of both hands, he managed to kick a tennis shoe airborne and barely avoided taking a header into a wide sectional recliner. Scanning the confined space while whirling about in a clumsy spin, he eventually spotted his prize lying near the cabin's lone entrance.

"B-bingo. Nectar of the g-ad ... gods."

Moments later, he sat at the kitchen table and emptied the first of what was to be several double shots of Jim Beam in two lengthy swallows as the faint echo of a portable generator unit hummed its disapproval from the rear of the structure. Located more than eleven miles from what could fairly be deemed civilization, that being the nearest two-lane highway, the Clifford family cabin retreat was the textbook definition of isolated. His father had built it nearly thirty years earlier as a place the family could escape the everyday ills of life. Just the thought never ceased to evoke the most hangdog of expressions from Joseph's weatherbeaten mug.

"Steady, Sarge, steady," he whispered, feeling the familiar burn coat first his throat and chest cavity and finally the pit of his belly, "deep breaths and mellow thoughts, that's what the Doc prescribed ... deep breaths and mellow thoughts."

He raised a forefinger airborne and waved it from side to side.

"Well, that, coupled with at *least* a pint of firewater per day and all your troubles will simply melt away, right, Doc? Riiiiiiight."

He did manage to shoot the alarm a blasé glance while diving back into the bed a half-hour later. It glowed with a defiant 2:08 AM.

No big deal, Joseph mused as the mattress began its nightly spin; it wasn't as if his snoozing until noon was going to cause even the most minute ripple in what served as modern society. No appointments to keep ... no places to see or people to meet.

The contents of the dream rarely if ever strayed in terms of content. Sixteen months and counting of the same exact scenario, a Greek tragedy played out in hazy black and white like some low-budget documentary. Though the timed duration of such mindbenders was virtually impossible to gauge, Joseph figured this particular stage play of the subconscious to be no more than thirty seconds in length; possibly a full minute at the outside. After all, it contained but a single location, two visual cast members, and virtually no dialogue save his own brief ranting. This being the case, such a short-lived series of images could be replayed ad nauseam over an eight- to ten-hour period, like a film clip promo stuck in an endless loop.

There were mornings (or early afternoons, depending on the severity of the hangover) that he would estimate trudging within the same nightmarish dreamscape at least two dozen times, if not more, and without the benefit of interruption by additional, unrelated images.

A few months following the incident, while undergoing mandatory psychiatric counseling, he'd been assured by a departmental shrink that such vivid imagery would fade over time with each detail slowly fragmenting until it would resemble an entirely different dream altogether. Several months (and countless "banshee shrieks") later, the same doctor had provided calm reassurance (along with several hand-scribbled prescriptions for various sleep aids and muscle relaxers) that such would be the case, though it might "take longer" than previously anticipated in such a traumatic case.

In the ten-plus months since that last office visit, Joseph was still waiting for the initial variation from the norm. In the meantime, boozing his way into a deeper state of slumber didn't seem to curtail the end result any better than the tranquilizers that had came before ... or the sleep aids ... or the prescribed narcotic ... nor the many attempts to refrain from sleeping at all (which he had personally dubbed the *Freddy Krueger Insomniac Method for the Hopelessly Deranged*).

Drifting off as the effects of the eighty-proof sleep enhancer kicked in at full bore, Joseph heard the faint howling of a coyote somewhere within the surrounding forest.

For at least the hundredth time since resigning himself to permanent cabin fever status, he prayed that he might run alongside such creatures in his dreams, relishing both the surge of freedom and lack of haunting guilt that occupied his every conscious and unconscious thought.

***

Propped against the dining table (merely the cheaper, flimsier twin of the kitchen table) while sipping a stout mug of steaming black coffee, Joseph lifted the notepad and studied his own writing as if it were some alien hieroglyphic carved into a stone tablet.

"O-kay ... lemme see here. Toilet paper. Bottled water. Bottled gin. Bottled vodka. Bottled Beam. Four large bags of ice. Takes care of the liquid nourishment. Canned beans ... canned chicken ... canned soup ... crackers. What the...?"

Lifting the yellow-shaded paper, even with his eyes squinting tightly, he couldn't help but grin in comical awe of his own horrific penmanship.

"Looks like ... tuna helper and ... *dill* pickles? Damn, I hate tuna helper. Sure can't trust my gut instinct when *Jack Black* or *Jimmy Beam* are calling the shots.

Strange cravings indeed, old Hoss. You'd think someone in the house was pregnant." The cabin's front door hinges groaned as he secured it with a light shove.

Hitching up his blue jeans, which seemed to be stretched wider with each wearing, he reached up to secure the baseball cap holding his overgrown bangs into place while simultaneously stroking a thick growth of gray-streaked brown beard coating his chin. Though his lack of height (five-eight in his stocking feet) would have never allowed the words "physically intimidating" to be used alongside his name in any standard description, his stocky, muscular build had once earned him the nickname "Joe Rock" by both service and departmental peers. It had taken less than ten months out of the weight room (not to mention countless missed meals and heavy booze consumption) to transform a cut, finely-tuned physique into a shell of its former self. Since the incident some sixteen months earlier, his weight had plummeted from a robust one-eighty-five to just near the one-sixty mark. Additionally, a once-healthy complexion appeared pasty and weathered, and the clean-cut look of old had been replaced by thick tufts of tangled hair that rarely saw a comb's teeth, much less regular shampooing. His beard and accompanying mustache were scraggly and woefully unkempt, looking more at home on a rock star gone to seed than a man once revered for an exceptionally neat outward appearance.

Strolling a bit unsteadily into the overgrown weed patch that served as the front yard, Joseph peered upward into an ominous patch of black clouds building overhead. The temperature was unseasonably chilly for late September, as if foretelling a hard winter to come.

"Gonna have to put pedal to metal. Don't want to get caught in a downpour with the windshield wipers on the blink. Bad enough driving around with this wretched hangover—adding blindness to the mix just might land you in the county lockup for a month of Sundays."

The late model Ford F-150 was the last of what he considered life's "luxuries" (fouled-up wipers not withstanding) that he'd deciding on keeping, since monthly payments had ceased less than two months before the incident that had so drastically changed his life. He'd recently noted that in the many months he'd occupied the cabin, the vehicle's mileage tally had increased by only four hundred eleven, or roughly a thirty-mile a month average. This was in stark (frightening?) contrast to the daily sixty- mile round trip trek he'd made while still an active, working member of society. Monthly supply runs into town were executed in streamlined fashion and with limited human contact, although of late the twenty-eight-mile round trip seemed to take an eternity. In fact, what had started as a slight annoyance in terms of even making the required trip was fast mutating into something more akin to *extreme* dread.

In recent weeks, Joseph's hold on both reality and his personal sanity were showing obvious signs of shredding at the seams. The prospect of enduring a fresh *clone phase*, as the departmental shrink had labeled the specific episodes, was less than reassuring and more along the lines of terrifying.

Barring inclement weather, the eleven-plus-mile ride down the narrow dirt and gravel trail to

State Route 43 normally took less than twenty minutes. From there, the local Winn-Dixie and Kmart stores were just under three miles and several bustling intersections away.

As luck would have it, the rain held off until his frantic shopping spree was complete approximately an hour and a half later. An initial wave of light sprinkles, accompanied by a sporadic thunderclap every ten seconds or so, didn't ensue until after he'd departed Kmart and pulled up to the gas pumps at a local BP station.

Removing his baseball cap to wipe a massive buildup of cool sweat from his forehead, Joseph propped his bulk against the truck's cab while filling the tank. As if suffering an intense bout of indigestion, he reached up with one hand to massage his upper chest. His breathing was just beginning to normalize, whereas he'd been on the verge of hyperventilating upon departing both the grocery and supply stores.

"You okay, bud?' the clerk had asked as Joseph had offered up a twenty with a tremor-wracked hand. "You're ... um ... looking a little green around the gills."

"Never been better, thanks," he'd replied nervously, a bothersome tick forming at the corner of his left eye. In raw frustration, he'd been ever so tempted to grasp the clerk by the collar and scream, *Can't honestly say that I am, pal. Ever been clone phased? Feels like my skull was shoved inside a blender and pureed. Probably end up crapping water for the next three days, not to mention all the quality sleep I'm apt to miss for the next several weeks. So no, to be perfectly candid ... I'm not at my best. In fact, truth be told, I feel a bit like hammered SHIT on buttered Texas Toast!*

By the time he'd departed the busy main drag for the sparse traffic of Route 43, both his breathing and pulse rate had almost completely stabilized.

"Damn, son. I do believe your public speaking days are long over," he mumbled, already feeling the fatigue-like symptoms that had become the norm following a trip into town.

Stop one had been a breeze. *The Firewater Station* liquor store was normally his last stop on the monthly shopping gauntlet, but on this particular day he'd unconsciously made it priority one for no particular reason other than perhaps a rather self-destructional sense of need.

Approximately fifteen minutes, four fifths, three quarts, and $138 later, the deed was done. Weatherwise, the light sprinkle had ceased, though the tar pit-shaded clouds above remained an ever ominous presence.

The meltdown had begun as it always did, roughly midway through his grocery list at Winn-Dixie, where he spotted a young girl of perhaps five or six sitting inside a shopping cart as her guardian plucked items from a nearby shelf. As if adhering to some eternal checklist set on autopilot, his head had begun to throb at the temples even as the palm of each hand grew slick with perspiration. Wheeling over into the next aisle as quickly as possible while attempting not to resemble an overmedicated lunatic, he came dangerously close to ramming a cart being steered by a preteen boy, who greeted

216

him with wide, fright-filled eyes and a warped, buck-toothed grin. Following a brief nod of acknowledgement, he'd sped past the bread and packaged desserts section and directly toward the dairy foods.

During checkout, he noticed the same small girl staring at him from an aisle over.

Averting his eyes to the cashier, he nonetheless felt his knees grow weak and a tidal wave of nausea wash over his midsection. By the time he reached his truck with a half dozen plastic bags tucked beneath both arms, a sharp tingling sensation had spread from his knees up his spine, and eventually all the way to the back of his skull.

Meanwhile, the light sprinkles had returned, accompanied by an occasional lightning strike from the east.

While picking up a few essentials across the street at a mostly vacated (the main reason he picked Monday mornings for such excursions) Kmart, he had just begun to recover somewhat when stage one of a particularly nasty *clone phase had* commenced. He spotted the first just past one of the hardware aisles, where he'd been loading his cart with generator fuel. Sucking in a series of deep, labored breaths, Joseph had practically sprinted toward the sporting goods section, temporarily forgetting that children's toys were located near that same corner of the store.

By the time he'd shuffled weakly to the checkout line, purposely omitting several items from the prewritten list in order to hasten his escape, practically every child below the age of ten that crossed his path had possessed the same identity. At least six or seven had jumped out at him near the toy and game section, each the same height and body size. Another trio had greeted him as he'd wheeled past the magazine and card racks, while an additional four or five had stared him down near the pharmacy.

As always, none had spoken or even gestured in his direction; they had instead studied him with slightly titled heads and sad, doelike expressions.

Unlike the relatively uneventful escape from Winn-Dixie, he wasn't able to depart the rain-slick parking lot before being bent over in a fit of heaving spasms that found him practically lying next to the truck's back left tire. He sped from the lot amid mass formations of cloned children, all lined up in military dress-right-dress fashion while engulfing the lot like an army of soldier ants.

In driving away from the BP station some ten minutes later, Joseph had allowed himself a final glance of the Kmart lot across the way. Mercifully, the ocean of clones had vanished; replaced by the parked cars that had been there all along.

Despite an unrelenting urge to do so sooner, Joseph waited until he pulled off of Route 43 and onto the unmarked dirt road leading to the cabin before gulping down three long swallows of Jack Daniel's straight from the bottle.

He had driven roughly halfway home when the sky had opened up in a typhoon- like deluge, complete with sheets of rain, golf-ball-sized hail, and wind gusts stout enough to cause the big pickup to shake and shimmy like a vehicle half its size.

"Swell. I'm beginning to think an amendment to *Murphy's Law* was written especially with yours truly in mind," he spat sarcastically, slowing to a halt as visibility became a virtual impossibility without working wipers.

"Thirty minutes at any repair shop, dumbass. That's all it would take. But noooooooo. Just can't manage the time. Have to rush back to the cabin and continue *operation pickled liver*."

Taking still another healthy pull from the black-labeled fifth, Joseph then sighed heavily and crossed his arms over his chest, happily resigned to wait out the storm for however long the duration. Clicking on the truck radio, he scanned various stations before settling on the local classic rock station, where the lyrics to The Who's *Behind Blue Eyes* struck him as sadly ironic.

Approximately ten minutes and three additional swigs later, the hailstorm was history and both the rain and winds had diminished substantially enough for him to exit the truck cab for a breath of fresh, pine-smelling air.

The road's deep ruts were filled to the brim from the downpour, though such an occurrence had never caused a traction problem in the past. Just such a dicey scenario had led him to sell the Mustang in lieu of keeping the pickup.

Removing his cap, Joseph tilted back his head and allowed the rain to pelt his face and forehead, the booze having already soothed his ragged nerves. Scanning the trail he'd just covered, he noticed an oak limb as thick as a telephone pole lying directly across the road.

"Well, at least I don't have to worry about moving that bad boy for another month or so. Instant roadblock ... instant privacy," he said, wearing a warped, Jack Black- produced grin.

He was in the process of hopping back into the truck when movement caught the corner of his left eye.

Squinting mightily, he stared past a deep rain-filled gully and directly at the base of an ancient elm tree whose upper limps were jagged and leafless from years of apparent decomposition.

"Huh. Must be the JD playing tricks with my—" he muttered just as a pale, clutching hand shot out from behind the thick trunk, apparently reaching for a fresh hold.

"Wha—the ... could ... whoa ..." he babbled, briefly stepping behind the truck's door as if to shield himself from whatever mystery lay beyond those splayed, grasping fingers.

Shaking his head vigorously from side to side, Joseph briefly considered the possibility of an alcohol/stress-related mirage, at least until the hand refused to vanish or melt away like dense fog struck by bright sunlight.

"Hey! Who—who's there? Show yourself now. I'm in no mood for games," he croaked a bit more timidly than intended, though feeling his law enforcement instincts kick in while creeping out from behind the truck door and making his way slowly toward the open bed. After blindly reaching over and retrieving a rust-coated lug wrench from near the left rear wheel well, he trudged toward the edge of the gully while keeping his sights trained solely on the mystery appendage.

"Hel-lo? Is anybody there? You hearing me? Sound off already!"

Just as his left boot sank ankle-deep into the gully, a body collapsed to the right of the tree trunk, literally vanishing into an overgrown patch of weeds.

Pulling his boot free with a moist plopping sound, Joseph leaped over the gully and onto the grassy bank beyond. He knelt over the body with the lug wrench held high in a striking pose before slowly allowing it to drop back down to shoulder level.

"Jesus Crow," he blurted loudly before reaching down to check the pulse of the fallen stranger.

"Weak ... but still ticking. Breathing's shallow, but sufficient. How in the world did she ... what is she doing in these woods anyhow? Just ... doesn't make a lick of sense..."

Placing the forefinger of his right hand gently atop her right eyelid, Joseph slid the lid upward while kneeling down ever closer.

"Unresponsive. Don't see any apparent wounds or trauma. No blood spatters on the skin or clothing..." he prattled, inexplicably whispering as if to maintain secrecy.

Standing with his hands locked on his hips, Joseph shot the fallen oak a somber glance before returning his gaze to the body lying prone at his feet.

"No way I'm budging that thing, and if I try to shove her aside with the truck, I'm liable to bury it up to the door handles in this mud. Got to get the chainsaw from the house, soooo…"

He gave her a final once-over before leaning back down to flip her into lifting position.

She was wearing only a mud-stained, sleeveless tee-shirt and black skin-tight spandex shorts (*cycling pants*, Joseph instantly deduced), and he couldn't help but notice the tightly muscled, meticulously toned physique, most noticeably around the calf, thigh and buttock regions. Her short, neck-length strawberry blonde colored hair was horribly tangled and matted to her skull and face in thin strips. He figured her to be no more than five-two or -three, and perhaps 120 to 125 pounds.

"Looks like you're gonna be a houseguest, Missy. At least until I can get that timber moved and drive you to the nearest sawbones."

Wrapping an arm around her upper back and another beneath her kneecaps, he heaved upward with two quick jerks, wincing as both knees moaned their disapproval.

"Lord girl, you're either a hell of lot more solid than you look, or I'm in the worst shape of my life," he groaned, stepping cautiously over a deep mound of wet leaves.

The rain fell harder as they reached the truck's passenger-side door, and Joseph struggled momentarily while reaching for the handle with outstretched fingers that had been tucked beneath the girl's limp legs.

"In we go," he huffed, propping her upright in the spacious cab before gently securing the door as if to provide her a comfortable lean-to.

Sprinting through the downpour to reach the driver's side, Joseph scanned the surrounding forest one final time before hopping into the cab, as if he were openly performing some felonious act.

He turned the ignition key as the steering wheel and dash were bombarded with raindrops from his cap's bill, then turned about to ensure the girl was sufficiently balanced for what was apt to be a rather bumpy ride.

"And away ... we go," he whispered apprehensively, checking the rearview and side mirrors as if negotiating a busy urban intersection instead of a one-lane dirt and gravel path leading precisely nowhere.

***

Watching the rain fall ever harder from the kitchen's lone window while sipping gin from an oversized coffee mug, Joseph rubbed his upper chest with a free hand and watched a shallow lakebed form in what served as the cabin's driveway, practically engulfing the truck's back tires up to the center portion of the hubcaps.

"May have to rent a pontoon boat to depart the premises at this point," he whispered sourly, shaking his head in utter disbelief. "Might as well face facts. There just isn't any hiding from society. Dig a hole on Mars and somebody would eventually fall right in on top of ya."

Raising the cup for a fresh snort, he halted in mid-sip as a low groaning sound reverberated from the living room.

Upon arrival, he'd laid the girl on the couch, covering her with both a sheet and wool blanket as the temperature inside the cabin had grown cooler as the day had progressed. With practically no insulation to speak of and a woodburning stove as the only source of heat (a source he wouldn't begin to utilize until mid-October or possibly even later), the cabin served as little more than a windbreaker during the fall months. Since he had taken up permanent residence smack-dab in the middle of a sleet storm in mid-January, an indoor thermometer reading of no less than fifty was considered downright snug.

As he crept nearer, feeling a bit like a cat burglar in his own abode, Joseph saw that the girl had turned over onto her back, her long, muscular arms hanging over the edge in a two-handed gesture of surrender. There was a small tattoo no more than four inches in diameter on her left shoulder, a variation of the familiar skull and crossbones one is apt to see on present or past military members. He couldn't help but be struck by just how strangely out of place such an image was on an otherwise unblemished appendage, though there was of course the possibility that other tattoos, not so easily viewed, did exist.

Tilting his head and studying her exposed facial features like one might a rare zoo exhibit, he couldn't help but think she looked vaguely familiar.

Squinting her eyes as if from sudden discomfort, the girl pursed her lips and released a muffled groan.

"Hmm ... celebrity lookalike, possibly," he said with a mischievous grin. "With all the reality crap on these days, she might've been on *Fear Factor* eating the bark off trees. At least that would explain why she was hanging on to that elm like a bear cub to its mam—"

"You ... in the habit of holding ... one-way conversations with the comatose?" the girl interrupted in a harsh whisper, her eyes remaining closed even as she rolled over onto her right side and almost off of the narrow sectional. "If so, excuse my rudeness."

Averting his eyes like a peeping Tom caught in the act, Joseph took an awkward step back and began shuffling his boots from side to side.

"Oh, um ... sorry. Didn't ... I thought you were..." "Comatose? As I was saying…"

"No, it wasn't like ... I mean ... I didn't mean to ... you were ... and I was just wondering…"

"Hey, it's all right, man. Don't ... blow a gasket over it."

Pushing herself upright as the thick wool blanket fell away, the girl coughed harshly into her left palm.

"Uh ... you feeling okay? Let me get you a glass of water..." Joseph blurted, his cheeks suddenly beet red and ablaze with embarrassment.

The girl nodded weakly while reaching up with both hands to rub her hazel- shaded eyes.

"That would be ... great. Tongue feels like a ... dried sponge."

By the time he returned with a tall glass filled with semichilled Evian, she was standing propped against the back of the couch with her hands atop her hips, blinking rapidly while stifling a yawn.

"Here you go. Best in the house. It's ... bottled."

The girl smiled, reaching gingerly to take the glass from his outstretched hand. "Gotta tell ya, at this point it could be ... truck stop toilet water and I wouldn't even ... hesitate."

She emptied the glass in four lengthy swallows, wiping her lips with the inside of her right forearm.

"Liquid gold, my brother. Thanks loads."

"No, um, problem," he replied cautiously, taking the glass from her without breaking eye contact.

Joan Jett, he thought crazily. *Bingo! The eighties rock chick of* I Love Rock and Roll *fame. Pretty much a dead ringer. Got the chopped hair, lip snarl, and tough as nails "chopper bitch" look down, though I have to say her substantially fuller figure's an improvement on anything ol' JJ of the Blackhearts ever displayed.*

"I won't be able to drive you into town until the storm lets up. That road has a tendency to fill up like a horse trough from a spring shower. Hope that's okay ... I mean, it isn't as though we have a choice."

"Town, huh? Uh, this might sound a tad ... maniacal, dude, but ... *what* town are we near anyhow?"

226

"Ridgecrest, about eleven miles to the south off Route ... um ... you serious?" Bowing her head, the girl studied her bare feet, which were coated in tiny welts, scratches, and dry leaf specks.

"I kid you not. Afraid that's ... not even the worst," she continued, massaging the back of her neck with one hand while eyeing him somewhat warily. "No reason to beat around the bush here. So ... are you my husband, brother, lover ... or what?"

As Joseph stood speechless with his mouth hanging open like a shutter with a shattered hinge, the girl sighed heavily and shot him a playful wink.

***

"So let me get this straight. Not only do you have no idea what you were doing traipsing around in over ten thousand acres of remote wilderness—"

"Not a clue."

"... but your own identity is equally mystifying." "Jane Doe at your service."

"No idea what you're even doing in the great state of Virginia?" "Your guess is as good as mine."

"So ... what we're talking is acute amnesia." "You're the doctor."

"Not even close."

"I'll take your word for it, Mister...?"

"Clifford. Joseph Clifford ... Joe. This is my ... cabin. Actually, it was my dad's.

He passed on several years back and I inherited the deed."

Sitting across from one another at the relatively petite kitchen table, the pair resembled poker

227

contestants in the middle of a particularly tension-filled match.

The girl had the blanket wrapped around her shoulders and torso and sipped a cup of steaming tea, while Joseph nursed a Jim Beam and 7UP from the same large- handled mug that had previously held a double shot of gin.

"More tea?"

"That'll work. Actually, you got any soup?"

"Got some cream of chicken, I think."

"I'd surely appreciate it. Gut's a little sour. No telling how long since the last fill-up."

"No problem. I'll fire up the hotplate."

Rising from the table, the girl shuffled over to the window and peered out. "Well, seems to be letting up somewhat. Still coming down pretty steady though," she said, lightly rubbing each eye.

"Real gullywasher, all right. Haven't seen one this severe since early spring. Late March or early April maybe," he replied, vigorously massaging his chest before inserting the hotplate's narrow cord into an open switchbox mounted onto the kitchen wall.

Visibly shivering, the girl sat back down with a heavy sigh.

"Kind of ... chilly in here. Is it ... is this fall, or...? My bones are telling me old man winter's alarm clock might be sounding off soon."

"You mean you don't..." he began, refilling her cup with from a steaming metal pot. "... Sorry, forgot the memory handicap thing for a second. It's September ... late September ... um, the twenty-eighth, to be exact."

Smiling kindly, the girl reached over and gently patted the top of his hand.

"Kind of like babysitting the world's oldest living toddler, I would guess. I ... truly appreciate everything you've done ... Joe, was it?"

"Y-yeah, Joe," he stuttered, bowing just slightly before stepping away to check the hotplate. "... Joseph Clifford."

"Well, at least I can recall your name, Joe 'Joseph' Clifford. It ain't much, but at least it's a start..."

"Not to worry. I'm sure it's just temporary. Doctor will fix you up, no sweat." The girl rested her forehead on the tabletop and released a low, purring moan. "Yeah, uh, sure. I ... guess."

***

"Sure you had enough?"

"Oh yeah ... just hit the spot. Thanks again."

"Hey, best soup heater-upper in the business, that's me."

Pushing away from the table, the girl lurched hard to the left before righting herself, then shambled slowly back toward the living room and sprawled out onto the couch.

"Mind if I nap for a while, Joe? Feeling a bit ragged."

"By all means," he replied, opening the door to a nearby closet and pulling out a large metal container. "I have to go refill the generator. Looks like we're stuck here until the rain stops and the water drains. I'm just glad you're feeling better. For a while there, I thought I was gonna have to toss you over my back and hoof it into town."

"Yeah, other than the obvious memory malfunction, I think some serious R&R is all the medication I require."

Joseph pulled his cap's bill down over his forehead and reached for the front door.

"I'll try to keep it quiet. Rest well."

"Thanks, Joe. I ... I'll sure owe you when all is said and done, and *Jane Doe* always pays her debts ... I think."

"Forget it," he grinned. "To be honest, I haven't felt this useful in eons. Back in a sec."

Upon reentering, Joseph kneeled to remove his boots and the socks beneath, all of which were equally soaked through, and could just make out the girl's soft, rhythmic snoring.

After topping off the generator's tank, he'd taken a short stroll down the rainsoaked drive and to the point where it widened a bit onto what his father had referred to as "Paradise Road" whenever they'd exited the highway for the cabin on summer vacation.

He'd halted further forward progress once he'd sunk his left boot ankle-deep into a pudding-like quagmire that served as starting point for the winding trail that eventually led to Route 43. Slogging back toward the cabin, Joseph's emotions ran the gamut from frenzied apprehension to soothing relief, a veritable obstacle course of mindbending garble that was, for the first time in months, utterly unaffected by the ravages of either alcohol abuse or past traumatic events. His heart raced; his temples throbbed; his midsection fluttered. The source of the meltdown was no mystery. There was something about the stranger occupying his cabin, other than her obvious good looks and endearing charm, that lit his every nerve ending ablaze in a way he hadn't experienced in years.

Entering the cabin's lone bedroom, he secured the door behind him and tuned the clock radio to the local Ridgecrest AM weather station. Through periodic waves of grinding static, he was able to hear a forecast that called for not only an additional twenty-four hours of moderate to heavy rains, but also a possible funnel cloud or two within the vicinity.

Stranded with a CAP-I-TAL S, it seems. Gonna be three, four days before that road's passable, maybe longer. Well, she doesn't appear to be in any immediate danger, healthwise. Nothing to do but wait it out. In the meantime, can't hurt to play a little game of Perry Mason and try to solve the identity crisis.

He cracked the door just a hair and could hear the sporadic snore over the generator's prattling hum. Placing his hands behind his head, he leaned back onto the crumpled mattress and fell into a fitful doze.

It would be nightfall before he would be shaken awake by a stranger's steely grip.

***

231

"Joe? Joseph ... you okay? You're dreaming, man ... wake up. Come to, man ... come to!"

"Huh ... wah? Whozat?" he blurted, jerking hard to the left and practically diving from the mattress onto the hardwood floor.

"Chill, Joe ... it's just me, remember?" the girl replied, backing to the bedroom entrance and pausing with her hands facing palms up. "The unknown chick, remember?"

"Oh ... y-yeah. Uh ... sorry. Wha-what's the matter? Is something goin—" "Everything's cool. It's just that you were ... shrieking like a coyote in heat and I wasn't sure what to do but bring you out of it. Sorry about that."

"*Banshee howls*," he mumbled, sluggishly crawling back onto the bed. "Excuse me?"

"My ... doctor used to call 'em *banshee howls*. Created, edited, and produced by Nightmares 'R' Us Incorporated, a subsidiary of Night Sweats INC. I ... apologize for the scare. I would've warned you, but I never intended to take such a lengthy afternoon power nap."

"Gotta tell you, Joe, you've certainly got a set of lungs. I practically executed a combat roll off that couch."

"Wish I could say such an occurrence was rare. Afraid it's more like Groundhog Day. I wake the same way every night ... sometimes more than once."

Folding her arms across her chest, the girl seemed to pause to study him momentarily before replying.

232

"Banshee howls, huh? You'll have to fill me in later."

"No big thing, especially compared to your predicament. I'd better go check the generator soon. Damn thing sounds like a train chugging up Mount Everest."

The girl smiled weakly and backed from the room to allow Joe a clear exit path. "Got any coffee, Joe? I could sure use a stout one."

"I'm sure I can dig some up, " he answered between yawns, turning to check the alarm clock before rising from the squeaking mattress.

"Damn. Seven-thirty. We were out close to five hours."

"It's done wonders for me already," she beamed, "I feel at least *partially* human again."

Centering the couch with her bare legs folded beneath her, the girl sipped noisily and grimaced.

"Smooth as a mountain stream, I take it?" Joe asked, wearing a comically stoic expression. Outside, a rumbling of thunder could be heard just moments before the living room window was briefly illuminated by flashes of nearby lightning.

"Hey, how does that old chestnut go? Better watch what you asked for, 'cause you just might get it? See, I can remember a vast array of useless, trivial crap, while such weighty matters as name, age, and place of birth completely escape me."

Joseph shrugged before gulping a mouthful of Jim Beam and Coke. "Speaking of which, I think I have a theory concerning the former." "Well, lay it on me, dude. Long as it doesn't involve prostitution or drug smuggling."

"Well," he began, setting his drink aside and wringing his hands excitedly, "since you've obviously stayed in great shape ... that is ... physically. I mean, as ... *toned* as you are—" he paused and cleared his throat—"... it only stands to reason that you're the athletic type. Maybe you were cross-training, hiking, or jogging, and banged your head somehow."

The girl took another sip and shook her head.

"Doesn't jive, Joe. Except for a sore shoulder and hip, there aren't any wounds apparent. Not a single knot or sore spot on the old noggin that I can find."

"Concussions don't bleed," he replied, tilting his head knowingly as a fresh set of thunderclaps sounded off beyond the cabin's thick log walls.

"Guess it's possible," she shrugged, scanning the area around them as if she'd just entered. "I ... I'm pretty sure the fitness thing is tied to whatever my job was ... *is*. I was kind of hoping this last nap might dredge up some clues via the magical realm of dreams. Funny, can't recall even a single image. Hope my inner tape deck isn't permanently warped."

"Had a co-worker take a shot to the head a few years ago. He suffered the same symptoms for a few days before it all started coming back to him in dribs and drabs.

Within a week he was back to his old self ... couldn't tie his shoes or remember how to shave, but other than that..."

The girl lowered the cup from her lips and shot him a worrisome glance, to which Joseph shrugged his shoulders and winked.

"Funny as a crutch, dude," she said with a frown.

After several moments of surprisingly comfortable silence, in which each drank from their respective cups as the occasional thunderclap blared out in the distance, Joseph found himself happily entranced by the mysterious, undeniably intriguing enigma occupying his couch. He saw her eye the lawn tools in a far corner, a sparse collection that included a small pair of pruning shears (never used), a garden hoe (ditto), and a long-handled sling-blade (possibly *overused* in light of a lack of anything resembling a lawn mower).

"Mean looking weed hacker ya got over there. Any other potential weapons I should know about in case of a bear attack?"

"Afraid that's about it other than a few butter knives," he laughed. "With all the booze and bad dreams, I find I really don't trust myself with sharp objects. More tea?"

"Whoa, no thanks. Any more and I think I just might float away. Could you point me to the nearest young ladies' room?" she finally asked, placing the empty cup on the room's lone table stand.

"Through the kitchen and to your left. Actually, it's the *only* room past the kitchen. You can't possibly miss it."

"Is there a shower? Methinks I'm beginning to reek," she added timidly, jutting out her lower lip in a seductive pout.

"Well, there is a tub. I'll have to plug in and tune up the hot water heater. Take about an hour and a half to heat up. Give me a couple of minutes to wipe out the tub."

She peered at him with a doe-eyed expression that instantly caused a throbbing at his chest.

"Sorry for all the trouble. I know just saying thanks isn't enough, but it's all I can offer for now."

"Hey, forget it," he replied, waiving her off as he stood. "As you can probably guess, I don't get a lot of company up here. Never really wanted any, truth be told. Surprisingly, I find myself enjoying it more than I would've ever guessed."

"Appreciate the kind words, even if it *is* the hooch talking."

"No way. Takes at least a fifth of eighty proof or higher to alter my thought processes these days. Just being honest. Who knows, you just might be the chosen amnesiac sent here to bring me out of my shell."

"Kind of gives my being here a purpose then, doesn't it?" she grinned as the room was again lit up by a vicious series of lightning strikes.

"Definitely. Now, let me plug in the water heater and get to that tub." Watching her run her fingers through her short-coiffed hair as he departed,

Joseph felt his heart inexplicably skip a beat.

My Lord, man. How old are you? Stop acting like a pr-teen boy with a grade- school crush. You don't even know this woman ... hell, this woman doesn't even know this woman. Get a grip already.

236

Still, as he wiped the porcelain tub with a rag coated in Lysol Bathroom Tub & Tile Cleaner, he found it virtually impossible to wipe the smile from his lips.

***

"Think I left about four pounds of moldy grime in that tub, dude. Looked like somebody had been panning for gold."

Sitting at the kitchen table, the girl talked between nibbles of a peanut butter and jelly sandwich and sips of chilled milk from a frosty mug.

"Feel like a new woman, whoever the hell that woman might be." "You do look refreshed. Hope the shampoo and soap were okay."

"Good to go, believe me," she replied, holding a hand airborne with the thumb and forefinger forming a circle. "I'll worry about the salon look at a later date.

Appreciate the new duds, too. Might be a size or two beyond my norm, but at least they're fresh."

"It does give you kind of a 21st century bag lady look, now that you mention it. I'll pick you up a few shirts and some jeans if we ever make it into town."

"Maybe there's a Goodwill store nearby. Like the old saying goes, I ain't too proud."

Joseph nodded while finishing up his own sandwich and washing it down with a mouthful of lukewarm Budweiser.

"Rain's finally let up. Nothing but light sprinkles falling. If it stops altogether, it might be dried out enough to give it a try by late tomorrow afternoon."

"I'm game ... I guess," she said, eyeing him curiously. "You sure have a hollow leg for the stuff, don't ya?"

Holding the beer can aloft, he cocked his head as to peek past it to meet her gaze.

"Years of intense training, my dear."

"Don't mean to be nosy. Guess it's my nature. Then again..." she quipped with a quizzical look, "...maybe it isn't."

"It's a loooonnnnnnng story. Don't think you could ever be that bored." "Depends on the level of cabin fever we reach in the next few days, I guess."

Stretching up and out with both arms, the girl yawned and lowered her head to the table.

"I do believe it's beddy-bye time, Joe. Feel like I've got ten-pound anvils hanging from each eyelid. I would try to stay up and watch some boob tube, but I didn't spot a set..."

"Sorry, no TV or computer-type devices allowed on the premises. Strictly prohibited by the hermit code I live by. No news *is* good news ... especially these days. Anyhow, you take the bed. I've already got it made up for you. New sheets, new pillow case ... the works."

"No, I've put you out enough, man. The couch is fine." "Hey, you're a guest in my humble abode. I insist."

Rising from the table with all the speed of a three-toed sloth, the girl stepped gingerly around

238

and leaned down to plant a light kiss on his left cheek.

"My shining knight," she cooed sweetly, though her overall tone reeked of obvious fatigue.

"I'll ... um ... get you an extra blanket. Radio said it's gonna drop to the low forties," he stammered, practically leaping up and out of the kitchen with the haste of a man escaping a burning building.

Following slowly behind, the girl was forced to brace herself along the way to prevent possibly keeling over.

"Whoaaaa, Nelly. Think I might've overrated the old healing process. Knees feel like melted rubber and I'm gradually developing the mother of all migraines."

"I'll get you a Tylenol. Might help you sleep."

"Lord, you're a sweet guy, Joseph Clifford. How is it there's not a wife and children present in such a fine man's life?"

He departed the bedroom, careful not to bump her as he passed by, strolling purposefully through the kitchen and into the bathroom.

"Again, chapter two in the lengthy tale department. Here's your pills," he answered, offering her two tablets with an upturned palm.

"Gotcha. We'll talk tomorrow. The Joe Clifford story. Hopefully by morning I'll have a few of my own to pass on. Perchance to dream…"

Backing away, Joe stood at the cusp of the living room and began scratching his scruffy beard with both hands.

"I get the feeling it'll all start coming back to you once you're good and rested." "I *pray* so, Joe. I really do. Well, goodnight then," the girl whispered, having turned toward the bedroom entrance with a wobbly gait. "'Night. Sleep well and as long as you like."

Taking up a position on the couch a few moments later, Joe removed his thick cotton shirt, as well as the tee-shirt beneath it, and gave each a vigorous sniff.

"Holy *mackerel,* man. Take a bath already before the girl has you quarantined for excessive BO."

Approximately two hours later, as the big-handed clock hanging in the kitchen ticked just past midnight, he lay prone with his ankles and feet protruding from the edge of the couch like overgrown feelers from a mutated insect.

As with earlier that afternoon, he could just make out the girl's barely audible snoring from behind the bedroom's closed door.

My girl Joan J. Just where did you come from and where in blazes do you go from here?

While gradually drifting into what would easily become the deepest slumber he'd experienced in months, Joseph secretly hoped the rains would begin anew and add an additional blockade to any possible evacuation plans.

How strange, he pondered just before sleep overcame him, *how one's perceptions can be so drastically altered in such a short period of time.*

***

"Talk to me, dude. Who knows, perhaps I held a psych degree in my previous life. If nothing else, it might be therapeutic."

"Screeching pretty good, was I?"

"Bat outta hell material. Didn't so much wake but *shook* me out of the bed."

Combing his hair and then beard with the splayed fingers of his left hand, Joseph took a loud sip of coffee before responding.

"No productive dreams on your end, I take it? Or did I possibly interrupt some of the—"

The girl shook him off and frowned. "A few faint flashes, but nothing that made any sense. At least I know I'm still capable. Headaches finally gone. Guess sleep was the best remedy after all. Good call, Dr. Clifford."

"Well, fatigue does have its side effects. No telling how long it had been since you'd had a decent night's sleep. Sorry I woke you so early."

"I got the full eight hours. Any more might've just prolonged my grogginess.

What ... time is it?"

Leaning back, Joseph nodded toward the wall clock, which read 8:16 AM.

She nodded acknowledgement without speaking, and Joseph found himself instantly entranced by the natural fluidity in her every moment, the grace of which he found amazing for someone enduring such palpable mental anguish.

As the girl paused to nibble a cracker layered in cheese spread, he inhaled deeply and took in the sweet, aromatic smell emanating from her, a soapy/perfumy mix he found utterly intoxicating.

"Anyhow, back to you and those night terrors of yours," she said after washing down a mouthful with a swallow of chilled orange juice.

"You sure you want to hear this? Might just serve to induce that grogginess you mentioned earlier."

"I'm bound and determined to hear it. Stalling will only serve to feed my curiosity.

So shoot already, that is, unless it really is something you'd rather keep private."

Emptying the remains of his coffee cup, Joe leaned back and placed his hands behind his head, his grayish-brown hair sticking out from behind his ears in hopelessly warped, uneven riffs.

"No, no ... you're probably right. Maybe enough time's passed that talking might actually help."

"That's the spirit, doc," she beamed, casually reaching up to brush back several tuffs of hair that had fallen over her eyes. "Let it out. Who better to confide in than a hopeless amnesiac who might well forget everything you've divulged by this afternoon?"

Pausing for several moments as to properly organize his thoughts, Joseph then sighed deeply before speaking.

"After six and a half years as a correctional officer, I decided to attend the Police Academy the day after I turned thirty. I can't honestly recall ever being interested in anything other than law enforcement. I never wanted to do anything else.

Even as a preschool kid my mom said I always talked about putting away the bad guys."

"You're a ... you were a prison guard ... *and* a cop?" the girl asked, propping her elbows on the table and resting her chin within open palms.

"Protected and served the good, god-fearing populace of Wheeling, WV for just under nine years, yes, ,ma'am," he replied, jokingly puffing out his chest.

"Wow. It's just that you don't ... look the part."

"Scary what sixteen long months of self-loathing can do for one's looks, not to mention a diet consisting mostly of distilled firewater and beanie-weenie."

The girl lowered her eyes briefly, her cheeks turning a light shade of crimson. "I didn't mean ... you don't look *that* bad ... I mean ... awww, hell…"

"Forget it, Janey. No offense taken," he said with a laugh.

"Janey? Hey, I like it. Please continue while I finish retracting the foot from my mouth."

"Believe it or not, I was considered a real golden boy in those days. Worked patrol for five and a half years; made corporal at three and sergeant at six. Had accumulated fourteen felony arrests and a handful of awards and decorations. A real go-getter, that was me. Mr. Self-Motivation; Mr. ... Self-Starter. Within the department, I was cherished by the upper echelon and pretty much despised by the lower.

"Somewhere in between I met a young woman named Melody, who'd been hired as a records clerk. We married a few short months later. I'll come back to that particular soap opera in a bit. Right after I'd sewn on my sergeant's stripes, I requested and received a transfer to the narcotics division. A few months later, we received a tip about a rather large meth lab operating near Filmore Heights in the low-rent district.

Working undercover for several weeks, I gained the confidence of the man behind the lab and was eventually taken to the location. It was early spring that the…" he paused, then inhaled and exhaled several times—"bust went down. Uh…"

Grabbing his mug as he pushed away from the table, Joseph walked into the kitchen and proceeded to pour himself a refill consisting of half black coffee and half Jack Daniel's Black Label.

"Sorry…" he huffed, retaking his seat, "need a booster shot with a little more kick than just plain java can provide."

"Understood," the girl said, openly enthralled as she shifted nervously in her seat. "Well…" he cleared his throat, "… the lab itself was in an old industrial warehouse that the owner was living out of at the time. Perp was in his late twenties with a wife and small child. Came from a very, *very* affluent family who had all but washed their hands of him years earlier once the arrests had piled up.

"Anyhow, the night of the bust, a trusted informant had assured us that the guy's family was off the property. We'd been given the green light to take the place down by any means necessary, to include deadly force. Guy had three known associates, all felons, who weren't beyond breaking

244

out the hardware when the shit hit the fan ... uh ... sorry."

Rolling her eyes, the girl snickered.

"I've heard worse, Joe, I'm sure. Go on…"

"To say the very least, things didn't exactly go as planned." He paused. "Sure looked good on paper the morning we plotted 'er out, though."

Pausing for several large gulps, Joseph then lowered the mug and leaned his elbows onto the table, his eyes growing distant and glazed, as if he were gradually entering a time machine viewable solely within his own mind's eye.

"It seemed the man had been tipped off not only about the bust, but the true identity of yours truly, possibly just hours before the incident. By the time my eight-man unit arrived, the joint had already been lit up."

The girl raised her right hand like a student asking for permission to speak. "Joint was ... lit? You lost me…"

"They had torched ... um ... set the place on fire to destroy the lab." "Oh ... gotcha. Man, this is just like *Dragnet*."

"*Dragnet*? Lord, girl, how old are you again?"

"Not a clue, remember? Have to chalk that one up to classic TV reruns, I guess."

Nodding, Joe flashed a bemused grin.

"Can't recall her own name, but images of Joe Friday come through crystal clear."

"Sad, ain't it?" she asked with a mild shrug.

Taking still another healthy swig from the mug before proceeding, Joseph seemed to be undergoing a marked physical transformation. His forehead was suddenly slick from building perspiration; his shoulders noticeably scrunched and his hands visibly shaking.

"They must've just lit the fire, since the place was only beginning to flame up. Being that it was an older warehouse, we knew it wouldn't take long to turn to ash. The lieutenant in charge, hard-nosed jackass named Jakes, figured the suspects were miles away by then, so there really wasn't much to do save to maintain our positions until told otherwise. We didn't dare move any closer than fifty yards or so, since meth labs are notorious for blowing sky-high and taking everything within a city block with 'em.

"I gotta admit, I was one disappointed pup. I'd hoped to bust 'em on the scene while in the act of cooking their ticket ... um ... the drugs. At that point, we were basically just waiting for the fire department to arrive on scene. It was about the time we dropped our collective guards that the first shots rang out. It seemed the man and his crew were still inside after all."

Pausing yet again, he lowered his head a bit before resuming.

"Chuck Talley, a twelve-year vet and the unit's second in command, caught a nine mil slug dead center in the left eye. We'd all donned our SWAT gear for the bust, complete with Kevlar vests and headgear with bulletproof face shields, but ... I guess Chuck had removed his helmet for a sec in order to converse with Lieutenant Jakes.

The Talley-man was one hardnosed SOB at times, but no one in that unit had a better friend or

246

could ask for a better leader. He ... had four kids ... two of 'em still in grade school.

"My closest friend in the unit, Jimmy Ezop, had the lower part of his jaw blown away by a thirty-gauge slug. Last I heard, he was about to undergo his fifth surgery. Messed up his nervous system pretty bad too, I guess. Went through the academy with the guy ... shared a boatload of cool brew and good times. Jimbo had a warped sense of humor, as I did in those days ... shot severed his vocal cords. Last time I saw him, been almost a year now, he'd had to scribble out messages with a Sharpie."

"Lord ... what a shame," the girl whispered, seemingly unaware she'd spoken aloud.

"Masterson and Kendrick, two officers on loan from homicide division, caught slugs in the thigh and leg, respectively. I'd already taken a nosedive behind our command post van by that time, but saw both of 'em squirming on the pavement, covering their wounds and ... searching for cover." He paused and sighed deeply. "Sorry, throat's a little parched." He took in another mouthful from the mug.

"Well, after another thirty seconds or so, the sniper fire finally eased up to the occasional round. Lieutenant Jakes crawled over to my position, along with Kerry Blachard, a patrol sergeant who'd arrived on scene just as all hell had broken loose. Jakes was raving mad..." He laughed bitterly. "... I'm talking the type of red-eyed rage that transcends merely pissed off. I sincerely thought the man's head was gonna explode ... you know, like the guy that that old horror flick ... um..." He snapped his fingers. "... *Scanners*, that's it! Thing was, the man's condition was definitely contagious. All I could think about at that moment was finding the sons of bitches responsible and taking them out, and Jakes' 'let's kill those cowardly bastards' rants were just adding fuel to the inner fire. I'd seen my best friend's face come apart like a jigsaw puzzle just two feet from where I'd stood. Had the man's blood spattered on my face shield and vest. In other words, it didn't take much along the lines of chiding to spring this boy's rear into action."

Leaning back with a bemused expression, the girl ran her fingers through her hair while watching Joseph pause for still another drink.

"I realize we've been acquainted less than twenty-four hours, but I just can't picture you playing SWAT at a meth lab raid."

"Janey, these days, I can hardly picture it myself," he groaned after a muffled belch. "Honestly. It's really like I'm talking about someone else ... or describing something I saw in a B-grade movie."

"Believe me, whatever it is ... it isn't B-grade. So what happened next?"

"Jakes ordered the rest of the team to storm the warehouse and extract the shooters by any means necessary. That was the official wording. Unofficial translation: find the murdering SOBs and make 'em pay. Believe me, no one present raised a single finger to argue. We were *all* stoked to take a life. Besides, rat bastards started it, right?

"Me, Brad Anderson, and Detective Kendrick took point, sailing into and through the front entrance and directly into a wall of flame. Thinking back, and believe me ... I do on an hourly basis most days, we were damn lucky the backdraft effect didn't turn all three of us into Colonel Sanders' extra-crispy entrees. Then again, it was obvious that no one was taking the time to *think* at all. The lieutenant had lit our fuses but good, tossing all logic and good sense aside like so much bagged trash, and when the insanity starts at the top, there's normally a good-sized section of hell to pay somewhere down the line."

"Hmm, seems I've heard a similar line..." the girl mused, glancing toward the ceiling as the kitchen grew suddenly dimmer around them. "... Can't place when or where, but it was almost word for word."

Rising to stretch, Joseph strolled over to the kitchen sink and leaned forward, peeking through the window as if recreating a particular scene in his mind's eye.

"More than likely a bad TV cop drama. Hey, looks like the morning sun's taken the high road. Could be more liquid misery on the way."

"You sure we're not in Seattle, dude? I can't recall seeing this much rain since..." She halted abruptly, cocking her head to one side as a deep frown creased her otherwise faultless features. "... Waitaminnit ... now I remember ... that's the whole problem ... I can't *recall* at all!"

Hissing laughter, Joe sat back down and began tearing into a package of powdered donuts.

"You're a real card, you are," he mumbled between chews, white powder coating the perimeter of his beard and the corners of his mustache. "You know, I'm beginning to think you just might be a loooong way from home, what with all the 'dude' talk and the lack of any southern drawl to speak of."

Her eyes widened in sarcastic glee, an expression Joe had already grown to cherish.

"West coast possibly? Surfer girl maybe? Failed model/actress? Porn star on the lam perhaps…"

"Geez crow, enough already!" he blurted, spewing a fine mist of white powder airborne.

"You're right … I've gotten us waaaaaaaay yonder off track."

Eyeing her suspiciously, Joseph's wry grin revealed a thick chunk of mushy donut tucked snugly between his two front teeth.

"And I truly appreciate the purposeful diversion, young lady. I … think I needed a bit of levity ushered into the conversation. Good timing, that."

"You're very welcome, Joe. Now, finish the damn story before I bust…"

Wiping donut remnants from his hands with a moistened paper towel, Joseph then nodded, cleared his throat several times, and commenced.

Outside the barely eight-hundred-square-foot log cabin, a light rain began to refill puddles that hadn't yet had a chance to drain into Mother Earth's woefully oversaturated soil.

***

"Like I said, the place was pretty much an inferno by the time we dived into her belly like a

250

trio of raving pyromaniacs. Place was packed with wood pallets and metal bins ... most of 'em filled with cardboard boxes and the like ... all burning like lit candles.

"The ... three of us separated once we got inside, all sprinting down separate aisles. It was like ... we knew ... *I* knew, deep inside, that I was running straight to my own death. I'm talking surefire dead as a hammer ... but ... we were ... I was beyond caring. Temporary insanity, I guess. Rage can do savage things to a man's mind.

"I had the stock of my short-barreled twenty-gauge tucked so tight to my Kevlar vest it felt partially embedded. I remember clearly, and I'm talking slow-motion crystal clarity, turning a corner and seeing a shadow crouched in an empty ground-level bin. I ... think I started to scream 'freeze' or some similar malarkey, and that was about the time it felt like someone had pelted me in the breastbone with the rounded end of a claw hammer ... I mean ... Thump! Thump! Thump!" He lightly bumped his upper chest with a closed fist. "...just that quick. Next thing I know, I'm flat on my back and struggling mightily to suck in a fresh lungful of smoke.

"It ... gets ... got a little hazy then. I ... somehow I lost my headgear ... maybe I pulled it off, who knows? Regardless, I was squirming around between brushfires trying to find the shotgun when I saw the movement out of the corner of my left eye. I turned away just long enough to retrieve Old Faithful, receiving second-degree burns from the red-hot barrel for my efforts, then tumbled over a flaming pile of pallets. Somewhere in between the roll and the landing, I'd let fly with both barrels." He laughed. "I'm talking John Woo action-flick territory ... A Quentin Tarantino special, yes, sir. On the move ... from the hip ... midair hot dog target practice at its best. Not that ... I remember actually performing such cinematic stunt-double heroics, but ballistics tests bore it out in all its grisly detail.

"Anyway…" He paused and cleared his throat while wringing his hands nervously. "The movement I saw just seconds before hadn't been some smoke-filled mirage or bleary trick of light caused by the fires blazing all around me. If ... damn, if only it *could* have been. No such luck. Nope, the well of good fortune had run bone dry for the Golden Boy on this night.

"No ifs, ands, or buttholes, no, sir. Dry as desert dusk. Dry as a lakebed in Hell. Dry as ... he…"

He froze in mid-word, his lips still quivering and his eyes wide and unblinking. "Joe? Joseph, you ... all right?" the girl asked timidly, reaching over the table to place her hand atop both of his, which were clamped tightly together like twin vises. "Um ... uh ... yeah ... yeah," he replied, licking his lips, which had seemed to visibly chap within a matter of minutes. "…Yeah, I'm ... just ... It's been awhile since I've ... I haven't gone the distance on this particular tale in quite some time. Sorry for the zone-out. I'll ... be back with you in a minute."

"Listen, if you're not up to this, I understand. You can finish it later, or not at all. I ... never meant

252

to make light of it. I had no idea, really," she pleaded, patting his hand more forcefully.

Joseph swallowed hard, finally able to meet her gaze. The smile was wrenchingly sad; a freezeframe photo of unbridled misery.

"No ... no ... this is good. I ... think I've ... I think I've been needing this. I just never ... found the right person to ... unload on before now. It never helped with doctors. Too ... damned pat ... too rehearsed. But ... it's different with you. Not really sure why.

Maybe 'cause I know you have no agenda.

"I have to finish. Can't leave this ... untold. Not this time."

"All right, but don't think you have to continue torturing yourself on my account," she replied, smiling weakly. "Heck, I might not ever *remember* it tomorrow."

Joseph shrugged, grinning devilishly as his eyes again grew vacant. "What's so funny?" she queried.

"Nothing, except ... well, it's kind of ironic, actually, in a pathetic sort of way." "What's that?"

"As dreadful as your condition might seem to you, and I have no doubts it is, I do believe I just might trade my very soul for a nice, long bout with *permanent* amnesia."

"Maybe later I'll sneak up on ya and belt you over the head with a log or something," she quipped with a menacing stare.

Planting a clenched fist beneath his bearded chin and rolling his eyes toward the ceiling, Joseph considered this for a moment before verbally responding.

"Why not, right? Always worked on television. Just don't let me know it's coming. Surprise me."

The girl reached over and delivered a firm slap to his left shoulder. "You'll be the last to know, Joe."

"I would appreciate it. Well, station break's over. Here we go ... back to the show..." He sighed, twisting his neck about as if preparing for a strenuous physical workout.

***

"The meth lab blew sky-high less than five minutes after they dragged my carcass into the street, at least that's what I was told once I woke up at County General three or four hours after the fact. They said the top of that warehouse went up like a guided missile.

"After the shooting spree, I'd passed out from smoke inhalation. That's what the medical report stated, anyhow. Personally, I believe it was a combination of stress, smoke, and the feeling that somebody had shoved a pair of pruning sheers into my chest that did the trick. All told ... eight people bought it that night, including all three suspects. Besides Lieutenant Jakes, we also lost Brad Anderson. Took 'em about two days of shifting through the charred remains of that warehouse to locate him, but its was damn obvious by that time that the boy hadn't sneaked out and caught a redeye to the Bahamas, you know?

"They kept me overnight for observation before releasing me the next morning. My section chief,

Captain Corey Phillips, met me there and escorted me home. As I recall, the man was pretty tight-lipped on the half-hour drive to my hacienda, a far cry from his usual talkative self. It wasn't until we were sharing a cup of joe on my back deck that Cap ... filled me in on all the details I'd missed while comatose. "

He sighed heavily and wiped building perspiration from his brow.

"Contrary to what had been reported, the main suspect had yet to relocate his family when the raid went down. Girl was in her early twenties ... little girl had ... just turned five. They, being the powers that be, figured that from the positioning of ... the bodies, well..." He paused and wiped his brow once again. "... The perp had spotted me through the smoke and flames and made a dash for the nearest exit, using his family as ... well, a human shield."

"Oh god," the girl whispered wide-eyed, covering her mouth with the palm of her left hand while reaching to caress Joseph's right forearm with the other.

"'Course, I had ... no idea. I was firing on instinct and ... out of blind fear and fury.

The human shield theory originated from the shot ... totals and patterns on each victim. The bodies had been singed but left intact, so outlining the origin of the various wounds was no problem. The woman had taken three, one to the left thigh, one in the abdomen and last to the breastbone. The little girl had..." He paused; his moistening eyes darted from side to side. "... one to the chest and ... one that had ... ricocheted off her right shoulder.

Meanwhile, Darren Danley, drug dealer, heavy user, and son of Douglas Ray Danley, one of the state's ten richest men, had taken but a single shot. A shot that essentially sheared the top portion of his head away. A shot that was later determined to be the same slug that had grazed his baby girl's shoulder. From all indications, it seems the man had been holding his own child airborne like a riot shield just to avoid ... still hard to fathom that ... it really, *really* is. I just ... can't get my head around such ... evil really existing, despite all I'd seen in previous cases.

"Positive ID was made via dental records, since the fire had burned their ... faces away by the time the bodies were discovered. I ... never saw either the woman or her daughter in person, just splashed across newspaper print for the next few months.

Local and national media sank their teeth in up to the gums once all the sordid details starting leaking out.

"I was placed on desk duty until the board hearing a few weeks later. Gotta say ... it was a moot point by that juncture. I was way beyond giving a shi—um, beyond caring. All I could see was the little girl's face, specifically the photo the local newshounds used; smiling all wide and toothy with her hair set in pigtails. Saw that smile everywhere; swirling about in my coffee cup in the morning and floating on the ceiling above me at night. After a while, I was seeing her more often at the bottom of a Jack Daniel's bottle. Every little girl I saw on TV morphed into her; every little girl on the street owned that very same smile; the same braces; the same damn pigtails.

Departmental shrink labeled my condition the 'clone phase.' Said it was simply the guilt feeding my subconscious, and that it would pass over time. Prescribed me a mild sleep aid and suggested nightly quiet time and deep breathing exercises for the stress. I recall reaching over to shake the man's hand at some point and congratulating him, in my best sarcastic tone, on such a phenomenal diagnosis. No wonder they get the big bucks, right? Doc 'Einstein' also said those midnight banshee howls would vanish about the same time." He laughed. "Hey, so far, so good ... NOT!"

"How long ago was ... the shooting?" the girl asked softly, stroking his arm a final time before removing her hand.

"A few scant days past sixteen months now," he groaned, while rubbing both eyes. "May sound overly dramatic to say, but there are days it feels more than sixteen years."

"I ... can only imagine. So ... you resigned your position?"

"My position ... my marriage, pretty much my life as I'd known it." "Your wife...did she try to support you through it all?"

Leaning forward, Joseph lay his forehead flush across the tabletop, folding his hands across the back of his neck.

"She gave it the token try, I guess. Can't honestly say I ever really noticed. I was in the deepest funk imaginable and not the easiest person to converse with.

Besides, we'd been on the outs long before all the shit came down at that meth lab. Sorry ... pardon the French. There is a rather bizarre side note to this sad, dreary tale."

"Go on..."

"The perp's parents, mainly his father Douglas, supposedly had Windy City mob ties dating back decades. Big money ties. Something to do with a gambling operation in Jersey. Anyhow, I was told there was an outside chance that a bounty had been placed on my head. Seems the suspect's father was none too thrilled that a local cop had shot and killed his granddaughter. None of this was ever officially substantiated."

"You're ... talking about a ... hit?"

"Yep. That was the scuttlebutt anyway. Can't say the talk ever really bothered me. I was so far into prescription sleep aids and Tennessee firewater by that time a cub scout could've smothered me with a pillow without much resistance. Gave me another excuse to push the wife away for good. Scared the hell out of her thinking she might open the hall closet one afternoon and discover a mob specialist waiting inside."

"You ... think about it much now?"

"Nah. I mean, it's been almost a year and a half. If they were gonna take revenge, it would've already happened. Old man Danley probably learned of my mental state since the shooting and figured killing me would be akin to doing me a favor."

"And ... you've been holed up here ever since?" Joseph scratched his chin thoughtfully.

"Personally, I prefer 'taking time to meditate and reevaluate,' but I guess holed up works just as well."

The girl leaned back and addressed him through tightly squinting eyes. "Sixteen months is a lot of meditation, dude."

Looking around instead of directly into her searing gaze, Joseph felt his scalp begin to tingle. It was as if someone had rubbed a handful of itching powder into the wavy rifts atop his bushy noggin. Some time later, while replaying the conversation in his mind, he would come to the rather unsettling resolution that the allergic-type reaction he'd felt was tied to nothing more elaborate than simple embarrassment. A deep-rooted shame had come to head, triggered by the most unlikely of sources; a mysterious female whom he'd known less than a full day. A woman without an identity, but who seemed to possess a toughness and internal fortitude he'd long since abandoned, replaced by self-induced bouts of depression and pity. He'd felt a rush of shame sweep over his senses like a viral infection. Shame over his appearance; his mental complacency; his truly pathetic existence.

"Well, there is that. It ... isn't like a part of me wouldn't like to rejoin society as a productive human being. Timing just hasn't been right, that's all. I'm ... shooting for January actually. New Year's resolutions and all that happy crap, you know?"

"Sound reasonable. Let's make it a double on the resolution part," she injected cheerily, lifting her coffee cup in a mock toast. "Here's hoping I at least

259

know my own name by the New Year, and maybe even a substantial memory or two."

Joe nodded kindly in response, temporarily lost in the deep hazel twinkle of her eyes. here."

"You up to some fresh air, Janey? I feel like a walk. Air's getting kind of stale in Rising from the table with a graceful stretch, the girl's knees and elbows cracked and popped from apparent stiffness.

"I'm with you, dude. Need to work out some mechanical issues. I get the feeling I was never the 'getting back to nature' type, but then again, I could be wrong. Let's go suck in some mountain air."

They departed the cabin some ten minutes later, the midmorning chill still evident in the frosty air seeping from their lips. As they stepped from the wooden porch onto the soggy grass, Joseph instinctively took the lead, and was subsequently shocked and elated upon feeling the girl's hand search out and find his own, filling his palm with soothing warmth as they trekked slowly down the gravel path leading to Paradise Road.

At one point, she turned and spotted a neatly stacked pile of firewood taking up space between two oak saplings.

"You fibbed," she said softly, suppressing a yawn.

"How's that?" he said, following suit but unable to refrain as he reached to cover his mouth.

"You said that sling-blade thing was the lone weapon in the grizzly bear-fighting arsenal."

"I'm not following…"

"Lot of chopped wood back there. You accomplish that with your hands, Kung Fu?"

"Oh, yeah…" he nodded as they split to circle around the squared remains of an ancient tree trunk. "… Got an axe hiding around here somewhere. Got to let off steam somehow, butterfly. Why are you so concerned with the lack of firepower?"

"Not really sure," she replied with a frown, "as with everything else, it seems."

They walked in silence for several minutes until the girl almost tripped over a fallen branch that had hugged her ankle.

"Sorry about the wardrobe, especially those shoes," he said apologetically, though unable to keep from chuckling at the sight of her. "Just tread slowly and veeeery carefully."

"Beggars can't be choosers, dude," she said, leaning to playfully nudge his shoulder. "Besides, look at the bright side. If we're swept up by a sudden tidal wave, these size fifteen clodhoppers of yours can double as pontoon boats."

Forced to overcompensate for the comically oversized boots by lifting her legs much higher than normal, the girl resembled the backwoods version of an SS storm trooper, goose-stepping her way clumsily forward.

"Just a pair of hopelessly lost souls, aren't we, Joe?" she asked softly, her hand noticeably shaking within his loose grasp.

"That we are, Janey. Only temporarily, though. Only temporarily."

***

"Maybe you were on the Olympic team," Joseph cracked, watching in awe as the girl began her third set of one-armed pushups in the center of the living room floor. Her arms and shoulders were noticeably pumped, and moistened with fresh sweat. "I'm exhausted just watching you."

"Must be the ham sandwich, soup, and coffee diet you put me on," she huffed, flipping over and immediately executing a frenzied set of crunches. "Whatever the source, I've got energy to burn."

Sidestepping by her to take a seat on the couch, Joseph held a lit cigarette in one hand and a jelly glass half filled with Southern Comfort in the other.

It was only his third taste of hard liquor since he'd bared his soul to her a day and a half earlier. Since that time, the two had spent literally every waking moment together, sharing the daily workload and the downtime in between while seemingly nurturing a tried and true friendship that had never before existed. To witness them together would be to assume they'd known one another for years, more than likely a married couple savoring a well-earned respite from the rat race while rediscovering what each adored about the other. Unbeknownst to his mystery guest, Joseph fought a constant battle to refrain from thoughts of attempting to consummate their budding relationship in a more physical sense.

"Amazing. Less than forty-eight hours ago you were as weak as a newborn kitten. Now you're the proverbial ball of fire. I still say it's a safe bet you were training for some 'Iron Woman' triathlon when you bumped your noggin."

Pausing between sets to catch her breath, the girl eyed him through her spread knees. Wearing the same tee-shirt and spandex shorts he'd originally found her in (having been hand washed in the bathroom sink the night before), her meticulously chiseled physique was on display as never before; pumped, cut and sculpted to near flawless perfection.

"Oh, I dunno, Joe. Seems a bit far-fetched. I ... can't pinpoint why, but I really don't think I have any ties to sports except on a purely recreational level. Heck, more than likely I spend my days counting corporate beans while tucked inside some dark cubicle, working out just to blow off excess stress *and* calorie buildup."

"Maybe you work at a gym ... personal trainer or aerobics instructor," he countered, puffing smoke from each nostril while bringing the ice-filled glass toward his lips.

The girl nodded as to possibly agree while leaping to her feet. As though driven by natural instinct alone, she began an impromptu session of shadow boxing, her clenched fists filling the vacant air with a succession of jabs, hooks, uppercuts, and combinations even as her feet shuffled gracefully from side to side like those of an experienced, skillfully trained boxer.

"Um, excuse me, *Sugar Ray* Doe, but what ... gives?" Joe asked, accidentally spitting a crushed ice cube onto his shirt in the process.

"Your guess is as good as mine, Dr. Clifford. Pretty good though, huh?" she retorted in a tone ripe with sincere astonishment, winding up her left arm in a mock Ali impersonation while shuffling backwards into the kitchen.

Her shoulders, arms, and upper chest gleamed with sweat, prompting Joseph to ask a question that he'd previously sidestepped as perhaps a bit too intrusive.

"So what's up with the skull and crossbones body art, anyway?"

Continuing to punch away with machinelike precision, her reply was predictably glib.

"You seriously expect an answer?"

"Oh, yeah, right. I keep forgetting. Maybe you were just fond of pirates. Think maybe you hail from Pittsburgh?"

She merely rolled her eyes in mock disgust and concluded the shadow boxing exhibition with a final, furious series of lightning-quick jabs.

Leaning over the back of the couch until he thought it might tip over from the strain, Joseph watched her pose near the kitchen table, then begin a complicated set of martial arts movements that were executed with a fluidity and grace he'd rarely witnessed.

"My lord, woman," he whispered before gulping down the remainder of his drink in two quick swallows, "where in blazes *did* you come from?"

***

"You sure about this? I mean, maybe they have some kind of radical treatment these days. Can't hurt…"

264

"I'll…pass for now, Joe. There'll be time for all the pokes and prods. I'm not denying the old skull massage isn't in my near future. It's just that, right now I can't think of a better treatment than the R&R I'm getting at the Clifford Bed and Breakfast, located smack dab in the heart of downtown Middle of Nowhere, US of A."

They sat across from one another at the kitchen table, sipping steaming cups of coffee while picking at separate plates of scrambled eggs and toast.

As had been the norm the past several nights, they had retired early (just after nine PM) and rose early (just past five-thirty). An early morning walk (also becoming a daily ritual) to the edge of Paradise Road had revealed still semi-boggy but passable ruts that had finally been allowed to substantially drain in the two rain-free days since the last downpour.

"Well, you know best," he sighed, lighting up his first smoke of the young day (though he would have normally sucked down at least three by breakfast's end). "I'll pick you up a few cotton shirts and a couple of pairs of blue jeans. What was that shoe size again … seven?"

"And a half … medium. Don't forget to save those receipts, dude. I'm paying you back with interest, whether you like it or not, " she barked sternly, holding an oversized mug with an inscription that read HOKIES RULE in faded black lettering.

"You can try, lady. Doesn't mean you'll succeed. Joe Clifford does favors for few, and doesn't want to hear a lot of guff about it later."

She was sitting on the couch as he strolled through the living room toward the front door, the truck's keys jingling loudly as he flipped the ring in a tight circle around his forefinger. The morning sun bathed her face through the spread blinds of the room's lone window, and she squinted just slightly while hugging her knees to her chest. As with just about every pose she struck or movement she executed, Joe couldn't help but be haplessly mesmerized as stout waves created of equal parts longing and lust clutched his chest in a binding vise.

"Janey, you sure you don't want to ride into town with me? Might just open up a few doors in the old memory bank. Besides, I still think you ought to see a doc—"

She waved him off with an open palm, her tone kind but stern.

"Maybe in a couple of days. I hope you don't mind. I mean, this is your cabin and I'll do as you wish ... it's just that ... I've ... I'm thinking I'm on the verge of remembering something."

"Really? You didn't mention—"

"Well, I really ... wasn't sure. I've been getting some really strange vibes since sacking out last night," she continued, her voice reeking with emotion as she hugged herself ever tighter. "There were ... flashes in the night. Not dreams really ... or maybe they were. Images, I guess you'd say. Almost like daydreaming when you're just on the very edge of sleep."

"I got you. Been there often," he replied solemnly through eyes that grew temporarily distant.

"I think a few more days of peace and tranquility is just what I need for those images to clear up ... to appear more concise until maybe they actually make some sense."

"See any faces or places that seem at all familiar?"

"Nothing concrete ... but it's coming, man," she answered in a flat, toneless voice that inadvertently sent shivers racing up Joseph's spine at breakneck speed. "The contrast is still bleary and littered in *swinging*, psychedelic colors, but gets a bit clearer every time it tunes in."

"Good," he managed in a hoarse croak while pulling the front door ajar, "good deal. Maybe you'll find the right channel while I'm gone."

"Don't be long, dude," she replied with just a tint of barely restrained desperation. "Becky Thatcher ain't shit without Tom Sawyer, ya know."

Walking out to his truck as his boots dug into and out of the moistened clay with loud sucking sounds, Joseph Clifford became acutely aware of two distinct facts, which there was no point denying.

Number one: he was head-over-heels, head-pounding, heart aching to the point of flatlining, flat-out crazy in love with the walking, talking female enigma presently sharing his forest retreat home. Since it had been so long since he'd felt anything but numbness toward society as a whole, the surges of pure elation he'd experienced in her presence the past several days had reopened doors he'd long thought permanently bolted from the inside. Best of all, he was almost certain she felt the

267

same way. He prayed she did. Prayed hard. It had been awhile since he'd bothered to address a higher power on subject matter not related to self-loathing and/or pity. So much for the good. It was fact *number two* that threw an anvil-sized wrench into the budding romantic works.

That being: he had a growing, gnawing fear, however illogical and/or ridiculous, that very soon someone or something was going to attempt to thwart the pair's budding relationship before it had hardly begun. Initially he'd chalked up such bleak thoughts to natural pessimism. Since the incident and breakup of his marriage, he'd long since become both a believer and staunch advocate of Murphy's Law. It was becoming apparent, however, that the feelings of stark dread gripping his gut on an hourly basis weren't merely the result of negative thinking. While navigating the pickup over multitudes of fallen branches and through foot-deep ruts on his way toward Route 43, Joseph tried unsuccessfully to pinpoint the origin of such outlandish and, as yet, unsubstantiated fears.

***

He purchased two pairs of size five blue jeans, three medium cotton tee-shirts in red, blue, and black, and a pair of Reebok tennis shoes, white with red stripes (size 7½) at Kmart, along with a medium-sized blue jean jacket and three pairs of ladies' socks.

As for groceries from the local Kroger-mart, the list of acquisitions included the usual (canned soups and vegetables, crackers, cereal), the unusual (fresh fruits, soymilk, yogurt), and the downright extravagant (fresh rib eye and sirloin steaks, baking potatoes), the latter items acquired solely for a surprise cookout he'd planned for that very afternoon. The hardware store was next, the truck bed soon lined with ten five- gallon containers of generator fuel.

Although not bypassing the stop altogether (such a potentially shocking act had, however, been briefly considered), the liquor store visit had been his least expensive, least extensive since his relocation to the cabin, with a single case of beer loaded into a truck bed that normally held at least three along with several fifths of assorted whiskies. Even the cashier had appeared to notice the marked dropoff, shooting Joseph a solemn *is this all*? glance at checkout.

Departing town at just past noon with the sun's rays warming his upper back and shoulders, Joseph marveled at both his own euphoric mood and in the miraculous wonder that there hadn't been a single clone phase incident since he'd left the cabin.

Truly, he deduced with a wide, toothsome grin, this mysterious visitor; this magnificent, alluring stranger; this enigmatic angel sharing his cabin was some sort of magical, healing muse, sent from the man upstairs to rescue his weary, battered soul. There simply was no other worldly explanation for such a rapid transformation in his way of thinking and feeling. Ten months and he'd only been able to push aside that little girl's memory for half-hour durations at best, and only then when so woefully inebriated that recalling his own name had been a Herculean struggle. Suddenly, out of the blue, out of literally *nowhere*, Jane Doe emerges from the forest and within a matter of days he is again able to interact with other people without breaking into a cold sweat or gradually losing the power of speech as every nerve ending in his body ignites in an electrically charged overload. Best yet, he is able to view the children he sees as they truly are; as individual souls and not walking, talking clones of a dead girl resurrected through his own inner guilt.

Still, despite all the positive vibes, Joseph realized the vital need to reel in, to refrain from overextending such joyful emotions in lieu of reality. There was, of course, the distinct (and therein logical) possibility that the girl's arrival and his newly discovered healing were complete coincidences; that perhaps the mere company of another human being after such a lengthy stretch of playing drunken introvert had assisted in turning the emotional tide. Then again, he also knew for certain how he felt about the woman, and it went far beyond any mere schoolboy crush. True, he knew nothing of her former life or what specific incident or incidents had landed her in his neck of the woods. The cold hard fact remained that he didn't even know her name, for cripes' sake.

Regardless, the connection had been made from the moment they'd met. Cornball as it sounded, fickle fate had intervened, and their meeting was meant to be, or whatever reason; a reason that might forever remain as mysterious as her past.

Roughly twenty minutes later, while turning off Route 43 onto the muck-covered, rut-ravaged trail leading to the cabin, Joseph did his dead-letter best to remain positive but not without allowing a wide length of slack for impending negativity. The inexplicable fear he'd felt upon departure was creeping back into place, almost as if putting distance between himself and the cabin had somehow cloaked its presence.

Swallowing hard, he allowed the truck's speed to increase just slightly. Despite the midday warmth, a sudden chill coated the exposed flesh of his face, neck and arms.

It wasn't until he'd neared an ancient, crooked oak that served as the halfway point down the trail that a fresh wave of dread punched his midsection like a heavyweight jab. Gasping, he temporarily lost the power to breathe. Thick clumps of mud slung airborne as he gunned the accelerator and barely avoided spinning off the trail into a deep, rainwater-filled ravine.

"I'm coming, Janey..." he mumbled between gritted teeth, gripping the steering column in a vise as the knuckles of both hands turned reddish-purple, "... just hang on ... I'm almost ... there."

***

From a distance, both the cabin and surrounding grounds appeared normal enough. He'd parked the truck a few hundred yards up the road and trekked the remaining way on foot, cutting through the saturated forest with a slightly rusted lug wrench secured tightly in a clenched fist. Sucking wind while leaning against the thickened base of a gigantic pine, he prayed the stout waves of paranoia that had triggered such irrational behavior would prove to be woefully unjustified. His pulse pounded like thunder at his temples and neck as he scanned the area a final time before pushing forward and sprinting toward the cabin, the lug wrench reared back as to strike.

Crawling onto the planked porch on his knees, he saw the front door was pushed slightly ajar. Creeping forward, his nostrils flared just as he reached for the knob. The scent of gunsmoke was unmistakable. As he lunged forward and crashed through with his left shoulder leading the way, Joseph was fairly certain his heart had temporarily ceased beating and taken up an uneasy residence at the midway point of his throat.

"Wellll ... Welcome back, Kotter ... I was beginning to worry," he heard the voice blurt out in a shockingly casual tone just as his combat roll ended at the center of the room with the rounded end of the lug wrench poking at his ribs.

The girl stood at one end of the couch with her hands propped definitely on her hips.

"Great entrance, though I gotta say you telegraphed the surprise with the preceding stakeout. Dude, it sounded like a herd of elephants thrashing through those woods. Either that, or I've discovered yet another hidden talent I had no earthly clue I possessed."

If asked under oath, Joseph would've confessed to hearing only a portion of his Jane Doe's dialogue, as the majority of his concentration had fallen upon the unidentified man bound and gagged to one of the high-backed wooden chairs normally kept tucked underneath the kitchen table.

"Um, J-Jane ... who the hell is ... that?" he babbled, scrambling unsteadily to his feet while pointing toward the stranger with the sharp end of the wrench.

"Joseph, I've been waiting rather impatiently for the past fifteen minutes to ask you the very same question," she replied, running a hand through her short-coiffed hair as her eyes darted from Joseph to the bound man and back again several times. "Not an old friend of yours, I take it?"

Pacing the sparse area behind the couch, Joseph kept the lug wrench reared back despite the obvious unconscious state of their mysterious visitor. She had literally mummified the man in duct tape, securing him at the chest, knees, and ankles. His hands had been similarly bound to the chair arms, and his mouth gagged by a tightly coiled, dark blue handkerchief. There was blood leaking freely from both the man's nostrils, as well as a series of deep slash marks across his left cheekbone.

"Never saw 'im before. You?"

Frowning, the girl shrugged her shoulders and turned her hands palms up. "No, but then ... I can't really know for certain."

"Sorry ... I ... forgot for a second. Shit, I could use a belt," Joseph retorted, briefly flashing a shaky smile while circling around the couch to join her at the far end. The girl sidestepped over and nudged him playfully, and Joseph allowed the wrench to gradually fall to chest level.

"I know the feeling, believe you me."

"Good lord," he groaned upon first noticing the overall condition of the living room, to which the term complete shambles came instantly to mind. "Where ... what happened? How did ... what did he do ... *how* did you—"

Patting him on the back like a consoling parent to a frustrated child, the girl's steely gaze nevertheless rarely departed her slumped, unmoving quarry. Meanwhile, Joseph's entire frame began to shake and shimmy as he took in the whole of the destruction; the shattered dining table and lamp stand, the overturned bookcase and splintered kitchen chairs. Shards of wood and glass scattered about as if blown apart by a detonated grenade.

"Whoa, just calm down and catch a breath, Joe ... just take it slow. Remember your training. Breathe in ... blow out. Inhale ... exhale."

"Well," he blurted angrily, stopping just short of slapping her hand from the pit of his back, "did he ... break in ... or ... or what?"

"Oh, yeah, he broke in all right ... breaking and entering in a most dramatic fashion, ya might say, with a dozen or more rounds of nine millimeter ammo leading the way. See his handiwork?" she said, motioning toward the front door and wall of the cabin. They were riddled with bullet holes, at least three of which had passed through to the kitchen to punch through the back wall.

"Dude, I was damn lucky to be in the kitchen at the time that initial round tore through these papier-maché walls. Spent the next two minutes playing cockroach, rolling and scrambling around on the floor in search of a suitable hole to leap into.

Needless to say, that was one tall order." "But ... how did you ... I mean…"

Looking to the girl and then back to the man several times, Joseph's pained expression was one of comical bewilderment.

"Correct me if I'm wrong, Joe, but I believe what you're trying so desperately to inquire is how come I'm still standing upright and Dirty Harry over here is the one who appears to have been ridden extremely hard and put away wet."

His shoulders slumping, he then nodded in apparent relief.

"It's a blur, really. I do recall the door flying open ... believe he entered using a bootheel key."

She paused in wake of Joseph's befuddled expression. "He kicked his way in," she added with a roll of the eyes. "Oh, gotcha ... go on."

"Well, from there bullets were being sprayed around and he was yelling something ... damned if I know what. He could've been reading off a Chinese menu for all I understood. At some point, I heard him pause to reload his peashooter and decided to come out of hiding and offer a proper greeting."

"And?" Joseph chimed in after a lengthy pause.

"Well," she shrugged, biting her lower lip, "from that point onward is where the blurry part commences."

"You remember tying him up?"

"Yeah, parts, though he wasn't in any shape to put up a struggle. I only left 'im long enough to police the grounds in case he wasn't alone."

Moving stiffly, Joseph ran a hand through his disheveled locks and stepped in front of the man before kneeling to better study the bonds securing him. In garnering a closer look, he noted obvious fractures of the pinky and ring finger of the man's left hand, both of which looked to have been severely twisted or perhaps stomped upon with great force. Scratching the back of his own neck, Joseph felt equal doses of awe and fear in terms of the woman standing just to his left.

"Any ID on him or did you look?"

"No ID, nope ... no wallet ... but ... um..." she responded timidly, seemingly wavering to complete the thought. The reaction was not lost on Joseph, who eyed her curiously.

"Well? What *did* you find?"

Sidestepping away, she paced behind the couch with her hands tucked at the pit of her back. Joseph noticed for the first time the dried bloodstains on her fingers and wrists and deduced the prisoner's facial wounds no longer a mystery worth pursuing.

"It's ... it doesn't look good."

"Jesus, Janey ... tell me. I need to get to the bottom of why a man I've never laid eyes on seemed damned determined to kill everyone or everything residing inside this cabin."

"From what you've told me of your past, it really doesn't take a neurosurgeon," she replied grimly, turning her back to him and bending down

276

to retrieve something from the fractured rubble of what had been the dining table.

"Pulled this little jewel from his interior vest pocket."

She turned and flipped him a yellow-tinted, legal-sized envelope that was folded neatly at the center.

"On one hand, it makes perfect sense. On the other ... well ... I don't have a blessed clue."

Joseph quickly pulled the contents free, tossed the envelope aside, and studied each item in equal ten- to twelve-second durations before turning his sole attention back to the man who'd originally possessed them. Other than a rather prominent nose and a set of close-set eyes, the man's overall looks held no special distinction. He appeared to be in his mid to late thirties, medium height and weight with dark brown hair thinning slightly at the top. Though difficult to be precise in such an overabundance of duct tape, the assassin's choice of clothing for such a desolate locale seemed logical enough; faded blue jeans, dark black tee with matching multipocketed vest and heavy-duty hiking boots.

"Well, shit. Looks like I underestimated a father's grief after all. Damn, I could sure use a stiff belt about now."

The girl knelt beside him, reaching over to reclaim the two photos from his open palm.

"So you think this Delaney fella you told me about arranged this?"

"Danley. Douglas Danley. Yeah, logically it's the only thing that makes sense, though I can't

277

figure why it took him so damned long to execute the plan. Surely to God I wasn't that hard to find."

Rising with a grunt, she held each picture in a separate hand and alternated glances at each.

"Yeah, I kinda figured as much but wasn't going to say until I knew we were both fishing at the same hole. So now I must ask you to riddle me this…"

Having been focused on a steady stream of fresh blood bubbling forth from their captive's right nostril, Joseph escaped the entrancement long enough to match her rather intense stare.

"Presuming you *were* this dude's prime target, photo number one makes complete sense. As for number two, how exactly do *I* fit into the plot?"

"How old do you think the picture is?" "You're kidding, right?"

"Guesstimate then."

"Well, hair's longer … kind of funky looking, hard truth be told … nineties retro at its worst. I dunno, Joe, could've been snapped five years ago or late last week for all I know."

Peeking out the bullet-marked front door, Joseph scanned the grounds for any movement or sound unrelated to a deep forest setting. Not surprisingly, the natural instincts of a trained lawman seemed to have returned with very little in the way of rust to shake off. Deep down there was a part of him that relished the rush of adrenalin, the stench of danger. He'd figured that particular gene long eradicated, burned away by countless gallons of alcohol and just as many doses of self-pity.

"Regardless, it's a lead-pipe cinch it wasn't taken since I found you wandering around in the forest."

"Safe bet there, amigo," she laughed, joining him at the door. "Anything moving other than the crickets?"

"Looks calm enough, but we'd better not hang out too much longer. Once this guy doesn't call his contact to confirm the hit, it's only a matter of time before a second wave moves in."

"Shit, this is just like a movie," she said, flashing a nervous grin, "only I've got the weirdest vibe that ... that I've played a similar role before. Damn, talk about your déjà vu all over again sensations…"

The brief, eerie silence that followed between them was broken by a low, muffled moan.

"What say we attempt to get us some answers, then?" Joseph asked with a wink as they strolled purposefully toward their captive, whose eyes remained closed even as his head began to bob and wobble.

"Sounds like a plan, and where better to start then straight from the horse's ass ...

I mean mouth…" she answered in an overly chipper tone that Joseph found both strangely exhilarating and a bit disturbing.

***

"Come to, jackass. We ain't got all day."

After flipping the coiled hanky over her right shoulder like some bloodsoaked bridal bouquet, she squeezed his lower jaw with her left hand and began to shake fiercely; first up and down and then from left to right.

"Jane ... Janey ... careful or he's gonna pass out again…" Joseph pleaded, stopping short of reaching over and grasping her arm.

The man's left eye popped open just as she removed her grip and stepped back.

The right soon followed suit, blinking rapidly as if to properly focus. The man's lips quivered and he swallowed hard several times before gagging and coughing up a blackish swirl of saliva and blood onto his chin and upper chest.

"Well, howdy there, Chuckles. What say we have us a little pow-wow?"

***

"Wh-what did you say? Please repeat minus the rolling marbles effect."

Between coughing fits, the man had mumbled something that only the girl had managed to partially comprehend. She leaned ever closer, until her right ear was mere inches from his trembling lips. Joseph, standing to the girl's right, was again unable to hear anything resembling actual words, despite the still, dead air within the tiny cabin.

"Shit!" the girl shrieked, jerking back and grasping Joseph's left bicep. Following her abrupt exit from his personal space, the man had clamped his eyes shut and winced as if expecting a physical assault.

"What? What did he say?"

"H-he ... called me ... by a name. He ... he knows me, Joe. He…" "What ... what else?"

"He ... asked me ... he asked me *why*."

Firmly removing her vise-like grip from his fast-numbing forearm, Joseph then turned her toward him and grasped her shoulders. He saw the blood had drained from her face; her eyes grew distant, obviously peering directly past him and into a plane of consciousness viewable only by herself.

"Asked you why? Why *what*, Janey? Why what?"

"My ... my name is Brandi. I ... think that's right. Yes, it is ... Brandi…"

He tried to snap the semi-hypnotic trance by reaching up and massaging her head on both sides and staring directly into her unblinking, startlingly bright hazel eyes.

"Okay, Brandi ... please focus. What did he mean by why?"

"You are o-one ultrafortunate s-son of a bitch," he heard the man grumble between garbled coughs.

"Say what?" Joseph barked angrily, temporarily forgetting the girl and whirling about on his right heel until he loomed directly over their prisoner.

"I said ... you are about the luckiest fu-fucker I've ... ever ... met…"

"And why's that, prick? Because I wasn't home to witness the precision and expert touch of such a great assassin? Hate to break it to you, pal, but you got your ass handed to you by an unarmed, 110-pound female amnesiac, so I'm not real sure you oughta be tootin' your own horn about now."

The man's raucous laughter was interrupted by the occasional hack, fresh tears spewing from both eyes, his tightly bound chest straining in disapproval. From the corner of his left eye, Joseph could see the girl mumbling to herself while constantly gesturing with both hands, as if in the middle of a particularly engrossing two-way conversation.

"Je—Jesus ... you know, for a former cop, y-you are ... you are one dense motherfuc—" he blabbered until the first round drilled a dime-sized hole into the center of his forehead. The man's head whipped back violently and then forward with equal force until his chin rested atop his chest, revealing a mass void where brains, skull and scalp once occupied. Just as he instinctively dropped to the floor, Joseph saw the second round strike the dead man's left shoulder. Covering his own head with both arms, Joseph crawled over to where the girl had been standing just as a third shot shattered the deceased man's left kneecap.

"Jan ... Brandi! Get down! Get..."

"Your brass is hanging out, Joe ... get back here!" he heard her bellow as still another round tore through the front wall and into parts unknown.

Wriggling forward on his stomach, he slid into the kitchen where the girl had turned the dining table up onto its side as a makeshift barricade.

"Looks like Chuckles had a partner after all," she growled while holding the table upright with a booted foot. As Joseph slid in beside her, he noticed the serrated kitchen knife she'd tucked into her spandex shorts' waistband.

"Planning on carving a turkey?" he quipped as all grew eerily quiet.

Dropping her voice to a harsh whisper, the girl shoved the square table forward until its elongated top smacked either side of the kitchen entrance.

"Hey, it was either this or a corkscrew. You ain't exactly prepped for combat, ya know."

"Well ... about *that* ... follow me. There's a space I never showed you," he replied grimly, scooting back into the far left corner of the kitchen and reaching up to retrieve a long-handled flashlight from an otherwise empty cabinet.

Pulling back a faded layer of grayish carpet to reveal a planked cellar door, Joseph sighed heavily before reaching down to grasp a small wooden handle.

"It's an old root cellar ... you might say I expanded it a bit upon my arrival at the cabin in a fit of paranoia ... hoped and prayed I'd never have to use it. Here, take the light and watch your step going down..."

"Not to doubt your motives or anything," she frowned, gripping the flashlight and peering over his right shoulder and into the blackness below, "but what exactly is the plan? Hide out in this hillbilly panic room until we're found, cornered, and executed?

Nothing personal, but this isn't exactly a mountainside mansion ... he'll find us soon enough, and we'll have nowhere to go."

"Jane ... um, Br-Brandi..." he stammered, placing a hand gently atop her shoulder and pausing momentarily to gauge the stillness, "... I promise,

283

we *won't* be cornered ... we *won't* be trapped ... and most importantly, we *will* be armed."

Leaning hard against him, she then stepped gingerly into the bleakness. "Now *that* sounds like a plan. You have another light source down here?"

"Yeah, three steps down and there's a pull switch. I'm gonna secure the trapdoor behind me."

"Damn, Joe," she exclaimed after flicking the switch, exposing a surprisingly spacious dwelling, "you obviously know your way around a shovel."

"Got my Ph.D. all right ... a full six weeks of digging, in between hangovers no less, eight hours a day just to add an exit. I think I swallowed as much dirt and clay as I hauled outta here."

Having secured the trapdoor and locked it from the inside via a steel crossbar lock, Joseph immediately strolled past the girl toward the lone object occupying the space: a three-drawer metal cabinet shoved flush against one side of the smooth dirt/clay wall. As he went about unlocking the top drawer from an overloaded keychain pulled from his jeans pocket, the girl walked ahead and shone the flashlight into a narrow, unlit tunnel.

"Ohh, no way, José..." she grumbled, quickly rejoining him near the cabinet. "What's the matter?"

"No big deal, really ... just a real shitty time to find out I'm claustrophobic."

"Not to worry ... it's a short trip to light ... I promise," he consoled, whirling about cradling a small armory. "Feel better now?"

"Oh, much..." she grinned, wide-eyed, while overlooking the available stock with the excitement of a small child at a candy counter.

284

"Hope I know how to use 'em."

"From what I've seen of you so far, lady, I have little doubt."

***

They stood at the outer edge of the tunnel, each loading their weapon of choice. For Joseph, it was his trusty .38; he filled all six chambers and pocketed an additional six rounds via a speed loader. He watched with no small amount of fascination as the girl loaded a nine-millimeter magazine with the precision and expertise of a veteran firearms handler. No small feat, considering her claustrophobic state of mind.

"So ... the name is Brandi ... I mean, for certain?"

"I do know that much for sure, yes. It ... rings true. I'm ... getting, was getting a few visuals, at least until this latest shooter made the scene."

"What else did he say ... you mentioned something about him asking you why?" "I'm ... not sure what he meant. Thought I had something for a second ... then lost it once the walls around us made like Swiss cheese."

"Guy in the chair is toast ... caught at least three ... one to the head." "No great loss to society, I'm sure."

"Point taken. You ready for the great outdoors?"

"Joe, I'd gladly jump out of a jetliner at twenty thousand feet to escape the close- knit walls of your root cellar/gun show ... no offense."

"None taken. With me it's heights. Allow me to blaze the old trail ... flashlight, please," he said, taking the long-handled light from her clammy grasp.

"Wish you'd made the hallway a bit wider, champ," she groaned with obvious apprehension, hooking her free hand into the back of his belt buckle for support.

"Just close those pretty eyes and think of the Grand Canyon and we'll be at the back door in no time flat. You know, a jigger of brandy would sure hit the spot right now ... actually, make that a dozen jiggers."

It took less than a full minute to navigate the narrow tunnel and reach said exit site, a spiraling metal stairwell leading up to a similarly steely rounded cover with a single squared handle positioned at its center.

"Looks like a manhole cover," Brandi marveled while standing on the bottom rung of eight such steps.

Joseph squeezed past her, aiming the light directly onto the door's handle. "It is precisely that, well camouflaged with at least a pound or five of carefully placed dirt and leaves. Actually, I hadn't bothered checking the outer cover in a while. Let's pray a fallen oak hasn't pinned us in."

"Cheery thought."

"Pessimist at heart, that's me. You ready?"

Not waiting for a response, he'd barely started up the winding well when a stout set of fingers reached out and gripped his left arm, stopping him cold.

286

"Joe, we can't just crawl out into the open thinking we're in the clear. These guys are pros, after all. We need some strategy in case we're spotted."

She could almost hear Joseph's smirk pierce the darkness between them. "I say something funny? By all means, then, let me in on the joke…"

"Brandi, once I lift the cover, you'll understand. There will be no sniper laying in wait, of that I can assure you."

"Well, you haven't lied to me yet. Press on then, but keep that pop-shooter cocked and ready."

"Done. All right then, away we go…" he said, lowering his tone considerably with the final few words before handing down the light and using both hands to push the cover gradually upward.

It raised easily enough and with only the slightest of squeaks. Watching Joseph tuck the revolver in his belt and pull himself out with both arms, Brandi was instantly taken back by the lack of bright light. Clicking off the flashlight and placing it under one arm, she ascended the stairwell with the nine mil tucked tightly against her upper chest.

Pausing just as her head was to emerge into the open, she saw Joseph's left hand shoot out palm up and heard his throaty whisper.

"Toss me the light."

She did so, then reached up and out to hook the door's outer barrier with her one free hand and pulled herself out with a single thrust.

"Clever, Joe … real clever," she exclaimed while crouched to the left of the opening that Joseph immediately reached down to reseal.

"Told ya. There was a method to my madness."

"Apparently so. I wondered where all the daylight ran off to."

From the bottom, the well appeared at least twenty to twenty-five feet deep, its circular design and bone-dry jagged rock walls a perfect complement to the tunnel they departed.

"Sorry for the additional climb, but I see it as the perfect getaway. Believe it or not, we now stand a full thirty yards, just over ninety feet, to the east of the cabin with dense thicket in between."

"Must've been a real bitch to navigate the dig where it lined up like this."

Joseph rolled his eyes before stepping over to retrieve a bulky burlap sack lying in a far corner.

"Dug from both sides, but it was still a migraine-inducer for sure."

"Whatcha got there? More surprises?" she asked, glancing from the sack he was untying to the well's opening, which from her perspective appeared no larger than a regulation basketball.

The four-pronged grappling hook appeared slightly rusty, though the accompanying metal chain complete with squared footholds shone as brightly as if recently polished.

"Glad I didn't settle on rope ... it surely would've rotted by now."

Punching him lightly on the shoulder, Brandi flashed a toothy smile while balancing the tip of the Browning nine-millimeter near her chin.

"Dude, you are truly my hermit hero. Toss that fishhook topside and let's shag some ass..."

Smiling despite himself, Joseph reared back as far as the limited space would allow and did just that.

***

"Brandi, what are you doing? The road to freedom leads in this direction," Joseph spat a bit louder than he'd intended, stopping just short of reaching out and grabbing the girl's bare, muscular arm and jerking her backward.

Having hardly broken a sweat despite the horizontal thirty-plus-foot climb from the well, the girl whispered a barely audible response while keeping a keen eye on the thick foliage ahead.

"I never meant to run, Joe. That just ain't me ... least, I don't think it is."

"Jesus, woman ... you said yourself these are professionals," he retorted angrily, though this time able to lower the volume. "I don't know how you managed to cold-cock the first one, but the odds of that happening a second time are precisely slim and none. Logic dictates the best strategy is to retreat to fight another day."

Sidestepping over with the handgun tucked snugly against her upper chest, Brandi leaned down and in until they were at eye level and practically nose to nose. Joseph took in her sweet scent and felt instantly woozy. Despite the obvious tension of the situation, for just a split-second he had an unrelenting urge to hold her tight and plant a big wet kiss on those permanently pouting lips.

"I realize my memory is lacking, but one thing I do know for by-god certain is that I have never, and will not ever, retreat. Besides, if we ... if I don't settle this now, we'll be staring over our shoulders every minute of every day. It ends now, Joe."

"Damn it, it's insane to…"

Reaching up with her free hand, she placed it lightly over his lips.

"I'm not being reckless ... I'm being a realist. Besides, I think ... no, I'm *sure* I know what I'm doing. I really do."

He stared into her dark hazel eyes for a few moments as she slowly dropped her hand.

"All right, but if we're going to do this ... it has to be planned damned carefully.

We just can't walk right into the bastard's line of fire. Now, I'll be on point until we reach the outer perimeter of the forest leading to the cabin…" he began, stepping forward and gesturing into the thicket with the .38's barrel leading the way.

The fierce pinch applied to his neck was, despite the immense centralized pressure, strangely soothing; a burning sensation that quickly spread the length of his back and turned his arms and legs to Jell-O molds. Just before all faded to black, his knees buckled and he felt a gentle cradling of his upper body and, incredibly, a light kiss atop his forehead.

Staring at her rapidly flexing right hand as if it belonged to someone else, she then smiled sadly when taking in his limp form lying at her booted feet.

"Afraid you're sitting this one out, Hero. Don't mind putting my own ass on the line, but yours is a different story."

After retrieving the .38 and subsequently tucking it inside her waistband, she then carried him several dozen yards in the opposite direction of the cabin and laid him atop a piling of oak leaves.

"Can't be sure how long that Vulcan neck-pinch thing will last, but I'm hoping it's long enough for me to take care of business and meet you back here," she said softly, kneeling down to peck his left cheek.

"Sweet dreams, hermit Joe. See ya soon."

A muffled snapping sound echoed through the surrounding woods as she jerked her head furiously to the left and then the right before concluding the brief muscle- loosening session with a trio of deep-knee bends.

Retrieving the revolver from her waistband, she performed a quick comparison of each weapon's weight before choosing the nine millimeter for her gun hand, that being the left. Trudging away from Joseph's prone form back toward the cabin, the woman named Brandi had many emotions bubble to the surface in a simultaneous tidal wave, yet the one conspicuously absent from the mix was that of fear.

***

Kneeling on one knee, she peered between narrow breaks in the thick foliage by using the weapons in each hand as limb-spreaders. The vantage point she'd chosen showcased the cabin at a

291

right/front angle with the hood of Joseph's pickup blocking a clear front door view. She approximated their absence from the cabin at a half hour to forty minutes. Ample time for a sweep of the tiny structure and a portion of the surrounding woods, she knew, especially if dealing with a true professional of the trade.

Rising cautiously, she looked to her left and right, then finally turned to the rear in deducing that the killer might well have discovered the underground tunnel and was tracking her every step.

She waited an additional three and a half minutes, standing statue-still while scanning the area for activity. Her senses honed to a razor's steely edge, she was forced to block out a flurry of forest-related movements such as the occasional windblown leaf, a swaying tree limb and fleetly exiting shadows created by the occasional bird flying overhead.

Reaching up with a bare forearm to clear the building perspiration from her brow, she briefly considered the possibility that the second shooter had already departed the area in the hopes that his random peppering of the cabin walls had surely done the trick.

"Yeah, right ... *assume* the target is dead," she moaned softly under her breath, "not unless they hire their assassins from Imbeciles 'R' Us."

Giving the thicket behind and around her a final glance, she blew out a lengthy breath and stepped over to a semicleared path that would lead her into a wide, foliage- free clearing between the forest and cabin.

Just before taking off in a mad sprint with the tailgate of Joseph's pickup as the desired destination, Brandi allowed each weapon to drop loosely to her sides. Though completely ignorant of its significance, she wisely chose to disallow any and all uncertainly and allow base instinct to carry the day.

Despite the ducking and swerving motion she purposely exhibited, the fifty- to sixty-foot trek was covered in a virtual blur, leaving her scrunched behind the pickup with the handguns' barrels pointed skyward and poised at either shoulder.

Crouching, she felt small shards of gravel penetrate the tender flesh of her bare knee and secretly savored the pain. Peeking around the pickup's protruded wheel well, she saw the bullet-riddled front entrance standing predictably ajar.

The first round grazed her left ear to ricochet off the dropped tailgate. As sticky warmth bathed her neck and shoulder, she dove to the ground and flattened out before rolling completely beneath the vehicle. She heard a second shot splinter glass, more than likely a side mirror, and then a third ping off either the hood or perhaps the front passenger door.

Rolling out on the opposite side, she repositioned herself back near the tailgate as two additional shots penetrated the windshield, the former causing a rippled, spiderweb effect and the latter shattering it altogether. Shoving the tailgate closed with a screeching thud, she placed her back against it with the handguns crossed at her chest. It was obvious the shooter was either inside the cabin or perhaps stationed on either side of it, since the pickup had been parked almost precisely on its center. She silently cursed the realization that the silencer being utilized was going to make pinpointing his whereabouts a remote possibility at best.

"Brandi, oh my ... is that *really* you, my sweet?" a male voice bellowed in mock agony. A voice sporting an accent of perhaps European origin; a voice she instantly recognized but could not, naturally, place. Smiling even as the throbbing wound at her ear continued its incessant leaking, she forced herself to focus instead on her attacker and his likely location.

"Oh, be still my rapidly beating heart. It is sooooo good to see you up and around, is it not? I so feared the worst for you. We all did..."

Refraining from taking the obvious bait, she pushed off from the tailgate and slid gradually over to the driver's side. Hooking the underside of the bumper with the nine millimeter's sweat-slick handle, she leaned over just enough to allow a partial visual with her left eye.

A portion of the taillight exploded mere inches from her scalp, forcing her to fall back onto the hard gravel with several new open wounds courtesy of an army of fragmented plastic slivers, at least one of which tunneled into her left cheek and stuck there like an embedded quill.

"My, such blatant recklessness. I could have so easily removed that gorgeous hazel eye, my sweet, but purposely aimed a bit high and to the left. Fact is, I've been avoiding doing the deed since you dashed so foolhardily into the clearing. Had you locked in more times than I'd care to say, in fact."

Wiping a fresh smattering of crimson leakage from the punctured cheek, Brandi once again used the tailgate as a barricade. Peering down at her blood-spattered shirt and matching shorts, she fought off a stout wave of cowardly regret by forcefully smacking the barrels of each firearm into her bared thighs.

"Call it sentimentality. Call it curiosity. I simply have to know *why*, my sweet. Besides, the powers that be will want ... no, demand an explanation of how things got so ... now what is it you Americans so affectionately call it ... so FUBARred?"

The wall of chopped firewood sat approximately twenty feet directly to her left, stacked neatly between twin pines. The pile itself was perhaps six feet in height, three deep in width and looked to have been squeezed together like bricks sans the mortar to hold them in place. She pondered a potential relocation while plucking a tiny yet shockingly long spear of hard plastic from just beneath her chin.

"You truly have nowhere to go, my sweet, and I can shoot that damned truck until it's more air than mass. So, what say we stop with all the usual formalities and discuss a better way to solve this rather queasy dilemma? It is so rare we are afforded an alternative, is it not? I'm game if you are."

Dropping her chin onto the gummy wetness of her upper chest, she then scooted around to face the wood pile and stretched into a track runner's pose.

The pile suddenly appeared a country mile away. Unfurling like a coiled spring, she extended both arms toward the cabin and commenced firing just as she cleared the tailgate and entered open space. Though each discharge of the .38 felt delayed and a bit clunky, the nine-millimeter unloaded with a smooth consistency, pockmarking the cabin's outer walls in a widespread circular pattern that, in the aftermath, appeared weirdly choreographed.

Leaping behind the stack head first, Brandi rolled to one side and planted her right shoulder against the pile's solid base, ignoring the fresh slew of cuts and scratches acquired along the way.

Tossing the still-smoking, emptied .38 aside, she wrapped the bloodsmeared fingers of either hand around the heated steel of the nine-millimeter.

"My *god*, girl, what has happened to you? Has the great outdoors softened you so? Once again, I pull back and spare you, all in the name of mutual respect. My patience, however, is wearing uncomfortably thin. Please, let us halt with the silly games and converse like the professionals we are."

Her mind raced, overtaking even her swiftly beating heart; overripe with random, frenzied thoughts that held no logical pattern from which to rationalize.

Like the professionals we are?

"One more chance, Brandi, my sweet ... that's all I can afford you. As apparently confused and out of sorts as you are, I still cannot take for granted the potential danger you present. Please, I ... we need ... we *require* an explanation."

296

"I got your explanation right here, jackass!" she screamed, tucked against the woodpile and assuming a prone position with her arms and hands locked in the classic shooter's pose. "How about you crawl out of hiding and prove what a professional you really are!"

Complete silence ensued for a full thirty seconds, save for an assortment of bird chirpings from seemingly all directions.

"As you wish, my dear," the man's voice boomed from the other side of the stacked logs, causing her to involuntarily flinch and instantly curse herself for doing so. "Damned if I ever could tell you no."

Pushing herself upward, she shoved her upper back flush with the splintered stack but remained low enough to avoid exposure to a possible head shot.

"Now, now, Brandi," he chided, "I've conceded to your demands. It would be quite rude to ignore such an obvious sacrifice on my part, don't you think?"

She paused to ponder what might well be the final plan of action she'd ever execute. Again, as when facing the first assassin or departing the safety of the surrounding forest to challenge the second, she felt nary a shred of fear. It was as if her involvement in such an ultradicey scenario was commonplace, or as Joseph might quip, the situation at hand was "far from her first rodeo. " Indeed, it felt downright natural.

Rising slowly to her feet with the handgun hanging loosely at her upper thigh, she took two strides forward before turning casually about.

"Ah, that's better. So very touching. A little trust between old friends," the man said through a grim smile, standing less than a dozen feet from the shoulder-high barrier separating them.

Brandi didn't have to study his dark, ruggedly handsome features for very long before a faint yet viable recognition came into play.

"You look well, my sweet ... a bit thin perhaps. Hope all that bleeding isn't too big an inconvenience."

Despite a more youthful appearance—slim build, slicked-back tar-shaded hair that was obviously the result of a color treatment of some sort—she somehow knew his age range to be in the low- to mid-fifties. Clean-shaven and muscularly trim, he flashed a bright toothy smile that was the definition of menace.

"I ... I recognize you," she blurted hoarsely, the sight of the nine-millimeter trained at the center of his forehead.

"Yes, I would surely hope so," he replied sarcastically, the smile fading a bit even as he dipped the barrel of the long-barreled Smith & Wesson .45 magnum from her upper chest down toward the abdomen.

"Rutger," she concluded, swallowing hard as a series of blurred images streaked into her subconscious only to exit at an equally rapid pace, none of which struck around long enough for proper evaluation.

"Brandi," he nodded, arching a brow while raising the gun's barrel back toward the center of her face.

"Didn't think introductions were in order. I mean, we aren't exactly strangers..." She took two steps to the left and stopped, the nine-mil's aim never wavering. "How ... how do I know you?"

"Oh ... my ... god ... that's it!" he exclaimed, wide-eyed, sidestepping over to match her earlier movement. "Well, a bout of total amnesia would certainly explain a lot. Many varied scenarios were discussed, but I seriously doubt memory loss was among them."

Brandi moved over an additional three steps, essentially eliminating the barrier between them.

"Glad I could solve your little mystery. Now suppose you return the favor."

Sliding over until they now stood directly across from one another, the man studied her through a searing gaze, his head tilted slightly to the right, nary a hair out of place.

"I suppose it's only fair, as I can see no logical reason why you'd feign such a malady."

"Take my word for it, Slick ... I ain't faking shit. Details please," she sneered, the multitude of open wounds she'd incurred throbbing with increased intensity.

"Now that sounds more like my sweet Angel of Death," he said with a smirk, raising his free hand palm up as if to surrender.

As with the name recognition of moments earlier, a similar batch of frenzied images spewed forth with the same frustrating, bewildering results.

"Good to see you haven't lost that sassy edge altogether. It was always so refresh—"

"Whatever," she scolded, inadvertently scooting back a half step. "Damn, you just love to hear yourself talk, don't ya? Well, do us both a favor and just give me the filed-down version."

The smile he'd so casually worn instantly vanished, replaced by a tight-lipped frown.

"Happy to oblige, my dear, though I must say, amnesia notwithstanding, that you are truly one disrespectful bitch toward the man who taught you every fucking thing you know."

Though she remained utterly motionless otherwise, Brandi's eyes widened considerably in response.

"Shocking, isn't it? Yes, I would think it probably is, considering whatever fantasy past your subconscious has created in the last few days. True, I am a man paid to eliminate other men. An assassin; a killer-for-hire, for those fond of such banal clichés. Then again, my sweet, so *are* you. I should know, as you were placed under my wing some eight and a half years ago, wherein I ... showed you the ropes, so to speak."

She could feel her scalp begin to tingle, the back of her throat suddenly as parched as the most arid of desert dunes. Though unaware of doing so, she began to nod her head from side to side in utter disbelief.

"You came to us with so much potential ... crude, unrefined, but with a natural instinct for the business. Thus, the powers that be fast-tracked you

300

directly to me—first for hands-on training and then the live-mission variety. In all my years, I never saw anyone advance so quickly, as if truly born to do the work. Within two years of signing on, you had climbed the ranks to near the top, passing numerous veterans of the trade as if they were rank amateurs. A born natural, you were. Mastered every weapon I handed you ... from knives to handguns to long-range rifles. Hand-to-hand was equally impressive; watched you take down men twice your size even before martial arts came into the picture. As for the poisons, you were like a goddamned chemist sans the actual degree."

"Bullshit ... it's ... it's all bullshit ... not a c-chance..." she stammered, the nodding having ceased even as her lower lip began to quiver uncontrollably.

"As for why you ended up marooned in this godforsaken wilderness, well ... it is kind of humorous in a warped sort of way..." he smirked, briefly breaking eye to take in the battered, bloodied whole of her.

"You were due a vacation, but handed a final assignment since it was considered ... on your way. It was ... seen as a minor task, as best, especially considering your growing rep. Fact is, you were viewed by many as the best female contractor in the states. That's what makes this so damn comical, actually ... the job itself wasn't even rated. It was a freebie, handed out free of charge to some real estate mogul for past favors. It seems this fellow wanted some ex-police officer torched for the shooting death of his son and granddaughter. An ex-cop turned recluse who'd been in hiding since the shooting. That, my dear, is where you came in…"

Utilizing her free hand to wipe away a fresh droplet of blood that had pooled in the corner of her right eye, Brandi suddenly recalled a name.

"Shit, it was Danley ... Douglas Danley. Joseph ... mentioned the old man and ... and the contract…"

"Now, now, my angel," he scolded playfully, waiving a forefinger back and forth, "you know the rules ... names mean nothing to the likes of us."

"I ... I was ... supposed to ... J-Joseph?" she continued, ignoring his baiting manner.

"Bingo, my dear. While on your merry way to whatever vacation resort you'd chosen for a well-deserved siesta, you were tasked to rid the world of said ex-cop. Obviously, somewhere along the line, something went horribly wrong. Once twenty-four hours had passed and mission completion had yet to be confirmed, the message came down for an immediate follow-up. Though such lowly procedural treks are normally below me, I volunteered for two reasons: one, I had a new trainee under wing and figured it to be a good experience. Two: well, you *were* my prize pupil, after all."

Dropping the nine-millimeter loosely to her side, Brandi was unable to refrain from breaking character as the first semi-clear image in what seemed like eons lit up her minds eye in glorious high-definition fashion.

She relived the sudden terror and impending trauma as the rented vehicle slid off the wet roadway, barreling down a steep, grassy hillside and into and through an overgrown thicket that served to effectively camouflage the vehicle from any and all passersby. Subsequent travels and all that followed remained a blank slate, all up to the point where she'd awakened inside Joseph's cabin.

Snapping to as the fog slowly lifted, she quickly moved to re-aim the weapon just as the man halted his forward progress less than three feet from her position. With the barrel of his magnum positioned mere inches from that of the nine-millimeter, the man flashed a wry, wholly insincere grin and briefly rolled his eyes.

"Whoa, steady, my angel ... *steady*. Now that the required back story is history, let us discuss how this ... rather awkward situation can be properly rectified."

Lunging forward, she planted the barrel directly under his chin while simultaneously groaning as the sensation of cool steel pressed her own flesh just beneath the right breast.

"Yeah, and how might that be, Slick?"

"Please, I'd prefer Rutger," he replied, baring teeth so white they practically gleamed. She could smell the faint scent of aftershave, a sickly sweet aroma that was nauseatingly familiar.

"Well then, *Rot*-ger, I guess it's time to put up or shut up, huh?"

"Simplicity in itself, my dear Angel. Give me the mark and then we'll get *you* the medical assistance you so desperately need."

"Who said I want help, *Right-guard* ... that is, considering all that's been revealed?" She felt an increased pressure at her ribcage but refused to acknowledge the obvious attempt at intimidation.

"Brandi, my sweet," he grinned, arching both brows, "let's not make this harder than it has to be."

"Afraid it's a moot point anyhow, *Rat-gut* ... since the mark you speak of is miles away by now."

"Could you please refrain from butchering my name so?" he asked softly, though the building anger reflected in his cold, unblinking eyes was palpable. "Trust me, my dear, it is for the best you give him up now ... no need to delay the inevitable."

"Son, I trust you about as far as I can toss ya, and like I said ... moot point. Joe took off to destinations unknown as soon as we ducked outta the cabin. Never saw a Caucasian male move so damn quickly and with such *'save my own ass'* determination. Good luck on tracking that boy down."

"I ... see," he sighed, momentarily staring up into the clear, blue skies. "It seems in your amnesiac state you formed a bond of sorts. Sad ... so very unfortunate…"

"The man saved my hide," she retorted irately, sliding the gun barrel gradually up his right cheek to settle near the outer corner of his eye. "Least I can do is return the favor."

As their eyes locked yet again, the smile he displayed appeared sincerely remorseful.

"You were the best I ever had the pleasure to train."

Brandi returned the favor, even shooting him a playful wink. "So you say, amigo."

Each shoved the other back at precisely the same time, her with a forearm and he with a flat palm. Unable to completely halt her backward momentum, she nonetheless got off the first shot before tumbling to the ground in a heap. The bullet pierced his left bicep just as the initial round from his magnum rocketed forth and dislodged a sizeable chunk of clay just inches from where her head had been at the conclusion of her fall. Completing her impromptu combat roll, Brandi leapt to her feet and sprinted toward the woodpile, firing blindly as she ascended and once again while diving head first over the stack. Impacting awkwardly on her left side, she felt a numbing sensation at the back of shoulder that she soon realized had nothing to do with the rough landing. Briefly peering down at the front side of the same shoulder, she clearly viewed the circular, bored-out wound from the shot that had grazed her.

Stooped on one knee, she was grateful for the temporary cover and took a moment to secure the weapon's magazine. Though unsure of how many rounds she'd expended, the guess was around a dozen of the available fifteen. She'd been pondering an exact count just as an explosion of splintered wood splashed her face.

Wiping away a tiny shard that had penetrated her lower lip, Brandi felt suddenly cornered with far too many angles from which the enemy could strike. Having already decided to make a run for the front of the cabin, she braced for takeoff and paused.

Within seconds, a series of high-pitched whizzing noises ensued, followed by hammer- like

305

thumps that filled the air with wood chunks and shattered bark. She darted as soon as the sounds of impact ceased, her deeply grooved boots kicking up a funnel of dust. Before clearing the side of the cabin, she whipped her gun hand around and fired a single shot for cover, though utterly blind to her enemy's possible location. It wasn't until she'd ducked past the bullet-riddled open door and into the cabin's front room, using the dead assassin's slumped form as a barricade, that she made a rather troubling discovery; the nine-millimeter had fired its last.

***

As she'd hunkered down in front of the dead man's tattered corpse, she'd attempted to fire a round into the kitchen area in the chance that her enemy had already taken up residence inside. A low, sickening click had been the response. The mag was spent. Her mind raced while scanning the ransacked room for a possible weapon.

Ultimately, she fixated on a long-handled blade propped in a far corner. What had Joseph called it? A *swing*-blade? No, a *sling*-blade. Crawling on all fours, she gently grasped the blade end, careful not to add to a growing collection of open, seeping wounds, and flipped it over until she could grip the slick wooden handle.

Kneeling in front of the motionless, strapped-in assassin with the newly acquired weapon resting across her lap, she sat in utter silence and listened for movement.

306

She'd been thinking of Joseph and hoping for his continued unconsciousness when the dead assassin's midsection practically blew apart and splattered her already bloodsoaked shirt with a fresh mix of shredded entrails and multicolored body fluids.

Rolling onto her back, Brandi was forced to reach up and wipe a spattering of gore from the corner of her right eye. Once her vision was sufficiently cleared, she pushed up onto her knees with the sling-blade held out chest level and peered upward into the shiny black barrel of a still-smoking forty-five.

***

"I am truly sorry it had to end this way, my dear. You were a tad rusty or the outcome might've been different."

The man who had, in another life, apparently been her mentor and perhaps even a lover wasn't the least bit sorry, she realized, despite his solemn expression and drooping, hound-dog eyes. True, there was nothing in his deportment that bore this out, but she somehow knew this to be gospel. It was, especially in their line of work, always preferable to be on the grip end of a firearm in lieu of staring down the barrel. The old saying *better you than me* was never more appropriate that in the life of an assassin.

"Just pull the damn trigger, prick ... anything to escape your jackass ramblings..." she replied with a smile that appeared blindingly white when compared to the dark maroon spatters covering the surrounding lips and cheekbones.

The forty-five did indeed discharge, and for a split second in time Brandi actually thought the man had purposely missed her despite the less than four-foot distance between them, perhaps toying with her in true cat-and-mouse fashion. It wasn't until she saw Rutger's head whip back violently as his knees apparently buckled, then watched his body become airborne over one of the sectional couch's overturned pieces that an altogether different theory swam into play. Standing with the sling-blade reared back to strike, she froze in midswing as Joseph crept up from the floor with the magnum cradled in both hands.

"Joseph? W-what the hell, dude?" she practically gushed, lowering the blade to chest level. Glancing over, she saw Rutger lying face first on the hard wood floor, his body motionless, a trickle of blood leaking from his exposed right nostril.

"It's called a body block," he huffed, his face and hair coated in so much dust he appeared some sort of cave-dwelling specter; "clip 'em and toss 'em all in the same movement. Not quite as effective as whatever you did to put *my* lights out, but it has its use."

She'd stopped just short of tossing the sling-blade aside and running over to give him a hug when her peripheral vision caught a flurry of frenzied movement from her left.

The weapon flew from her grip just as Rutger's size-eleven hiking boot plowed into the right side of her ribcage, shoving her into the nearest wall and essentially voiding all oxygen from both lungs in the process.

Having bounced from the cabin's log wall like a ricocheting pinball, Brandi landed face first on the plank floor and immediately rolled onto her back and drew her knees into her chest in an attempt to regain the capacity to breathe. Forced into the role of hapless spectator, she watched Rutger engage Joseph in a hand-to-hand duel she feared held but one logical outcome. Though a street-toughened ex-cop with adequate fighting skills, Joseph possessed little formal training and exactly zero speed when compared to the soulless killing machine facing him down.

Still unable to suck in a helpful amount of air, Brandi watched Joseph step forward and throw several wild, random punches, the majority of which were slapped casually away.

In turn, the grinning demon serving as his opposition seemed resigned to remain on the defensive, backing up and swatting away the blows in a cruel, mocking fashion that only served to fuel Brandi's anger tenfold. Then again, Brandi could only hope and pray that Rutger's cocky, asinine behavior continued until she fully regained the use of her lungs.

She (breathing still horribly shallow) saw Joseph, no doubt out of sheer frustration, attempt a front kick that Rutger caught in mid-air and then released with a raucous howl. She (still shallow but improving) saw Joseph back and scream 'ASSHOLE!' before rushing forward and tossing a combination left jab and right hook that the other man blocked with little effort. She (rapidly improving) saw the smirk depart Rutger's face, replaced by the stony frown and tightly squinted eyes normally associated with an impending kill. It was, she realized, an expression she'd witnessed countless times before just before someone was to expire by unnatural means.

Her breathing almost normal as her strength rapidly built, she saw Joseph scoop up a broken chair leg complete with a jagged, sharp edge and wave it back and forth challengingly. Rising to one knee, she also saw that Joseph was sucking wind like a freight train trudging up a steep mountainside. Standing, albeit wobbly, she knew Rutger was a man of many assorted death blows, and deduced she had but moments to intervene if Joseph was to be spared.

Scanning the carnage around her, she saw Rutger first bow and then spring forward just as Joseph reared back with the chair leg as if prepping to toss a tribal spear.

A high-pitched groan permeated the cabin air just as Brandi reached down to retrieve the object of her search.

***

She was unable refrain from gasping aloud as Rutger stood over a dazed Joseph with a boot planted to his chest and the sharp end of the jagged chair leg a mere thrust away from penetrating the ex-cop's exposed neck.

"What was that I heard, my sweet?" Rutger spat sardonically, hardly out of breath and not even bothering to acknowledge her armed presence less than three feet to his left. "Was that a cry of shock? Of outrage? My god, woman, you actually *care* for this man?"

"Leave him be and I won't kill you," she replied stoically, the sling-blade cocked back and ready to ascend.

Turning and tilting his head about just enough to view her from the corner of his left eye, Rutger cocked a brow at the sight of her before releasing a muffled snort.

"I am to presume that the Angel of Death will show mercy if and *only* if I do the same?"

Her tone was ultracalm, her expression shockingly bland. Though utterly impossible to gauge via the human eye, she inched the blade slightly forward as her grip on the slick handle tightened.

"You came here to kill, Rutger, not me ... and not him. Let him up. Let us *go*.

Tell the powers that be that we escaped. Surely they won't question you. Not with the track record you've established. No one would know."

"No, that is probably true. Problem is..." came the cold, emotionless reply, "... *I* would know. Your memory fails you on what I am, Brandi ... on what ... we are. Others live to obtain wealth ... most live to merely survive from day to day. We live to kill ... to complete the assignment. For us in the profession, there is nothing else. It is what we do ... what we were *born* to do. Exterminators of

311

humankind ... the genuine oldest profession, you might say."

Following the spear-tipped shank to the small pool of blood it had drawn from just beneath Joseph's chin, Brandi saw her friend's eyes flutter as he fought to regain consciousness.

"Enough speeches, asshole," she snarled, cocking the blade back until she resembled a ballplayer hovering over home plate to await the next pitch. "It's real simple; you kill him ... I kill you. You decide if the *assignment* is worth the consequences."

"Brandi, ah, my sweet dear Brandi..." he mocked, turning his full focus back to Joseph's prone, unmoving form, "... the consequences for those such as you and I involve nothing less than eternal damnation ... but then, why bother sweating the *little* things?"

His left arm, the one brandishing the shank, visibly tensed. With that, she lunged forward and swung the blade down with the serrated edge aimed directly at the back of his meticulously shaved neck. Displaying feline quickness, Rutger whirled about just as blade began its final descent, effectively redirecting the blow with the shattered portion of chair leg before discarding the hopelessly splintered remains. Knocked off balance as the blade sailed from her grip, Brandi leapt back and barely avoided a vicious backhand aimed for the center of her throat that instead only grazed her already wounded left shoulder.

Growling like nothing remotely human, Rutger kicked away the remains of a badly broken bookcase and stood at the center of the room with his legs spread wide and his back slightly hunched. His clenched fists rested at his outer thighs.

Remarkably, Brandi noted the man had yet to break anything remotely resembling a sweat.

Circling around the sectional to essentially front Joseph's body, she assumed a defensive martial arts fighting stance she had no earthly memory of ever learning.

Apparently reading the temporary confusion in her eyes, Rutger threw his head back and howled.

"Oh that's priceless! Don't have a clue of your own skills, do you, my sweet?

Well, you just waltz on over here and give Uncle Rutger a hug…"

Instead, he plowed ahead fearlessly, reaching her in two purposeful, robotic strides.

Initially shocked, Brandi easily sidestepped his lunge and delivered a quick series of straight jabs to the left side of his rib cage and a badly timed left hook that punched only air.

Having grunted mildly in response to the blows that did connect, his retaliatory move consisted of a cobra-quick leg whip that effectively chopped Brandi at the knees and sent her thumping to the hardwood floor with her upper back taking the brunt.

A quick rollover avoided the heel of his boot by mere inches, followed by a leg sweep of her own that he evaded by timing his hop to perfection. Back to her feet, Brandi stepped in close, ducked a right hook and landed an elbow to his chin, followed by a solid uppercut to the groin that drove him to one

313

knee. Desperate to take quick advantage, she leaned back and then drove forward with her head lowered like a charging bull. The result of the perfectly executed head-butt was a resounding crunch, his mutilated nose literally spewing forth fountains of blood from both nostrils. Flailing back, Rutger cupped the damage with both hands but managed to regain his balance upon impact with the bullet-riddled wall.

Screaming like an enraged predator with its legs crushed from the jaws of a steel trap, he charged forward with extended arms and grasping fingers, the center of his face a bloody, blackened mask.

Despite being afforded several seconds to brace herself, Brandi was caught off guard by both the man's surprising quickness and brutish strength. He blocked her punches with sickening ease, leaning in and wrapping his arms around her upper torso.

Pulling her close, his screams soon transformed into a sexually charged series of low, guttural grunts. In trying to break his grip, Brandi found the man's anaconda-like embrace literally unbreakable. He slowly began to squeeze, and she heard several muffled crunching sounds originate from between her shoulder blades. His blood spattered her face and into her eyes, and she shook and spat furiously to escape the deluge. A coppery aroma filled her nostrils as she strained to turn her head away from his leaking nostrils and the putrid stench pouring from between his parted lips. She found no wiggle room to attempt another head-butt, and her pinned arms had gone numb from the constant pressure from his ever-contracting, tentacle-like arms.

In a last-ditch effort as precious energy ebbed away, Brandi tried to knee his groin but found that he'd apparently foreseen such an attempt and had tucked his legs together for protection.

Just as the last of the air fled her lungs and a flurry of black spots dotted her vision, she was abruptly released to collapse to the planked floor like an overstuffed sack of laundry.

Sucking in several deep breaths that only served to feed the hacking cough that soon followed, Brandi peered up through a grayish, bleary haze to see Rutger tumble to his knees. The man's eyes were pulled saucer-wide, his mouth hanging agape and spewing forth a blackish-maroon tidal wave. Though the image was vague and bathed in shadows, Brandi could just make out the figure poised behind Rutger's kneeling frame.

Backing away instinctively as to put more space between them, Brandi's vision began to clear even as her lungs regained the power to regulate air. She watched Rutger fall to all fours, the flesh between his shoulder blades flayed neatly apart. The fact that his lower back appeared as drenched in his own leaked fluids as his neck and chest made it all the more astounding to witness the man rise to his feet and whisk about to face his attacker.

Blinking rapidly to clear away the final batch of cobwebs, Brandi watched her savior emerge into the light swinging forth what she first thought crazily to be a samurai sword.

She heard Rutger growl a final time a split second before his skull was neatly halved down the center, his body toppling forward like a downed tree from a woodman's axe.

Stepping over the still twitching corpse, Joseph had the black-handled chopping axe resting atop his right shoulder, its shiny silver edge dripping ooze.

Lifting her feet and legs to avoid the massive spillage of bone, blood and brain tissue, she eventually managed to stumble to her feet and brace against the cabin's lone undamaged, spatter-free wall. She felt faint from the sudden movement and momentarily struggled to remain upright.

"Brandi, you all right?" she heard Joseph ask from what sounded like a great distance.

"Ye-ye—I ... ye..." was the garbled reply as she crumpled back toward the floor only to be intercepted halfway by a pair of strong, sure hands.

"Don't worry ... I gotcha. What say we blow this slaughterhouse for greener pastures?"

Closing her eyes as she was lifted from beneath the knees and the small of her back, Brandi's battered senses were soon assaulted by the sweet scent of fresh country air, her clammy flesh instantly replenished by a double whammy of warm sunlight and cool mountain breezes.

"I ... see you ... found your axe," she finally murmured, having tucked her face into his neck and shoulder to relish the faint scent of aftershave found there.

Petting her blood-soaked hair, Joseph's sudden belly laugh served to warm her inner soul even as the sun's searing rays had heated her outer shell. He had carried her to the front porch, where they sat in tranquil silence for several minutes.

"So, what now? I mean, will they keep coming for us?" he finally asked in a tone ripe with dread, as if he already knew the answer.

"We'd be fools to think otherwise, Joe," she replied, her head resting in his lap while his torso so effectively blocked the sunlight from her still-bleary eyes.

"They ... that last one acted as if he knew you. I mean, we were both targets, right?"

For one terrible second, a complete confession perched on the end of her tongue like a great, crippling weight. She quickly swallowed it without regret and lied instead.

For the time being, it seemed the only option. In time, perhaps the truth could be told. In time, perhaps the potential ramifications of said truth would lose a bit of their razor- sharp edge. For now, he meant too much to her. Losing him in light of such a bitter truth was a definite non-option.

"Most assuredly," she said, staring into his eyes and reading the befuddlement they held, "the first one had photos of us both."

"But ... how did they know we'd be together out here? It doesn't make a damn bit of sense."

"Nope. Not at all," she sighed, breaking eye contact. "I sure must've pissed somebody off."

He huffed in frustration, slamming a palm onto the planked porch and whipping up a cloud in dust in the process.

"It had only been a few days since I'd found you wandering around in the woods.

317

What's the connection?"

In the wake of his building anger, she felt less guilt in the act of fibbing. "We'll probably never know. At least, not unless I wake up one day with a heaping helping of total recall."

"Wait out here," he said after a long pause, moving her head gingerly aside as he arose to reenter the demolished cabin interior. "I'm gonna grab the first aid kit. Have to clean those wounds of yours."

"Do it quickly, Joe," she added earnestly.

"Yep. We gotta make tracks posthaste. I'll pack a few things." "Water would be nice."

He nodded in agreement.

"For sure. As for old smoky here, we'd better leave as little evidence of our stay as possible. Generator fuel oughta do it."

"You're the doctor."

"Back in a jiff with a Band-Aid or twelve."

"Hey Clifford," she chided, reaching out to slap his left calf as he started to walk away. "That's at least twice you've pulled my bacon from the pan. Thanks…"

He shrugged weakly and smiled, reaching up to tip the bill on a nonexistent cap.

As haggard and spent as he appeared, she believed she'd never laid eyes on a handsomer man.

"I once took an oath, ma'am, to serve and protect."

Lying flat on her back, looking as though she'd hitchhiked through the bowels of hell, Brandi slapped one hand to her heart and placed the other palm out over her forehead.

318

"Ah, my humble hermit hero," she exclaimed in a faux southern drawl that was suitably awful.

Perched in the tip of nearby oak, a crow bellowed out a shrill concerto while eyeing an approaching storm cloud of mammoth proportions. Minutes later, as the black cloak ceased movement and seemed to hover overhead like some mist-impregnated spy, two battered and bloodied individuals limped from the ruins of a log cabin from which tall plumes of smoke arose. As crackling sounds filled the air and yellowish flames grew taller, the blackish tendrils reached skyward as if to greet and merge with their foreboding kin. As if accepting the offer to unite, the rain held off until all that remained at ground level was a few charred logs and a wide black smear. Once engaged, the downpour that followed was of biblical proportions.

BOOK 4 - SEVENTEEN YEARS LATER

Just as she'd prepared to circle around the counter to lock the front door and flip the sign to read CLOSED, she heard the door chime sound off.

"Whew ... just made it, didn't I?" the man asked cheerily, bowing slightly to shake the buildup of snowflakes from his shoulders and short-cropped hair. The tall collar of his ankle-length parka was flipped up and covered the bottom portion of his earlobes.

"By a whisker all right ... I was actually heading to the door to lock up," she replied, trying not to sound annoyed but failing miserably. It had been a long day, and her knees and shoulders seemed to be locked in a fierce competition as to which throbbed the worst.

"Sorry ... had one hell of a craving. Would've been here half an hour ago but for navigating the tundra."

He gestured toward the glass door, the outside view virtually obliterated by waves of heavy snowfall.

"Nice town you got here ... if you're a polar bear."

Ignoring both the remark and the man's openly sarcastic tone, she managed a smile while stepping past him to secure the front door deadbolt.

"Oh, you get used to it ... over time," she replied, pausing to wipe a clear circle into the condensation build-up on the door and briefly peering through the space provided. Upon receiving no reply, she pulled down the shade covering the length of the door before turning back to him.

"A visitor to our fair city, I take it?"

"Oh, yeah, and I sure as hell don't plan on sticking around any longer than I have to. Heard you got the best cream buns in the state. My sweet tooth's been aching to test that particular rumor."

Strolling past him a second time, she noted he appeared even younger than earlier speculated. His cheeks were not only cleanshaven, but utterly stubble free, as if the use of a razor had yet to be a daily requirement. Blue-eyed and full-lipped, the manchild reeked of cheap cologne and cheaper smokes.

"Believe I still have a cream bun or two in inventory. Let me get you a sauc—" "Nope, afraid not," he interrupted politely enough, "gotta have a fresh one to properly test the theory. Hope it's not asking too much, but I'll pay double whatever you charge ... triple even."

Stationed back behind the counter, she placed her palms flat against the counter and forced yet another weary smile.

"I'm sorry, sir, but all the dough has been packed away and the ovens turned off.

Like I said, I was just getting ready to shut her down when yo—"

"Lady, you got shit in your ears? You don't seem to be hearing me. I said ... cook me a fresh one," he snarled angrily. "Better yet, *fuck* the cream bun. Think I'd rather feast on something a little fleshier."

Reaching into his coat, he pulled free a serrated combat knife. The blade, perhaps six to seven inches in length, glistened and gleamed with each calculated twist.

"Listen, kid ... there's not much in the register. I mean, the haul certainly won't be worth bragging about," she said calmly, keeping her hands glued to the slick tiled counter.

Taking two cautious steps forward, he displayed the tip of the knife like a chalkboard pointer, closing the distance between them to a scant four to five feet.

"You really ought to know better. Such blatant ignorance doesn't befit a legend."

Frowning, she cocked her head to one side and peered deep into his sparkling blue eyes as if studying a particularly mystifying entity of unknown origin.

"Legend? Kid, if I was such a legend, I'd have my own cooking show on the food network."

"Please don't play stupid with me, Monica ... or shall I be so bold as to refer to you as Brandi?"

She offered nothing more than a mild shrug, retaining the same glassy-eyed stare.

"Kid, put that pork-slicer away and you can call me anything you damn well please."

"Right," he nodded, stepping back while casually flipping the knife from hand to hand, "rumor had it you might be playing some sort of amnesia bit. Whatever ... act or not, I gotta say it's one shitload of a disappointment."

"Disappointment?" she queried with a creased brow.

322

"What are you now? Forty-five, six? Still, not bad for an older chick, though you are looking a bit portly. Guess using a bakery as a front might naturally lead to a widening of the ass."

"Please just take the money and go," she pleaded, sliding her hands back so slightly that the movement was practically impossible to ascertain with the naked eye.

"Anybody in the back room, Brandi?" he asked, looking past her to the kitchen's propped open double doors. The darkness beyond seemed to indicate that the interior lights had already been shut off.

Her eyes briefly darted to the same location, then back to him. "I run the place alone."

Sidestepping over until he was directly across from the entrance, he reached into the interior of the parka once again and retrieved a long-barreled Ruger Blackhawk .357 with accompanying silencer.

"Uh-huh. Must be tough hiding out without Joe as your right hand man. Sorry to hear of his passing. Colon cancer, was it? So young still ... and such a horrible way for a man to die."

Though a severe challenge, her expression remained suitably bewildered. In the meantime, she'd managed to pull her hands back another full inch toward her body.

"That said ... it saved me the trouble of gutting the ex-pig, though I'm fairly confident the pure pleasure of doing the deed would've surely outweighed any effort expended."

Her teeth gnashed together like ivory magnets, and she could no longer refrain from breaking character.

"Joseph Clifford could *shit* bigger than you, punk."

"Whooah now..." he grinned, spreading his arms as if to surrender, "... the Angel of Death speaks. Bought ... damn ... time. Appreciate the verification of ID. I couldn't be sure by that grainy-ass photo I was given. Now I can earn my paycheck..."

He pointed the Ruger level with her chest and paused to line up the twin sites, as if target shooting despite the ultraclose range.

"Are you serious?" she blurted angrily, lifting her hands and waiving them about frantically. "Old man Danley *still* has a boner for me after all these years? I figured that miserable old son of a bitch kicked the bucket years ago."

Lowering the barrel several inches, the young man paused. "He did, in fact ... 'bout a decade back, I heard."

"Then ... why track us ... why now?"

"It ain't some rich old crank that's been sniffing the globe for you, lady."

Standing defiantly, she folded her arms around her chest and scoffed. "Educate me then, asshole. Eighteen years and at least as many stops later ... from one state to the next ... one coast to the next. One border to the next. Somebody is either extremely persistent or persistently nuts."

"Let's just my ... *our* employer casts a cold light on those who kill their own kind.

324

Heard they were especially pissed about that Rutger dude."

Shrugging casually, he repositioned the handgun's sights to the center of her face.

"Sorry, seems there ain't no *statute of limitations* where those dudes are concerned, babe. Can't just hide away and play Suzy Doughnut Maker and hope it all just goes away. Eventually, the past does catch up ... least, that's what I've heard."

Lowering her arms to her sides and thus out of view, Brandi remained otherwise motionless.

"Guess that goes for you too, mister. Good luck with that…" she said with a slight nod, as if utterly resigned to her fate.

A faint buzzing sound shot through the tiny space between them, followed by a resounding garbling noise as the young man dropped the serrated blade to the tiled floor and reached up to his own throat. Tugging at the slim black handle protruding there, he staggered back, inadvertently triggering the .357 several times. The first of three shots, all muffled effectively by the attached silencer, ricocheted off the floor to parts unknown; a second struck a tabletop before shattering a wall mirror; a third blew a sizeable hole into the hardwood counter less than a foot from Brandi's left kneecap. By the time he'd discarded the weapon and pulled the shiny metal shank free from just below his Adam's apple, prompting a virtual geyser of bloodflow, Brandi had brandished a tiny twenty-five-caliber Colt from underneath the counter.

The front of his parka drenched in crimson, the man's eyes went glassy while he stumbled about, knocking over tables and finally collapsing against a back wall with both hands wrapped around his ravaged throat. Appearing as though he were literally trying to strangle himself, his terror-filled eyes were still somehow able to focus on Brandi as she leaped over the counter and sprinted toward him.

"G ... ga ... h-h-ho-how? Wh-w-who?" he stammered, his lower lip and chin now as saturated as the parka's fur-lined collar. His knees suddenly buckled, though with the wall's support he somehow managed to remain partially upright.

Holding the diminutive pistol mere inches from his heaving chest, Brandi pumped two shots into his chest before raising the barrel several inches and drilling a dime-sized hole into his forehead. With a final gasp, the young man crumpled to the floor with both hands still cradling the initial wound.

Brandi remained locked in a shooter's stance for several moments, the trance broken only by the intrusion of a frantic voice that sounded on the verge of hysteria.

"Is he ... is he down?"

"Yes, honey. He's ... down ... he's finished."
"Are you ... are you sure?"

"Very. Listen, sweetie ... just stay in there, all right?" "N-no. I ... I want to see."

Securing the twenty-five in her apron's front pocket, Brandi kneeled down and ran a hand through her color-treated strawberry blonde locks.

"You don't have to, sweetheart. I'd rather you ... didn't."

Seconds later, she heard the shuffling feet at her back. A shaking hand landed atop her left shoulder.

"He was ... gonna ... I mean I ... didn't know what else to do…"

Reaching up, Brandi gently patted the hand before giving it a comforting squeeze. "You did the right thing, honey, or we'd both be dead."

"I ... I heard him threaten you, and I ... I looked for something to use. I was trying to be ... as quiet as I could ... then I saw the shears…"

"You did good. That throw was ... like a miracle."

"I ... had to separate the blades before I ... before I threw it. I never ... never thought ... dreamed I'd, like, actually ... hit him."

"It was meant to be, that's all," Brandi said, tilting her head to rest atop both their hands. "It wasn't our time. It wasn't *your* time."

"I heard ... the popping noises ... d-did you?"

"I finished him, hon. I made sure he wasn't going to get up."

"So ... s-so ... I didn't ... I didn't kill him, did I?"

"No, I did. You injured him, but *I* killed him. Remember that, okay? You're still clean. You'll ... always be ... clean."

"But ... it was self-defense, right? You ... we had to?"

"Yes it was, sweetie. It was him or us. God was on our side."

"It's ... it was all about that thing before ... with you and daddy at that cabin?" "Yes, sweetie. It was."

A short pause ensued, wherein the echo of a faraway car horn was heard. "We'll have to move again, won't we?"

"Yes. We'll have to ... leave before ... too many questions are asked." "Will this be the last time, you think?"

"I pray so, sweetie. I truly ... pray so. Now, we have to plan ... to strategize. Are you up to it?"

The young girl rolled her eyes in true teen angst, the tears already drying on her reddened cheeks.

"I'm not a child, mom. Just tell me what to do."

"Lord, if you don't have a lot of your father in you," her mother said with a smile that reeked with an inner sadness and loneliness she prayed her daughter would never know.

Rising to her feet, Brandi hugged her offspring close. Her daughter, whom Joseph had affectionately named Janey, would soon turn the still-tender age of sixteen. Janey, who so acutely resembled her mother at the same age. Janey, whose battle- weary mother prayed so very hard could someday escape the hellish existence her own flesh and blood had created.

As snow continued to fall fast and furious outside the locked doors of JC's Sweet Tooth Bakery, a mother and daughter stood together and plotted out yet another fresh start, the third such time in the past decade they'd been forced to do so.

Less than an hour later, they would utilize the blizzard conditions, treading potentially dangerous roadways to front their escape to whatever destination awaited. Along the way, a body would be tossed into a frozen lake from the edge of an iced-over bridge. Along the way, the bond between parent and child would grow ever stronger.

Soon enough, a destination was chosen and life did indeed begin anew. Hope sprang eternal again, as had been the norm with previous relocations.

Unfortunately, so did an underlying feeling of dread, of suspicion, of distrust in the faces of strangers.

Throughout whatever turmoil this caused, Brandi could always find an inner peace in memories of the only man she had ever loved or *would* ever love.

A man she would someday rejoin in a more tranquil setting, free of the ghastly memories of a past life she was still unable to either recall or fully accept.

For now, she had but one goal; protect the precious life she and Joseph had created, for that was truly all that really mattered.

THE ISLE OF TRANQUILITY, PART IV

Well, if nothing else it sure served to help sober me up ... but I suspect I'll get over that in pretty short order ... ha! Pretty decent yarn, I must say. At least he ignored all the overly campy supernatural elements that plagued his later works, according to the critics, that is. Couldn't say personally ... never cared enough to read any of his last five or six books. Gotta admit, I always dug anything to do with assassins, especially of the attractive female variety. Perhaps I had something in common with the old man, after all. Before this, I always thought the lone thread was our bad taste in choosing women.

And speaking of such, it is now 4:06 PM and still no sign of the little woman.

Gotta figure my campout theory of earlier might just hold true. Whatever ... better exit the tub before I resemble a walking prune. Besides, it's high time I regained my long- lost buzz. Following a quick but edible enough supper consisting of tuna fish on rye, I do believe a rather tall gin and tonic is in order, yes, sir, followed by yet another tale of terror and intrigue from my recently deceased benefactor.

Huh ... looks like Jen picked the wrong night to play runaway beachcomber, 'cause unless I miss my guess, those are some downright badass storm clouds headed this way. Better batten down the hatches, my love, or be scooped up, carted off to sea, dragged under and tossed into Davy Jones'

locker! Ha! More power to ya, you loopy bitch!
Hope you and Mother Nature enjoy a great big wet
kiss!

Seventeen minutes later:

Yeah, buddy ... that's the ticket ... hits the spot
dead on. Nobody, but freakin' nobody mixes a gin
and tonic like this boy! Sometimes ... hell, let's be
honest here ... many times I find myself in awe of
yours truly. Oppositely, Jen never has been very
impressed by my drink-mixing skills, much less my
inbred ability to toss 'em down like nobody's
business. Lord, how exactly did I end up married to
a teetotaler? Kinda like pairing up a cannibal with
a vegetarian. Just doesn't make sense in terms of
strengthening a relationship. If Jen would just
loosen up and have a belt with me every now and
then, maybe the whole apocalyptic thing wouldn't
depress her so. Nothing like a nice lingering buzz to
ward off one's worries, and even the hangover that
eventually follows manages to enhance the
psychological cloaking, albeit a bit miserably. The
sad fact is ... I need a drinking buddy and I'm stuck
with Mary Freakin' Poppins. Sadder still is trying
to dredge up even the faintest memory of when we
last shared the sack for something other than
slumber. Not since we landed on Slacker Isle, that's
for damn sure, and possibly several months prior to
the planet's transformation to a deadhead all- you-
can-eat buffet.

I mean, I know I don't exactly resemble your
everyday matinee idol, but hey, beggars ain't

supposed to be choosers, right? Didn't hear me bitching when Jen started packing on a few extra pounds. More to grab and hang onto, I say. Always search out a ray of sunshine inside a raging shitstorm, that's Randall J. Striker in a nutshell ... especially when he's about half lit. If only I had a partner that felt the same. Well, no need to keep whining over spilled gin ... no better place to ride the storm out than what Pop labeled the "panorama room" surrounded by hurricane-proof picture windows on all sides. Can see practically the whole north side of the island from this bad boy, so with any luck I'll be able to spot Jen as she sails by, tent, backpack, and all!

Meantime, it's back to Papa Striker's last published work for still another entry. I may be no rocket scientist, but the running theme isn't hard to spot. Seems the old man was locked in on introverted behavior with a passion. Hmmm ... perhaps he unintentionally dedicated 'em all to his lone offspring!

Well, better make it a good one, ya grumpy old som'bitch, 'cause from the looks of the colossal thunderboomers building on the horizon, it damn might well might be my last ... ha!

BOOK 5 - THE GUARD SHACK

The day began like all others. Like so many before and those fated to come.

Any variation, however minute, from the daily rituals would be purely accidental.

He awoke to the sound of blustery wind gusts pounding the outer walls like an impatient solicitor, the consistency of the barrage doled out in a freakishly synchronized rhythm. As always, his heart had initially skipped a beat upon reality setting in. As always, he silently cursed and fought back a wrenching sob.

Leaning up a bit awkwardly, he extended his bare feet from the cot's edge and allowed them to gingerly pat the chilled stone flooring. Following a lengthy yawn and accompanying stretch, he arose with a muffled groan as the sound of popping bones mixed uneasily with that of the steady gusts reaping havoc outside.

Following a normally sluggish first few moments of consciousness, during which time the bladder was sufficiently drained and the initial pot of coffee prepared for brew, his movements gradually achieved a marked level of fluidity; an almost choreographed grace birthed from a singleminded sense of purpose.

Leaning forward and resting his forehead against a padded rest, he peered unblinking through twin eye-portals, using one hand to adjust the camera angle while the other reached up to complete a minor picture adjustment. As had been the general rule of late, the visual at hand was a debris-laden mystery; like staring into the swirling belly of a raging funnel cloud. Sighing, he nonetheless gave the outer fringes a second look with similarly unspecified results. A quick gauge check revealed nothing unusual in terms of bucking recent trends; hazard levels graded as extreme exposure deemed potentially fatal for durations exceeding one hour. Again, he reset the codes for the obligatory double-check of said info. Following strict procedure in such a situation might seem ludicrous to an outsider looking in, but veterans understood the need. It was, ultimately, simply a matter of both pride and respect for those who came before.

Pulling on a pair of skin-tight thermals, he soon stood before the latrine sink and splashed his face with handsful of lukewarm water. Leaning up, he stared into the mirror and ran a palm over his scarred, stubble-coated dome. As in the sleeping area, the faint scent of her was maddeningly pervasive. Sniffing the air like a trail hound, he felt a vise-like tightening of the heart that was equal parts pleasure and excruciating pain. The lovely daze was broken, as always, by the fervent whistling of the coffeepot.

Two full cups, each tar black and stout, were ingested between a return trip to the latrine to shave and defecate, respectively, the latter act still unable to completely eradicate the sweet, lingering smell of her. Protocol dictated the coffeepot's steaming contents remain stored in a massive thermos, along with a similarly bulky, thickly insulated water bottle and a handful of protein bars. A package of the latter was subsequently ripped open and sucked down to serve as breakfast, the very act of self-nourishment no longer associated with pleasure but merely a stopgap measure to maintain the life source.

The day's ensemble was soon laid out atop the neatly made bunk, followed by a frenzied series of, in order of completion, push-ups (three sets of fifteen repetitions), crunches (two sets of thirty reps), and squats (a single set of thirty). A round of shadowboxing ensued, roughly equal to perhaps a full round of actual sparring, and finally a two-minute running-in-place session that, despite great effort, left him only casually winded.

The interior of the parka smelled strongly of her, even more so than the shack's cramped interior. It was as if she'd just removed it and the warm, sweet fragrance still remained. Impossible, he knew, since the jacket was tailored for him and thus several sizes too large for her, but such factual disclosures meant little in the wake of filling his senses with her memory. He hardly needed an excuse to revel in fantasy. His every waking moment ... every surviving moment ... was tied directly to such memories. She populated not only every waking moment, but his every dream, no matter how bizarre the setting or confusing the plot. He spotted her and her alone among the plethora of bleared faces and oceans of otherwise unrecognizable humanity. No matter the dozens upon dozens of fellow warriors and close friends he'd watched die in combat; many of whom he'd considered closer than any blood relative, Katreena was the fuel to his inner fire. A fire that would've long since extinguished without the faint hope of her eventual return to the guard shack to which she'd once been assigned.

Appropriately decked out in knee-high mukluks pulled over steel-toed combat boots, insulated coveralls, the aforementioned thermal undergarments, and a multilayered parka engineered to withstand temperatures of forty below, he completed the ensemble by donning a clear filtered mask that snapped easily into place within the parka's fur-lined hood.

Slinging the backpack over one bulky shoulder, he hoisted a long-barreled rifle over the other, the firearm protected by a layer of instant air-bubble sealant easily removed by the press of a button. In checking the wrist watch tucked snugly beneath the outer edge of his thermal gloves, he noted the time and sucked in several deep breaths before securing the face mask and ensuring a sufficient level of oxygen existed. The door's inner latch released with a loud pop and upon closing echoed similarly, though this was easily drowned out by winds that roared and screeched like an army of runaway freight trains skidding off their tracks.

The trek to what had been his assigned shack was usually a twelve- to fifteen- minute excursion, depending on the elements. On this particular morning, while trudging blindly forward in a veritable wind tunnel, he estimated twenty to twenty-two, but surely no more than twenty-five, barring some unseen roadblock. Despite the less-than-ideal travel conditions, he felt little in terms of apprehension. After all, he could literally find his way with both eyes closed. It was more a matter of repetition than instinct, a textbook practice-makes-perfect scenario. So often he'd considered forgoing the daily routine, going as far as delaying the trip until late afternoon and thereby risking full blackout status. Yet again, to refrain from shirking one's duty was simply a matter of honor. The check had to be made—needed to be made, and the security manual regularly updated per regulation. Just as important, he refused to be called onto the carpet and accused of being derelict in his duties if such an occasion arose in the near future. Elements be damned, he'd find a way to ensure perimeter alarms remained unbreached, though the question of who or what exactly would bother to infiltrate a long-abandoned, seemingly forgotten site did occasionally rise to the forefront despite his best efforts.

Trudging forward in a steady, purposeful gait, he was forced to sidestep or, in several cases, climb over the scattered remnants of the former base. A tattered fence post here ... a dented fuel canister there, all being blown about like weightless confetti by the constantly shifting winds. Weeks earlier, in the initial days of what he referred to as the "season of swirl," he'd even been pelted by a paperback book, smacked so forcefully at the center of the faceplate that he'd tumbled back and barely avoided ripping his suit lining on an upturned section of jagged metal. The other seasons, dubbed "Days of Tundra" and "Shake 'n' Bake" by a former base commander, offered their own challenges, mostly of the extreme temperature variety, but neither came equipped with the potential danger a sudden wind gust of seventy to eighty miles per hour provided.

Leaning forward with his head bowed so as to safely navigate each step through the shifting carnage, he struggled to remain on familiar ground, stopping several times as a particularly nasty gust blew him to one side or the other. It wasn't until he stepped onto a slightly warped metal sign with dark blue lettering that a sense of familiarity and relief washed over him. A half dozen additional steps and he stood before the guard shack entrance. Lifting a thick metallic cover away from a mounted keypad at the door's center, he quickly entered a four-digit code and was practically shoved inside by a ferocious blast of air.

Discarding the cumbersome gear, he quickly initiated the necessary security checks. Unlike Katreena's, he considered the shack to which he was originally assigned a bit of a tomb—a cold, impersonal workstation, nothing more. Though he'd spent ample time within its squared walls upon assignment, he felt nothing in the way of sentiment upon departure. No, it was Katreena's shack that was home. Her things were there to be touched ... fondled. It was there he sensed her presence ... her very aura. His shack contained bound regulations, checklists, and the necessary technical equipment to complete the task at hand, nothing more. It even smelled a bit rank as opposed to the lingering sweetness of the other.

The necessary perimeter checks complete and unchanged from countless days before, he started to redon his gear but hesitated upon hearing the increased fury of the current storm. Wearing only the thermals, he tossed the next layer of clothing aside and stepped to the viewfinder for a quick peek at the source of the ruckus. Groaning in frustration, he then lumbered over and sat down hard on the bare cot. It sounded and appeared as if the storm had doubled in ferocity, leaving him temporarily stranded in his own shack. Lying back as the cot squeaked in apparent disapproval, he pulled the top sheet, faint sour scent and all, over his upper body and blow out a long, laborious breath. Perhaps as much due to his own inner boredom as to the internal heaters rapidly warming the surrounding air, a sudden bout of extreme drowsiness ensued, followed soon thereafter by a series of rich, vivid dreams that were, at least initially, strangely soothing in their familiarity. That is, until their inevitably frustrating, horror- filled conclusion. A conclusion that he seemed permanently helpless to alter, the aftermath a black cloak of depression he would wear for days on end.

***

Katreena sat across from him in the oversized tin can that served as the base dining hall, slowly forking in tiny bites of canned peaches while eyeing him seductively. As was the case whenever off shift, her short-coiffed, regulation-cut brown hair had been casually brushed behind each ear. She wore little makeup save for a dab of blush atop each naturally rosy cheek and a sparse outlining around

339

each almond-shaded eye. Perhaps to the average male eye, his Treena might rate no higher than "kinda cute" on the beauty scale, but as far as he was concerned, she was the complete female package, all rolled into a petite five-foot frame whose flawless curves were usually being held hostage by the most unflattering of military-issue clothing. Better yet, and despite opposite upbringings, they shared similar senses of humor, however warped to the outside eye, and had meshed effortlessly as both work partners and off-duty friends since the day of their initial meeting. Never, in countless other relationships, had he felt such comfort in another's mere presence, truly as if they'd shared a similar kinship since childhood. Simply put, she had "gotten" him from minute one, as had he her. As for the sexual attraction, it had been a gradual build. It wasn't as if it hadn't existed from the start, just boiling beneath the surface, but the actual act hadn't been unnecessarily rushed. They had taken their time, in both a figurative and physical sense, and the wait had been worth every minute.

Peering down at the metal tray before him, he registered a half-eaten slab of roast beef and an as-yet-to-be touched serving of mashed potatoes. He jabbed the potatoes as if testing their liveliness before sitting the fork aside without ever taking a bite. In brief scanning the mess hall, he noted perhaps a dozen other troops spread out over the forty or so seats currently available. As SPs, he and Katreena shared similarly strange on-duty hours, thus the added bonus of enjoying less crowded mealtime formations once said hours expired. As grueling as the seven-day-a-week, fourteen- hour "shack" shifts were, it wasn't as though the tiny, ultraremote base camp offered much in the way of off-duty entertainment. Thus, though never considering himself a deeply religious man by any means, he truly felt it a genuine godsend that they'd found one another. He heard Treena giggle girlishly, hands-down his favorite sound, and looked back up to visualize an alien landscape so dramatically altered it appeared in fragmented spurts, as if he were literally falling in and out of consciousness during its unveiling.

Gazing through a thick, drifting gray fog, he was unable to positively identify any of the shadowy objects floating nearby, and his frantic cries to Katreena seemed to hang at the base of his throat as he began to cough uncontrollably, swinging his arms and hands about in windmill fashion in order to clear away a portion of the blinding haze.

He stumbled forward just as a series of stout, frigid breezes soon cleared away large sections of the swirling smoke to reveal imagery equally bonechilling. He stumbled back in the face of the scattered carnage, unable to mentally compute the horrors even as yet another potential shriek remained haplessly locked in his rapidly tightening chest.

Amid countless freshly blown-out chasms of unturned earth stood jagged spears of metal protruding from the cracked, mutilated earth like quills. From several hung the torn, detached, bloodied appendages of his fellow warriors, while

341

others housed their impaled, permanently posed corpses fully intact. Stepping cautiously forward to avoid sinking knee-deep into a freshly blasted crater, he reached over with a shaky hand (several knuckles of which were stained in pork gravy) and secured a handful of hair from one such impaled casualty before gently lifting the bowed head. The slouched meat, as was the popular terminology for the recently deceased, belonged to Private First Class Gene "the Gabber" Gentry, a painfully young pup of perhaps nineteen whose unlimited energy and constant optimism had been infectious within the unit. Held upright by the sharp-tipped steel pole penetrating his chest cavity and missing the entirety of his lower jaw, it went without saying the youngster's inspiring days were long over.

Turning from the horror as the bands around his gut tightened a bit more, he spotted the tabletop he and Treena had shared, their trays miraculously untouched, a cube of sliced fruit still protruding from the edge of her fork.

To his right and a mere trio of steps away lay Sergeant-Major Jared Powers, a grizzled, twenty-six-year combat vet who commanded respect not merely with his steely gaze and gravelly voice but through an infamous, well-documented battlefield record.

Alas, once an imposing figure at just over six-five and two hundred fifty-plus pounds of tightly muscled bulk, having one's legs blown off at the thigh and the top of his skull sheared off at the eyebrows had a way of permanently eliminating such intimidating traits. War was the ultimate humbler, ofttimes reducing even the grandest of warriors to unidentifiable shreds of carrion.

Jogging past similar carnage, he glanced skyward between steps, weary of continued bombardment. He felt a rush of hot air pelt the exposed flesh of his neck and skidded to a clumsy stop at the edge of the fiery ruin that had, just moments previously, been the dining hall entrance. Whirling about on wobbly legs, he watched in utter silence as a patch of ground just to the right of Private Gentry's propped torso detonated, practically disintegrating the dead soldier's remains and leaving, fittingly, a grave-sized crater in its wake. Three similar explosions ensued, none of which his shellshocked ears were able to detect, with each growing closer to his present location. Peering upward for the source of the mayhem, he was only able to visualize a long, lean shadow streak by before leaping behind what had been one of the metal double doors leading into the mess hall.

Kneeling down and using the badly bent door as an impromptu shield, he attempted to shake the maddening deafness by vigorously shaking his head from side to side. Once resigned to the condition, be it temporary or permanent, he eventually found the courage to stand erect and peek around the door's outer edge.

Unconsciously allowing his makeshift shield to fall away, leaving him exposed to whatever flying shrapnel roamed the surrounded airspace, he thought his heart actually paused between thunderous beats. It was Treena, zigzagging past the mangled bodies of their unit and headed directly

343

toward him. As fresh eruptions of earth and rock filled the sky from the continuous onslaught, he noted the expression she donned. It was a mask of pure grit and diehard determination he knew only too well. Reckless but damned admirable, he'd always quip of such qualities, both of which an effective soldier must possess to some degree. Frantically waving her over like a maniacal third-base coach to a ballplayer sprinting toward home plate, he wasn't sure she had even spotted him as her gaze suddenly froze skyward and she skidded to a stop directly in the path of a severed leg, void an attached foot, which stuck from the mangled dirt like a makeshift surrender flag.

He watched her pull the twin firearms from her belt and commence firing wildly into the overcast sky as the occasional shadow whizzed by at supersonic speed.

Though equally shocked and impressed by the level of valor on display by his lady love, the emotion he most felt was a shockwave of terror that instantly transformed his legs to overcooked noodles as he attempted to dash forward to her aid. Even more bizarre, the more distance he covered the farther away she appeared, as if he stood atop an escalator traveling in the opposite direction. Katreena continued to fire both weapons in perfect synchronization, never altering her line of sight from the space directly above her, the need to reload apparently no longer mandatory as it was obvious the number of rounds fired were far past a realistic count for handguns that held no more than six per pistol.

He saw the earth split between her splayed legs, as if someone were literally slicing the ground apart from underneath. Dropping the weapons to her sides, the barrel end of each spewing slender tendrils of smoke, Treena finally appeared to take heed of his presence. The solemn, hangdog expression she wore just seconds before collapsing into the widening chasm was one he could easily identify as regret; the same hapless, gnawing, gut punch of remorse he felt at the realization that such a potentially special relationship was about to end so abruptly. Her standing freefall was so swift he never saw her pose alter as one might expect. There had been no flailing arms; no head-whip, no lingering scream that grew fainter as distance to the surface grew greater. She had simply been there one second and gone the next, as if magically teleported.

His next act wasn't about bravery. It had little to do with heroism. It was the act of desperation, pure and simple. The final act, if need be, of a man with nothing left to lose. Leaping forward as the top edge of the ever-expanding sinkhole reached his position, he swan-dived headfirst into the unknown. What he found there wasn't his tumbling lady love, whom he groped so wildly for while careening downward, but a river of darkness like no other; an infinite, smothering cloak of despair from which there existed no eventual landing to end one's misery. Twisting and contorting his body in sky-driver fashion, he kicked out with both feet and windmilled his arms in hopes of scraping a wall, moistened rock, anything tangible, without success.

As before, the building screams hung at the base of his throat as if corked, though he was fairly certain his mouth stood agape in mid-bellow, just as his eyes bugged out to mutated proportions despite absolute blindness. As for the total loss of hearing that had plagued him, presumably due to the sudden barrage of high explosives, it was no longer an issue once he felt an impossibly strong grip clasp his left ankle in an unmerciful vise.

Initial evidence of this came with a series of sharp crunching noises as his lower leg splintered from the intense pressure being applied; secondly came the high piercing shriek that accompanied it, the first of the long-bottled screams to make it to the surface. Finally, the soft, familiar voice that whispered so sweetly in his right ear.

"You saw what I really did, lover, and you did nothing to stop it," it cooed seductively with icy cool breath, the familiar sweet scent of which was unmistakable. Treena had always favored spearmint as her choice of gums. The fingers that wrapped around his neck were equally chilled, the pressure applied gradually until his air supply dwindled to a choked gasp.

"We are truly one and the same, then, are we not? Two rotted peas in a pod ... with only one logical destination ... for infinity... "

With that, his head was twisted severely to the right, the last audible sound that of snapping bones and mangled vertebrae.

***

346

Tumbling from the cot with both hands fumbling about the underside of his chin and neck, he landed atop the cool stone floor with a pained grunt before rolling off his bludgeoned left shoulder and onto his back. Sucking in a series of strained breaths while simultaneously reaching up to wipe away a building moistness from the corner of each eye, he allowed himself the luxury of a full two-minute respite before attempting to regroup. It wasn't often the dream awakened him so rudely. Normally a low shriek or the occasional wild flinging of arms ensued, but rarely a full-fledged abandon cot.

Rising with a grimace, he reached down and flung away the sheet that had wound so effectively around his lower calves and ankles. Moving quickly to shake off the cobwebs, he had already taken note of the still-present but obviously weaker winds currently battering the shack. A quick peek through the viewfinder confirmed this, as visibility had returned to perhaps a six- to seven-foot range during the span of his unplanned nap. Feeling predictably regenerated, he dressed with renewed vigor and soon departed, making the return trip to Treena's shack in a record time of just under twelve minutes. Basking in the homey atmosphere, so drastically altered from the tomblike vibe of his own shack, he began preparation for midday chow, humming a lively pop tune fondly recalled as one of Treena's favorites. There would be no magical premonition of the drama soon to unfold, as even the steadily weakening winds seemed to dictate a rare siesta of tranquility.

"Radar reports sector six cleared, sir." "What's our window, Sergeant?"

"Looks like a three- to four-hour span, sir, before a new wave of nastiness moves in."

"How far out are we?"

"ETA to target area is approximately ... twenty-one minutes, sir."

"Let's roll it forward then, Sergeant, while we've got the luxury." "Should I and the corporal go armed, sir?"

"Affirmative, though such measures are hardly necessary unless he plans on *stoning* us to death. Still, regulations dictate otherwise." "Yes sir, Major, strictly by the book, then."

"Despite such unregulated circumstances surrounding said case, Sergeant Walker, yes indeed, it's by the book all the way."

***

The dull aching at his chest having subsided substantially in the hours since the dream, he sipped steaming tea from a ceramic cup adorned with various images of wolves; another of Treena's many passions. A collector of anything and everything lupine, the girl had pillows, blankets, shirts, various framed photos and even a pair of wolf-shaped flower vases. Not surprisingly, her assignment to such a desolate, remote base site was in no small part fueled by an inner craving to experience a similar lifestyle as her canine brethren. She had, in fact, following one of their many after-hours trysts, confessed to said motivation in being sent to what was popularly considered one of the three worst permanent duty assignments available. Unlike roughly ninety-nine percent of the post's eighty-five or so occupants, she had actually volunteered, citing the nearby mountains and utter lack of modern civilization as the top draws. Being a city boy through and through, he could hardly relate, though he did his best to at least humor such bizarre thinking.

Stripped of all clothing save his camo pants and wool socks, he flipped casually through the second of three photo albums Treena had stashed away. It was his personal favorite, showcasing mostly his lady love at her prior duty station in various poses of youthful exuberance, most of which involved beverages of the alcoholic variety. It so reminded him of his own such experiences, and had helped them connect despite the age difference, though it had occasionally struck him strange how little she divulged about her life before the military. When queried, she could abruptly turn cold, distant.

Still, he had never been one to push. At the time, he'd figured they would have ample time to cover their individual pasts. An immense drowsiness soon escalated into a deep slumber that was, for once, dreamless.

***

"So how many search and captures does this make, sir? That is, if I'm not treading in top secret waters."

"Four, Sergeant, two in the last six months. I've tried several times to have him moved to a maximum facility to prevent such treks."

"You got the goods to show 'im this time, Major?"

"Yes, Corporal, all printed out in black and white inside this handy manila folder." "Think he'll buy it this time? I mean, it's gotta be a strain to stay in such denial, right?"

"Corporal, the man isn't in denial ... he's deranged. A shattered psyche such as this isn't capable of what we consider normal emotional debates. I've shown him the same evidence many times. Eventually he'll wear down, but he'll never, ever believe."

"Jeez, doc ... I sure don't envy you brain-pickers ... um ... pardon the term..." "Not a problem, Sergeant ... in times like these, I'd rather be a plumber."

***

"Oh my sweet Jesus," he cried, warm tears streaking down both haggard cheeks. "I knew it ... just a matter of time ... of being patient. I told 'em ... told 'em all. Nobody believed ... nobody understood. It's ... destiny ... f-fate ... and you ... can't ... fight ... destiny."

Completely nude, he rose with outstretched arms, the attached hands shaking like those of a wino in the final stages of detoxification.

"Thank you, lord ... oh, lord in heaven, tha-thank y-you..." he blubbered, falling hard to his knees but utterly oblivious to the throbbing pain that followed.

***

Rising from the cot to refill his mug, he froze in midstride. Tilting his head a tad to the left and thus utilizing the ear less damaged by past combat scenarios, he winced as if struck by a sudden wave of intense abdominal pain. Despite the passage of time and lack of recent exposure, there was little mistaking the still faint but slowly building sound of an approaching engine. Tossing the empty cup into a far corner, he sprang forth in a streaking blur toward a metal locker shoved against the shack's far wall. As the hum of the approaching visitor grew ever closer, the finely honed survival instincts of a career warrior took center stage. Whoever or whatever their uninvited guests might be, he mused grimly while briefly showcasing a double thumbs-up' gesture, the surprise was definitely going to be on them.

***

"Main guard shack's empty, sir. Appears as though it's been uninhabited for quite a spell. Did

351

notice a few boot tracks that seemed fairly fresh leading to and away from the entrance."

"Fine, Sergeant. I didn't expect to find him residing here. The second shack, *her* assigned shack, was at the back perimeter of the post, just over the next hill about thirty clicks."

"Hard to believe they're still upright at all compared to the rest of this rubble pile." "The guard shacks in these sectors were usually constructed like fallout shelters.

Besides, they were rarely a prime target in aerial attacks. As a rule, the divers and droppers concentrated on the main HQ building and the troop barracks."

"Makes sense. We ready to roll, sir?" "By all means, Sergeant."

"You ... sure about this, Major Ogilvie? I mean, we could go ahead on foot in case of potential conflict."

"Conflict? Sergeant, he has no weapons to speak of. He's been cooped up for over two weeks with spare provisions and little in the way of protection from these damnable conditions. There'll be little in the way of sparring other than verbal.

"Besides, by now he's undoubtedly made note of our presence. Please proceed."

"Yes sir, you're the doctor."

***

Having only donned camo pants and spit-polished combat boots, he remained otherwise uncloaked. After a quick check of the pants' side pockets, he grunted in apparent satisfaction and pushed back, allowing the high-backed chair to incline back until it struck the metal locker for support. A tense moment passed, broken by a heavy sigh and slight bow of the head. Several minutes earlier he'd spied the trio of intruders depart their vehicle and trudge slowly in his direction. Two walked on either side of the third, each armed and sufficiently decked out in combat garb befitting professional warriors. The man at the center, however, appeared ludicrously out of place in both appearance and gait, the former laughably formal considering the surroundings and the latter shockingly casual, as if treading through a picturesque park setting. Strange how vaguely familiar the man seemed, though putting a finger on exactly why would be risking potential mental fatigue. At this juncture, any and all such resources must be used sparingly, much in the same category as generator fuel, bottled water, or toilet paper. *Waste not, want not,* went the old saying. Soon, he would need all his faculties operating at well-oiled-machine levels, meaning not only mental and physical, but verbal as well. The sincerity of both voice tone and mannerisms; the dialogue crisp and concise with no hesitation or, heaven forbid, stuttering in responding to whatever clever interrogation techniques might be employed. He had the necessary training and, lord knew, the experience to back it up. It was simply a matter of execution; of follow- through; and most important, of timing. Timing would, indeed, be *everything*.

Allowing for a quick glance to his immediate right, he flashed a broad smile.

"Just like we mapped it out, right? Well-oiled machines, babe ... never lose a step, no sir. Well-oiled machines."

He heard the shack's outer door rattle, gently at first and then with increased fervor. He smirked while folding bare arms across a tightly flexed chest in the realization that, for once, the consistently howling winds of Sector Six were definitely not a suspect.

Following a brief pause, wherein a series of clicking noises ensued as the entry code was initiated, the door pushed inward with a low metallic squeak. Clearing his throat, he briefly closed his eyes and took a moment to mentally prepare. It was, after all, *show* time.

***

"I ... we appreciate your cooperation, Tim. I know this isn't ... easy for you." "Just ... give me a moment to ... pack a few things, huh?"

"Take your time, Timothy."

"A little privacy ... please. I ... need a minute to ... reflect."

"I'm afraid we can't leave you ... unattended at this particular juncture, Tim. Corporal Jakes will stay, his back turned, while the sergeant and I stand out front; is this ... acceptable?"

"I take it I don't really have a say."

354

"I truly apologize ... regulations, you understand." "Only too well, Major. This ... won't take long." "Like I said, Timothy, there is no rush."

***

"Pardon me for asking, Major, I mean ... brain matter puzzles ain't exactly my bag, but why is it he doesn't recognize you? I mean, considering your extensive history together."

"I have no easy answer, Sergeant. A fractured mind is just that."

"Damn, but it reeks in there. How's he managed with just a rickety old cot and a few dozen protein bars? No plumbing, no lights, nada, but he was jabbering away about the equipment and gear, like it was still intact and he could just go on living inside that fourteen by sixteen tomb for years. Again, sir, I'm sure no expert, but you think it could all be an act?"

"What purpose would such a guise serve? Don't think I haven't considered the possibility ... many times, but it never seemed plausible within whatever warped universe Tim ... *Master Sergeant Wills* views as reality."

"So ... this little tragedy plays out pretty much the same every time?"

"With little variation, though normally between the padded walls of the sanitarium.

Astonishing he actually makes it back to the original site intact. Such determination is almost ... otherworldly. Perhaps now the brass will finally reconsider reassignment to a more secure ward."

"Have to say it freaks me out just being here, sir. Jeez, read about this place ... *The massacre at Sector Six* ... when I was in grade school. Never thought I'd actually tread the hallowed grounds, or ever have reason to."

"I was in OTS at the time. Saw the file ... and accompanying photos years later.

Believe me, the brutality and sheer horror of the attack's aftermath lived up to everything you've heard. One only has to witness the behavior of its lone survivor."

"Damn, he really must've loved that chick. Talk about loyalty ... delusional as hell but loyal nonetheless."

"I feel I know her almost as well as Tim, more from his stories than her personnel file. Despite obvious character flaws, Corporal Katreena Whitlock was a fascinating woman."

"And they never found her remains?"

"The Corporal and six others were never identified amid the ruins of the base, no.

Their deaths were ultimately listed as *total disintegration by force*." "Meaning exactly what, sir?"

"Meaning it was determined that each suffered a direct hit from falling artillery, leaving nothing behind but a bloody smear that soaked up rubble like a sponge and eventually blew away like so much passing dust."

"Damn. Grisly shit ... sir. Pardon my French. Hell of a way to buy it."

"No one died easy here, Sergeant Walker. In retrospect, perhaps those six were the lucky ones."

356

"Well, if he dug his lady that much, I can sure understand the breakdown, if not the duration of said crack-up. So he just ... waits here for her to return?"

"Convinced that since her remains were never found, she was captured and thus might someday return to the place their relationship began and ended."

"Captured? Shit, *rescued* maybe. Anyhow, Mills is a lot ... older looking than I imagined."

"Fourteen years is a lifetime when every minute is spent in misery, Sergeant." "You think he ... well, poses any threat despite the fragility? For a second there I thought I detected a gleam."

"The only weapons at poor Timothy's disposal are strictly in his mind, much like the atmospheric gear he thinks is so vital to his survival."

"Kinda like the daily perimeter security checks with alarms and cameras that no longer exist?"

"Bingo, Sergeant. All part of the routine that keeps the overall dream alive." "Um, Major Ogilvie ... you think he's had enough time to pack whatever he's bringing back, or *thinks* he's bringing back to the sanatorium? Jakes has probably nodded off by now, and it's a long haul back to civilization."

"True enough, and we do need to beat the incoming storm. Let's take a peek, but keep it nonchalant. I've seen the man flip out, Sergeant, and it isn't a pretty sight."

***

357

At initial glance, Corporal Carlton Jakes appeared to be casually leaning against the shack's main console with his back facing the entrance, his head tilted slightly to the left. Apparently positioned so he could monitor the structure's tiny latrine, the sliding door to which stood partially ajar, the corporal sat slumped atop what was once commonly referred to as the "watcher's throne," that being a rolling, high-backed leather chair provided for the sentinel on shift.

"Jakes, straighten up, for shit's sake," Sergeant Russell Walker whispered harshly, stepping gingerly through the entrance while shouldering his rifle. "You napping on company time, boy?"

"Where's Wills?" the major asked fretfully a few steps to the sergeant's rear, his widening eyes frantically scanning the minuscule confines.

"You hearing me, Jakes? Son, you'd better snap to and display some professionalism before my size twelve steel-toe finds the crack of your—"

"Damn it, Walker, where is Wills?"

"Relax, Major, he's probably just draining the lizard, right Ja—?"

Stepping between his young charge and the latrine entrance, the sergeant's lips froze in midword, his warped, bug-eyed expression as still as a painted image on canvas.

"Jesus Crow, J-Jakes..." he finally managed to groan as the major stumbled forward and practically rammed into his left side, the larger man barely registering the other's clumsily executed halt.

"Dear g-god..." the senior officer stuttered in surveying the fresh carnage on display. "W-Wills..."

The first of two rod-iron spears, each perhaps six inches in length and two in diameter, protruded from the center of the young corporal's neck directly between his collar bones, seemingly sealing itself upon penetration as only a tiny amount of blood had spilled near its rounded perimeter. The second had punctured his right eye with meticulous aim, shoving said orb deep into his skullcap while again, as if inserted by the hands of a master surgeon, limiting the amount of escaping fluids. The corporal's left hand, curled at his lap, twitched and flexed every few seconds as if timed to do so, and the odor of recently released bowel slowly filled the surrounding air.

"Sergeant, wh-where's his weapon?"

Twisting slowly around toward the latrine while slinging the rifle free from his shoulder, the sergeant reached back with a free hand that quickly found his superior's upper chest and began to forcefully shove him in the opposite direction.

"Major, get back! Move!"

The door slung open from the inside with a resounding screech a split second before a series of booming retorts split the otherwise deafening silence. Instantly collapsing onto all fours, his teeth snapping together painfully from the brutal impact of kneecaps against rock flooring, the major quickly rolled onto his left side as the tiny structure filled with the thundering echoes of live fire. Propelled by frantically pumping elbows, he turned just as a trio of quarter-sized holes opened up directly between the sergeant's shoulder blades, propelling the veteran NCO backwards with his arms flailing. Crashing hard against the squared console, Sergeant Russell Walker continued firing into the shack's rock-shell ceiling, sending chunks of displaced stone raining down in jagged clumps. Attempting to straighten his awkward gait by using the high-backed chair as an impromptu lean-to, he instead slid down to one knee as the chair pinwheeled in the opposite direction.

"Sergeant ... head for the door!" the major shouted as his noncommissioned bodyguard flashed him a wild-eyed glance, the chest and abdomen areas of his camouflage field jacket soaked in dark maroon. For a terrible moment, their eyes locked in mortal desperation; two doomed, hapless souls at the cusp of unlocking the mysteries of an afterlife neither was prepared to greet. As yet another projectile effectively obliterated the center of his face, leaving little more than a pulped crater in its wake, it became sickeningly obvious that the good sergeant would be the first to wander such an enigmatic realm.

Rolling over onto his back as Sergeant Walker's bloodied corpse toppled forward a mere three feet away, the major used the heels of his boots to scoot toward the entrance door, where his upper back soon made solid contact. He then took a deep, labored breath and craned his neck, peeking cautiously toward the latrine door as if the act of squinting might deflect an oncoming shell.

"Ti-Tim? Timothy? This is Major Ogilvie ... Ran-Randy. Listen, Tim ... I ... I just want to talk."

Reaching up, the major's tremor-racked, gloved hand found and tightly clutched the door's inner knob and gradually began to twist clockwise.

"There's no need ... no need for this type of aggression, Tim. I'm ready ... to listen to anything you have to say."

Slithering up the cool metal surface like a predatory reptile, he heard nothing but the occasional gust of wind pelt the outer walls with renewed fervor.

"I realize ... understand your point of view. Loyalty is indeed an admirable trait.

You have demonstrated that time and time again…"

A low, hauntingly familiar clicking sound ensued, followed by the unmistakable snap of an armor-piercing rifle being locked into automatic firing mode.

"I'm here to help, Tim. You have to believe that. Not to threaten or challenge your beliefs. I ... I just need you to meet me halfway. Can you do that, soldier? Can you meet me halfway so we can discuss this like ... well, like the old friends we are?"

Wincing as his left knee popped with a muffled crack beneath the thick camo coverings, the major twisted his body the better to flee once the door was pulled ajar, while careful to maintain eye contact near the latrine as to not give away his change of positioning. Glancing over to the sergeant's still form, where a widening pool of blackish red continued to spread out like a seeping oil spill, he briefly considered retrieving the dead NCO's rifle. That is, until he took note that all but the final few inches of its still- smoldering barrel lay pinned beneath the dead man's bloodied torso.

"I know how special Corp ... Katreena was to you, Tim. You may not realize it, but you and I have spent countless hours discussing the special bond you two shared all those years ago. Your ... need to reconnect ... to rekindle that bond is overwhelming, I know. I'm ... here ... came here to help. You have to believe that."

In mentally mapping the winding trek back to the parked Hummer, the major felt a faint surge of hope. Before departing for the ruins of Sector Six, the assigned trio had sat through the usual survival and safety briefings, wherein each had been informed of a hidden location where an emergency spare key for the vehicle had been planted.

"There's no need for the bloodshed, Timothy, after all ... hasn't enough been spilled upon this very site?" the major crooned, purposely enunciating each word in true Shakespearian actor style as to stretch each syllable to the max while simultaneously pulling the door gradually inward.

"Hasn't there been enough unnecessary death doled out on these haunted grounds?"

As the space grew to just past six inches in width, the major stuck out a dust- coated boot-tip.

"Fresh kills didn't ... won't bring Katreena back, Timothy, if that's the theory..."

The space between door and doorway grew to a full foot, and he leaned out with his left shoulder, though careful to keep his voice aimed toward the latrine door.

"... the woman you loved was a great but flawed warrior, Tim ... her dedication to her cause unquestioned. As painful as it might be ... the subject must be breached ... discussed for you to reach closure, you understand?"

The whole of his body now poised on the exterior side of the door save for his craned neck and head, he fired off a final sequence of dialogue even as his knees bent slightly and his lower body tensed for the impending sprint.

"... if she *were* here now, Tim, I think Katreena would advise you to drop the weapon and allow those who care to intervene ... to help you cope. If she were here now, Katreena Whitlock would advise you to stand down, soldier, and take a knee..."

Twisting about and lunging forward with his head bowed and both legs and arms pumping, he briefly froze in place as for one terrifying moment the outer doorknob caught the inner lining of his partially unzipped field jacket. Pulling free with a low tearing sound, the major proceeded, only to halt yet again, skidding forward and braking with both bootheels before scrambling madly in reverse as a high-pitched, rather feminine whine erupted from between tightly pursed lips.

"G-good g-od..." he croaked weakly, having tumbled down onto his back and forced to spider-crawl in reverse, "... y-*you*? But ... how did you ... can you ... be he—"

"Should have listened, doc ... I tried to tell you ... didn't I try to tell you? Stubborn as a mule ... never listen ... only what you *wanted* to hear," a familiar voice chimed, stepping forward as the major struggled to backtrack. His former patient stood stiffly with his booted feet planted wide apart and a recently obtained rifle propped casually atop one shoulder. His bare chest was smeared in blood, as were the hands that gripped the stolen firearm. Backing away with a dramatic bow, Timothy Mills whipped an arm back as in introduction. His grin stretched; his eyes lit up, his face taking on a ruddy tone from an apparent rush of pure, unbridled glee. He viewed the entity hovering at his side with unabashed pride, despite its rather ghastly appearance.

Strands of tar-black, seaweed-like hair hung from its fleshless scalp, the smell of decay as thick as the waves of primal fear pouring from his veins. Its spindly arms bounced and jiggled like those of a mangled marionette, its equally withered legs flapping in the breeze like twin kite strings. The tattered clothing, what little remained, hung in barely recognizable camouflage strands so fragile that the occasional section would flake off and crumble like ash.

"Worst part is, I'm powerless to intervene here," he beamed, rolling his eyes in mock exasperation. "Ya see, Treena never did exactly cotton to your kind, and I ain't about to contradict my sweetie ... no sir-ee. The little woman surely did not appreciate the label you people pinned on her so

364

posthumously, and I can't say I blame her in the least, patriotism be damned.

"Whatever plan of action she takes, major, sir, I'm bound to back her up, or at the very least back off and let her have her jollies."

Timothy Mills shrugged before bowing his head, raising a forefinger to casually draw through the fresh layers of blood and draw the rough outline a heart at the center of his chest. Peering back up, the toothy sneer on display was anything but sympathetic.

"I'm fairly certain this may not end well for ya, Major..."

"Wha—Tim ... who ... what are you say—" the major stammered, his lips coated with chalky froth. He'd fallen onto his left side and was pointing at the levitating monstrosity overhead with one hand while using the other to claw and grasp at the hard clay ground.

"What-we can ... I can get you h-help, don't you underst—please just g-give me a ch-chance..." he whimpered, the shack entrance just a few scant feet away.

"I ... *am* here ... now ..." the creature bayed, its voice as toneless and hollow as its pupilless eye sockets from which a bloated beetle wriggled free to scamper down a jawline littered with a swarm of equally plump maggots.

"And ... I think for all ... the skull ... fucking you ... administered to my ...

Timothy ... through the years ... it 's high time *you* took ... a knee ... Major Ogilvie..."

Sergeant-Major Timothy Mills stepped back, wearing a grimace of disgust as the levitating thing's head shot down toward the major's exposed face in a manic blur, its slavering maw opening impossibly wide to reveal rotted, toothless gums from which pus leaked like yellowish lava.

As a cloak of total blackness enveloped his senses, the last detailed memories Major Randall Ogilvie recalled were the sound of raucous giggling and a mysterious aroma; the smell; an atrocious, overwhelming odor of gangrene-type infection that, even on the verge of merciful unconscious bliss, triggered his gag reflex. He felt enormous pressure at the base of this throat and breastbone and could faintly make out a series of moist ripping sounds that were accompanied by a level of hellish, excruciating pain he never knew possible.

***

Hours later, as darkness fell and a blazing bonfire provided the lone source of light, two figures danced in the flickering glow, though only one provided the expected shadow.

"I never bought into their lies, Sweetie. Not for a New York minute," Timothy Mills whispered through a wide, warped smile, the dark circles that had for so long underlined his fatigue-laced eyes having miraculously vanished, a renewed spring in his step he hadn't known since that faithful day when his world, his reason for being, had been so viciously stripped away. "Oh, they tried like hell to drill the notion into my brain, but I recognized the rhetoric for what it was; propaganda—a fictional tale of espionage created by people like Ogilvie to better sweep away the facts; that somewhere up the chain of command somebody dropped the ball but wasn't about to take the blame."

As he continued to box-step around the flames, the surrounding air pregnant with the scent of burning flesh, he didn't dare break eye contact with his dancing partner in fear of her suddenly disappearing upon attempting to reconnect. He'd waited far too long for such a magical reunion for it to end so abruptly.

"You were an easy target, simple as that. Born on enemy soil; grandparents as hardline extreme as it got and parents only a shade more respectable. You had two strikes against you the minute you took the oath. Bet it didn't take 'em long to choose a scapegoat once the base was flattened. Got their greedy mitts on your personnel file and bingo! Family of terrorists equals budding spy in the making and voilá! The perfect scapegoat."

Mills paused, his throat clicking emotionally as in the background the flesh of three fresh corpses popped and crackled beneath the billowing flames. Hanging from the pile with his scorched skull just out of the fire's reach, the image reflected in Randall Ogilvie's dead eyes was but of a single dancer who spoke and reacted to empty air; the same single dancer who had murdered two men inside the guard shack, then crawled out from a tiny latrine window to surprise him outside the entrance.

The same lone, demented dancer who had then so calmly reached down with gnarled fingers to rip out the major's throat and tear his chest cavity to shreds.

The same delusional dancer who would continue to celebrate long into the night, until the time when yet another group of intruders would dare infiltrate the deserted ruins in search of a trio of recently missing comrades.

The same insane, terminally lovesick dancer who would then retreat into the shadows for yet another assault on the shattered grounds of what he'd come to think of as their "happy home." A crazed, lone dancer filled with newfound joy that his battles would no longer be fought alone.

The same hopelessly mad dancer who had so casually tossed a manila folder labeled *Personnel File 2345D: Corporal Katreena Whitlock* into the bonfire without so much as flipping it open—a personnel file containing insurmountable evidence that a certain female corporal had indeed given away the base's secret location to the enemy all those years ago, thus dooming all but the clueless, lovesick soldier she left behind.

Crouching behind a crumbling rock wall as enemy headlights approached the ruins, former Sergeant-Major Timothy Mills gripped the recently procured, fully loaded firearms in both hands. His breathing properly regulated, his eyes sharp and focused, he peered over and shot his lady love a appreciate wink.

In response, the dead space to which he had gestured seemed to swirl and hiss with a life all its own.

THE ISLE OF TRANQUILITY, PART V

Wow, what a deranged, sick pup of a man you were, father. Mere words cannot express my disgust, though once again, that ending alone almost made the whole sickening ride worthwhile ... emphasis on the almost. You always were partial to spewin' off about the horrors of war, being the decorated vet and all. Never could let me forget all those past heroics either, or anyone else bored enough or forced to listen.

Gotta say ... Whatever family gene you possessed to be able to drudge up such grind-house horrors is certainly one I'm grateful to have evaded. Can't begin to imagine the sleepless nights, though maybe in Pop's case such evil writings served as a sort of built-in relaxant. Yep, I can see Papa Striker sleeping juuuusssst fine after a night of penning countless decapitations and dismemberments. Some people get drowsy from turkey meat ... my dad dozed off after a good, old-fashioned fictional drawing and quartering.

Come to think if it, he always was partial to cookouts ... the bigger the better. Used to grill chops and burgers for hours on end in that moronic "King Cook" hat and the lily-white apron with the fake blood spatters that read "Greet the Meat" across the belly. Makes me wonder what kinda zombie ol' pop would make ... or is making. Now there is one goosebump-raising thought. Anyhow, I repeat ... one unbelievably sick, sick pup ... so who'd have thought such derangement could pay off so big? I repeat...wow.

Meanwhile, looks like the storm of the freakin' century is only an hour or so away from hammering the island full-force. Sky's as orange as a grapefruit peel ... butt-ugly and full of potential carnage. Palm trees are gonna be bending to the breaking point soon. Makes one long for the Weather Channel and their "on-the-eights" updates. Not that there's a helluva lot I can do to stop or prep for it. Got a basement the size of a football field but I'll be damned if I'm gonna take the chance of the entire mansion imploding and landing on my noggin.

One thing's for sure ... watching that army of monster waves build on the far horizon has certainly served to sober my drunken ass up, and it'd probably take guzzling a half gallon of Beam to reanimate that particular buzz.

All this of course begs the query ... where the hell is Jen as a freakin' hurricane of unknown strength preps to transform Slacker Isle into Slaughter Isle? Guess I'm as surprised at my concern as I am shocked by her utter recklessness. I'll give the hardheaded bitch another fifteen minutes ... until exactly 5 PM ... before deciding a next move, the loopiest of which would of course be an impromptu rescue mission. Hard as I might try, the fact that she is my partner in marriage keeps nudging its way to the forefront. Shit ... if only I'd done less reading and more gulping, I'd more than likely be snoozing through this freakin' mess without a care in the world. After all, there are

370

worse ways to go, especially these days, than drowning in one's sleep.

Looks like I got time for one final, brief tale from pop's maniacal crypt. What the hell, right? Can't be half as scary as what's brewing right outside these walls...

BOOK 6 - THE REUNION

Part One: *Pre-Reunion (The Day Before)*

Little Billy had grown to despise the annual family get-together. Having just turned twelve less than a week prior, Li'l Bill, as he was so affectionately known among the kinfolk, figured it was high time he had a say in whether his attendance was mandatory to said gathering. As usual, he figured wrong. Oh, so wrong. So incorrect in such a bold assumption, in fact, that he'd narrowly escaped a proper throttling from mother. On the flip side, his father (Big Bill, naturally) had initially seemed agreeable to his son's request, at least until mother had flashed that certain stern glance that always seemed to instantly alter Big Bill's opinion. Thus, with slumped shoulders and a reddened face, Little Billy accepted defeat yet again. His presence was indeed mandatory, it seemed. This gathering, he'd been told, would be different. This one, his mother reiterated time and time again, would be *special*.

Little Billy was given his instructions and instantly felt the fear grip his brittle soul in a steel vise. His mother doled them out sternly but in a caring, loving tone he'd hardly recognized. Frightened as he was, Little Billy also felt a brief swelling of pride in what was expected of him.

As for the relatives, perhaps as many as thirty or thirty-five—counting whatever newborns or new spouses had been added to the mix since the previous year—would descend upon the family abode early the following morning. Once the intrusion began, Billy would be stationed near or around the front door wearing a wide, faux grin along with a belly full of fluttering butterflies. By the time the last of the stragglers had departed, normally around 8 or 9 PM, he would be sufficiently fatigued from both a mental and physical standpoint, a haggard condition it usually took several days from which to properly heal.

The problem wasn't merely with the relatives *per se*. Fact was, Little Billy found nothing but discomfort in the company of others, be they complete strangers or immediate family members. Little Billy didn't appreciate camaraderie, conversation, or kinship, even with those among his own age bracket. In school, this ultra-introverted behavior had had garnered him the nickname 'Silent Bill,' though the other kids rarely spoke this aloud in fear of possible retaliation. After all, at six-feet-two and a strapping one hundred eighty-five pounds, Li'l Bill was anything but amongst his peers. He was, however, no bully or playground ruffian. In truth, Billy had no history of fighting or ever laying his hands on anyone in anger. The factors behind his natural ability to intimidate the other kids were twofold: his size was obviously first and foremost; then there was the searing, intrusive stare that he so obliviously flashed that shrieked of pent-up anger and unbridled rage. As far as the physicality, that had been inherited from Bill Senior, a six-foot-six, two hundred seventy-pound giant of a man with barrel shoulders and biceps as thick as tree trunks. The mad stare was Mother's, plain and simple, though in her case it wasn't as much a habitual expression but a potentially dangerous one.

Regardless, Little Billy was, for the most part, happily isolated within the school walls. Friendship, he'd long since deduced, was an overrated myth from which eventual disappointment bloomed. Content in his own private enjoyments, he felt no need to share or have another's forced upon him. Besides, forging kinships with outsiders was pure folly. No such relationship could possibly last considering the circumstances.

Little Billy had birthed from a long line of loners, true, though in his case the inherent tendencies seemed a bit more on the extreme side.

He often daydreamed of inhabiting his very own desert isle, or perhaps an isolated igloo located on a desolate mountain of ice. A mountain found on no manmade map—a mountain virtually unreachable by land, air, or water. The surroundings themselves weren't nearly as vital as the element of solitude. Simply put, little Billy wanted to be alone, *all* alone, and despised a crowded house full of kinfolks most of all. Despise or not—dread with every fiber of his being or not—the following day's torturous rites were inevitable. Bent over by a sudden wave of nausea, Little Billy promptly threw up into a thicket of bushes. Down on his knees, he wiped the steaming bile from his trembling lips and wondered if he could truly survive yet another family reunion.

Part Two: *Pre-Reunion (The Night Before)*

Sleep eluded him until well past midnight, despite a relatively early turning in time of just past 9 PM. He spent an hour or more rehearsing his words, understanding the importance of sounding sincere but not overly needy. The call had to be brief ... concise ... not overly dramatic so as to raise suspicion. Both his mother and father had conveyed their extreme confidence just before bedtime.

"You can do it, son. No problem. It's past due," Big Bill had relayed with a toothy grin.

"Of course he can, silly," mother had chimed in, playfully bumping father with an extended hip, "he's our child, right? Why, he was born and bred for this day."

Once he was able to succumb to the Sandman's unwavering pull, the dreams were predictably garish, considering the battering his subconscious had endured the past several days.

He stands stiffly at the center of the family living room, decked out in his best (and only, truth be told) suit and black dress shoes that squeeze his feet into painful submission. One by one, as if attached to and pulled forward by some invisible rope, the kinfolk file in to greet him. It is, he realizes, the usual murderer's row of blood relatives that he annually ranks as the worst of the clan. Tensing to the point of rigor mortis, he so wants to scream out as they draw closer but is only able to release a rather pathetic inner shriek that serves little purpose. The aforementioned clan, in order of appearance and matching annoyance, are as follows:

Uncle Tim, he of the dead (glass perhaps) eye, caterpillar-fuzzy eyebrows and the aftershave that smells of bug repellent.

"Damned if you ain't sproutin' like a spring weed, son..." he bellows while reaching out to roughly pinch Little Billy's left cheek.

Aunt Flora, she of the snow-white bird's-nest hair, breath that reeks of stale mints, and thickly layered makeup that any mortician worth his salt would forever deny applying to even the ripest of corpses.

"Oh, sweet Billy-boy, you are the spittin' image of yore daddy..." she squeals before kneeling over and planting a saliva-coated peck on the opposite cheek.

Cousin Benny, he of the pear shape, multiple chins, and cleanly shaved but badly scarred dome that resembles a rut-infested roadway.

"Hiya, shrimp. How's she hangin'?" he blurts, nudging Little Billy's shoulder with one pudgy paw.

Cousin Marilyn, she of the grape-sized chin mole, massive bosom, equally colossal midsection and straw-thin legs.

"Ain't you a cutie now!" she proclaims, shoving him forth into those two heaving, gargantuan water balloons, where he briefly ponders an escape through suffocation.

Grandpa William, he of the lengthy nose hairs that swirl and levitate with a life all their own, crimson-shaded, vein-infested jumbo ears, and the always-present aroma of stale urine.

"Chip off'n the old block, ain'tcha, boy?" he growls, utilizing fingers that better resemble the skeletal appendages of a daddy longlegs to rub a permanent cowlick into Little Billy's already mangled coif.

Grandma Helen, she of the milky left eye that one cannot help but stare into like some enchanted crystal ball, the paralyzed right hand that is curled into a permanent claw, and the almost completely toothless maw that, when opened beyond a tight smile, brings to mind a rank, foreboding cave.

"Give ol' granny a smooch, you handsome lil' devil," she croons. He does so with great trepidation, her leathery, sandpaper-rough skin instantly reminding him of his badly aged baseball glove.

Predictably, as seems to be the case with all good nightmares, the worst of the bunch is saved for last.

Uncle Sid, he of the constantly pinching, poking fingers and forceful shoulder punches; he of the consistently unfunny jokes, the majority of which he either tells incorrectly or has forgotten the punch line outright; he of the fishy breath, twirled mustache and greased-down hair.

"You're growin' into a real brute, kiddo," he chides, first pinching a knot into Little Billy's left bicep and following up with a forceful pinch of the right breast, an excruciating little maneuver sometimes referred to as a "titter-twister."

Billy woke grasping his chest only to find such a malady non-existent. "Tomorrow," he whispered hoarsely before lying back down with a huff, "tomorrow the hurt will be real."

Once dusk gave way to a dreary, cloud-infested dawn, Little Billy made the call.

Part Three: *Running with the Herd (The Day Of)*

"You did the right thing, Billy. I'll ... we'll just see if we can talk this thing out, all right?"

"Y-yes, sir. My folks have been wanting to meet with you, it's just that ... well, my dad travels so much it's hard to get them both together at the same time. Anyway, t- thanks for coming."

"Don't give it a second thought, young man. After all, I'm a counselor ... it's my job. Miss Ridley had spoken to me concerning your falling grades of late. Maybe between you, me, and your parents, we can get to the root of the problem."

"O-okay, Mr. Gregg. T-thanks again."

"No, thank you for having the courage to call to set up this meeting, Billy, and for finally realizing ... *understanding* that you couldn't ... that you *shouldn't* have to face this kind of situation alone."

Adrien Gregg was a middle school science teacher/job counselor. A short (five- five), obese (two hundred fifty-plus pounds), balding man in his mid to late forties, he was forced to reach with a slight upswing in order to place a pudgy arm around little Billy's left shoulder.

"Is this—" he cleared his throat—"your residence, Billy?"

378

"Yes, sir. Sorry about the yard. I was supposed to mow this weekend but the rain…"

"No, no … that's fine," Mr. Gregg said nervously as they strolled through a shoulder-high, rod-iron entrance toward an ancient three-story, Victorian-styled abode. "It's just … that it's so … roomy-looking. You say just you and your folks live here?"

"Yeah, just the three of us."

"Well, you certainly aren't cramped for space, now, are you?" "Nope. Plenty of places to hi—um, to get off to yourself and think."

They began to ascend a planked staircase leading to the front porch and Mr. Gregg was obviously a tad winded from the effort.

"I'll bet this place holds some real history. Must be a hundred years old or more," he panted, turning to scan the surrounding grounds. Though there had been a trio of other homes nearby, he was unable to visualize them due to a head-high wall of thick foliage that cloaked the residence like a privacy fence melded from overgrown grass, vines, and shrubbery.

"I dunno. I guess. My family's owned it a long time. Only place I ever lived." "Well, then,…" Mr. Gregg blurted cheerily after a short pause, "… it's about time I met your folks." He took a step toward the home's front door, a badly scarred, dark-stained pine entrance in dire need of refinishing, when he felt a gentle tugging at the shirtsleeve of his left arm.

"Mr. Gregg?"

"Yes, Billy?"

The boy's eyes were huge.

"We'll ... have to go around back. They ... mom and dad are working in the cellar."

Wearing a deep frown, Mr. Gregg eyed the boy curiously.

"Working in the cellar? What are they up to down there, mmm? Doing some preserving, I take it?"

"Yeah, that's it, I reckon," Billy replied with a strained grin before averting his eyes to the far right end of the rounded porch, "Mom always plants flowers this time of year and forces Dad to help. They said they'd be potting some veggies when we got here."

"Then we'll just see if they need some help ... c'mon," the big man said with a wink, allowing the boy to blaze the trail toward the back of the house via the winding porch.

Once they descended a narrow, spiraling metal stairway toward the cellar entrance (Mr. Gregg finding the going uncomfortably snug), Little Billy abruptly halted, as if waiting for the adult to take the lead.

As the cellar's dented metal door was pulled slightly ajar, a partial, mostly obscured view of the murky interior was allowed.

Mr. Gregg squeezed past the boy and began to sniff as if prepping an impending sneeze. His checkered tie had blown onto his left shoulder from a sudden gust of wind.

"Ugh ... something has certainly turned for the worst down there."

The boy giggled through splayed fingers, peering past the large man's bloated midsection into the waiting dimness.

"Yeah, I told mom some of the potatoes were rotting. Dad is always saying we were gonna clean it out."

"Whew-weee!" Mr. Gregg exclaimed, waiving a hand in front of his nose in apparent disgust. "Maybe once you're in there for a few minutes, you get used to it. You ready to get down to business then, Billy-Boy?" he asked.

Billy again retained eye contact for only a sparse moment before staring down at his own grass-stain smeared sneakers. A twenty-one-year veteran in the school system, Adrien Gregg could hardly recall meeting a shyer, more introverted youth.

"Yes, sir ... ready as I'll ever be ... I reckon."
"Well, then ... let's do this."

Mr. Gregg turned to face the entrance and took a single, purposeful step forward. He paused, sticking his head into the darkness while laying the palm of his left hand flat against the door. The shove he received was gentle, almost caress-like, thought sufficiently forceful to send him flailing forward with both arms waving.

Little Billy heard the rotund man shriek as he stumbled through the opening and vanished into the murk. The next sound, following a surprisingly lengthy pause, was a resounding crunch as the science teacher landed atop the cellar's stony floor.

Turning back toward the stairwell from which they came, the boy winced as a chorus of cheers reverberated at his back. In keeping with the ritual, he would return to the house and enter the cellar from inside. In truth, it was the only viable option in order to avoid potential injury, as the outer entrance's inner staircase had been removed decades earlier, leaving a fifteen-foot dropoff onto hardened cement.

For the briefest of moments, a mere heartbeat in time, Little Billy considered flight.

It wasn't the ritual itself he dreaded so horribly, but the personal attention he would garner at being the reunion's chosen guest of honor.

In the end, while trudging forth like a death row inmate toward his own execution, he sadly conceded the fight. Strolling through the dusty, cobweb-infested interior of the mansion toward his preordained meeting with destiny, Little Billy began to begrudgingly accept who and *what* he really was, and that as irritating, annoying, and downright maddening as they sometimes were, the clan waiting in the cellar were his family.

Hermit tendencies be damned, they were his blood, one and all, and he would by god learn to tolerate ... no ... he would learn to *accept* their peculiarities just as he hoped they would accept his own. For, to paraphrase a rather odd but seemingly factual saying he recently ran across in his school reading assignments, *no man is an island.* Certainly then, no mere preteen child could qualify as such.

Sailing down the cellar steps with a newfound enthusiasm, little Billy was greeted with catcalls, whistles, and clapping hands.

382

His father and mother stepped forward and offered a group hug, with which he happily complied as the rest of the clan slowly spread out to allow a path toward the center of the room, where the celebration had already begun in earnest. All save for Little Billy were completely nude, their outer clothing piled into a far corner like shed snakeskins.

Led through the cheering clan to the feasting table by his smiling, jovial parents, Little Billy displayed a wide, gleeful grin of his own while taking in the generous offering laid out before him. His nostrils flared wildly as the coppery scent assaulted his highly tuned senses, and a thick layer of drool bubbled from the right corner of his mouth onto his pointy chin.

"We left the best for you, son," his father announced proudly, spitting a sliver of bone fragment from between his teeth before reaching over and giving the nape of his son's neck a firm squeeze. "The choice cuts, you might say."

"You did good, sweetie. Real good. You're one of us now. Enjoy the spoils of your labor..." his mother added, reaching up to wipe a trailing tear from her crimson- stained cheek.

"We've been ... worried about ya, kiddo," Uncle Sid said with a wink, his moustache dripping gore. "Thought ya might turn out to be the black sheep with all that weird-ass loner crap. Sure was glad to see ya prove us wrong."

"My boy, I couldn't be prouder," Grandpa William added between chews, a pencil-thin strand of moist, jagged flesh hanging from his chin like shredded confetti.

"This is the best damn meal we've had in the last five or six reunions."

"You're right as rain, dear. This handsome little cuss is gonna grow into a hell of a man ... a born leader, he is," Grandma Helen cooed before gumming a meaty mouthful held out from her permanently clawed hand, her sagging breasts drenched rose red.

"Oh yeah, Billy's a natural all right," Cousin Benny exclaimed between echoing burps, his shiny bald head coated in dime-sized, blackish/maroon spatters.

"Kid even made sure no loose ends were danglin' about by making the call from a pay phone. Figured that one out all on his own, too. Sharp as a tack, he is."

"Sheeeeeeeit. All that dadgum worryin' for nothin'," Aunt Flora bellowed happily, a rather large shank of bone fragment tucked inside her high-coiffed hair like the skeletal remains of a deceased insect trapped within a spider's web.

"Yep, Bill Junior is definitely one of us after all," shouted Uncle Tim as a grouping of meaty shrapnel sprayed from his parted lips, the bushy hair growth around his groin inundated with tiny specks of discarded flesh.

"Go on ... dig in, son," Big Bill chided, playfully nudging his son forward, "you deserve it."

Reaching forth with greedy, clutching fingers, Little Billy first went for the eyes, leaving the true delicacy for last.

Despite being the youngest by far of this particular clan of ghouls, Little Billy knew well the feeding rules of the sacred ritual.

Thus, it was the (still faintly) beating heart of Adrien Gregg that would serve as the final portion consumed at the annual family reunion.

THE ISLE OF TRANQUILITY, PART VI

Aww, freakin' perfect! How tragically fitting, one might say! Flesh-eating ghouls, no less. It is to laugh ... nervously! I'd use the word prophetic, but the official meaning escapes me, and I'd surely hate to misuse Webster's with the specter of Papa Striker roaming nearby. Pretty sure that one word does sum it up in a nutshell, though. No doubt, were he still alive today to witness my breathless, wide-eyed reaction, Papa Striker would be busting a gut with rolling howls of sarcastic laugher. Freaky, but the circumstances feel almost ... somehow ... planned, even though, logically anyhow, there ain't a chance in hell they actually could be. Shit if I ain't as stone sober as I've been in months. Waaaay too sober, in fact, and just in time to play meet and greet with what has to be, at the very least, one badass tropical storm. That weird orange hue has given way to pitch-black skies, and the ocean itself looks to be one highly pissed off mofo with the worst of intentions.

Much as I'd love to duck down, take cover, and ride this out by my lonesome, thereby enhancing my ultraselfish rep, it just ain't in the cards. The way the walls are starting to shake, I figure I've got ten, fifteen minutes tops to find and drag Jen's lunatic ass to safety, or at least what professes to be safe during such dicey scenes.

Sooooo, despite my inner coward screaming its freakin' lungs out, I'm gonna pull on the old raingear, grab a flashlight or two and hit the beach.

If nothing else, I can stand at the pearly gates and claim I went out a hero ... ha!

Eight Minutes Later:

Okay, this ain't ... can't be right. Nope ... no way this is the least bit kosher.

Mud-sloppy and indistinguishable as they are, those are definitely ... footprints. Booted footprints, looks like. Oversized booted footprints spattered onto the tile that do not in any way, shape, or form resemble either mine or Jen's: oversized mud- and sand- coated footprints leading from the front foyer, through the living room, and toward the kitchen.

Wellll, simple logic dictates I follow the slug trail in order to unmask an originator, but with that in mind, why is it that my aforementioned inner coward advises to sprint in the opposite direction as fast as humanly possible? Methinks a brief detour is in order...

Four Minutes Later:

It's times like these that I adore Pop's legacy of raging paranoia. Man had a gun collection second to none, always thinking a crazed fan was gonna show up at his doorstep with a copy of one of his novels in one hand and a butcher knife in the other.

Regardless of my woeful lack of expertise in its actual use, this Smith & Wesson blue-steel baby sure has a comforting feel to it about now. Never mind I probably couldn't nick the side of Mount Everest with a single round ... it's all about intimidation, baby ... intimidation and peace of freakin' mind.

Now, just gotta be careful to soft-shoe ... step light and easy ... can't believe I'm actually grateful for the howling winds and shaking walls.

Kitchen lights on ... and I know ... well, pretty sure anyhow, that I powered her down after that last refill. It seems somebody's rustling up a midnight snack ... time to quell my shaking gun hand and find out just who that somebody is...

Well, here goes nothing ... hands up, assho—

Oh ... m-my ... freak ... freakin' ... g-god... "D-ad?"

Three Minutes Later:

I ... think I ... nailed 'im with that last shot ... can't be s-sure but ... I think I saw its ... his ... skull snap back ... thought I heard a few bone fragments ... nail the far kitchen wall.

It ... was Pop ... no freakin' doubt about it ... nothing but a walking, moaning skeleton on stilts ... but I know ... knew that stare ... saw it too many times ... the slight tilt of the head, the hunch of the shoulders ... som'bitch is just as sarcastic in death as ... he was in life. Can't believe he'd even ... dug out that damn barbecue hat and apron ... like he was ... mocking me ... by wearing 'em ... no one else would know to push those specific ... buttons ... no one else could ... know how such a ... fucked-up image could warp my psyche. He was ... playing with me ... toying with me like only that crazy... old bastard could.

No way I ... imagined it ... right? Out of the question ... but how ... how is he ... did he possibly ... get here to the island? Backstroke maybe?

Never freakin' mind, buddy-boy ... you ran outta ammo and balls at the ... precise same time ... the second Papa Striker slung that unidentified slab of meat toward you ... and lunged forward like you were next on the freakin' menu.

Just ... focus on trucking toward the hangar ... without breaking your fool neck ... just keep picking 'em up and putting 'em down, soldier ... get to the plane first and worry about attempting a takeoff in hurricane winds second...

Four Minutes Later:

Winds are ... gotta be reaching typhoon levels at the very ... least ... fifty-sixty MPH ... gusting to seventy ... tear the wings right off the ... the...

Jesus wept ... mystery ... solved. Unreal ... simply un-freakin'-believable ... my kingdom for a tall glass of Beam. Looks like a Piper ... maybe an S33. Damn things are light as a dried leaf and just as quiet upon approach and touchdown.

Forgetting for a sec that the old man's been fucking DEAD for sixteen months ... there's ... no way he landed in this storm ... or even navigated through it, meaning just one thing. He flew in hours ago ... probably hit terra firma while I was dozing off on gin and tonic. So ... what the hell was he doing all that time? I would assume it's damn hard to enjoy a ... leisurely stroll across the beach with ... only a single leg intact.

Listen to me ... a skeletal corpse manages to fly a plane across hundreds of miles of ocean and ... I'm doubting it can take a freakin' walk?

Ahh, who the hells cares what mean and skinless was doing to bide his time ... before crashing the party ... need to tuck my happy ass inside that hangar and hope ... the walls don't give in before this storm passes ... then fly the hell off haunted isle and find a new place to nest. Somewhere ... anywhere ... anyplace ... that Papa Striker can't track me down. Swell ... at least the outer walls seem to be holding up ... now to duck inside and wait it out.

Seven and a Half Minutes Later:

Superfine ... got 'er fueled up and ready to levitate. Winds ain't letting up an iota though. Might be a long, bumpy night, buddy-boy. Well, at least I don't have to worry about Papa Chalky-Bones breaking into the hangar. Triple-bolt locked the only entrance save the hangar door, and he ain't about to raise that heavy steel bad boy without a hydraulic jack. Now to tuck myself inside for a quick instrument check and pray that nothing vital's rusted from a year-plus of inactivity.

Whew ... smells like spoiled pork in here ... guess I should've aired 'er out a while back...

Waitaminnit ... didn't that hatch door have a bad habit of sticking? Pulled open like it was freshly oiled ... damn, but it reeks in here ... some kind of coppery stench ... and w-what ... what's that on the seat? Sticky ... like oil ... n-no ... it's blo...

390

"Oh … shit … is that…?

I … w-wasn't going to leave you behind, I … I swear … I was just g-gonna prep the bird before … s-searching you out…"

Lord god, her left arm's miss-missing below the el-elbow … probably the mystery appendage that Pop tossed at me … and her throat … t-torn open … and those eyes … dead fish eyes. She's turned … already turned. She probably saw the Piper land and greeted it with open arms … and the sadistic son of a bitch turned my wife … fed on her … then planted her here to … to … shit…

"Its g-gonna be all right, Jen … I'll fly … get you to a doc—a doctor. You just … try to relax, okay?"

Dear lord she's salivating … she's f-frothing and I'm tr-trapped like a freakin' rat in a trap…

"I love ya … you gotta believe me … I always loved ya … can you … even understand what I'm … what I'm saying?"

Crying … crying like a baby … crying like a spanked infant and I can't stop. Hell, this is no way for a g-grown man to go out … but … maybe … just maybe … it's what I deserve…

"C-come and get me th-then, Jenny. Come and give your husband a great big ol' hug…"

Two Minutes Later:

Strange, the pain isn't as bad as I'd … feared … maybe it's all the b-booze serving as an analgesic … ha … ha … a-at least Jen appears …

to be enjoying herself... savor-savoring every b-bite...

I'll be d-damned if the ... old man d-didn't have the ... l-last word after all....

THE END

www.ingramcontent.com/pod-product-compliance
Lightning Source LLC
Chambersburg PA
CBHW010821250626
47172CB00004B/956